KU-622-503

BENJAMIN MARKOVITS
CHRISTMAS IN AUSTIN

faber

First published in the UK and the USA in 2019
by Faber & Faber Limited
Bloomsbury House
74–77 Great Russell Street
London WC1B 3DA

This paperback edition published in 2020

Typeset by Faber & Faber Limited
Printed in the UK by CPI Group (UK) Ltd, Croydon, CR0 4YY

All rights reserved
© Benjamin Markovits, 2019

The right of Benjamin Markovits to be identified as author
of this work has been asserted in accordance with Section 77
of the Copyright, Designs and Patents Act 1988

*This is a work of fiction. All of the characters, organizations, and events portrayed in this novel
are either products of the author's imagination or are used fictitiously.*

*This book is sold subject to the condition that it shall not, by way of trade or otherwise, be
lent, resold, hired out or otherwise circulated without the publisher's prior consent in any form
of binding or cover other than that in which it is published and without a similar condition
including this condition being imposed on the subsequent purchaser*

A CIP record for this book
is available from the British Library

ISBN 978-0-571-33976-1
US PAPERBACK ISBN 978-0-571-36596-8

FSC
www.fsc.org
MIX
Paper from
responsible sources
FSC® C020471

10 9 8 7 6 5 4 3 2 1

With thee to go,
Is to stay here; without thee here to stay,
Is to go hence unwilling . . .
Paradise Lost

SATURDAY

"There are too many of us," Liesel told her daughter, but it also gave her pleasure to be able to count them: "Fifteen, including Bill and me." She had spent the morning getting the house ready for Christmas, washing sheets and towels, moving some of the boxes out of the spare room into the attic, to make space for the crib. Jean, her youngest, helped. She had flown in from London the day before and was up early with jet lag anyway, wild-haired, bright-eyed. You had to pull the attic ladder down with a hook. Liesel was too old to climb the foldout steps, but she watched and worried as Jean backed down the rungs.

"I couldn't do this on my own," she said.

And Jean said, "You don't need to." Afterward, she crouched on the floor in the "wooden" room (it used to belong to the au pair and sat over the old *porte-cochere*); she put the pieces of the crib together. She was a very competent person. I don't know where she gets it from, not from me. Liesel stood in the doorway, useless. She had things to do but she hadn't seen her daughter since August.

"Isn't Cal too old for this?" Jean asked. The floor was cluttered with large pieces of wood. Childless herself, she had learned to play the helpful aunt, to have opinions and secondhand expertise—otherwise you got excluded from the new family drama, the second act. "I mean, I'm happy to build it, but he's four."

"It's what he's used to, I don't know anymore. I want everything to be familiar." When Liesel was tired or anxious, it came out as indecision. Her brown handsome face, under white hair, showed emotion easily.

"It's fine," Jean said. "That way it's there if he wants it." When the crib was built, she stood up painfully; even her youngest wasn't young anymore. "You know we all think you're nuts."

"Who is we?"

"Well, everybody but Paul. God knows what he thinks."

Before Bill left for the office, Liesel reminded him that Cal and Dana's flight was landing at noon. He was sitting at the kitchen table, scribbling; one end was covered with breakfast things, the other with pieces of paper.

"I thought Jean wanted to pick them up."

"She said she could, but I told her not to bother. She went back to bed, she's been up since three in the morning. I think she thinks . . ."

"Why doesn't Paul do it?" Bill asked, and Liesel gave him a look. Dana was Paul's ex-girlfriend—Cal's mother.

"What do you have to do in the office? Nobody will be there."

"My secretary promised to leave me something . . . It's too complicated, it's not important," Bill said. And then, giving in: "Do you want me to pick you up on the way?"

Maybe he was nervous of meeting them on his own, for understandable reasons. Liesel would have collected them herself, but she never liked driving on the highway, even before the last few years of macular degeneration—it was like pressing a thumb to a screen, there were spots of blurriness, lines shifted and bent, telephone poles, street markings, it could be very disorienting. Even so, at the old airport, which was a fifteen-minute drive away, she might have done it, she was still perfectly legal. But Bergstrom felt too far.

"Yes," she said. "Okay. I think that would be good."

A few minutes later, the front door slammed and she watched him descend the portico steps and get in the car. Her study was on the other side of the living room; she could see him through the side windows, or rather his shape, between the leaves. When he walked he bent over, as if he were hurrying, even when there wasn't any hurry. I need to cut his hair, she thought. His beard is getting out of control. Another thing to do before Christmas, and she felt rather than heard the old Volvo clank at the dip in the driveway, reversing. He backed into the road, turning slowly. The house was quiet now; she had a few hours.

Liesel had semiretired from teaching and was working on a book—a sequel to her stories about growing up in Germany during the war. The trouble with her eyes gave all of this a greater sense of urgency. But even the capacity for urgency comes and goes as you get older. She spent most of her days at home, which made her a little stir-crazy, and she was often glad of excuses to get out of the house. Also, she worried about Dana. She was anxious about the visit and wanted to send the right signals from the start. And she wanted to see Cal again. She hadn't seen him since the summer, when he spent a month with Paul in Wimberley, which was about fifty minutes from Austin in the car, although she didn't feel comfortable driving there on her own anymore. Either Bill drove or Paul came to them.

Her editor had made positive noises, but there was nothing under contract. And Liesel sometimes felt, as she chipped away at the computer, one finger at a time, that she was indulging in something, playing around. Keeping herself busy. All of which was fine by her.

Sunshine streamed in, bright wintry Texas sunshine. You could feel it translating into heat against your skin, but Liesel also sat with a blanket on her lap. Her study was formed out of an old sleeping porch and got very cold. The screens had been turned into windows; it was like sitting in a glass box. From her desk, she could see the side of the garden by the kitchen extension (they built it after Bill got tenure). When they first moved to Austin, in the summer of 1975, she tried to grow vegetables there. The ground was so hard, she had to flood the earth, standing with the hose limp in her hand while mosquitoes chewed her, before she could get a shovel in. But nothing would grow, not even grass. And now ivy covered the dirt by the concrete footpath.

Steps led down from her study into the yard, but her desk stood in the way and she never used them. Liesel was happy enough just looking out—along the bamboo hedge, past the pagoda (there were leftover sacks of fertilizer lying underneath it), and across the sharp-leaved St. Augustine's lawn to the shack where they kept their gardening tools. It stood in the shade of an old pecan tree, which fruited every two years, and Bill had spent at least an hour yesterday combing the grass, trying to rake the nutshells out. She had watched him when she couldn't think of anything to write. He wore his Cornell sweatshirt and a pair of dirty cords, what used to be his teaching pants. The acidity ruined the soil, he said. But also, every time the kids came home, Bill wanted the backyard to look like it used to look when they were kids.

The woman they bought the house from told Liesel that her mother's servant had lived in that little shack. (Her mother was dead. That's why they were selling up.) A few years after the Essingers moved in, a man rang the bell and introduced himself. Sam Mosby—for some reason Liesel remembered his name. He said he used to visit his father in that house and wanted to look around again. At first Liesel thought, when she saw him through the door window, a young black man in chinos and a collared shirt, he's trying to sell me something or maybe he wants a job. But he explained himself very naturally. He said the old lady used to give him licorice or pecan brittle every time he came over. Before leaving, he offered Liesel his card—he had recently started a painting business in East Austin.

His father's old cabin was really very small. You could hardly fit more than a single bed in there, one chest of drawers and a hard chair. She wondered if as a boy he ever slept over.

One of the first things the Essingers contracted for was to fix the roof—Liesel had an idea that the kids could use the cabin as a playhouse. A long limb of the pecan tree rested its weight on the shingles and had to be cut down. The foundation needed work, too, and the contractor found a nest of copperheads nearby, under the roots of a eucalyptus. Mr. Mosby must have lived with them for years.

These are the stories she wanted to write about now. A young

German woman, raised during the Second World War, making a life for herself in America, the land of plenty. Arriving first at Cornell, on a Fulbright, where she met Bill and got married—to a Jew. Then trailing after him for several years on the academic roadshow, renting houses, looking for joint appointments, before moving to Texas with three small kids and finding . . . the kind of thing you read about the South in books. A black servant who sleeps in the shed. The house itself was a 1920s plantation-style colonial, with white clapboard walls, blue-shuttered windows, pillars holding up the roof to the veranda. You learn to live with the sense of estrangement. Because even the weather can seem like a stranger to you, the heat, the sudden storms (flash floods they call them), and the days like this in late December, when the sun is out, the sky is clear of clouds, and it might be spring in northern Germany, except for the leafless trees.

Probably Liesel was as old now as that woman when she died. When you start out somewhere you have no intention of ending up there, too. Maybe that's not right. Intention doesn't come into it. But you can't imagine . . . that's not right either. You spend your life imagining. From the first you think, in thirty years, will I sound different, what will my children be like . . . my Texan Jewish children. When Liesel told her mother about Sam Mosby, and the nest of copperheads, about trying to grow potatoes in the hard ground, and the grass so sharp it almost hurt to walk barefoot on it, her mother said, *I don't think any of this was written into your stars at birth.* But already Liesel felt inside her a little resistance to her mother's sympathy. This is my home, she wanted to say. She had made her own life. And took a certain pride in pronouncing all the German names like everyone else: Mueller like Miller, Koenig like Keenig. Her mother probably felt what she was supposed to feel, gently pushed away.

Whatever you did to your parents your kids do to you. Liesel knew she was in the middle of an ongoing argument with Paul, the kind of argument where you don't have to say anything. Because she couldn't tell him what she felt, almost ashamed, though maybe that wasn't the right way of putting it. The kind of unhappiness you don't want to look at or admit to. The idea that one of her children would walk out on his family . . . was unspeakably . . . but then again, she didn't have to say anything, because Paul knew what she felt about it anyway. You don't have to say anything and still they blame you for it, they get mad at you. Just for having a point of view. Jean told her, it's not enough not to say anything, you have to stop thinking it, too. But how do you stop thinking something. Jean said, you stop.

But it's not even true that Paul was mad at her. He rarely mentioned any of the legal problems or stages or decisions. Around his parents he always sounded careful and considerate, almost polite, which wasn't easy to keep up, for any of them. They saw him maybe once a week. More when he had Cal. But how can you say to someone, "You don't seem happy to me," without its sounding like a reproach? So she said it to Bill instead. If you want to walk out on your marriage, she said, okay, I don't like it. But you have to walk *into* something, I'd almost rather he was having an affair. Instead of . . . whatever he's doing. Buying that concrete box in Wimberley. *Outside* Wimberley. I don't understand what he does with himself all day. I really can't imagine. There's nothing for him there, he's just running away. And hiding.

Bill, who was just as unhappy about all this as she was, couldn't help correcting her. They had a disagreement, he said, about certain life choices. "He wasn't running away, it's just that Dana didn't want to come along. He didn't want the life they had in New York, which I can understand."

It was Liesel in the end who kept up contact with Dana, and not just for Cal's sake. She had a slightly embarrassed feeling that Dana herself wanted to stay in touch. Embarrassed because, Liesel also felt, if it comes to sides, I know whose side I'm on. But it didn't come to sides. Mostly they emailed each other, Dana sent pictures of Cal. It was Dana who told her, Paul's going to see him at New Year, he's coming to New York. Liesel got the sense that these visits were fraught for all of them. Confusing, too; it was a small apartment. And so she eventually wrote, *Why don't you come for Christmas. That way, Paul can see Cal here, but there's no other pressure — you can stay with us. He lives fifty minutes away in the car, you can see as much of each other or as little as you want. And Cal can spend time with his cousins, there will be kids around.*

For the first time, Paul blew up at her. "You're interfering," he said. "This is none of your business."

"No, it isn't. You're right." She also thought, Jean never gives me credit for biting my tongue. But I'm biting my tongue now.

"Every time we make an arrangement, there are negotiations, and every time we change an arrangement, we have to have more negotiations."

"There's nothing to change . . ."

"How long is Dana going to stay?"

"I don't know . . . a week. She says she wants to be home for New Year."

"I was supposed to have Cal for New Year."

"So he can stay for New Year, too."

"Without Dana?"

Liesel hesitated. "She can leave him here."

Paul shook his head, almost amused. "If she leaves him here, I have to fly him back."

"Yes."

"I don't think you thought any of this through."

"Maybe I didn't," she said.

"You should have asked me first."

"I should have asked you." And then she gave the real reason, which was also the honest truth. "I didn't think she would say yes."

Liesel seemed to find out about their separation, if that's what it was, by stages. Paul never exactly told her anything; maybe he was ashamed, too. He obviously talked to the other kids, to Nathan, his big brother, about the legal and financial details, but there were things no one passed on to Liesel or Bill. Whatever went wrong started at the US Open. Her first reaction, when Paul lost to that guy (she couldn't remember his name), was, well, at least that's over. This is what she said to him afterward, when he met them in the players' lounge, still wet from the showers.

"You've done much better than anybody thought. I'm proud of you, I still can't believe it. My tennis-playing son."

Paul patted her on the head. There was a wide window overlooking one of the courts, with a match in progress, crowds filling the bleachers, an umpire, ball boys, the whole back and forth. He wasn't paying attention to what she said.

But Jean took her to task for it later on. She was standing up for her brother in some funny way. "That's not strictly true," she said. "Maybe he did better than *you* thought he would."

"*Das stimmt gar nicht.* I always . . ." Somehow, Liesel had to defend herself on the long unhappy train ride back to Manhattan. Paul had offered to drive some people in his car, but in the end only Cal and Dana rode with him. There was a kind of deference shown, which Jean later felt bad about. Maybe she felt bad already, abandoning her brother like that (Like what? Liesel thought—to his family?), and this is why she picked a fight with her mother. Who knows. They had one of those stupid arguments. Liesel had to justify her . . . level of expectation for her children. "It's not that I don't think the world of you. Of all of you. Of course I do. But I don't care about these . . . stupid . . . measures of success."

"You have to realize," Jean said, "that these are the measures of success that matter to us. This is what Paul cares about. You can't understand what's going on here if you don't accept that."

The fact is, whenever Liesel used to watch him play, she felt almost unbearably tense. Tense and bored and somehow sorry for him. That he wanted to win so much. But after it was over, she could never remember anything. The name of his opponent, the final score. Paul would talk about this point or that point, and everybody seemed to know what he was talking about. Even Susie, his other sister, who otherwise had no interest in sports. But afterward, none of it mattered to Liesel, she was just glad it was over. And now the whole thing was over. She wanted to show him some sympathy, some of which she felt, but mostly what she felt was relief. Now you can get on with your life.

Bill, of course, kept pestering Paul to postpone whatever decision he was going to make until his head had cleared. "That's a long time to be retired."

"My head is clear," Paul told him.

He flew out to Austin and stayed with them for several days. Just to finish up the paperwork on this house he was buying near Wimberley. Also, he wanted to take a contractor around. The house was only ten years old, one of these modernist boxes, all glass and concrete, which had lately become fashionable in Austin. But the trouble with minimalism is that it puts a lot of pressure on the quality of craftsmanship, because everything stands out—any asymmetry or loose wires or leaks or rust. The property ran down to the Blanco River. The boathouse needed work, too, and not just a lick of paint.

Liesel asked him, "How's Dana doing? How's Cal?" But he only said, "Inez is around, she's got help."

By this point, she was deep in the middle of teaching—her last full year. She was going through her own retirement doubts. Maybe she didn't pay enough attention. She also thought, he probably wants to be left alone. And they had a nice time together. They went out to restaurants, the restaurants he used to love as a kid, Fonda San Miguel, lantern-lit, with bright tiled floors and potted trees inside. Ruby's BBQ, just behind their house on 29th Street—you could smell the smoker from their backyard. He let himself eat whatever he wanted to. In the evenings, he sat with Bill and watched baseball on TV. Paul was never their most communicative child. He was always very level. He went jogging in the mornings to stay in shape. He made decisions about the house. He spent a certain amount of time on his computer. And then after a week he returned to New York.

Bill kept worrying about Paul, about what he was going to do. It's a long time to be retired, he kept telling people on the phone. Mostly the other kids. It became a kind of refrain. But Bill was a worrier, Paul seemed fine.

When Liesel asked him what his plans were, he said, "Right now, I'm taking a break. It's just nice waking up in the mornings without anything hurting. But I'm talking to people, I'm looking at some options."

This seemed to her perfectly sensible. His face was still his face, handsome and finely drawn, sun-damaged, an athlete's face, but she could see the boy in it, too, who doesn't want to have to talk. They Skyped sometimes, for Cal's sake—Liesel liked to keep tabs on her grandchildren this way. Mostly Paul set the computer on their living-room coffee table. She could see the sofa and the plants behind it, on the windowsill; the skies of New York in the window, maybe a few tall apartment buildings, depending on the angle of the screen. Dana came in and out of the picture, she said hello. Inez was sometimes there, too. It all seemed a little crowded to Liesel. She could imagine people getting on each other's nerves. When you're young, when you're that age, it's important to have a few money worries, something to strive for, to get you out the door in the morning. A mortgage. But Paul always looked very relaxed.

When he flew back to Austin a few months later to take possession of the house, he came on his own.

The Volvo pulled into the driveway, clanking against the dip in the other direction. Bill stepped out, in his teaching jacket and a faintly striped shirt—one of her presents to him. The collar was new enough it still stood out around his neck. She used birthdays and

Christmas to replace certain items of his wardrobe because he never bought anything for himself.

She waited for him to climb the steps, she waited for him to open the door, and then he was in the house and calling to her, "Are you ready? Liesel? Liesel? I don't want to be late."

But she had to find her purse first, it wasn't in the hallway. And she had bought a little something for Cal, which she wanted to give him. She couldn't find that either.

"You can give it to him when we get home."

"It's just a little thing. But it will keep him busy in the car."

"Come on," Bill said eventually. "Let's go. You don't need your purse."

"It has chocolate in it. I'm hungry. Dana might want some, too, after her flight."

"And what you really want, when you're traveling with a baby, is for people not to be late."

"He's not a baby—he's four years old."

"Even so," Bill said.

Maybe he was right; but still the idea upset her, having gone to the trouble of buying it, of not arriving with the present in her hand.

"Come on, come on," Bill said again; but, in fact, he wasn't in a bad mood. Just the thought of a full house cheered him up. More than the reality, sometimes. "Move 'em on, head 'em up," he started singing. And he found Liesel's purse, with the present inside it, sitting on the bench in the kitchen under a dish towel.

"What are you so anxious about?" he asked her, when they got in the car.

He backed into the wide empty road. All of the lawns were yellow, all of the trees were bare. The sunshine on this bareness had a curious effect. The temperature was mid-sixties, very mild; it was as if everything had died for no reason. The sun kept shining and cast little sketches of shade across the asphalt, from the twig-thin branches. Funny how a neighborhood grows old. People with kids move in at the same time, the kids grow up and move out. Now couples with babies couldn't afford to buy here anymore. Dodie, the old lady across the street, had turned ninety-three; she was still hanging on and remembered the woman they bought their own house from, she knew Mr. Mosby. But these links keep breaking.

They passed the law school building and Bill avoided the turnoff for I-35. Instead, he drove under the highway, two raised improbable tracks curving above them, swoops of concrete. He liked to take the old road, Airport Boulevard, even if it meant stopping at a few lights. Liesel looked at the parking lots, the single-story businesses, car washes and Family Markets and taco shacks. When she first came to Austin, thirty years ago, she couldn't understand how Americans could live this way, from parking lot to parking lot. Her parents visited and she watched their reaction. Quiet neighborhoods split by five-lane roads. On the near side, out of her window, Liesel could see backyards, small houses, picket fences, chain-link fences. The corner plots of residential streets. Everything had a temporary feel, which she now found attractive. The landscape sloped here and there, trees sprouted, grass grew, you put down houses and streets where you found a space. And there was plenty of space.

"We have to get a tree today," Liesel said. "Susie told me not to wait. Last year we waited and there was nothing good left."

"With Dana?"

"If she wants. Cal might like it."

"They just got off a plane."

"Then she doesn't have to come. Jean can come. I'll need a little help."

But it's also true the city was changing. Local government did its best to deal with all the newcomers, but sometimes she got the feeling there was a two-tier city—for the young, good-looking, successful types, who wouldn't be out of place in Brooklyn or San Francisco. And for everybody else.

Take any route out of town and you came across signs for new

housing developments, people kept moving in. Cheap-looking houses where you had to drive forty-five minutes to get to work. It was
hard to meet anyone who grew up in Austin anymore. Not the guy
at the checkout at the co-op grocery store or the waitress at the new
Italian restaurant or the lawyer you went to after your old lawyer
retired. When Jean was a baby, Bill bought her one of those *Native
Texan* T-shirts, in red, white, and blue. She was the only one of the
kids born in Austin, at Seton Medical Center in Bryker Woods. One
of the older neighborhoods, which meant that some of it was developed in the 1930s. The other kids were all East-Coasters. Sometimes
Liesel thought, this made a difference. But what the difference was,
who could say.

Henrik was coming after Christmas. Another thing for her to
think about. She had never met him before, Jean's married lover. Apparently he was in the process of a divorce. But Liesel's information
was usually out of date, she didn't like to keep asking. It could have
happened already.

"What exactly do you expect to accomplish?" Bill said. They were
stuck in the lane merging with 71. For a second, she couldn't figure
out what he meant. But then he added: "By inviting her like this."

"I don't know. I don't know what's going on. Nobody tells me.
And if I ask Paul, he gets defensive."

"That's why I don't ask."

"He says to me, there's a reason we didn't get married. This is the
kind of thing he says. We wanted to keep our . . . separate lives. I
don't know what Cal's supposed to make of it."

"My understanding is that when Paul visits them in New York he
stays over."

"Who told you that? What does that mean?"

"Nathan said something last night. We were discussing sleeping
arrangements."

"What else did Nathan say? Does Paul expect to stay at Wheeler
Street?"

"I don't know. He thinks Paul has taken his retirement pretty hard."

"Jean says he talks sometimes like one of these self-help evangelists. I haven't heard it. He sounds like Paul to me."

"Well, the least we can say is that Dana is extremely tolerant."

"Maybe she should be less tolerant," Liesel said.

Her older brother, who was retired and living in Hamburg, had recently sent her a document he had put together, photocopies of their parents' letters to each other, when they lived apart during the war. Their father was stationed in Gotenhafen, now part of Poland. The Russians were advancing and Liesel's mother caught the last train out with the kids—they lived in Berlin for a year with one of her uncles, a minor government official. Later, when the war ended, they shifted to Flensburg, which is where Liesel eventually grew up.

The letters were upsetting for several reasons. Her father wrote things he shouldn't have written, about their prisoners of war, about shooting the deserters and the outcomes of certain battles . . . things she didn't want to read. But you have to make allowances. People living in the middle of history are in a tunnel they can't see out of. It's the difference between saying what you think in your own home, among friends, and expressing yourself in a public place. The past is a very public place. When you write a book about your family, when you publish your memoirs, people keep telling you stories— they send you things. Even your own brother. In spite of everything, they want to have the facts recorded. But Liesel also thought, reading over her parents' letters, she couldn't help thinking, my father would never have left us the way Paul has left his child. It took a war to keep them apart. But Paul has these expectations, he has these ideas, about how you can live your life, how you have to be honest and do what you want, which are more shameful than anything my father wrote.

They had been living in Flensburg for several months, with her mother's parents, when a man showed up at the door in uniform. Liesel, seven years old, had answered the bell and called back over her shoulder, to her mother, who was in the kitchen: "There's a soldier at the door who looks like father." It *was* her father. She knew as much when she heard her mother's footsteps; she was running. Liesel thought, what does Cal think when he sees Paul.

Around the airport, the landscape is very flat. The skies are wide but somehow flat, too. You feel like you're a long way from anywhere. Then a huge hotel appears off the highway, the airport Hilton, and the traffic thickens on the access road. You can see the control tower, its little bleeps of light, and the parking lot stretching out away from the terminal—all those brightly colored cars in the sunshine, lined up as if by some obsessive child, in little rows.

She said to Bill, "I was going to put her in the au pair's room, but if Paul is staying, too, we'll have to think of something else."

"Put her there for now."

The curbside pickup lane was semi-underground—the road sloped into a cool shady concrete-colored world. Everything seemed to slow down; the speed limit was 10 mph. Cars pulled in and pulled out again, with their lights on. Through glass doors, Liesel could see the baggage carousels rolling along. People waited outside, smoking; there were wide stone benches, but mostly they paced around or sat on their luggage. Enjoying the mild Texas air. But she couldn't see Dana or Cal. For security reasons, you weren't allowed to park outside the terminal anymore. So Bill had to circle, into the sunshine again, along brand-new mostly empty roads, in the middle of nowhere.

"I don't know what I want to happen," Liesel said.

"So long as we get through with nobody getting sick, it'll be a triumph." Bill was still in a good mood, looking forward to it.

They had to circle three times before Dana was waiting for them. Liesel saw her first, standing by a brand-new suitcase, the kind you can pull along the ground. Like a stewardess, Liesel thought. She had forgotten how handsome Dana was, it was disconcerting. She wore a short tweed skirt over cream tights and a bright red turtleneck—the sort of woman who can go to her hairdresser and flip through the magazines and realistically ask them to make her look like one of the photographs. Without any delusion or vanity. Cal had been dressed up for the occasion, too, in skinny corduroy pants and a fancy plaid shirt. But he seemed tired and bored; he kept playing with the suitcase, trying to release the handle, to make it work. His nose was running. Bill pulled in behind one of those new pickup trucks, almost an SUV, big and aggressive, totally clean and white. The guy in the passenger's seat had rolled down his window—he said something to Dana, who said something back as they drove away. Then she saw Bill and smiled and made eye contact with Liesel, too. She didn't look very unhappy.

Cal had made a mess of his lunch on the slippery seat-back tray and so Dana took him to the bathroom when they landed and tried to clean him up. There was rice-in-tomato-sauce all over him. She even changed his shirt after the suitcase came through, which is partly why they were a bit late and why he was grumpy. Even though she knew Liesel didn't care about these things and was just as likely to be put off by . . . presentableness as endeared by it. But Dana couldn't help herself. What you do when you're stressed is what you do.

The last thing she wanted was some guy trying to pick her up while she waited for her in-laws to arrive. Or ex in-laws. Or not even that. But he was perfectly sweet. The kind of earnest sensitive bearded type who spends a lot of his free time in the gym. His wallet was full of business cards and pictures of his little girl. Her mother was just a one-night stand but he was doing his bit. They sat next to each other on the flight—he gave Cal his pack of sour cream pretzels. One of the reasons she changed Cal's shirt in the bathroom was to get away from him, but then he was waiting outside anyway when she walked out.

His brother came to pick him up. The guy gave her his business card as he left. "If you ever need anything while you're in town," he said.

"What am I going to need?"

"A greener greener lawn." He sold eco-friendly irrigation systems; it was a company slogan.

Then Liesel called out, "Dana!" with an exclamation mark in her voice. It was like switching between costumes in a play, except worse, because you have to do it on stage. Liesel tried to get out of the car, but Dana wouldn't let her.

"He'll be happier with me in the back," she said, before realizing, maybe she isn't offering. Maybe she just wanted to give you a hug. Anyway, that's not how you should have turned her down.

Bill pushed himself out of the driver's seat to walk around the car and open the trunk. There was an air of slow-motion hurry about the whole thing—cars pulled in and out, cops waved them on, people were waiting on the curb, coming home for Christmas, looking for their ride, everybody inching forward, hanging back, getting in line. Surging off. Bill bent down for the suitcase and Dana tried to embrace him or stop him, even she didn't know. But Bill won. He grunted and lifted her suitcase and threw it in the trunk. Afterward, he put his hand on Cal's head. "Hey, son," he said. "You all right, kid?" Cal didn't respond—he was annoyed that Bill had taken the suitcase away. "That's okay," Bill said. "Not talking while the flavor lasts."

There was a car seat in the back, but it wasn't set up, and Dana spent a minute trying to figure out the mechanism. Feeling strangely hassled and anxious, as if this were a test of motherhood. At the same time worrying that it might seem like a reproach to Bill and Liesel for not setting it up themselves. When they were both buckled in and ready to go, she reached forward and squeezed Liesel's shoulder from behind.

"It's nice to see you," she said. But the gesture seemed wrong, somehow both too intimate and too formal. The kind of thing a daughter would do to her elderly mother, which wasn't their relationship.

"I've brought something for Cal," Liesel said. "Something small and stupid. And I've got a piece of chocolate for you, if you want. I'm going to have one."

She turned around to reach them over, and smiled at Dana—her broad round face, under her short gray hair, seemed almost brimming with good intentions. Dana felt something hot on her cheeks, like a blush.

The toy was a small plastic airplane, with a propeller in front that you could wind up. A typical Liesel gift, which probably cost two dollars. She bought these sorts of things for herself as well—her desk was full of them. This one made an airplane noise as it unwound again, a rushing takeoff sound, a sort of whee! Maybe after all it was a little babyish for Cal, which Liesel seemed to sense.

"He can play with it in the bath," she said.

"What do you say?" Dana said. "Cal. What do you say."

"I thought, since he just got off a plane . . ."

"He thanks you," Dana told her.

And in fact he played with it happily enough—stopping the blade with his finger, and annoying everyone with the noise. One of the funny things about learning to talk is that it makes kids more private than they were before. They don't want to look at you because they know you might expect them to say something. At least that's how it felt sometimes to Dana. That Cal was retreating more, was more boyish, concentrating on stupid little things, and not listening to her. But he probably had other reasons for that, too.

"Jean said she would meet us back at Wheeler Street for lunch," Bill said. "I don't know about Paul."

"Are you excited to see Daddy?" Dana said to Cal. She didn't want them to think that she was poisoning him against their son. But even so, it seemed like the wrong thing to say—the wrong tone. She felt like she was on one of those landings with too many doors. All her feelings seemed to get in the way of each other.

The car drove out from under the shadow of the access road above them, and the landscape opened up. There was yellow grass between the highways, that wide flat sky. Dana rolled down her window and closed her eyes against the mild inrush of air. She said, "When we got outside this morning it was about six in the morning and twenty degrees. The car service had cardboard laid out on the floor, which was just . . . mush. Everything was just dirty and cold."

"Welcome to paradise," Bill said.

"That's what Paul always says."

On the drive through Queens, she had stared out the window at the traffic, hurrying in both directions, people trying to get out of the city before Christmas, commuters commuting in. She saw snow piled up by the railings, the elevated exit lanes, held up by heavy purplish walls, the yards of row houses backing onto them, bordered by chain-link fences. The world looks harsh and depressing at seven in the morning, during a Northeastern winter. Who would live in this place, maybe Paul was right. Cal kept repeating something, he was trying to remember something: one rhinoceros, two elephants, three pigeons, some story he read, maybe, but Dana didn't recognize it. All gray, he said. All gray. Maybe a game he played with Inez. Another thing to worry about. But somehow when you're in a taxi, heading to the airport, nothing matters much. This isn't your life, you can get out.

"I don't know if Cal would like to help us pick out a Christmas tree," Liesel said. "I don't know if he's too tired."

"Cal, what do you think. Should we pick out a tree?"

One of those strange overlaps between what he was thinking about and what they were talking about had taken place. "Are there any . . . are kids . . . coming, too?" he asked.

"He wants to know if the cousins are around."

"Susie gets in late tonight," Bill said. "Nathan's coming tomorrow."

Dana stroked her son's hair. "Not yet," she told him.

"Is Daddy there?"

"I don't know."

"Why don't we just call him," Liesel said. "I don't have a phone. Call him and tell him to come to lunch. He should be there. Or call Jean, she can tell him."

"I don't want to make him . . . make any plans," Dana said.

✳

For the rest of the week, until she flew home again on the 28th, Dana kept going over in her head a conversation she wanted to have with Liesel, an explanation or confession, which she wanted to have in person. If the circumstances seemed right, and she could get her story straight. But then her story kept changing; what she wanted to say kept changing.

Part of the problem was that she didn't have enough to tell them. I mean, she thought, you wouldn't always believe it, from an outside point of view, how little Paul and I have discussed what's going on. It seems like this big decision but I don't even know really who made it, or when it got decided. It's just . . . it's not that it just happened, but . . . these are the sorts of phrases that ran through her thoughts. But there were also things she wanted to conceal from Liesel, which it was going to require an effort of courage on her part *not* to conceal.

The first stage of their separation, if that's what it was, was also the easiest to identify. Paul bought the house in Wimberley—he flew in to Austin five days after losing to Borisov and arranged the bank transfer and signed the contracts. Dana was welcome to come along, he told her, and bring Cal, if she wanted to . . . but the fact is, they had argued about buying the place and he had won the argument simply because he had the money, more money than he knew what to do with, and she couldn't reasonably stop him from using it. Also, it was pretty clear to her at the time, if not clear to him, that he was going through something—some kind of trauma or post-trauma, which involved a certain amount of denial about its own existence, which was part of the problem. In other circumstances, she might have fought harder, if for nothing else than the view of their relationship that meant they should make these decisions together. But she let him go; and he went.

Now she realized that maybe this was a mistake. Because when you buy a house it's not a one-time decision or transgression, it's only the beginning in a long line of future decisions and transgressions, which is what it turned out to be.

Paul started spending more and more time there. He hired a contractor to fix up the place, but he also brought in various architects to discuss other projects. The house came with twenty-seven acres of land, much of it along the Blanco River, and part of Paul's ambition for the property involved building a cluster of houses with enough bedrooms and facilities (kitchens and bathrooms and laundry rooms) for everybody he knew—or at least everybody he liked or everybody who was genetically related to him—to stay and hang out in their own private space, which was easy enough to arrange. But he also wanted shared or communal areas, which meant that if they wanted, large numbers of people could go about the business of daily life together. Cooking meals, eating them, looking after kids, playing games together, watching movies.

All of which occupied an increasing share of his time and attention—talking to architects and contractors and city planners, soliciting and receiving bids and designs, discussing his ideas with his brother and sisters, but also flying out to Austin to go over these plans on site. Dana understood that after you give up on one career, which took up all your energy and time (and he was used to being on the road, away from both of them, often six months a year), you need something else to fill the vacuum. But it seemed to her that what he was filling it with was a deliberate attempt to replace the perfectly viable family he had in New York with other people. Specifically, his old family—who, so far as Dana could tell, had little interest in the project and were mostly humoring Paul, if that, and were also very worried about him and kept calling Dana to find out what was going on.

"What do you want me to say," she said. "I don't know. I just figure—I don't know—it's his money. If that's how he wants to spend it. What can I do."

Which isn't to say that she didn't also pick fights with him. She did that, too. So that it got to the point that he didn't want to bring up anything connected to the Wimberley house in her presence. So they stopped talking about it. Dana resented the fact that every time he flew to Austin, she was left holding the baby, holding down the fort, whatever you want to call it. But Paul, reasonably enough, pointed out that she had Inez five days a week, she was hardly over-occupied at the moment. And in any case, he was very happy to take Cal with him, if she didn't want to go.

"What am I supposed to do with Inez?"

"That's not a—that's not a reason for me, or for you to—I mean, she can come along, if this is the kind of job she wants. But I'm not going to hang around New York for the nanny."

"That's not what I mean. I'm thinking about Cal. He has his routines, he's got his little friends. This is where he lives."

"He's more moveable now than he's going to be at any other point in his life. Trust me on this one. And there are kids in Texas. There are routines for him in Texas."

This line of reasoning had the effect that maybe Paul wanted it to have—she stopped complaining about being stuck with Cal. Until the second stage of their separation, when these sorts of details had to be part of the discussion.

Along the way, while all this was going on, it was very hard to tell how much Paul liked her. Whether he liked spending time with her or her and Cal together, and whether he was angry with her or not. She really couldn't tell. He didn't seem very happy, she almost never saw him particularly happy, but she never got the sense that he was unhappier around her than he was with anybody else. Not that he seemed in any way obviously or measurably depressed—Paul was always a low-key kind of guy, very easygoing, somebody who didn't get too worked up about anything. For example, he very rarely lost his temper with her. Almost never. Rarely enough that this seemed an almost-conscious decision on his part, a piece of strategy. Not because he used to get mad all the time, but because when they were getting along better, or if not better, more intimately, little fights just seemed like part of the deal, something you couldn't entirely avoid at close quarters, they just came up from time to time, and escalated, especially when Cal was very small and nobody got enough sleep.

But these conditions weren't quite the conditions under which they seemed to be operating. Cal slept through, almost always; in any case, both of them had gotten used to the broken nights by this point. They didn't matter much anymore. But she also got the sense from Paul that whatever decisions he had privately reached he was also waiting for her to make her own decisions, maybe to take the burden off his hands; and in the meantime, he had honorably reflected, it wasn't fair to get mad at somebody for not being what you had already decided they weren't. So he reined it in, he reined himself in, he had that look of a man in training who decides on how much sugar and alcohol he will permit himself, and the answer was, at least in terms of their intimacy, not much.

Sometimes, it's true, they still had sex—mostly when she initiated it, but not always. One of the chillier aspects of their relationship, one of the things that freaked her out most, is that when he commenced sexual operating procedures (a phrase which, in their happier days, he had used to describe whatever he used to do to show her he was in the mood) and she put him off, by kissing and releasing him a heartbeat sooner than he'd like, or any of the other physical gestures you learn to make in the course of a long relationship without any need for verbal reasons or indications, he never pressed her anymore. He never forced her to give him those indications and reasons, he simply accepted it. The atmosphere in their bedroom was friendly and almost polite and about two degrees lower than room temperature. You had to look pretty closely, with extremely finely calibrated instruments, to realize not just that they weren't getting along very well, but that the level of human communication between them, in all its various forms, had sunk to record lows.

On the first night, when he flew back from Texas, after a few weeks away, they usually had sex. With some need, some appetite for the act. And sometimes it felt impersonal, people making use of each other for practical and not dishonorable purposes, and sometimes it felt like more than that—a reminder, an expression of deeper urgency, but it wasn't always easy to tell the difference. And after a while, the difference didn't seem to matter very much to Dana.

At some point, of course, they had to talk about what was going on. And it was never Paul's style, as inward and self-sufficient as he tended to be, to shirk these conversations. It was a point of pride with him, not to be the kind of guy who refused to admit there was anything wrong as a way of sliding out of a situation. If you want to talk, let's talk, was his attitude. Let's go over the whole thing from the beginning. But she got bored of his tone. She wanted something else from him, she wanted it to cost him more—which you couldn't really express in those terms. At least, when she did, he seemed unusually reasonable in his replies. I can only be as unhappy as I am about what's happening. I can't be more or less. I don't want to pretend or fake it just . . . to be polite or something.

Dana, throughout the year and a half the slow process of their separation took, had the sense that she was playing one of those defensive specialists who keeps winning points just by getting everything back, until you lash out and overhit, just to end the point, one way or another. Because you can't keep going back and forth this way. You start running out of legs. You stop caring. At least, this is what happened to her.

Her friends, her girlfriends, insisted from the very early stages that he was seeing somebody else. That he had a girl in Texas, an old girl-friend, somebody he had met on tour, whoever, that he kept coming back to. This is what all those airplane trips are about; this is why he keeps having to meet up with the contractors and the architects in person. But Dana shook her head. She genuinely didn't think that this is what was going on. Part of her wished that he *was* having an affair—because it would suggest some reasonable ambition or desire on his part, to live a kind of life she could recognize, to make up for whatever was missing in their own relationship, which she could maybe address, in one way or another, after the inevitable upset and recrimination and heartbreak of finding out. Sometimes she even asked him about it, just to provoke a response. "Please," he said. "You know me better than that." And she thought she did.

But it was an argument along these lines that eventually produced the third stage of their separation—because he figured out, or insisted, that maybe what was going on here is that Dana needed someone else to fill the gaps. "You're trying to push me away," she said. "This is what you *want* to happen." She had been rejected before along these lines, she was sensitive to it. In spite of the fact that she was very used to the attention of men, she had also become accustomed to their inattention.

"What I want here," he told her—they were having this conversation on the phone. For some reason, most of their intimate conversations happened on the phone. And in this case, something she said had forced him to go under the skin, at least a little; to admit part of what was going on. His tone had changed. He sounded on the edge of tears, not because he was actually going to cry, but because he was always weirdly susceptible to the idea of honest conversation, of breaking through in this way—the idea itself was enough to move him. But maybe that was just her own cynical take. "What I want here," he said, "is something that you have made pretty clear to me that you don't want. Which I don't blame you for. I want to get out of all of this competitive . . . living, I don't want to do it anymore, and I don't want to put Cal through it either. But that's not entirely my choice here, which I freely recognize."

"Look, Paul. You're just going through something right now, which is understandable . . ."

"Of course I understand that's what's going on. But just because it takes a certain life event to make a point of view possible, doesn't mean you can dismiss it on those terms."

"Well, yes, that's what it . . . that's why they . . . I mean, when you were a kid, this is what your parents call a phase. At least mine did."

"And when you were a kid, it annoyed the hell out of you, right?"

"It did. Of course it did. But I mean, they turned out to be . . . They were right, right? That's what you figure out."

"I don't think that's what I figured out. I had fifteen years of being exposed to a very specific worldview, about what counts and what doesn't, and what you should strive for, and . . . what it should feel like to strive. I'm talking here about learning to endure really pretty high levels of physical pain on a daily basis. Now, I realize, I'm not an idiot, that this is . . . like I said . . . an extreme form of what's generally going on out there . . . but even at Cal's age, when you see him with the other kids. I can run faster than you. You're stupid. You don't know how to read. You can't even spell your own name. It's . . . totally relentless . . . And what I feel like saying to these kids is basically just that . . . all of you suck. Not just now but in the future. This is what your life experience is going to teach you. That at everything you care about and want to get good at the world will turn out to be full of people who are much better than you are. And it's pointless."

"I don't know what you expect me to do about any of this, Paul. I mean, this isn't something I can fix."

"I don't expect you . . ."

"And we can't fix it for Cal, either. If that's what you're thinking."

"Look, that's just not . . . Look, I mean, what we have, through no virtue of our own. What I have. Is a lot of money, by any reasonable standard. And the truth is, you *can* buy your way out of a lot of this kind of existential trouble. That's what I'm trying to do. Whether you want to . . . whether this is something . . ."

"Paul, all that you're doing here is moving to the suburbs. Or the country. Or whatever. Someplace outside Austin, I don't know what it is. Suburbs or country. But I mean, people have done this before. This is not some radical solution. This is just another thing that people get competitive about."

"If this isn't something . . ."

"What do you expect me to do?" she said.

"You should do what you want to do. You should feel free to do that."

That was really as explicit as they had gotten on the subject. And the next time he called, the next time she saw him, other things came up. The circumstances that had produced the mood that had produced the conversation were not repeated. And since both of them, maybe for different reasons, were slightly embarrassed by the conversation, which felt much more important and philosophical at the time than it did to Dana afterward, when it seemed to her the kind of intense exchange you have in college late at night with some guy who is probably too awkward to make a move on you, and keeps putting off the moment, until you don't really want to make out with him anyway.

The funny thing was (though it was absolutely predictable, too) that Paul seemed to spend all his ridiculous amounts of free time training or staying in shape. There was a group of guys around Austin, semi-celebrities Jean called them, who used to meet up and go running together. Along the river, or around Decker Lake or out by Zilker or along the greenbelt. Lance Armstrong was one of them. According to Jean, he was like the leader of the pack, and Paul started biking with him, too; maybe once a week or once every couple of weeks, a bunch of them hit the road together and tore up the miles. Afterward, they swam a few laps at Barton Springs. Lance was getting serious about the triathlon, although at this point Paul was mostly just along for the ride.

But his whole physical shape had started to change, the impression he made or the aura he gave off or whatever. Obviously, he was never fat, he always looked like what he was, a physically confident and athletically able young man. But tennis required a certain amount of upper body bulk, which is partly what attracted Dana to him, physically, in the first place—the strength of his forearms, the way his shoulders moved inside a collared shirt. But all that was changing. He was now like one of those skinny guys who looks like he can run forever. And when he smiled (somehow he seemed to smile more these days, though maybe this was because most of their conversations happened over Skype, he was staring at them out of a computer screen, and maybe he felt like his facial expressions had to do a lot of the work of communicating with Cal), she could see the skull under the skin very vividly. His mouth was a jaw, his eye sockets protected his eyes, the whole structure, foundation and purpose of his face seemed visible to her. He didn't look good, she thought. He looked like somebody who believed in something and had a purpose. And even when he seemed particularly happy or charming, it was like his whole countenance was lit up by a candle flame which flickered behind it, and that he was aware of this precious flame and wanted to show it to the world. He reminded her of some of the good-looking ultra-Christian guys she knew at Sidwell Friends, who responded to the embarrassment of class privilege with a kind of self-denying and aggressively happy humility. Some of those guys could be real assholes about sex, she knew firsthand. At least Paul wasn't.

And what made the whole thing hard on her was the fact that in spite of everything, and indeed sometimes because of what he was going through, and what his response to it was, she really liked him. He was a decent guy. One of the things you learn as an athlete is the kind of self-discipline that allows you to practice what you preach. And Paul had become extremely good at doing what he said he was going to do. If he said he was available to Skype with Cal at three o'clock on Sunday afternoon, Dana knew perfectly well that the little buzz-ring of her computer, one of those manufactured happy sounds that genuinely did the trick, produced the emotion it was meant to suggest, would buzz and ring at three o'clock on the dot. When they bought the apartment, they set up a joint account for mortgage payments. Paul almost never used it these days, but it was always full—he clearly kept an eye on it, and topped it off months before she might have wanted to ask him to. He never mentioned this either, and so they never needed to have a conversation about money, or the larger conversation that the money conversation would have included. This was just something he did. If he said he could take Cal for three weeks in August, he would fly to New York on the agreed day to pick him up and then either stay a few nights in the city with Dana, to acclimatize Cal to the changeover, or take him back to Austin on the afternoon flight, whatever it was they had decided beforehand.

Plus, on some level she genuinely believed everything he was saying, about competition and striving and the pointlessness of it all. Paul had had the same reaction to his competitive athletic ability that she had had years before to her own physical attractiveness—that it was superficial and occasionally useful maybe, but also something you have to learn to put up with, and which can easily become a distraction from things that matter. After a while you realize that every time you enter into an intellectual conversation with some guy at a party, or even with one of your friends of long standing who should have known better, just the fact of your prettiness seems to them to be making promises that you have no intention of keeping. Every time you confess a feeling or make a joke, you give off these promises. And there's nothing they can do about it, there's nothing you can say to them or explain in advance, because whatever you say or explain they just keep hearing more promises. So on some level you realize that whoever you actually are, whatever it is that you are actually like, is so tied up in the complicated but ultimately predictable way that other people react to you (women, too, whose expectations based on your looks are usually different from but not always deeper than the expectations of men), that you genuinely can't tell anymore if you're funny or interesting or honest.

Moving to Wimberley, or to a house outside Wimberley on the Blanco River, seemed to Dana like an extreme reaction to this problem, or whatever version of this problem Paul was responding to, but it also seemed to her like an understandable reaction. She just didn't want to move to Wimberley.

Which meant that when she *did* start seeing somebody in New York, she was more shocked and upset by the sudden realization of what was ending, or what she was giving up, than she had expected. The depths of this realization, the emotional frame of mind it put her in, the vulnerability it exposed, gave off more of those promises to the guy in question (like a scent or a body odor, intimately connected with you, but which you also have only limited control over), so that everything in both directions (retreating from one lover and advancing toward another) happened faster than she could internalize or digest. She had reached, in ordinary daily life—the decisions you make, the places you go, the people you see—the kind of hyper-speed unpredictable reality of accident scenes, in which instincts you were only dimly aware of suddenly emerge and become visible, act in the powerful ways they are capable of acting, before submerging again and leaving you to cope with or come to terms with their appearance.

The guy in question was a TV producer. He was older, he had been divorced twice, some of his shows were pretty successful, though most of that was in the past; and in fact he seemed much less sure of himself, more touching and awkward, than any of the obvious ways of describing him would suggest. Which didn't prevent him from being fairly persistent in his pursuit. They met through friends—his daughter worked with one of the photographers Dana also sometimes worked for. Stephen had a big apartment on Third Avenue, a nice place, though in other respects he seemed to Dana fairly hard up, in an attractive way. He had inexpensive tastes in restaurants, this was his own phrase for it. Most of his money was what he called "old money, from the 1990s"—his current income fluctuated between modest and nonexistent. But he also didn't seem to care that much about any of this stuff. In that way, he resembled Paul. He had made some decent television programs he was still proud of, he had worked on a couple of turkeys, too; in any case, that side of his life was probably behind him, a fact that he had painfully come to terms with. But he was still ambitious in other respects. After you've been through two marriages and two divorces, after you've raised two kids, at the age of fifty-three you realize, you have a limited time left, you've got

limited vitality, to do the stuff you want to do with your life. This
was all part of his pickup routine, part of his sales pitch, which he was
self-aware enough to flag up even while he was making it.

They still hadn't slept together. In that respect, it was all much
more innocent than she could have imagined. They made out once,
in the back of a cab; but she broke it off, a fact about which he was
surprisingly understanding.

"Look," he said, "I get it, I've been through these things, through
the ups and downs. It's also true that I can probably control myself
now a little better than when I was twenty years old."

"I need to make a few things clearer, in my own head," she started
to say. "Not just in your head, sweetheart," he told her. "These things
aren't just in your head. What you want is a note from teacher. That
it's okay. But nobody's teacher anymore."

For some reason, it didn't annoy her to be talked to this way. But
he was also very tender toward her, very solicitous. And somehow
the innocence heightened the intensity of feeling. What it felt like was
kindness, a kind of generosity, very simple, which she hadn't been
able to show toward Paul in a long time; and she got the sense, from
his side, that something similar was going on. They listened carefully
to each other, they explained themselves carefully. The way you do
when you're young. She also realized that before anything else happened, she needed to talk to Paul, she probably needed to see him;
and she wanted to talk to Liesel, too.

———

The houses around Wheeler Street have big front yards. People
work hard on them, and even in winter there are red pyracantha
bushes, pansies in the grass, bright ornamental cabbages, pots of
geraniums on the stoop, and lots of Christmas lights. A park at the
bottom of the road has a creek running through it, overgrown with
weeds and bedded down between limestone walls. Not so much a

park as a grassy field. Since she first got together with Paul, Dana had come to Austin a half-dozen times, and she felt a faint sting of home-coming as Bill turned the Volvo up the familiar curved street that led to their house.

What surprised her, and upset her more, is the way Cal ran out of the car as soon as they got there. "Is it the swing house?" he said, and she realized (which she knew perfectly well) that he had come more recently than she had—that he spent time there with Paul.

Liesel, lifting her bad leg out of the car, explained: "We had Mario put up a swing on the front porch."

Cal had already run down the side alley, past Liesel's study, into the backyard. It was nice to see him running after being cooped up on the plane all morning, staring at a screen; but it hurt a little, too. One of those premature ways that divorce or separation forces you to accept that the kids have their own lives. Bill started dragging her suitcase out of the trunk, and Dana took over.

"That's all right," he said.

"It wheels," she told him; and he let her pull it up the driveway to the front door.

When they got inside, Liesel led the way upstairs. "I've put you in the wooden room," she said—a token of intimacy, which Dana heard and understood. It meant she knew the family jargon.

"I don't know what he sleeps in at home," Liesel went on, a little breathlessly. At the far end of the landing, she opened a door. "But when Cal's here he likes to sleep in the crib. Paul had it until he was four. He refused to sleep in a bed and in the end, it didn't matter—he could climb in and out perfectly easily. It didn't seem worth fight-ing about." She looked at Dana; her eyes were bright. Whatever awkwardness she might have felt had been translated somehow into something more sentimental. "Well," she said. "I'll leave you to it. I'm making coffee if you want some. Jean should be back soon, she said she was bringing lunch. I'll go see what Cal is doing. He's fine out there, he doesn't do anything dangerous."

Dana sat on the freshly made bed when Liesel was gone. She looked at the shelves, which were full of old books, a showpiece collection of leather-bound Walter Scott novels (not in very good condition), but also kids' books, the Hardy Boys series, Nancy Drew. Whatever nobody wanted ended up here. And in front of the books, on shelf after shelf, she saw trophies. Mostly the cheap kind, with painted marble bases and plastic golden figures screwed into the top. For second place in the AISD Geometry Competition, 1985, Nathan Essinger. Also, some of Paul's tennis trophies, the early ones. Bill was a serial buyer of cheap antiques, *Schnäppchen* he called them: willow-pattern plates, Kilim rugs, barometers and oil-paintings and prints. The room was full of those, too. It looked like a junk shop, but in a pleasant way. On top of a rocking chair, gathering dust, lay three volumes of the *World Book Encyclopedia* 1978. That kind of thing. Just the stuff you pick up along the way, in a long life, which has many children in it. Dana felt weirdly emotional. The story in her head, the confession or explanation she wanted to make to Liesel, had shifted again, and it was tiring, constantly, on some level of consciousness, to keep rewriting it.

Jean turned out to have strong opinions about Christmas trees. Dana had been looking forward to seeing her. Of all the Essinger kids, not including Paul, Jean was the one she felt she had most in common with. When they were in Austin together, which didn't happen often, they liked to duck out the backyard gate and walk to Trudy's for a margarita and sometimes even a quick cigarette. But what Dana felt when she saw Jean again was a strange kind of disappointment, which she found it hard afterward to put her finger on. (Her boyish friendly face, under the short hair, looked like Paul's; she dressed like a boy, too, in Levi's and a T-shirt, and gave Dana a fraternal hug.) Maybe what had weakened or disappeared was the sense she sometimes had in Jean's company that they were conspiring together about something. Or against something—the other Essingers. Or gossiping about them. But that door seemed to be shut.

But it was fine anyway, it was nice seeing her. It was totally fine. Jean brought in a bunch of random tacos from Changos, a Styrofoam box of nachos, a couple of soups, and a cheese-and-bean quesadilla for Cal. Apparently, this is what he liked—this is what Paul said he always ate at Changos. Another one of those little facts that, as his mother, you have to digest, you have to come to terms with. Bill said he wasn't eating, there was a meaningless football game on TV in the room next door, but then he came in and ate anyway. He finished up.

Jean looked well. Dana told her so. Not necessarily skinnier than usual . . . though she was always emerging from or entering into some diet or other, which she tried out not from any great conviction or desire to lose weight, but partly because her friends in London were all on these fashionable diets and there was nothing you could do except join in—if you wanted to cook for them or eat out with them. But the part of it she liked, the part she enjoyed, was coming up with edible possibilities out of the ridiculous sets of constraints, whatever they were. Only green vegetables and fats. Or no fats at all but only complex carbohydrates. It was like a challenge. It was like writing a sonnet, where for no particular reason you have to limit yourself to rhyming words every other line. Anyway, when she came back to Austin, she just wanted to eat. Not that Austinites weren't just as faddy about this kind of thing as everybody else. Probably more so.

All of this banter seemed like a way of putting something off, other kinds of conversation, whatever else it might seem obvious for them to talk about. But she did it very naturally, very confidently—Dana couldn't really be sure if Jean was holding back on her or not. Then they went out Christmas-tree shopping together. Cal came, too, which took a certain amount of persuasion. He kept asking, where are the kids, when are the kids coming. Late tonight, Dana told him. When you wake up tomorrow morning they'll all be there. Or some of them will. Which kids, he asked. That big one, that big boy? He meant Susie's son Ben. Yes, Ben will be there. They're flying in late tonight. With a baby. Little baby May. You won't be the baby of

the family anymore. *I'm not a baby* . . . Most of these reactions are
predictable, but you walk into them anyway. They got him in the
car with a square of peanut brittle Jean had been saving for some
occasion like this. He didn't actually like it, he made his what-weird-
thing-have-you-put-in-my-mouth face, but it got him in the seat.

First they drove to the lot on San Gabriel, five minutes around the
corner, where the Austin Optimist Club raised money every year by
selling trees. This was kind of a family tradition, but it was also a kind
of family tradition to show up too late when all the good trees had
gone and spend about half an hour kicking around the pine-needley
yellow grass and making jokes about the shitty trees. Holding one
up and saying, how about this one, while Liesel looked on semi-
despairing and starting to worry that this year we really won't get a
decent tree. Cal had a pretty good time. Part of what became clear—
Dana knew this already but said that every year she forgot—is that
the Essingers just had a different taste in trees than she did, different
standards. What Dana liked is the kind of Fraser fir you saw in the
window of Madison Avenue shops, covered in tinsel or fake snow, all
fluffy and bushy. Whereas the Essingers used real candles and needed
something sparser.

"Every year we have this argument," Dana said, to be a sport about
it. But then realized that just saying this, in the way she said it, was
making claims, about her rights in the family and what had happened
in the past and was going to happen in the future, that she wasn't in a
position to make anymore.

But Jean, who was sensitive to this kind of awkwardness, and good-
hearted, said in response what she would have said anyway, that Dana
had no taste, or she had the kind of glitzy, expensive but basically
low-brow American taste that you get from growing up in a city like
New York. In fact, she went on, because she was also sensitive to the
possibility that just by teasing Dana the way she always teased her,
by being friendly, you could also go too far. "What's really happening here is that I'm channeling Susie, who will judge us for what we

come home with today. And I don't want to be judged. I like Frasers, too. They're like the Christmas tree that Charlie Brown would want, except he always ends up with that scrawny kind where the branches are too weak to hold up the decorations."

It was tiring, for everyone, paying attention to all these claims you couldn't help making, and the possible misinterpretations. After San Gabriel, they drove out along North Lamar to the big Whole Foods between Fifth and Sixth. But they were sold out, too. So they doubled back and tried the Christmas tree farm at Papa Noels on Mopac, which wasn't any better. By this point Liesel was getting genuinely upset, Cal was tired and hungry, and there was a running argument, where Jean kept taking the high ground, about whether or not they should put up with something obviously substandard or keep going. "I don't mind doing this myself," Jean said. "If Cal is tired."

"Cal's going to be tired anyway. He can fall asleep in the car if he wants to," Dana said. And in spite of everything, all the new subtlety and complex etiquette involved, what was happening was real and ordinary and annoying, and fine, in the way it would have been anyway; and Dana felt, whether she was imagining it or not, that Jean was softening toward her, or opening up. Or not even that, but that whatever relationship they had always had in spite of or independent from Paul was surfacing again.

There's a Home Depot on Mopac, too, out past Papa Noels. By the time they got there, it was a little after five o'clock, the sudden subtropical winter dark was in the process of falling, where you go from a mild sunny winter day to actual streetlamp-lit night in the space of about twenty minutes. In the parking lot, which was half-empty, but filled with or seemingly surrounded by the highway noise, they found a wide green tent fenced off with metal barriers. But there were still a few trees left inside it, decent trees but too big, which nobody wanted. Cal snuck under the barrier—Dana climbed over. Liesel stood outside, worrying and feeling cold. That faintly dementia-flavored but basically also existentially accurate feeling you get in the dusk, near highways, had descended on everyone—like, What am I doing here? Where am I? I need to get somewhere quickly where the artificiality and frailty of all this human-settlement stuff isn't so obvious. There were electrically powered cutting tools lying in the tent, which probably explained the barriers. Jean went inside to find a guy. Eventually—it was dark by this point, proper dark—Jean and the guy came out and they bought a tree. He cut it down for them, pruning the lower branches, too, so it could fit in the stand, in the light of a Klieg lamp, or whatever they're called, which was lying on the ground in a tangle of wires. It was cold enough that the heat the lamp generated misted in the beams of the light it generated. They pulled the tree into the trunk of the Volvo, half of the backseat had to be folded down, and Dana got into the other half and put Cal on her lap. They drove home.

Paul was there when they got back. He had been waiting around for several hours longer than he had expected to, which always made him unreasonably angry. This fact alone was upsetting to him. The new laid-back self wasn't supposed to care about these slight affronts or revealed indifferences, but somehow he was stuck with the old self that did care. When he was home he sometimes went out into the backyard with a tennis racket and ball. Behind the playhouse there was an odd extra bit of land, tacked on because of the angle of the road, with a solid concrete wall at the far end, supporting the parking lot of a cooperative grocery store. For some reason the level of the stores on the main drag was fifteen feet higher than the level of the residential streets. Bill, when the kids were kids, turned this extra bit of backyard into a small court and Paul used to hit balls against the wall by the hour. This is where he spent his childhood, every day after school more or less regardless of the weather. Hitting a tennis ball into a concrete wall.

So he went there now and banged a ball around and worked up a sweat—the winter sunshine was warm enough for that, he was wearing jeans and a T-shirt. When Liesel told him she had invited Dana to come for Christmas his first reaction was to have no reaction or to have as little of a reaction as it was possible for him to show. In general, this was his policy when discussing matters that affected him intimately. If you care about the honesty of your reactions then there's always this slight delay—you have to register what you actually feel, you have to check your sources, and the upshot of all this due diligence is that it makes it almost impossible to have honest reactions. But Paul still preferred the slight artificiality or coldness of people who measure their words to the alternative, to be one of those people who have to keep apologizing afterward for misrepresenting their positions in the heat of the moment. Also, Liesel was his mother, she was seventy-four years old, she loved him, she meant well, and he had no deep-seated resentments or reproaches to work out against her. His childhood was pretty great. Anyway, it was usually Jean's job to take her to task for clumsy interference.

Half an hour later he went inside to get a drink and they still weren't there. It was now almost five o'clock, getting dark and cool. He could have called Dana on her cell to find out where the hell everyone was, he wanted to see his son, but they didn't have the kind of phone habit anymore that would have made this a normal thing to do. It would have suggested pent-up resentment, which is what he felt and could not have kept out of his voice. Bill was in the TV room watching a football game. There was half a watermelon on the counter by the sink, lying in its Saran Wrap, beaded with condensation or juice, and Paul cut himself a slice and joined his father. One of those meaningless pre-Christmas third-tier bowl games, the Collision Repair and Auto Painting Bowl or something like that. Boise State was playing, those guys in the bright blue and bright orange uniforms, totally chemical-looking. Third quarter, already a wipeout, Boise State was running away with it and Bill said, slumped on the sofa, half-lying down, with his feet kicked out on the footstool, "They should have been ranked higher. All year long they were telling everybody, we can do what we do against anybody, any of the big-name conferences, and now it turns out they were right."

Paul sat down on the rocking chair and picked at the seeds in his watermelon slice with a fork. When you're basically unemployed, this particular dead patch of the year, when everybody else is just glad to get to the holidays, to kick back for a few days before the pressure of Christmas itself starts to tell, is especially depressing, because your whole life is like this, a kind of waiting around for other people who are busier than you to intersect briefly with your life. Even though whatever keeps them busy is rarely very satisfying to them, even though they complain about their jobs and lives and pretend to envy you, somehow they leave it to you to work out the problem of what to do with existence in the absence of meaningless small goals.

"I don't know." Paul took a piece of the watermelon on his fork—it was still cold. The watermelon was pretty good. "What usually happens is they play against some mid-conference team from what turns out to be one of the weaker major conferences and then it's not surprising Boise State can run up the score. Didn't they lose to TCU?"

"TCU has a pretty good football team this year," Bill said.

The front door opened, you could hear it from the TV room, a click and then the sound of voices, and Jean was walking down the corridor saying, "Sorry guys, *Paul*!, sorry we're so late, we could use a hand with the tree . . ." and Paul felt his heart rate accelerating in spite of himself, and without, it seemed, any sympathy or participation from his conscious mind, though whether it was because he was going to see Cal or he was going to see Dana he couldn't tell.

Liesel followed Jean into the TV room. "It's a big tree," she said.

"Where's Cal?" Paul asked, getting up and setting his watermelon bowl on the floor.

"Dana's taking him to the bathroom. He was very good."

"Pick up the bowl," Bill said. "Someone's going to step on it."

"How's Dana?"

"She's fine," Jean said. "She's in the bathroom. It's an okay tree, we got lucky. Every year we leave it too late."

"That's because you kids always want to help," Liesel said.

"Pick up the bowl," Bill said.

"The only person who really cares is Susie and even she agreed that this year she was arriving too late."

"I want to put it in a bucket of water," Liesel said, and then, to Paul: "Maybe you can help Jean carry it around the back."

"I want to see my son."

The TV room was part of the kitchen extension, which included the breakfast room next door. Paul walked down a hallway into the old part of the house. The toilet was under the stairs. Dana stood outside the opened door, watching Cal, who was sitting on the pot and looking totally chilled-out on the pot and not in any hurry. Dana turned around when she heard Paul. He hadn't seen her in a month, since he flew to New York at Thanksgiving to spend a little time with his son. Whenever he saw her after an absence there was a buildup of static charge, the kind that gives you an instant and consistently surprising slight jolt on contact. She hugged him dutifully, two arms but little pressure and a quick release. Then Cal stood up and bent over, and Paul said, "That's all right, I can do it," and leaned into the bathroom to pick a piece of toilet paper from the roll.

"You always do it so it hurts," Cal said.

"I'm sorry, kid. I like a clean butt."

"I like it more when Mommy does it."

"Is this any way to greet your father?"

But he wasn't sure for whose benefit he was saying it, Cal's or Dana's or maybe for Jean, who was now standing and waiting in the hallway traffic jam, and said, "You ready to move the tree? Liesel's fricasseeing about putting it in water."

"What does fricasseeing mean?" Dana asked.

"Nothing. Not what Jean thinks it means."

"I know what it means."

"All right. All done. Now wash your hands," and Paul washed his hands in the sink while Cal pulled up his pants. Dana was looking at him when he came out. That patina of strangeness which their changed relations had allowed to accumulate, week by week and month by month, seemed to add a gloss or maybe he just saw her again for what she actually was, an extremely handsome woman, tall and skillfully and fashionably dressed, the kind of woman you hesitate to approach at a party because of her obvious good looks, which makes your reason for speaking to her seem a little obvious, too. "Hey," Paul said, "it's nice to see you," and then turning to Jean, "Come on, let's get this over with," because on some level he had realized that playing the casual brother at home with his family gave him some advantage over Dana or might put him in a more attractive light than she usually saw him in these days.

Paul stayed for supper; he wanted to put Cal to bed. This involved some negotiation because Cal was used to sleeping in Jean's old room when he stayed over at Wheeler Street and it had to be explained to him that Jean was actually there. "I don't mind," Jean said, "if he wants to sleep with me. We can move the crib in. Until Henrik comes." But this wasn't really a serious offer and nobody took it seriously, including Cal. They let him go downstairs to watch TV for a bit, which meant that Bill had to switch the channel from his football game, and then they tried again. In the end, Paul gave up and let Dana deal with it. It didn't seem to help to have two of them around. Bill was driving out to Sunflower, the Vietnamese place off 183, which was Dana's favorite restaurant in Austin, to pick up some food and Paul offered to come along.

Dana sat with Cal until he fell asleep, which wasn't long, because they'd had a very early start that morning. With the time difference, his bedtime had been pushed back anyway. She lay on the bed next to the crib, in that funny crowded charming little junk-store room, and almost fell asleep herself while she listened to his breathing. But in fact she lay there awake and tried to get a hold on her impressions and feelings. It was nice to take a break from the Essinger atmosphere for a few minutes, or maybe fifteen or twenty. But she also liked knowing it was there, that she could step into it again whenever she wanted. At home in New York, unless she made special arrangements, she was stuck in the apartment every night after Cal went to sleep. Liesel had said to her, "If you ever want to go out while you're here, just go. We can look after Cal, he's pretty used to us by now. Even if you just want to sit in the Spider House after putting him to bed."

The Spider House was a café and bar just two minutes' walk from the back gate—it had firepits in the winter and lots of colored lights and rusty outdoor furniture, it was a nice place to sit. And part of what Dana was thinking as she lay there was, Jean and I could go and get a frozen margarita. Or I could just go by myself. She was trying to work out which she wanted to do and if it was rude to go alone and ended up doing neither, she just lay there listening to Cal and thinking, Paul looks skinny. Whenever they talked on the phone he sounded totally unchanged but every time she saw him he looked skinnier and skinnier. It was nice to have Cal lying next to her because without him she would have felt a long way away from her own life and right in the middle of Paul's. Almost deliberately, almost consciously, she started narrating to herself these feelings and observations in the form of a conversation with Stephen, and then, feeling weird and a little heartsick, stopped. *It's like, you have to understand this family, it's like, with them you're always in the middle of some argument, not an argument, but it's like that, and everyone's having it together, and whatever you say it's connected to something somebody else said, and has a different opinion about, and so on. And it never ends.*

———

They took North Lamar out to 183—most of the stores had Christmas lights in the window. When Paul spent time with his parents he reverted to high-school mode. In high school, he was a pretty good kid, he never rebelled much, he kept his own counsel, and that's what he was like with them now. Bill was always an errand father. He was one of those dads who drove you around and picked you up, and his idea of hanging out was the car ride on the way to practice or the restaurant. The rest of the time, the time at home, he was happy to watch TV and mostly shut up, but in the car he liked to talk.

He said, "The ALEA is meeting in Austin this year."

It was easier talking like this, with both of you staring ahead at the road or looking off at the side streets passing in the dark. The radio in the car hadn't worked in years, otherwise Paul would have turned it on. It was warm enough he lowered his window for a minute, just to feel the air, and then shut it again.

"I don't know what that is," he said. You forget sometimes your parents are people, too, with their own self-obsessions. It's amazing how little as a kid you care about what their lives are actually like.

"It's the law and economics society. Nathan is giving a talk this year. So am I."

"Well, can we listen to you? Is there a . . . public gallery?"

"You can come. I don't know how much of what I say you'll understand."

They passed the old Highland Mall, where Susie used to go as a teenager to meet her friends and eat ice cream among the indoor plants. But the parking lot surrounding it was dark now, there were unused grassy areas, it looked depressing. Susie was the only mall rat among the kids; she felt the pressures of socialization more than the rest. Highland was the first mall in Austin, but now all the hipsters had rolled into town, with their independent boutiques, and nobody wanted to go there. Bill said, "They're closing it down. The community college is taking over the site. At least that's what they say."

"Americans," Paul said. "They don't want to shop anymore. They just want to learn."

"Anyway, the ALEA is putting on a panel this year. About my work."

"That's great," Paul said. "That's nice."

"The way it goes, I give a paper, and they invite a couple of people to respond to it. It's up to me to pick the guys."

Bill was an economist—the kind who, he liked to say, had spent his life trying to prove what economics *couldn't* tell you about the world. This hadn't always made him popular in the profession.

"You want to hear something funny," he said. "UT is going to publish these responses online, alongside my original paper." Bill paused a little, he made a kind of laughing noise, like a humorous sigh. "Yesterday I get an email from the editor. My secretary prints it out for me. You know what he wrote?"

He waited for Paul to say, "What?" You realize after a while that everybody's internal lives are full of this kind of thing, it's endless, all you get are glimpses of it in other people. Paul said, "What?"

Bill told him—a long list of redactions made because the material covered in his paper "duplicates" some of the arguments in the talks. I mean, they're supposed to be responding to *me*. So Bill has to go through the redactions, item by item. That's what he was doing this morning, before picking up Dana and Cal from the airport. It takes him three hours in the office and he's halfway through. This is how you spend your life. Nobody ever reacts to these stories the way people want you to, and Paul knew that he had failed to react in that way.

"What's Nathan talking about?" he said, after a minute. It was nice just sitting in the car—he could feel the day's run in his bones. And also, what he felt for his father was something else, a complicated form of identification. So this guy is also out there hitting balls against the wall.

"The legality of drones. They've put him in Dwight Auditorium, which seats about five hundred people."

North Lamar came to an end and Bill merged onto 183, one of those elevated highways that curves around the city. Even at that time of night, it was full of cars, people heading home, into the dark flat increasingly developed countryside north of Austin.

"This city keeps growing," Bill said, and then: "You know where they've got me? The Ronald B. Koenig Seminar Room at the business school. Capacity thirty-five."

"There's a whole panel on your work. I don't feel that sorry for you."

"Your brother is in demand," Bill said. "I am in supply."

But he was in a good mood—this is the kind of thing he liked, talking like this, making jokes. Deprecation had the effect on him of genuinely cheering him up.

"Well, join the crowd."

The raised highway was about the level of the treetops, Paul could see the roofs of houses and warehouses between the leaves. Somewhere out there, in the streets below them, was the medical complex where the dentist he went to as a kid worked.

"Cal seems happy enough," Bill said. "He's excited about seeing his cousins."

Maybe this is the conversation he'd been waiting to have. Bill's attitude from the first had been noninterventionist. He had more sympathy than Liesel, as a general rule, for the reasons men and women choose not to live together anymore. But Paul also had a fairly good idea of what his father thought about the whole thing.

"I guess. I didn't see much of him today. They spent all that time . . . picking a tree. It's hard to find one where you can put the candles on."

"One of these days they're going to burn the house down," Bill said.

They exited 183 and turned at the off-ramp quickly, doubling back almost, and parked outside the restaurant, which was practically under the highway, you could hear the traffic noise thrumming overhead, and went inside to get the food. Bill said that Paul could wait in the car but Paul came in anyway. There was a fish tank on the counter. He looked at the fish, feeling a little fishlike himself. Like he was staring at everything with his mouth open, not saying much. Bill as always chatted up the waitress, who lifted a couple of steaming bags over the counter, plastic inside paper, and they headed out again, into the mild night, and got in the car.

"I like Dana," Bill said, pulling away. "I don't always get a lot out of her, but I like her."

"She's very smart." For some reason, Paul wanted to defend her. "She was Phi Beta Kappa at Amherst. Already by her junior year. When she left."

"I'm sure she is, but there's a WASP quality, which in its way is very attractive, although I also find it hard to penetrate."

"That's just what she's like," Paul said. "There's nothing really underneath it that's very different."

He thought he was protecting her, against some accusation that Bill hadn't exactly made, of phoniness or superficiality, but he realized after he said it that what he said didn't sound like a defense. Anyway, it ended the conversation and they drove in silence back the way they had come. Eventually Bill said, turning off at 32nd Street, between the limestone pillars onto the darker and greener neighborhood streets, and then turning again onto Wheeler, with its familiar curve: "The Longhorns are playing at the Erwin Center. Nathan wanted to go with the kids. Cal seems to me old enough now to get something out of it. Should I get you tickets?"

"Sure."

"What about Dana?"

"You can ask her," Paul said.

They drove into the driveway, clanking at the dip, and Paul, who had been holding the food on his lap and at his feet, waited until Bill got out and handed it to him, before getting out himself. His lap was slightly damp from the heat of the bags. Walking into the house, Bill called out, "Soup's up," and Paul said to him, "Cal's probably asleep." They walked into the kitchen and Bill put the food on the counter. "Soup's up," he said again. Dana and Jean were laying the table; Liesel was already sitting down, sewing something. She had her glasses on and a little roll of needles and threads on her plate, which she put away.

"My favorite food," Dana said, a little loudly.

Supper was weirdly normal, it was weirdly like the suppers they used to have before their separation. Dana didn't talk much, it wasn't easy merging into the Essinger family conversational traffic. But that's how it used to be anyway. Jean and Paul had an argument, which wasn't really an argument, about a TV commercial that Jean had walked in on while Bill was watching sports. This is the kind of thing they talked about, endlessly, like it was politics or art, or something that actually matters. Speaking of Nike, Jean said, in a different voice after standing up to get more food. Henrik wants to meet Lance Armstrong when he comes over. If that is at all possible. Paul said it was just a question of timing, their regular Sunday morning ride was on . . . and they tried to work out the date. The thirtieth, if it was happening, which Paul assumed it was. Lance tended to stick to his routines, at least when he was in town.

"When does Henrik get in? We just have to find him a bike," Paul said.

"I don't know if he's up for a twenty-mile ride," Jean said. "He's still pretty weak."

"Well, he can come along and say hi."

At one point, while they were working this out, Dana turned to Paul and said, "What's he like?" and there was something about the way she said it, like an attractive acquaintance at a dinner party trying to break into the conversation, trying to interest you . . . that had a powerful effect on him. Because he realized, something he knew perfectly well, that she was alone in his family, slightly adrift, that she was probably doing her best, but also, and this was part of the effect, it struck him again what an attractive stranger she was. It was like some of the unfamiliarity had grown back, and he could see her again the way a stranger would see her, as a tall pretty well-dressed woman who asks questions and listens to your answers.

"He's like . . . in some ways, he's this typical Austin guy, kind of chilled-out and relaxed, but basically in an extremely intense and competitive way."

"Do you like him?" Dana asked. She sat very straight at the table, always, and she looked at you when she spoke.

"I like him. Somehow that doesn't really come up, when people are famous. Everything they do has a slightly different moral weight. Just the fact that he goes riding on Sunday mornings with a bunch of guys like us makes him a good guy."

"I'm a fan," Jean said.

Later, when supper was over, and Bill had moved over to the TV room to watch the Spurs game, Paul and Jean and Dana were clearing the table, and Paul said to Dana, "Do you want to come out and see the Wimberley place while you're here?"

"I've seen it before," she said.

"Okay . . . it's a little . . . the work on the house is finished. And they've started building some of the cabins. The foundations are dug. Cal likes going out there."

"Sure," Dana told him. "I'll come if you want me to." There was a silence in which something had to be said, to fill it, and eventually Dana said, "I think I'm going to check on Cal. It's stupid but . . . I don't want him waking up and thinking, where am I."

"I'm sure he's fine. He sleeps here all the time."

"Go check on him," Jean said.

Paul put a hand on her shoulder as she turned away—a kind of apology, but maybe it came across as something else. He noticed her calf muscles under the cream tights, the way they took the strain, and had a faint sexual response, or more like an appreciation. She walked well, she walked like an athlete. What Bill had said in the car came into his mind. About the fact that Dana was hard to read, she didn't give much away. Because of her Waspiness or Waspishness, whatever the right word for it was. The idea that for one week his family would live with her, see her, judge her, come to conclusions about her, without his full-time presence to deflect their judgments was suddenly painful to him. But what could he do. He didn't want to be there either.

After she went up, Jean said to him, "What's going on there?"

She was filling the garbage with empty Styrofoam containers, which crackled in her hands, the juices dripped. Paul picked up the bag and lifted it from the trash can and pulled the edges open, so that Jean could fit the rest of the containers in.

"Nothing, it's fine. We get along fine." He sounded defensive when he didn't mean to, but he also sounded, to his own ears, something else: lightweight or superficial, like somebody who doesn't take life seriously enough. Which wasn't what was going on at all.

"That's what I mean. People who get along fine usually stay together."

"Is that right?" Paul said.

Jean took the garbage bag out of his hands and stood in the kitchen doorway for a moment, looking at him. Her eyes were a little shiny. She looked at him like you look at someone departing in a car, after they can't see you anymore, then she went outside to put the garbage in one of the cans.

—

It's about a fifty-minute drive to Wimberley, most of it along I-35. But there wasn't much traffic, which allowed his thoughts to run on a little, he could cover plenty of ground.

For the first few weeks after moving back home, Paul was just happy to be home. He slept at Wheeler Street a lot of the time, while work progressed on the house in Wimberley, he slept in his old bed, touched the same window he used to touch when he woke up, and jogged around the neighborhood where he used to ride his bike. And the truth is all of these things made him actually happier. He had a feeling of rightness, even the weather felt like the weather in which he belonged. Hot until early November, when the first norther blew in and knocked the leaves off the trees, then variable, drippy sometimes and mildly cold, or sunny and hopeful, even with the dead grass. And so on, all year round, one season after another, the seasons he grew up with. But after five or six months, maybe even sooner, after a couple of months, when the boredom kicked in, and not just boredom but something worse, like some kind of leukemia of boredom, a disease of the blood and bone, he realized that even if you decide to retreat from the world you need something to do. Otherwise you have no reason to get out of bed, you have no reason to get out of the house. A couple of his high-school friends had stayed in town. One of them had kids, and he used to hang out at their house, feeling like, I have a kid, too, I have a home. There was a limit to how much time he wanted to spend at the periphery of other people's lives.

Sometime after New Year, a mutual friend, a sports columnist at the *Austin American Statesman,* put him in touch with Lance, and Paul started joining Lance and several other guys on their Sunday morning bike rides. He couldn't keep up at first, he had let himself drift out of shape, and for two days after his first ride he could hardly walk around the house. Just sitting down on the pot caused a heat map of pain to spread from his knees to the left side of his lower back, and he had to push himself up afterward with his hands on the edge of the bathtub next to the toilet. At this point he figured, I could go either way, and the way he went was to get back in shape. He started running again in the mornings, first around Wheeler Street, around Barton Creek, and up to Shoal Creek, and along the greenbelt, and later, when he moved out to Wimberley, along Lone Man Creek, a tributary of the Blanco River that formed the southern perimeter of his property, and sometimes down Red Hawk Road into Wimberley itself, through various neighborhoods with spread-out houses and back again, farther and farther, until he was routinely logging fifty miles a week.

All of which kept him busier than just the hour and a half a day he spent on the road or on the bike, because you've got to recover and wind down and eat right, and shop to eat right, and so on. It's a process that involves a certain amount of concentration on the self, a certain kind of intense and painful loneliness, and if you stick with it long enough, and push through the first five or six weeks where the pain barrier is all that you can think about, something semireligious starts to happen. You realize first of all that you're a physical human being, that you live in a *body*, a fact which, as an athlete, he had always been more or less aware of, but then his body was always a means to an end, taking care of it was part of his job, but not the part that got measured, whereas now . . .

If you push through the boredom, if you push through the depression of the boredom, if you manage to find a purpose, or not even a purpose, if you manage to give a shape to your days, something to do when you get up in the morning and something to think about when you lie down, eventually a new kind of life starts to kick in, a new frame of mind. You start to see your relation to the world more clearly, what matters and what doesn't, which is something that Lance had been coming to terms with and was willing to talk about. Some of the other guys they rode around with had semi-famous pasts, too. There was an actor who dropped out of LA after drawing a blank in pilot season, and thinking, all right, I don't need to spend my life waiting around for people I don't particularly respect to say yes to me. There was a retired baseball player, there was a NASCAR guy, people who had settled in Austin because it's a nice place to live and not totally off the beaten track in celebrity terms but not in the spotlight either. In other words, people who had been forced into some clear perspective on the meaning of worldly success. But he didn't talk about this stuff with his family, maybe with Jean, but even with her not much, because he was aware that they didn't respect this kind of pseudo-philosophical enlightened calm and also because on some level he realized he was making use of it as a stepping-stone toward something else.

The irony, which he was perfectly willing to admit to, was that as soon as he decided to drop out of the world the people he started hanging out with were all these B-list types, instead of ordinary civilians, guys like his high-school friends, who tended to view what he was doing as an example or side effect of decadence and privilege. He could see it from their point of view. But he also had a point of view.

Which is just that, for reasons unrelated to any kind of deserving, he had made a lot of money, and what this money made possible for him is that he could live a life entirely of his own choosing. So the question becomes, what do you choose. This is not an easy question to answer. You can choose to help other people, and in fact, every year, after conversations with his accountant and Nathan, who had a sophisticated sense of the charity market and where you get the most bang for your buck, he gave away roughly a hundred thousand dollars a year. (Enough for him to feel a pinch, a slight constraint, given the fact that he didn't expect to earn anything but interest and dividends for the rest of his life, and was living off the capital.) But this also seemed to him like a way of avoiding the question. Because obviously there are people who need quantifiable things, like clean water and prenatal care and access to the internet, which money can supply. But the question he wanted to think about, the question he wanted to answer by example, is how should you live when all of these material concerns have been met? There's got to be a kind of life possible that would seem to him worth living.

At the moment, he was reading a lot. In bed, on the toilet, on the exercise bike. Different kinds of books, he had bought a Kindle. High-end self-help stuff like *Thinking, Fast and Slow* and *Blink*, neither of which Nathan or Susie or Jean had much respect for. But also biographies. He was fighting his way through the Caro volumes, the stuff about LBJ's early days in Texas interested him, the way the century changed around him. You grow up in one time and learn certain valuable lessons, whose application to the time you end up in, as an adult, isn't always immediately obvious. Books had a way of leading on to each other, and without Cal around he had the leisure and headspace to follow the tracks and see where they would take him. But there were certain premises he had firmly established in his mind. That the feelings he had now, of pointlessness, of randomly directed anger, which flared up and disappeared almost instantly, of disillusionment, were of a relatively recent growth, that they did not have their roots in his childhood. That his childhood was meaningful to him in a way that no subsequent life seemed meaningful to him, not the couple of years he spent at Stanford, or his tennis career, or even his relationship with Dana. That everything apart from his feelings for Cal was corrupted by this sense of pointlessness, or colored by it, and that what he needed to do was find a way to reproduce, not the innocence of childhood (because he had no interest in innocence; guilt was not the problem, he rarely felt guilty; besides, as everybody knows, children are full of cruelty), but something like the meaningfulness or authenticity of childhood. Though these were clearly the wrong words, and the fact that he couldn't find better words for what he was after might be part of the problem.

You turn off I-35 at Mountain City, and when you get through that, end up on the dark roads, in the deep middle of Texas nowhere, where even the land looks like nothing much, not like farmland or anywhere you'd want to build, made up mostly at that time of year of dead grass and dead bushes and a few low trees, driving along Old Kyle Road, where there aren't any houses or stores or shacks by the side of the highway, just telephone poles. There aren't any streetlamps, and for several miles you think, this is what it feels like to travel through an unknown continent, until the outskirts of Wimberley appear.

Maybe love was one of the words, though that seemed a stupid way of putting it. But what he meant was just the thoughtless unquestioned feelings of brothers and sisters for each other and for their parents, people you're basically stuck with and *didn't* choose, your simple relations with them and physical lack of embarrassment (he still pissed in front of Cal, he wiped Cal's ass), even if what went along with those feelings in many cases was boredom and shortness of temper (on the parents' side) and endless trivial competitive rivalries on the kids'. The boredom of love on the one hand and the battles of love on the other, which is maybe why, for the rest of your life, boredom and fighting seem like indicators of honesty or sincerity or the real thing, and everything else feels like playing around.

Okay, what he had taken so far were a few long- and medium-term steps, like buying the house and trying to develop the land. He was reading up on permaculture, too, which was making a move in Texas, in spite of the climate. There was a school in Plano he had made some initial contact with, though it was a long way from Wimberley, about four hours in the car. Not that he really intended to enroll—you get these ideas, but somehow the content of them never lives up to the shiny surface. As soon as you start to follow through with anything it becomes clear why you didn't want to bother in the first place. And he realized somewhere along the way that who he was explaining himself to was probably Dana, though not all of the time, that he was listening to Nathan, too, and Jean, and other people, who occupied critical points of view on whatever he thought, but it was mostly Dana, who just seemed to sit there at the back of his mind and listen to him. Without saying much.

There weren't many houses on his stretch of Red Hawk Road, just above Lone Man Creek, and the few there were lay spread out enough you couldn't see your neighbors. Irregularities in the land got in the way, trees got in the way, and as he pulled up the drive to his house, which didn't look like much from the front, just a concrete shed with a horizontal window under the eaves, like a two-car garage, the faint, faint fear of living this far out on his own pressed in on him. Even after a year and a half of living like this he felt it. Movement-sensitive lights, which lined the drive, flared on, which was both a source of comfort and mild anxiety, because every time you came home at night it was like a big announcement. In New York you get sick of all the people crowding in on you, sharing walls and sidewalk space and subway air, so that you can't even shout at your kid, not anywhere, not at home or the street, without feeling like you're under observation. But out here you had the opposite problem. The distances around you were so great and so empty that you yourself became a kind of witness to yourself. There was nobody else to do the job, and you developed, at least Paul had developed, a weird kind of double-consciousness, where every step he took, between the car and the front door, felt semi over-deliberate. You wondered what was out there watching you, so it was like you yourself were watching yourself. But this was part of the point of it all, this is what he wanted to get used to. At night in the hills the temperature dropped and you could smell the cold air over the river at the foot of the yard. He was glad to get the front door closed behind him, and to turn on the lights.

The telephone rang just as he walked in, and he could see the red light blinking on his answering machine. The house had poured concrete floors and exposed limestone walls, big single-pane windows, and even after Bill brought over a couple of rugs to lay down, from his years of hoarding (more lay rolled up under the pool table in the back apartment at Wheeler Street), noises echoed. Paul picked up the handset and sat on the couch, looking mostly at his reflection in the glass, which shone and glared a little under the overhead lights. Behind this reflection, dimly, you could see the bent reaching arms of the live oak tree outside the patio porch, and behind it, sloping away, the yellow wintry grass that led to the river. On the far side, vaguely, the green outline of a hill.

Bill said, "I got you. I was expecting to leave another message."

"I just walked in the door."

"Listen, I wanted to tell you because I've told everyone else. Except Susie, who's in the air. Your Aunt Rose is not very well. She has pneumonia, and other complications I won't go into. The hospital called just after you left. Jean is booking me a flight right now, I think the earliest leaves at something like six forty-five. Anyway, I wanted to let you know. She may be fine. On the other hand, she may not be. I don't know how long I'll be gone for. Over Christmas."

"Do you want me to come?" Paul said.

"That's sweet of you, son."

"I can come."

"You've got enough on your plate right here. Okay, there's some-one on the other line. Hold on a minute."

Paul waited, not thinking of anything much, and then his father's voice returned—you could hear a faint shift even before his voice came through, indicating a different kind of access, like a key fitting and turning in a lock. "That was Nathan, I should get back to him, he's trying to persuade me to let him book his driver. To pick me up from the airport, which I don't need. Listen, have a good time, okay. Give yourself a break. Try and have a good time."

"Give Rose my love," Paul said.

But Bill still didn't hang up—he wasn't good at getting off the phone. "She was very proud of you," he said at last. "Of all you kids. She took a real interest. Just the fact that, one of the Essingers, seeing you on TV. She loved watching you play."

"Okay, Dad, thanks for calling. I hope it's all—I hope it's fine. It's good of you to go."

"Well, what can you do. All right," Bill said, and then the phone went dead in Paul's hands.

Afterward, he clicked on the answering machine and heard his father's voice again, more or less repeating himself, except of course that it had happened the other way around. "Listen, give me a call when you get in. I wanted to tell you because I've told the others . . ." At the end, Bill signed off with: "It was good to see you today. It's nice to have Cal in the house. All right. Just call me when you get in. Dad."

Paul got up then poured himself a bowl of cereal, some kind of granola, and took the cold milk from the fridge—an industrial-sized unit, all stainless steel, which hummed audibly and was parked against the limestone wall. Nathan was very envious of this fridge. At least that's what he said. "Well, it came with the house," Paul told him. "I wouldn't have picked it."

"You're an idiot. This is a restaurant-quality fridge," Nathan said. "What does that even mean?" Paul asked him. But sometimes when he opened the heavy door, he heard his brother's voice. You're an idiot, this is a restaurant-quality fridge . . . He took his bowl of cereal onto the patio porch, which meant setting it down on the concrete floor for a moment, unlocking and pulling the sliding door that separated his living room from the backyard. When you live alone you have to make these deliberate efforts to use different parts of the house. Outside, in the cool air, he slurped his cereal and drank up the sweet milk. The creek at the bottom of the property was really just a different kind of blackness, a sense of vague movement between the trees. Only at this time of year could you stand outside without getting bitten by mosquitoes.

When Judith, Rose's daughter, was thirteen years old, she flew to Texas on her own and visited them. It was a big deal for her, an only child, visiting her family of cousins. Getting on a plane for the first time by herself. None of the Essingers was particularly nice to her. Nathan was closest in age, but she got on all their nerves — complaining about the heat, about the air-conditioning, about the mosquitoes. Bill brought in bagels from Einstein's bagels, to make her feel at home, and Judith said, "These don't taste anything like New York bagels, I wonder why that is." As if she were genuinely curious, that kind of thing. She was just a thirteen-year-old kid. Paul had a four-foot-long rubber rattle snake, which he put in her bed. Judith spent half an hour on the phone to her mother afterward, in tears. Saying, *Nobody likes me, everybody's mean.* Paul overheard her, maybe she meant him to. The truth is, he was just a kid, too, they were all just kids. But every time he saw his Aunt Rose he felt . . . some residual . . . not guilt. A reminder of his father's childhood. How far he had come. Bill had said to him before, given Rose's general condition, at some point I expect to get a phone call, telling me . . . He spent his life in expectation, not of bad news exactly, but of the inevitable eventualities, so that when they came, he was ready for them, almost cheerful, he seemed prepared.

SUNDAY

Jean set the alarm on her phone for five a.m. so she could drive him to the airport. "It doesn't matter to me," she said. "With the jetlag, I'm awake anyway. This gives me something to do." She put the phone in her bed, she slept with it next to her pillow, so that it didn't wake Susie and the boys, who were getting in late the night before.

When she came downstairs, Bill was lying on the couch in the TV room, with his shoes on, draped over the armrest so that he didn't get the fabric dirty. "Okay," he said, when Jean came in. "Okay," repeating himself, still half-asleep. The TV was on, some movie.

"Have you got everything?"

His suitcase was in the front hall. The morning was windy and damp. When you're tired, you feel the coldness more. Jean took his keys (they were driving the old Volvo), adjusted the seat and mirror, and turned on the heating. It was dark on the road and the lights of the other cars suggested a kind of conspiratorial intimacy. Under the low white sky, heavily overcast, the streetlamp glow didn't get far. On Airport Boulevard, they passed a gas station, Dan's Hamburgers, a tire-change place (While-U-Wait), and a church no bigger than a taco shack, with a sign like a drive-thru billboard sticking up in the parking lot (Salvation Is Cheap). There used to be a branch of Dan's outside Jean's high school, where the cool kids liked to go for lunch. Jean thought, they weren't actually cool, this is just how you thought about people with friends, back in high school.

Bill was awake in the passenger seat, looking out. Unshaved— his beard hadn't been cut in several weeks, one of the things Liesel planned to get around to over the holiday, and he looked like a hippie rabbi or a student radical, except older and thinning on top. In his teaching jacket and button-up shirt, a real Seventies Jew. Which is probably why I always feel nostalgic watching old Dustin Hoffman movies. *Tootsie*, when he's not in drag. *Kramer vs. Kramer*. Neither of my brothers looks like this, half-goys. It's funny to be driving your father, one of those things that brings home to you, the relationship has changed.

Jean said, "How bad is it? Did you talk to the doctors? Is that who called?"

Since Henrik's illness, she had acquired a capacity for absorbing and processing medical detail, in spite of her own low-level health anxieties, because this is something you have to do if you're going to behave competently toward people you love in ways that benefit them. Bill started to explain. Rose's thyroid issues were only part of the problem. The medication she was on affected her heart, she suffered from palpitations, she couldn't sleep, which was another explanation for the weight gain. Also, maybe, for why she overate. When you're tired and housebound, you spend all day putting food in your mouth. There's only so much you can say. It doesn't help that she's borderline diabetic. Two weeks ago she fell at home getting off the pot—fell against the bathtub edge, and broke her hip. Just got dizzy. I'm so stupid, she said. She called me from the hospital. Just a stupid thing. One of the side effects of the thyroid medication is osteoporosis. Anyway, she broke her hip, and at her age, and weight, and given her general frailty, even routine operations have a certain level of associated risk. A hip replacement is no joke. But the doctors were satisfied, they kept her in for a week and let her go, a therapist came to the house to help her with the rehab, but the first day she came decided to take Rose right back in.

Rose wasn't making sense, she was badly dehydrated. When this woman took off the bandage to have a look, there was a rash, the whole area was infected, and since then they've been putting her through tests to find out what's going on. Judith called me last night, she only found out yesterday afternoon. For some reason the hospital had her ex-husband's cell phone number. One of the things you forget to do when you're going through a divorce is change your details as next-of-kin on your mother's medical records. It's all a mess; Rose's whole life is a mess. So for two days she's been lying there unconscious with nobody to see her. Judith is arriving this afternoon. We get in around the same time; she's made arrangements to leave the boy with his father. But all of these communications are painful for her, she doesn't like asking him for help. I asked her, should I call Alex, or are you going to talk to him. Because somebody should probably tell him. So she says, can you. Judith is not a coper. Maybe that's not fair, but she doesn't make anything easier for herself. And this is her business, calling her father is really her business. So last night, at eleven o'clock, I phone Alex, who's asleep in Tempe, with two small kids, and say to him, "I don't expect you to do anything about this, but I thought you should know, your ex-wife may be about to die."

"What did he say?" Jean said.

"Excuse me?"

"What did Alex say?"

"He said what you'd expect him to say. Thank you for letting me know. If there's anything I can do. I have no problem with Alex, we've always gotten along fine. I thought when Rose married him he's a bit of . . . he's not the kind of guy to appreciate her. But that was Rose's fault, too. She was complicit. And by the time he walked out, well . . . You forget, you never knew her then, but your aunt was an extremely attractive woman, in her way. Very funny, too. She's still very funny. When she's not unconscious."

Jean pulled up outside the JetBlue check-in desk. There was a little podium outside, on the concourse. Even at six in the morning, taxis were arriving, the 10 mph zone was busy with trucks and cars. She had to wait to find a spot. Bill said, "Let me just get out here," but Jean wanted to park and help him with the suitcase, she wanted to give him a hug. Then she sat in the driver's seat and watched him walk through the sliding glass doors. She thought, he's sixty-eight years old. The suitcase wheels, he has his ticket and passport inside the pocket of his sports jacket. He'll be fine, she thought. He can look after himself. She remembered, when she was little, the way they used to travel to Europe every summer: with suitcases and boxes, always at the upper limit of what was allowable (Bill used to study the legal fine print), four kids in tow, everybody harassed, short-tempered, and basically cheerful. When Bill was her age he had a tenured job, a house, he was married with two kids. She pulled out into the slow traffic, it was still dark, and reversed her journey. The flat Texas landscape surrounded her, dawn was an hour away.

When she got to the house, the lights were off, except for the upstairs bathroom where she had brushed her teeth an hour ago. A pale, slightly dingy, flowery blind over the bottom sash. The pyracantha hedge had gotten out of control, it reached in bunches almost to the second floor. An indicator of something, the way your parents, as they got older, let things go; but it was also a sign of growing privacy. When the kids leave home, the parents can retreat. She drove past the house and turned onto 32nd Street and then on to Guadalupe, which was relatively quiet at that hour, so she pulled across the median and started heading south. If you're going to be up early, you may as well come back with breakfast.

But the baker on Rio Grande looked closed. The street was just about a block and a half long, lampless, there were maybe a dozen houses, some old and poky, some new and big, with trees growing out of the front yards and getting tangled in the telephone wires. The kind of street where a kid could ride his bike. On the corner stood Texas French Bread, like a brick warehouse, with pleasant blue shutters fronting the sidewalk. But the windows in the bistro section were dark, and only at the back of the parking lot, where the bakery operated, could she see any signs of life. Well, it's barely after six o'clock, almost lunchtime in England. Henrik was driving to Bristol to pick up the kids.

This was his year to have Christmas with them—last year, which was right after everything went public, his wife took them home to her parents. But things were now proceeding on a more rational basis, with stuff like holiday time fairly parceled out. He had rented a cottage in Pembrokeshire; it was Jean who found it online, and then on Boxing Day he would fly to Austin, that was the deal. Are you nervous, she asked him. About meeting your parents? He shook his head. Maybe I will be. (He said this almost to be nice to her.) Who knows. For a minute she closed her eyes and when she woke up again it was a quarter to seven and somebody was cleaning tables in the front room. She got out of the car, in the cold, in the dark, and put her face to the window of the side entrance. Two tall stacks of dried wood lay in cages by the door. She tapped the glass and a young guy with a broom in his hand opened up.

"I'm sorry," he said. "We're closed. I haven't even fired up the coffee machine."

"I don't want coffee. Just something to take back home for breakfast."

"Well, let me see."

He had a well-trimmed beard and black glasses and wore a denim shirt. She thought he sounded Californian or Pacific Northwestern or something, which meant he didn't sound like anything much. There was a tray behind the counter already stocked with scones and croissants, and Jean asked for several of each. While he was bagging them, she told him, "My mom says that during the French Revolution the first thing they did was ban morning bread. So that the bakers didn't have to get up so early." Her voice sounded strange to her, like she was reading from a book, not quite natural.

"It's quiet," he said. "I don't mind. I just kind of . . . do my thing."

By the time she pulled into the drive at Wheeler Street, the neighborhood trees had started to lighten, the sky was the color of concrete, birds made their noise, but sunrise was still half an hour away. Rose was dying, Henrik was coming in three days. Bill was probably already in the air. The bread was still warm in the bag as she walked up the porch steps and into the house. Everyone else was still asleep.

—

Dana woke up, a little after five, when Jean used the bathroom—
the door was catty-corner to her bedroom door, the floorboards
creaked, it was an old house. She lay in the strange room feeling
strangely happy. Cal was still out cold. He barely fit in the crib anymore, his head and feet lay oddly angled, it seemed weird to her that
Liesel put him in one. But who was she to pick fights. And she liked
being in a house with other people in it, even if they were her sort-of
ex in-laws. The apartment in New York felt very . . . just to go out
for a newspaper or a carton of milk she had to take Cal with her. His
bedtime was at seven-thirty; after that she was stuck.

Last night, after checking on Cal, she waited for Paul to drive away.
She thought, it might be easier when he's gone. But in fact what she
felt, after coming back down, was something else—a sense of intrusion. The phone rang, Jean picked up and then called for Bill, who
was half-asleep on the couch, watching a basketball game. But he
woke up quickly and started pacing with the handset. When one conversation ended, he dialed again. Liesel hovered in the background.
He was speaking to Nathan, he was leaving messages, and when Dana
looked for Jean to say good night, she found her in Liesel's study, on
the computer, booking flights. "His sister's in the hospital," Jean said,
and Dana made appropriate noises. She said, "I'm going to go to bed,
unless there's something I can do," and Jean said, "Go. You've had a
long day," but her attention and sympathy were elsewhere.

When Dana crept into her room, Cal was snoring, breathing heavily
through his mouth—his nose was still stuffed up. She changed in the
dark and threw her clothes on an old leather club chair, which was out
of keeping with the other chairs in the house, and probably belonged
to Bill before he got married. The room was outside-temperature,
mild for a New York winter, but freezing by indoor standards. The
heating vents didn't work properly; they were covered in cardboard

boxes or rolled-up rugs or broken suitcases. Liesel had left a wool blanket in case Dana got cold, which itched a little when it touched her skin and smelled of mothballs. The whole room smelled of storage. And yet, and yet, as she lay in bed, tired but sleepless (first night syndrome, even though they'd had an early start), she felt the presence of accumulated life, which was missing in her own life, and had been missing through much of her childhood.

Her mother was the kind of woman with one shelf of books (a few recent bestsellers, a dictionary, an atlas, and other than that, mostly cooking and travel books, a few museum catalogs). She didn't like the clutter. The New York apartment in which Dana spent her first twelve years was rent-controlled, and when her dad got a job in D.C. they bought a newly built house in Bethesda, which was much too big for them. It had four bedrooms, an eat-in kitchen, a separate dining room, a den, a living room, they never filled it. She never had any siblings. The kitchen floor was tiled marble, you had to take off your shoes, every footprint showed.

And now she was in the middle of family messiness, urgency and intimacy and crisis, only it was someone else's family. What am I doing here, she thought, staring into the dark, at the shape of the overhead fan against the wooden ceiling. It's a little weird. Maybe what you're trying to do is break up with them. Though that's not what it felt like. And anyway, there's Cal, they have a right to . . . Maybe it's the opposite, maybe you're just trying to bypass Paul. Who needs him. She had various explanations on the tip of her tongue, things she wanted to say to Liesel. Just because Paul and I . . . doesn't mean . . . whatever happens. The cousins should get to know each other. I mean, it's perfectly possible, the way things are going, that Cal isn't going to have any brothers or sisters. And I know what that's like.

You have to prepare yourself for these conversations. Otherwise, the Essingers . . . you have to be ready for them. Thinking these thoughts, preparing herself, she fell asleep, and then, after Jean and

Bill drove away (Dana could hear the old Volvo coming to life, and clanking in the dip in the pavement as it backed onto Wheeler), she fell asleep again.

When she woke up, the birds were making a tremendous amount of noise, like rusty scissors, scraping back and forth, and Cal was looking at her, in the half-light, filtered by wooden blinds.

"Hey, Buddy," she said, which is what Paul called him. Snail tracks of dried snot covered his upper lip; his nose was crusted.

"Is it morning?"

Now that he was talking, there was something strangely formal about the way he put together sentences. Even his voice seemed small and clear, very careful.

"I don't know. Let me look."

Her watch lay wherever she had put it the night before—among her clothes, on the club chair. It took her a minute to find it.

"Are the . . . kids here?"

"What kids do you mean?" She was teasing him.

"You know," he said. "Those kids."

"You mean Ben and William? And the baby?"

He looked at her. Sometimes she worried that because of the way he was living, sometimes with Paul, in Texas, sometimes in New York, the people in his life coming and going, he had learned to be too self-contained. But maybe he was just her son. Men used to call her cold. She used to feel the same about her mother.

"I don't know their names," he said. "Those big kids."

"I think so. I think they got in last night. Did they wake you up?"

He was climbing out of the crib in his pajamas.

"Don't wake them up," she said. "They got in late. They'll be tired."

"I'm not." (Indignantly.) "I'm going downstairs."

"What are you going to do downstairs?"

"Watch TV."

"Who says you can watch TV?"

"Bill."

"Bill's not there."

"Bill always lets me," he said, and opened the door.

She listened to his footsteps in the corridor, thinking, I should go, too, he's got nothing on his feet, he's got a cold. Also having a minor reaction to the fact that he felt comfortable in the house without her. But she waited a minute anyway, still sitting on the bed. Leaving the room meant facing everybody again. All right. All right. She put on her slippers and a robe and emerged. The door to Susie's bedroom was shut; so was Liesel's. There was a kind of galleried hallway running to the head of the stairs, and cloudy morning light came in from windows overlooking the side of the neighbor's house. Cal had disappeared. She went to the bathroom (Jean had left the door open at 5 a.m.) and brushed her teeth and checked her face in the subtly distorting mirror over the sink. The faucet dripped a little; the old mint-green floor-tiles hadn't been changed since the Essingers moved in, forty years before. Dana felt fine without makeup but liked to know what she looked like before she showed it to anyone else. Fine.

Jean was in the kitchen, washing her hands in the sink, when Dana came downstairs. "Morning," Dana said, from the doorway. "Did Bill get off all right?"

"Fine."

"Is there any news?"

"I don't know. Everybody's still in bed."

Dana could hear cartoon noises coming from the TV room at the other end of the hall. The flicker of violent light shone in the glass of the narrow double doors, so she went to check on Cal, who was sitting where Bill usually sat and staring at the screen. Above him, and behind his head, one of Susie's undergraduate paintings filled the wall space. An Essinger family portrait, all of the kids lined up against a reddish background, sitting in the same room, on the sofa, and watching TV: Nathan, looking handsome and unhappy; Paul in his skinny teenage youth, with a big head of uncombed hair and slightly out-of-perspective hands; Jean, maybe ten years old, fat-cheeked but not quite innocent anymore, smiling too much to show that she was still the baby of the family; and Susie herself, hovering somehow behind them in the background, sad-eyed and slightly crazy, like the woman in the attic.

Dana thought, staring at Cal underneath it, What have I gotten you into? His face was intent and completely expressionless.

"He said he was allowed," Jean said, when Dana joined her in the kitchen.

"Allowed to what?"

"Watch TV. I think he meant that Bill lets him."

"He makes that stuff up. I don't mind though."

"I de-snotted him," Jean said. "The scones are still warm if you want one."

Dana made her *thank you, I'm a bad mother* face. She put her hand on Jean's shoulder, as Jean turned away, looking for a paper towel. Dana couldn't tell if she was mad at her about something, or if Dana herself was just being tired and paranoid. Maybe not mad but distant, not quite on her side.

The rest of the morning passed in a series of appearances and exits. Liesel came down in her dressing gown and put the coffee on. Her silver hair looked vaguely electrostatic; her eyes were bright and well-intentioned. Dana by that point was picking up Cheerios from the carpet from Cal's breakfast—Cal was still eating, he had a face full of jam.

"Coffee?" Liesel asked.

"Yes, thank you," Dana said.

"You're always so polite. My children were badly brought up."

Jean had gone for what she called a "very slow not even a run more like a walk like when you have to go to the bathroom." She banged in the backdoor, looking red in the face, and grumpy about it, too. "I hate running," she said. "I'm not any good at it. I don't know why I do it."

"Have you tried . . ." Dana began, and they spent the next ten minutes in a pointless argument about fitness fads. Spinning, hot yoga, that kind of thing.

"When the kids were younger it was jazzercise," Liesel said at one point, which Jean referred to in a friendly but also mocking way as "a surprisingly relevant contribution to the conversation."

The family atmosphere, which always took a little getting used to, comforted Dana, too. As if nothing that had happened with Paul made any difference to them. But maybe that's not what she wanted. Cal kept bugging her to wake up the "big kids" and she had to restrain him. Which he responded to by asking to watch more TV, so they had a fight about that, which Dana won. But only at the expense of spending the next half hour on her knees in the TV room, on the rough old carpet, building a tower and bridge with blocks, getting kind of into it, and then trying to restrain Cal from knocking it down, and thinking, oh what's the point, who are you doing it for, while he knocked it down.

Jean and Liesel read a newspaper next door, at the breakfast table, talking, about Bill, about Rose, about the shooting in Sandy Hook. And all the time Dana's mood went up and down, she was glad to be there, she was bored already, she felt at home, this wasn't her family. Then Ben came in and said, "I'm watching TV."

He wore glasses, he looked friendly and disinterested, and Dana realized she didn't have the status to contradict him. He was twelve years old, it was his grandparents' house, he had found the remote control. So Dana left Cal to join him on the sofa and went in the kitchen to give Susie a hug. She had May in her arms, feeding; her dress was pulled down, her shoulder was bare. She looked good, post-pregnant and sleep-deprived, her belly and breasts still carried a little weight, but she looked good—hassled, but in the middle of life, biologically active or whatever, and somehow because of the baby more sexually exposed or public than she would usually permit. William, her other son, dug a waffle out of the ice mess in the freezer.

Breakfast happened in several stages, it lasted several hours. Liesel started with a cup of coffee and a bowl of cereal, she ate a Ryvita cracker, spread with one of the several unusual jams collecting mold in the cupboard behind her (fig, quince, lemon curd), and only graduated to one of the pastries after Susie came down. People set the table piecemeal. Bill's work, a stack of scribbled-on typed-up pages, was first pushed to one side, and then resettled on the large wooden chest under the window. Liesel refilled a jug containing red-berried pyracantha twigs with water from the faucet, and placed it in the middle of the table, on the tablecloth, after Jean insisted on clearing the plates from the first sitting and starting again. Silver napkin rings, all of them antiques, none of them related to each other, were identified, filled with fresh napkins, and parceled out. Eventually Ben walked in from the TV room, picked up a scone, and started to eat.

Susie said, "Get a plate, sit down."

Cal insisted on sitting next to him. He had been staring at Susie and May. Dana felt vaguely relieved.

Meanwhile, the morning wore on—people argued. Jean and Liesel came back to their discussion of Sandy Hook, until Susie, with tears in her eyes, asked them to stop. Not in front of the kids. "I don't mind," Ben said. "What do you think kids talk about?"

"William is six," Susie said.

They talked about what they wanted to do, about where they wanted to eat lunch, and Dana remembered again, like someone putting on wet clothes, the sensation of entering into another family's life. The Essingers seemed less friendly than her own but maybe more intimate. Dana had to explain what her parents were doing, which was really an explanation of why she was spending her Christmas in Texas, since she wasn't with Paul anymore. "On a cruise," Dana said. "In the Caribbean." She could tell they were being judged for it, though nobody said anything, until she added: "According to the brochure, there's an adults-only sundeck. I don't know what they're doing." Jean laughed politely, and Dana felt she had betrayed something.

The weather turned from cold and white to cold and white and drippy, but William went outside anyway, and Dana tried to get Cal to join him. The age gap was just over two years—this is the friendship she hoped to depend on for the next few days. William looked like his father, pink and fattening, barrel-chested, fair-haired, and had his father's energy. In the kitchen, he drove everybody nuts after breakfast by kicking a tennis ball against the trash can, trying to make it bounce away at an angle, into the corridor. This is why Susie sent him outside. "If you want to kick things, kick things there. Put on your coat, it's cold." But he just stomped out and Susie let him go.

"Do you want to kick a ball around?" Dana said to Cal.

But Cal was more interested in the baby, who kept dropping things out of the tray of her high chair. He started picking them up, Cheerios, her spoon, her sippy cup, it turned into a game. For a while, Dana and Susie sat around, pretending to read the newspaper but mostly just watching the two of them interact. Liesel was upstairs getting dressed, Jean was showering.

"He's very sweet with her," Susie said, in the voice she used among women, which Dana responded to because she couldn't help it but she didn't like it much. This is how her mornings disappeared, sitting around with women.

Then David came in, Susie's husband, unshaven, overweight, but strong, too, looking as he always looked, tired and happy. He sometimes referred to his "unintellectual body"—he meant that he looked like a laborer, and actually, in his 20s, before he knew what he wanted to do with his life, had spent several summers working on farms in Spain and South America. Susie liked to explain, this was a typically upper-class thing to do. His parents were gentleman farmers. They owned cattle in Hampshire. David went to Winchester and Oxford. He said, "Who wants coffee?"

"We've all had coffee," Susie said.

"Who wants real coffee?"

He was offering to pick something up from one of the food trucks near the Spider House Café. There was a blood bank parking lot next to it, with several berths—you could get coffee, churros, Greek gyros, Japanese ramen, depending on the weather.

"Ben, you coming?" he shouted, in the general direction of the TV room. But nobody answered and David said, "See you in a minute," and went out the back, letting the screen door rattle behind him and some of the cold air in. There was a gate at the end of the yard that led to the stores. Dana had asked him for a cappuccino.

"Check on Willy," Susie called after him. And then: "Ben, turn off that TV." In a different voice, she said to Dana, "What's actually going on with you and Paul?"

"I don't know."

Cal had wandered into the TV room. Liesel came down. It was eleven o'clock. The leftovers of several breakfasts had accumulated on the table: plates sticky with maple syrup and pastry crumbs, used cups of tea and coffee, soggy bowls of children's cereal, warm glasses of milk and juice. Susie, sighing, said, "I was really hoping for a little sunshine. We've had twenty inches of snow so far in Connecticut."

"It's supposed to clear up this afternoon," Liesel told her.

And so the day went on. Nothing much happened, except for moments of lurching progress in several ongoing arguments. They decided on somewhere to eat lunch. Jean got her way, Ruby's BBQ, a bright-yellow low-roofed restaurant behind the house, very run-down-looking inside, with a kind of indoor/outdoor seating section, protected from the weather by hanging clear-plastic flaps. You could sometimes smell the smoker from the backyard, depending on which way the wind blew. It took about half an hour to get everyone together. May needed a diaper change, William had to be lured and then pulled out of the bamboo hedge, Ben was doing something on the iPad. Everything takes time.

"Has anyone called Paul?" Jean asked, but nobody had. "What did you arrange?" And she looked at Dana, who made her helpless face. "Okay, I'll call him," Jean said and left a message: "We're going to

Ruby's." It was Sunday—he usually went biking with Lance.

Then just as they were on their way out, the phone rang. Liesel ran hobbling back to pick it up. She thought it might be Bill, but it was Nathan on the other end. "Have you seen the weather reports?" he said—his voice sounded just like his father's, and like Bill he took a kind of cheerful practical pleasure in disaster. A huge snow front was expected to hit the northeast around midnight; people were being advised against nonessential travel.

"What about Bill?" Liesel kept saying.

"He's fine, he should have landed by now, and by the time he gets to Yonkers, what are we talking about. It's a ten-minute drive from Rose's house to the hospital. Anyway, I wanted to let you know." Know what, Liesel thought, and then Nathan told her. Their flight had been canceled. Part of him was tempted just to show up at the airport and see what they could get. Now, before the storm hits, but it's a bad time of year to wait around for standby. Plus, there were the kids—they needed four seats.

Each of the Essingers came to the line at different points, and Dana overheard Jean saying, "How about TF Green. I think they fly to Atlanta." Susie for some reason kept shaking her head. "He always does this." *What*, Dana didn't know. But Susie explained, "The truth is, he prefers having Christmas in Cambridge anyway. Clémence likes to be at home."

Dana saw tears in Liesel's eyes as they walked to the restaurant—across the damp grass of the backyard, past the gazebo and the little water-lily pool (the fountain had been turned off), under the old pecan. Nobody else seemed to notice. Jean and Susie were arguing about something, Cal and Ben and William had run ahead, and so Dana hung back for Liesel, whose progress across uneven ground was always slow.

"First Bill and now Nathan," Liesel said, smiling but wet-eyed. "I'm sorry."

"I'm sure something will work out."

"Probably not. Everything's already overbooked."

"Nathan is very persuasive."

And Liesel made her thank-you frown. There was a stack of fire-
wood at the back fence, black with rot; the grass around the foot of
it had edged away. Liesel, as she held open the gate, said, "Paul keeps
saying we have to get rid of it. It's a snake trap. He says he'll do it
himself but then he doesn't."

Dana walked through and waited for Liesel to shut the gate behind her. The dead end of a dead-end road was on the other side.
It was a funny sort of street, very wide and quiet. Dana could see,
over fences, into the large backyards of expensive houses, but there
were also more modest bungalows and student apartments, with
bikes and old sofas on the porch. And arching over everything, the
trees—mostly live oaks but also sycamores and sumacs, Japanese
maples. Very old Austin, Paul once told her, the first time she visited. The kind of place where you can rent somewhere cheap and live
off not much and nobody bothers you. You can do your shift at the
co-op grocery store or some data center and come home every night
and listen to your vinyl collection or read your old comics and sit
outside on warm evenings, drinking beer and thinking, Fuck it, life
is pretty good.

Liesel said, as she stepped down carefully from the curb, "I don't
know what he does. I don't think he is very happy." Everyone walked
in the middle of the road, on the pitted asphalt—even the kids, who
were waiting with David at the intersection, maybe a hundred yards
ahead. Jean was there, too; she had taken Cal by the hand. Susie, carrying May, followed slightly behind. "I think," Liesel went on, "he
went a little crazy when he retired. He didn't know what to do with
himself. He gets these . . . even as a kid, he was very easy, very undemanding, he went along with everything, ninety-five percent of the
time, but from time to time, he would get an idea, and there was nothing you could do, you had to give in."

"Well," Dana said.

"And now he has this idea about . . . living in Texas, about, I don't know, building a house where everybody can live. But nobody wants to. He's all on his own."

"Maybe that's what he wants."

Liesel stopped and looked up. Her round face, very brown under the white hair, seemed exposed somehow, less protected than other faces. She wore a tarnished silver necklace among the wrinkles of her neck. Her large eyes were still rimmed with red, but she also looked cheerful enough, she recovered from her emotions quickly.

"I hope not," she said and bent her head down again, walking on, as if one of her many small jobs for the day had been done.

Over lunch, while waiting for the food to come, Susie started complaining about Nathan. "He always does this," she said. "It's typical. He leaves everything to the last minute."

"You're being completely irrational," Jean told her. "You guys came in late last night. He was scheduled to fly in tomorrow. A snowstorm hit—it could have happened to you."

"He always has to make this grand entrance . . ."

"Whatever," Jean said, and when Susie looked at her, she went on: "This is some first- and second-born thing, I don't know what. I mean, I should just leave you to it."

"Be nice to me. I'm just disappointed for the boys. They don't get to see their cousins as much as I'd like."

"I'm disappointed for *me*," Jean said. "I don't get to see my brother."

For some reason, this set Susie off—her face crumpled, she turned away. "Just ignore . . ." she began, in a different voice. "I haven't slept. We got in at one in the morning and then May wouldn't go down. She slept too long on the plane, she's a good little girl. But then I had to keep feeding her all night, so she wouldn't wake up everybody else."

"I don't mind," Dana broke in, not sure if she should, if it was her business. "I mean, if that's what you're worried about. Cal never wakes up."

They were sitting inside, on a couple of rough wooden tables pushed together. A waitress started bringing over trays of food, chopped beef and onions, pickle chips, on wax paper; ribs and brisket, soft tacos, sliced sausage, half a chicken. Little plastic bowls of beans and potatoes. Jean stood up to get drinks and silverware from the counter, she asked for extra bread. Most of the other adults were occupied with their kids, trying to find something they would eat. Liesel, having sat down and swung her knee under the table, couldn't get up again easily. Jean passed around mottled plastic cups of iced tea and water. Everybody was eating, everybody was silent, when she joined them again and reached over shoulders to put together her own tray of food.

But slowly it emerged what was going on. David had been on the phone to England, that's why he was late coming down. With his fat stubbly face, his bald head, his glasses, he turned to Jean and said, "It's all my fault. I've been causing trouble."

When he ate you could see the strong workings of his jaw. He took a lot of pleasure in food, he took nothing very seriously. Sometimes, it's true, he shouted at the kids, he lost his temper, but in a kind of careless way, it didn't matter much. When Ben was born, twelve years ago now, Jean had lived with them for two weeks, helping out Susie with the baby, taking the late shift. She got along well with David, but he also had a way of treating her like staff.

A few weeks ago his old Oxford college had approached him about a job—they wanted someone to run the American Institute. They would give him a room in Mansfield and an office at the Institute, which was across the road. He would have almost no teaching duties, just the odd graduate seminar. It meant moving to Oxford. He had said yes that morning. At the moment their plan was to rent out their place in Connecticut, at least for a year or two, to see if they wanted to make it a permanent move. It was a chance for the kids to get to know their English grandparents—David's father had recently become too frail to travel. To get to know their Englishness, generally.

Jean said, "Well, it will be nice for *me*," looking at her sister tenderly and apologetically. There was a cheap coach service running all night long between London and Oxford—it stopped near Notting Hill Gate. She was renting a flat with Henrik in Kensal Green. The 52 bus took you straight to Notting Hill. You could do the whole journey, door to door, depending on traffic and connections, in under two hours. I can come at the drop of a hat, I can go for the day. "I'm sorry it's upsetting to you."

"You're the main reason I agreed."

It was left to Dana to offer congratulations—nobody else had said anything nice. Liesel kept asking everyone to repeat themselves, she couldn't hear. The restaurant was filling up. She kept saying, "But what's going to happen to the house?"

Susie's house was acknowledged in the family as the nicest piece of Essinger real estate. It was also the thing on which she had spent the energy she might have spent on a career—an old saltbox, almost three hundred years old, painted gray and deep red. Some of the windows contained the original glass, they shimmered in sunlight. It sat around the corner from a gas station, which doubled as a liquor store, and just off the highway that slowed down in Durham village to become the high street. A lake at the bottom of the property didn't belong to them but they swam in it anyway, every summer.

When they bought the house, the kitchen hadn't been touched in forty years. There was a breakfast nook, with built-in benches and table, under the window that overlooked the front yard. For that and other reasons, the whole place reminded Susie of the trim postwar cottage that Liesel had grown up in, in northern Germany, which lay off a dirt road and whose garden also ran down to a body of water: the Flensburg fjord. These connections or continuities meant something to her. To give up the house, to leave it behind, meant stopping or editing out one of the stories you tell about yourself.

Cal wouldn't eat anything but the sausage; it was the only kind of food on the table he was used to. Even the potatoes had vinegar or mustard in them. At least he liked the white bread—Dana made him sausage sandwiches. Susie had to wrestle her phone away from William, who afterward climbed under the table and sat there. Liesel pretended not to notice. She always had to bite her tongue where the kids are concerned. Maybe you just forget. I don't think my kids behaved in this way. But it's also true that everything tires you out after a while, especially noise.

Susie said, "You don't even have time to react to anything that matters, because you're so busy reacting to all these things that don't."

"There's time," David told her. "We don't have to move till the summer."

The weather started clearing over lunch; they could see the sun shining on the cars in the parking lot outside. Jean held everyone up for a minute by buying merchandise, a Ruby's baseball cap. She needed one, if it was going to be sunny; she wanted to bring one back to London anyway, as a badge of home. Her short hair stuck out of the sides. She wore one of her T-shirts, black jeans, and an old suede jacket from the Gap, which she had inherited from Susie years ago—the kind of thing Susie stopped wearing when she had kids.

Liesel said, "You look cool."

"*Thanks*, Mom."

Jean and Susie went ahead on the way home. Dana could see them—Jean had taken her sister's arm, and for a moment Dana felt a pang, of jealousy, to be excluded from all the petty fighting and the casual loving making-up. Also, this meant that she had to look after the boys. David was occupied with the baby, letting her walk, holding her lightly by the hand. When she lost her balance, she swung around like a flag on a pole. You forget all the stages, they don't last long. Ben was old enough to take care of himself, but since Cal wanted to go with him, Dana had to chase after them both.

William and Liesel were walking together.

"Are you sad about leaving Durham?" she asked, but he kept his head down.

His father used to have the same blonde hair, cut like an up-side-down bowl—you could see it in his prep-school pictures, which his parents had hung in the bathroom under the stairs in their house in Hampshire. David, with May's little fingers sweating in his palm, heard Liesel's question and looked up at his son, who was three or four steps ahead. In a few years, his hair will probably darken, like mine; his accent will change; he'll be an English little boy.

Liesel slowed down to cross the road. She reached for his hand, and William let her take it. "When I was your age," she said, "maybe a little older, I lived in an apartment in Berlin. We had no garden but the windows went from the bottom of the floor to the top of the ceiling. They were really doors, you could open them, and step out onto a balcony. Not very big, but big enough for flower pots. I used to sit out there and watch the people in the street go by. There weren't many cars then."

They crossed and entered the wide quiet road that dead-ended on their backyard. In the sunshine, you could see the printed shadows of twigs and leaves shifting over the rough asphalt surface. Jean and Su-sie were already at the gate, followed by Cal and Ben. Dana, lagging a little behind now that the road was safe, had taken off her jacket. The afternoon was transformed by radiant heat—the winter sun felt very close in the sky. "Then the war ended," Liesel went on, "and my mother took us all on a train, it seemed like a long journey, to the house where I eventually grew up. With a big garden, by the sea."

"Did you miss the old house?" William asked. His voice had a slight thickness to it, as if he had a mouthful of yogurt; his hearing went through phases of better and worse, they were still doing tests. He didn't seem to mind much.

"I was happy in the new house. But all my life I've wanted to live in an apartment with windows like that, and a balcony like that."

The back gate was open, and William let go of Liesel's hand and ran into the yard. By the time Liesel followed, she couldn't see him any-more—he was hiding again in the bamboo. David, who had picked up May by this point, her face was in his neck, she was very fair and he didn't want her to burn, said to his mother-in-law: "I'm sorry to take them all away from you."

"You're not taking them away. It won't make a difference to us, Connecticut or England. But Susie will be sad about the house."

"Yes," David said.

Paul was waiting for them when they came back. There was a patio with a picnic table on it, outside the kitchen backdoor. A crepe myrtle tree gave it shade; leaf-matter tended to gather between the pebbles of the poured concrete.

"Hey, Buddy," he said to Cal. "Want to hit a ball?"

He wore his biking gear, a Lycra top and shorts, and shoes that clicked against the pebbles. There was dried salt around his eyes, his hair had taken on the shape of his biking helmet, he needed a trim. In his playing days, Dana used to run the electric razor over his scalp. He sat on a kitchen chair on the bathroom tiles and the short segments of keratin scattered around his feet, like iron filings. She felt the grain of his hair in her hand. Whenever she saw him, she had a physical reaction. Somehow his body had become more distinct to her since their separation, she noticed him the way she might notice a stranger at a party: a muscular, intense, not-very-happy-looking guy.

A new kids' tennis racket lay on the picnic table, with a canister of balls.

"I brought you something," he said to Cal. The boy looked down.

Dana felt suddenly angry. "You can't just show up whenever you want," she said. "He's got to know when you're coming and going."

Sometimes his temper was just as quick as hers—it came out of nowhere.

"What are you talking about. This is my house."

"Don't act like you don't know. I'm a guest here."

"What's that got to do with anything."

"Oh, Paul," she said, shaking her head. "If you can't see . . . I mean, the whole time he's looking over his shoulder, where's Daddy gone."

"That's just not true. He doesn't even care. I mean, look at him." Cal had followed Ben into the TV room.

"No TV!" Dana called out, her anger spreading, like something spilled, and Paul went in to get him. After a minute, he came out again, carrying his son, so he had to push open the screen door with his butt and turn around on the steps, while at the same time closing the door delicately behind him.

"You can't make him," Dana began to say, and then let it go.

"Come on," Paul said, in a different voice, to the top of his son's head, to his fragrant hair. "It's Daddy time."

Cal was letting himself be carried, unprotesting, but not helping out much either. So Paul picked up the racket and balls with the kid still in his arms, and clicked his way across the patio and into the thick St. Augustine grass. Strong memories returned to him. The direct early afternoon light made the skin contact with his son, Cal's cheek against his neck, feel hot, and he had to duck against the outcroppings of the crepe myrtle. After his bike ride, his knees hurt, his back hurt; the kid was heavier than he used to be. How many times did he walk this walk as a boy? Under the pecan tree, past the playhouse. Paul was maybe six when Bill put in the court at the back, with the high net on one side and the concrete wall of the parking lot on the other. For hitting balls against. He could still remember the guys pulling the cement mixer, which had wheels, through the back gate and across the lawn, and watching them from the window of the playhouse. Mexicans, wearing baseball caps, which they took off and put on again; they laughed, he couldn't understand them. In summer the sunlight was so intense that it obscured rather than illuminated — colors faded, a bright glare spread over everything, the green of the grass, the pale gray of the poured concrete.

"Is it dry?" he kept asking his dad. "Can I go on it?" And finally Bill said, "Okay, okay."

One thing his father was good at was repetition. He could be very patient, and held out the tennis ball in his hand, to show his son. "Now I'm going to throw it in the air. Now I'm going to let it bounce. You have to wait for it . . ." And then, "That's it, that's it," as Paul knocked it into the fence, into the grass, into the pebbles laid down by the side of the court. The son had inherited his father's appetite for repetition. "One more time," he would say, even in the heat of the day, the two of them standing there, six or seven feet apart, the dad throwing, the son swinging, something in the DNA both being passed along and mirroring itself, a capacity for concentration, for taking pleasure in simple contact, between the two of them, between racket and ball, while Bill's neck grew red under the sunshine. "One more time"—again and again.

When they reached the court Paul let his son slide out of his arms. He wasn't sure if Cal would make the effort to land on his feet, or if he would stay in limp protest mode, but the kid stood there, not very steadily, blinking.

Paul said, "I always loved the smell of tennis balls when you open the can."

In the past few years Bill had let the court run to seed. The sycamore by the drinking faucet had stretched its branches farther and farther across the playing surface, interfering with the telephone wires and dropping leaves and twigs. These snapped underfoot and contributed to the erosion of the rough green paint, which had started to crack in slow wrinkles. But the tree cast shade, too, and even on a winter afternoon, a few days before Christmas, you could feel grateful for it. Paul set the racket on the ground and gave the can of balls to Cal, who took it.

"You pull at the tab," Paul said. "You have to pull it . . . here, like this."

And he tried to show the boy, who told him, "I want to play with Ben."

"You can play with Ben later—"

"I want to watch TV."

"Nobody's watching TV, it's a sunny — "

"Ben is."

"No he's not."

"He is. Let me see."

"Look, you can watch TV later . . ." And so on, until Paul pulled the tab off himself and let the balls roll out onto the concrete. "Can you smell them?" he said, holding the opened canister like a flower against his son's face. "They never smell that way again." Cal just looked at him.

Paul stood up (he had been crouching down) and felt the ache in his back shift. His muscles were cold from recent exercise; he needed a shower. You can't force this kind of thing but you don't want to give in all the time either just to win their temporary approval. Which isn't worth much anyway. "I bought you this, as a present," he said at last, sounding lame even to himself, and unzipping the racket bag. William, he noticed, was watching them from the other side of the net, pressing his face against the mesh, so you could see the lines of it on his skin. "Hey, Willy," Paul called out. "You want to play, too?" Thinking, maybe the presence of another kid, especially an older boy, another cousin . . . and Willy stepped around the net and picked up one of the balls that had rolled away.

"Here, throw it here," Paul said, and the kid threw it.

Paul put the racket into Cal's hand, feeling the small fingers and wrapping them around the grip. "Hold it like this," he said. "That's right, and stand like this." All of which involved a certain amount of intimate rearrangement, of fingers and feet, which Cal passively accepted.

"Watch the ball, I'm going to throw it to you in the air," Paul told him, hearing his father's voice and seeing himself at the same time, standing in front of himself, though Cal had his mother's face, pretty and small-featured, and his mother's long neck. Paul tossed the ball toward the racket head, which bounced against it and rolled away and Willy ran to get the ball. "Look at that," Paul said, in a dad voice of wonder. "But this time I want you to try swinging." When it happened again, Willy said, "Can I try?" so Paul said, "Can Willy have a turn?" and Cal eventually gave him the racket. Paul threw the ball, and Willy, two years older, hit it hard in the air and away into the grass. "You want to get that for me, kid?" Paul asked his son.

Cal watched it rolling away. "Can I go now?" he asked.

"You can pick up the ball, the way Willy got the balls for you," Paul told him, losing his temper.

"After that can I go?" Cal asked, not chastened at all or angry in return.

"After that you can go."

"Can I watch TV?"

"Whatever. You can do whatever people are doing."

"But can I watch?"

"Okay," and the boy ran to pick up the ball and then walked back to put it in his father's hand—looking up for the first time into his face. Cal had blue eyes, like Jean, like his mother. "Okay," Paul said again, "Thank you," and the kid took off, rounded the corner of the playhouse and was gone. Paul said to Willy, "You can go, too, if you want," but Willy wanted to keep playing, so for the next half hour that's what they did. Paul, holding the ball underneath, by the palm, tossed it lightly at Willy, who knocked it away, and every four balls (that's how many came in the can), uncle and nephew ran to chase them down and start again. Willy was pretty good, he had a good eye, and swung naturally along the line of his hip, not up and down but horizontal, which gave him a reasonable chance of making decent contact. Neither one of them spoke much. Willy was concentrating; Paul was rehearsing in his mind various arguments against Dana. If the kid misses me so much he's got a funny way of showing it. The way he gets cooped up in that apartment all day in New York, I mean, no wonder. The only thing he knows how to do is watch TV. And so on—but without much conviction.

Jean sat in Liesel's study at her computer—she could see Cal running back into the house, on his own. He ran like his father, vaguely knock-kneed, but powerfully, too, as if he might stop or change direction at every step. His heels kicked out behind him, he seemed to be running downhill, and she could feel some of the kid-pleasure in being fast, in having the energy to get where you wanted to go as quickly as possible, and then he disappeared up the back steps into the kitchen. From inside the house, faintly, she heard the slam of the door and waited to see if Paul would follow. But sunshine fell on the empty lawn, the switched-off fountain, the bare trees, and the mesh of the screen window gave a faint impression of something etched and printed in its frame, a picture of a winter garden. Dust in the air of her mother's study moved slowly through the green light of her computer as she shifted her attention.

Paul didn't want to spend his afternoon teaching his sister's son how to play tennis. He stuck it out for a reasonable time, and then he said to Willy, "I need to take a shower, should we call it a day?" But Willy by this point had learned to hit the ball two or three or sometimes four times in a row by himself against the concrete wall and wanted to keep going. So Paul left him there like that, bouncing the ball, hitting it, waiting for it to bounce back and hitting it again and mostly losing it in the weeds that grew up at the edge of the court. Running after the ball and starting over.

Dana was sitting at the kitchen table, reading the *New York Times* and drinking coffee, when Paul walked in the backdoor. "How was Lance?" she asked him, and he stared at her for a second before replying.

"What do you mean?"

"I thought you went out biking with him. That's what Jean said."

It was the kind of question she might have asked Nathan, friendly and interested. He thought, I guess she's doing her best. But this is also what her best looked like, a bit polite.

"I don't know," Paul said. "He talks a lot."

"And he's boring or what?"

Maybe she wasn't being polite—maybe this was just another kind of dig. So this is who you spend your time with, famous people. Instead of me and your son.

"It's not just that, it's that you have to let him talk. Because he's Lance. Whereas . . ." He was trying to explain himself, he wanted to explain himself to her. "Everybody else . . . There's a hierarchy, which everybody accepts. But Lance is okay, it's not his fault. He's very competitive."

"I thought you wanted to get away from all that."

"I wanted to get away from all that," Paul said. "Where's Cal?"

"I don't know. He was watching TV with Ben. And then Susie came in and turned it off. So they've gone away somewhere."

She sat with her legs crossed, at an angle to the table, because her knees wouldn't fit underneath it. Her skirt was long and high-waisted, but he could see her fresh-shaved ankles and the straps of her leather sandals—she had a dancer's muscular feet. The newspaper lay scattered over the stained oak.

"Where's Susie?"

She looked at him, smiling, and shrugged. She was thinking, when Susie wants to turn off the TV, she turns it off. I'm a guest in this house. But Paul didn't seem to understand.

"Where's Liesel?" he asked.

"Taking a nap, I think. On the living-room floor."

"Where's Jean?"

"She said she was going to call Nathan. Anything else?"

"I'll go see what Cal is up to. And maybe take a shower."

He stood in the doorway still, with the screen door closed behind him; but now he shut the housedoor, too, and felt somehow that he had to lower his head, to duck his gaze, just to get out of the room. Still in his biking shoes, he clicked across the wooden kitchen floor, and Dana had a flash of feeling, watching his back, that maybe he really was a pretty odd guy—in his Lycra shorts and shirt, thirty-five years old, too skinny, with his strong and hairy legs, and slightly saddle-sore way of walking. Not unlikable or anything, but the sort of guy who confessed things to you in a way you didn't totally trust. It was like the thought you get on a subway platform, that maybe you should jump. Maybe this is what he's like.

The bathroom was upstairs, but Paul sat down on the lower steps first and took off his shoes, which he left in the entrance hall, where his backpack was. It had a change of clothes and he picked it up. Quietly, then, he poked his head around the living-room door.

As children, they were never allowed to go in—the living room was off-limits, except on special occasions, like Christmas. After dinner parties (which they didn't have often), Bill and Liesel would bring their guests back here and sit around the coffee table (covered in a sequined Indian fabric) and eat crème de marrons with whipped cream. An old backgammon set, never played on, served as coaster or ornament. The lamp hanging over the coffee table was Art Nouveau, the light inside seemed always twilit, even in the middle of the day. Three tall windows looked darkly out on the bright front yard, shaded still more by the screen porch. Paul felt, entering, something like his old childish sense of a world of adult privilege, secrets and appetites and conversations, from which he was excluded.

His mother lay on the carpet outside her study, on her back, very straight with her arms beside her and her white hair spread out on the rug. Maybe she was fifteen feet away, on the far side of the room. She looked heavier than she looked in normal life. (He thought of this because he imagined having to lift her for some reason, to carry her, in case she needed help.) Her sleeping face seemed somehow very German, frowning and patient, as it breathed in and out.

Sliding glass doors separated the living room from her study, and Paul could see Jean sitting at their mother's desk and tapping at a laptop computer. Then Jean noticed him and made a face, spreading her mouth without opening it, so that her lips widened and thinned, in a kind of frown or smile, while she looked down toward the floor where their mother slept. He nodded and walked out. Upstairs he found Cal in Jean's old room, watching his cousin play Minecraft on an iPad.

"How long have you guys been playing?"

"I'm not playing," Cal said.

"It's all right," Ben told him. "My mom said it was okay."

His pale, somehow English face looked very assured; his glasses reflected the images on the screen.

"I don't want to sleep in a crib," Cal said. "I want to sleep in a bed."

Paul looked at them both for a moment—the twelve-year-old boy and the four-year-old boy, sitting on an unmade bed, in the dark room. "Okay," he said and left them there. The green-tiled bathroom was at the end of the hall, and he locked the door and set his backpack on the floor. Undressing, he glanced at himself in the mirror over the sink, then under the hot water he closed his eyes.

Jean was looking for flights out of Boston that afternoon, something with possible connections to Austin, or even Houston or Dallas, or flights out of TF Green—anything. Nathan had promised to try; he and Clémence were getting their bags packed, they hadn't expected to leave until the morning. When Jean wanted to call him, she stepped outside. Liesel's study had French doors that opened onto the balcony, a corner unprotected by the porch roof, which meant that for nine months a year it was too hot to use. Leaves ended up gathering there, nobody swept it, but it was pleasant now to stand out in the bright winter sunshine and talk to your brother on the phone.

She could see down the curve of the street toward Hemphill Park, where she had learned to ride a bike on the short grass, pushed by Bill, hour after hour, though he couldn't ride one himself—and feel the peculiar transposition of jet lag, since two days ago she was sitting with Henrik on the top deck of the 52 bus, moving in traffic along the

Harrow Road, after going out for dinner. Always, she was aware of the time of day in England, eight at night, Emil's bedtime, Henrik would be turning out his light, and could feel it in her body, too, the split time zones, two biological clocks ticking at once. When Nathan picked up, she said, "How long will it take you to drive to Providence?"

"At this time of day, at this time of year? Anything from an hour to whatever, depending on traffic. You've got a lot of people leaving the city. I-95 gets pretty packed."

"Okay, so you need to get in the car now. In the next half hour."

"Look, Jean," he started to say.

"There are five seats left on a flight out of TF Green, which gets into Charlotte around seven o'clock. From Charlotte you can catch a plane to DFW—there's a two-hour layover, you should have plenty of time. And with the time-zone change, it won't even be that late when you get in."

"Get in where?"

"To Dallas. It lands at ten."

"Look, Jean," he said again. "I've been thinking about this. What we should really do is find somewhere to stay in New York and help out with Rose. We should spend Christmas with Bill."

"Have you spoken to him?"

"The number he gave us for the hospital room isn't answering. I don't know. I expected him to be there by this point. Clémence thinks that maybe we have a cell phone number for Judith—she's checking her email. I don't know. What do we do when we get to Dallas? I mean, after a certain point, it gets a little crazy. When's the last shuttle to Austin?"

"You'll miss that, but it doesn't matter—"

"You know we don't drive long distances at night. I just fall asleep—both of us do. We could check in to an airport hotel, but it all adds up. I mean, at that point it becomes a two-day trip."

"I'll pick you up. It doesn't matter."

"You can't pick us up. It's six hours in the car."

"It's three hours. At that time of night, maybe less."

"I mean, both ways. This is sweet of you, but at a certain point . . ."

"What do I care," Jean said. "What else am I going to do. I'm jet-lagged anyway. So I listen to NPR for three hours, and on the way back, we can talk. We can spend some time."

"I want to see you, too," Nathan said.

"Liesel was in tears at lunch when she heard you might not make it. After Bill left this morning."

"I understand that, but really, if it's a question of that . . . Let me see if I can get in touch with Bill, let me see if I can find out what's going on."

"By that point, you'll miss the flight."

"There'll be other flights."

"I'm not sure there will be. Let me buy it now—it may already be too late."

"How much is this going to cost? Two thousand dollars, maybe more? When the marginal utility is . . . debatable, given that Bill could probably do with some company right now."

Jean, staring at their neighbor's front yard, where the father of one of her old school friends was trying to clear out the leaves from the heating and air-conditioning unit, said, "No, that's true, that's probably true."

"Let's just—maybe it's best just to admit . . ."

"It means a lot to me that you come." There was a silence at the other end of the phone, and after a moment, Jean went on: "Henrik is flying in on Boxing Day. Anyway, it means a lot to me. But you're right. You should go to Bill. In which case, you probably want to set off pretty soon anyway. To beat the weather."

Nathan, at the other end, speaking into her ear (he sounded very close, a presence in her head), said: "Give me five minutes. Let me talk to Clémence. I'll call you back in five." And he hung up.

Jean waited on the balcony with the phone in her hand—her ear felt hot from the pressure of the handset, she must have been pressing it hard. When they were younger, this neighbor guy looked like all the other dads, he was just a category of person. Now he had put on weight, he had lost his hair, his scalp looked pink and smooth, and there were white tufts of uncropped hair around his ears. And yet at the same time, he seemed to have changed very little, he moved more slowly, but he was always deliberate, and the weight gain had kept his face unwrinkled.

He noticed Jean on the balcony and stood up to wave. Jean waved back and he called to her: "Daryl's flying in next week. How long are you around for?"

"That's nice. Till the third. Where's she coming in from?"

"Sioux Falls. She's staying with her in-laws out there, the kids like the snow."

"That's nice."

"They get Christmas, we get New Year."

"That's how it goes."

"Everybody's at that time of life."

He pressed his hands against his lower back and stretched out, frowning. The clothes he wore were the clothes he always wore, jeans and a white T-shirt and a collared shirt unbuttoned over the T-shirt. "You're in London, Bill tells me."

"That's right."

"How's that?"

"Wet," Jean said, and then felt ashamed of fobbing him off with this kind of answer. "I like it. It's one of those cities where . . . everybody's doing interesting things." But this isn't what she felt either.

He looked at her for a few seconds, waiting maybe to see if she was going to say something else. "I'll tell her you're around," he said eventually and went back to his work, turning away from her and leaning over.

Jean went inside; she wanted to check the ticket availability anyway and sat down at her mother's computer to refresh the page. Liesel collected old glass—there was a bookshelf full of it next to the desk, decanters and crystal goblets but also champagne coupes and a row of faintly cranberry-colored water glasses, with an odd bubble or two seeming to rise against the surface. The bookshelf itself was the old-fashioned kind, dark wood with rickety hinges, and glass shields that could be lowered or raised. Liesel had wedged photographs into the jambs, and while she waited Jean looked at them. Part of the point of coming home was the density of association, you seemed to move through a thicker material. There was a picture of Paul, maybe five years old, dressed from head to toe in red oilcloth—his fireman's suit. A picture of Jean, too: standing in rubber boots in a pile of snow. Must have been taken in Europe. It almost never snowed in Austin, and even if it did, it didn't stick. Nathan at his high-school graduation, just a Polaroid, very poor quality. He was smiling the way you smile when you're a teenager, not quite in control of how you come across. And one of Susie's little watercolor sketches, about the size of a postcard, of the house in Germany where Liesel grew up: a tall, peaked tile roof, red bricks and white window frames, on a green lawn with the sea behind it, and Denmark, a thin green line across the water.

Next to it, and partly tucked behind, was a black-and-white photograph of Liesel as a young woman, her long dark hair in a braid, she looked thin and nervous and happy, and prettier than either of her daughters. Hard to say where it was taken—maybe Berlin, in her student flat, the one she shared with her cousin. Now she lay fifty years older sleeping on a rug on the floor five thousand miles away.

When the phone rang, Jean thumbed the receiver and pressed it again to her ear—the seats were still free, the price hadn't changed, she stared at the screen.

"Hey," she said.

"We're getting in the car. If you could buy the tickets now I'll pay you back later. Just email them—to Clémence's account, not mine. Okay. We'll call you from the road."

"I'll see you in Fort Worth."

"I'll see you in Fort Worth."

"I'll see you tonight."

"With luck."

He didn't say anything else but he didn't hang up either, and eventually Jean said, "I'm really pleased," and he said, "Me, too. Thank you. All right, I should go," and the line went dead.

Liesel had been woken by the ring and lay with her eyes closed, still out of it but vaguely aware that her daughter was talking on the phone. There's a kind of half-state, before full consciousness, when reality doesn't press very hard. She felt the floor under the rug under her back; she knew where she was, but in the darkness she wasn't really committed to any of it, and wondered for a moment if she might drift back to sleep. She liked listening to Jean's voice and tried to work out from the tone of intimacy who she might be talking to, a puzzle that pulled her slowly back to consciousness. Henrik maybe. She heard her say, "I'm really pleased," and felt a pang of brief anxiety at the thought of his coming visit. Maybe it was just as well Bill wasn't around. He had less patience than she did for . . . irregular arrangements. The fact that Henrik was so much older, almost closer to their age than to Jean's, didn't help. For a moment, she thought of her daughter as a thirty-two-year-old woman, making choices about her life, the way other women make choices. Taking on another man's kids, at least part-time. But she didn't recognize her in this light. It was all a kind of elaborate pretending, which everybody for some reason went along with . . . But this is foolishness, she told herself, it's wishful thinking. Okay, okay. Okay. You should get up.

She opened her eyes and the filtered afternoon sunshine fell in two streaks against the wall. There was a watery effect from the waving of a tree branch outside—the wind seemed to disturb the surface of the light. Standing up was mildly painful. She had to roll over first on her side, and then use her hands to push herself up from her knees. Jean, pulling at one of the sliding glass doors, put her face in the gap. She said, "I'm sorry, that was my fault. Did I wake you up?" But she didn't wait for an answer and went on: "That was Nathan on the phone. I found a flight that gets them into Dallas around ten o'clock tonight. I said I'd pick him up."

"Oh good," Liesel said, flooded suddenly with strong emotion. "Oh good." And then, in German: "You're my good girl. *Mein tüchtiges Mädchen.*"

For the rest of the afternoon, they followed Nathan's progress by various means. He called from the airport in Rhode Island—they took the Concord Turnpike out of Cambridge and missed most of the Boston traffic. It was fairly plain sailing after they crossed the mess of exits around I-90. Anyway, they made good time; security took an hour to clear, but they were now giving the kids late lunch/ early supper at Famous Famiglia's Airport-Style Pizza—for them, it was basically an adventure. Susie wanted to decorate the tree, Paul (showered, dressed, in jeans and T-shirt) had helped her carry it in from the backyard and move some of the furniture around in the living room. They pushed the side table into a corner, they lifted pictures from the wall. While Nathan was talking, people kept walking in and out, the phone got passed around. Susie said to him, "I'm glad you're coming. I didn't even have the heart to tell the kids that you might not. Safe flight. One of you should stay up to talk to Jean, I don't want her falling asleep." And then, in answer to something Nathan had told her: "No, that's probably true."

When it was her turn, Liesel found she couldn't hear with all the noise and carried the handset out on to the porch for peace and quiet. Then she closed the French doors behind her and sat down on the rocking bench with a sigh. From there, she could see—through one of the living-room windows—Susie holding up the tree, Paul, crouched underneath, adjusting the stand. Nathan said, "Has anyone spoken to Bill? We tried to call the hospital number but nobody picked up."

"I haven't heard from him." It was cool on the porch, under the roof, in the shade of the pyracantha bush. Paul had said they should put in those restaurant heaters, but Bill was opposed. We're talking about two months a year, he said, where they might get some use.

And Liesel, hearing this argument in her head again, said, "Jean's been looking up hospital reports. Apparently where Rose has been brought has a very poor record on MRSA. There are a number of specialist centers in Yonkers . . ."

And Nathan said, "Listen, I should go—people are starting to board. We don't even know what state she's in. This seems to me premature."

"Nathan?" She could hear the PA system announcing a gate change for the flight to St. Petersburg, the distinctive echo of a public announcement, as evocative in its way as the smell of a swimming pool, which shifted the space in her head, so that for a moment she felt like her bags lay around her, she was catching a flight. "Jean says this is an area where the doctors have very different rates of success, and it's worth . . ."

"She may be right. There's nothing I can do right now. I'll call when we get to Charlotte."

"Nathan?" She couldn't tell if he was still on the line. "*Ich freue mich sehr. Dass du kommst.* I'm happy you're coming."

"Me, too," he said and she was sitting again on a shady porch in Texas, with the sunshine falling brightly on the empty street outside her house. After a few minutes, she pushed herself off the bench and went inside.

Susie had gone upstairs to find Ben—it was something they always did together, decorate the tree, a mother and her firstborn son. He used to have tremendous patience for this kind of job, cooking, wrapping presents, baking cakes. But lately Susie felt . . . she was losing him somehow to his father's way of . . . a certain cheerful carelessness, which Ben had adopted as a useful strategy for getting out of chores. At the top of the stairs, she heard him saying to Cal, "You can't get on my bed until you blow your nose. I mean, look at you. It's disgusting." And when she walked down the corridor to his room and saw the two of them, Ben said to her, "Somebody needs to clean his nose. He's disgusting."

"We're decorating the tree. Come here, Cal." And she picked him up, shifting him onto her hip. There was a box of Kleenex on Jean's old desk and she pulled out a tissue and spread it against his face. "Blow," she said. "That's it. As hard as you can." Really, he was too big to carry like this, too heavy, and she put him down and threw the tissue in the wastebasket by the door.

"Okay . . ." Ben said, in his mildly ironic puzzled voice.

"I want you to help."

"I'm reading."

"You're playing Minecraft. Come on, Cal. You, too."

"I want to play Minecraft," the kid said, and Susie gave her son a look. Like, busted. Ben shrugged his shoulders.

"This is something I love to do with you," she told him and reached over to take the iPad away. He fought with her a little, he was strong enough to fight harder, and tested the waters longer than he might have, then gave in and lay back on the bed, while Susie, feeling strangely upset, tried to shut off the device.

"Don't be a pane of glass," he said.

The button she pushed kept reverting the screen to its home page, but then she found the off switch and heard the satisfying artificial click. "I hate this . . . thing. Come on, Cal," and she took his hand, which in its smallness seemed somehow trusting.

"What about Willy?" Ben asked.

"What about him?"

"Why can't he help?"

"He's playing in the yard. I don't know, he never likes this kind of thing. You do. You . . . it's not a chore . . ."

"Well then."

"Do what you want." And then, to Cal: "You can help me hang up the *Kringel*. *Kringel* are like chocolate."

"I don't like chocolate," he said, but allowed her to lead him away.

"Give me the iPad," Ben called after her, but Susie only waved it in the air, in a kind of triumph, like the spoils of war. Ben, watching her go, felt less pleased than he might have expected to. The news about moving to England was not upsetting to him, really—it satisfied a sense he had of himself, of being slightly apart or distinguished in some way, though he realized already that he was thinking about it in terms of the people he knew at school now, in Connecticut, who wouldn't matter very much when he was gone. Still, he felt his parents owed him something, for what they were putting him through. And it made him feel better to hang out with Cal and order him around. Part of what he liked about the iPad is that it required a kind of concentration that seemed to conceal him from other people. Though he also had a vague sense that this was unhappy behavior and he should snap out of it. He lay back on the bed and listened to everyone talking downstairs.

Dana had joined the others at the tree-side. When Susie came down, Paul left to check on William, who was still apparently hitting balls against the wall out back. "You never do what I say anyway," he said, meaning the decorations. Susie had strong specific tastes and opinions, but the truth is, Paul didn't really care. David had taken May for her afternoon walk. (She liked to sleep in her stroller, and he was planning to go to a coffee shop and work.) Jean had carried her mom's laptop into the living room to find out what she could about her aunt's condition. She rocked in the old rocking chair, newly upholstered in a kind of Klimt fabric, soft bright yellow, while Liesel sat on the sofa with a pile of *Kringel* on her lap—German Christmas decorations, chocolates and sugared jelly-candies shaped like little donuts. She was threading them with silver and gold loops of string, for hanging on the tree.

"Hey Cal," she said. "Come here. Want to try one?"

And the boy was walking toward her, squeezing between the chairs, when the phone rang. Dana, doing nothing much but standing around, picked it up in Liesel's study. Bill said, "Well, I'm here."

"Hi, Bill. It's Dana."

There was a silence while he adjusted his thoughts. From where he stood, in the hospital corridor, he could see through a gap in the plastic curtains into Rose's room. His sister lay on one of those mechanized beds, a quarter upright, the angle at which you display fruits and vegetables in the supermarket. Maybe because of this she was hunched in slightly, lying partly on her side, a protective position; wires and tubes proceeded from her, hidden under the folds of her sheets, and connected to monitors and plastic sacs of liquids—some going into her, some coming out. On the screen Bill could read various accounts of what was happening to her or inside her, pulse and blood pressure, and it was hard not to overreact to changes in the data. When people don't talk, when they just lie there, when their only form of expression is the medical readout, every blip or adjustment feels like a communication from the deep. Whatever it is that's going on in there, dreams or sensations. The battle you spend your life fighting played out at the micro level, gang warfare of cells and bacteria. From time to time a broken connection in one of the wires set off a persistent beeping, which the nurses, passing by, largely ignored.

"Hey, Dana," Bill said, "who's around?" and immediately felt bad. But he wasn't prepared for any kind of small talk or jumping over conversational fences. Nobody used the hospital phones anymore, people relied on their cells. He had had to buy a calling card from the gift shop—the guy at the counter was surprised they still sold them. All of this involved a grappling with practicalities that wasn't Bill's specialty. Who would have thought, with your sister lying there like that, that reading numbers off a thin plastic card, following the instructions, waiting for the automated voice, could be the thing that stresses you out. Standing in the hallway, he held the stretched cord in his hand. For some reason, he didn't want to talk in Rose's presence. He didn't want to wake her up or act like she wouldn't wake up anyway. For the past two hours she had been like a body lying in the water. Sometimes with her head in the air she could respond, but then she would dip down again, below the surface, and you had to try to make contact through a very thick medium.

"Everybody," Dana said. "Anybody you want. We're decorating the tree." And he heard her announce, into the living room, "It's Bill." And then his wife's voice, "Bill?" rising in a kind of pleased panic, as she made her way between the chairs. And then, as if she had really moved closer to him, across the distances, her words in his ear: "Bill? Where are you? How is she?"

So he told her, keeping his voice down. One of the nurses sat on a swivel chair, maybe five feet away, typing into a computer and eating a sandwich—a late lunch. Asian, straight black hair, pretty; she sat there like she was sitting in a coffee shop. Everything echoed off the marble tiles, but sounds also lost themselves in the echoes. The privacy of public spaces. While he was speaking, two men wheeled a cart full of medical equipment, containers of some kind, on balky wheels. They pulled and pushed and had to start again. One of them had left a clipboard on the top—Bill worried it might fall off.

Judith has come and gone already, he said. She showed up straight from the airport and was almost angry with her mother for not being in a critical condition. Anyway, she went home to drop off her suitcase and shower. Yes, she's staying at Rose's. I don't know, I guess I'll sleep there, too. We may as well take it in turns, she said. The truth is, she's angry with her mother anyway. When I arrived she had been sitting in the room for maybe half an hour. The first thing she said to me was, she must weigh two hundred pounds.

Yes, I brought some work along. It's okay, I sit and scribble. There's a TV in the room, but I don't like to turn up the sound. MSNBC.

She woke up. She wakes up. She's in and out. Yes, she knows who I am.

In fact, Rose hadn't said his name, but there was no surprise on her face to see that he was there. As if, of course, when you come round, not knowing where you are or what has happened to you, Billy will be there. Your brother. (For the first ten years of his life they shared a bedroom. Every time they woke up, when they opened their eyes . . . until they moved to the house on Roosevelt Avenue.) When the nurse arrived he thought he traced a different reaction, a faint . . . manner. If you told her to sit up, she could sit up. If you asked her, would you like to watch TV, she could shake her head. Her robe, as she shifted, sometimes parted in the middle. Bill saw her stomach, discolored and pleated from any little application of pressure; it was also covered in the soft hairs of obesity. Her breasts hung down like balloons filling at the faucet. There are things you can't turn your eyes from. Just to look is doing a kind of human duty, because it means, okay, I see you, you're there. The skin of her shoulders had a peculiar milky pallor and softness, like a baby's skin or worn stone.

The nurse herself seemed grateful to have somebody else to communicate with—other than Judith. Judith liked to think of herself as a person who got what she wanted from these relations. There was also the fact that she had spent two years in medical school, training to become a doctor. At a certain point in life you become one of these people who, regardless of the situation, has some vanity at stake. Her voice carried and she spoke at full volume, even in the little curtained room, in the presence of medical personnel. Every time I come to the house I have to throw out all the sugary foods; she says she buys them for Mikey but it isn't true. She eats them herself. But I guess you have to let your parents make their own mistakes. And the way she laughed conveyed to Bill in some unmistakable way the impression she had of herself, as charming and tolerant, among friends. These people, people like Judith, need constant support; unless you agree with them they think you're stabbing them in the back. But he laughed, too, or made a grunt of amusement; he felt sorry for her. She was his sister's child. The truth is, the two of them, Judith and Rose, were still locked very much in the same battle. Which he had somehow, in his own life, in relation to his own parents, escaped.

Liesel, responding to Bill's silence, tried to keep him on the line. "How was your flight? Did the driver find you all right?"

"I told Nathan not to bother. I rented a car."

"Bill. You're too tired. You didn't sleep."

"I'm fine. I slept on the plane. I can sleep now. There's one of these mechanical reclining chairs in Rose's room, which is perfectly comfortable. What else am I doing."

"Nathan said he was going to call his driver."

"Well, I figured I'd need a car anyway. When I got here."

This is also the argument he had with Nathan. He told his son, it's a half-hour drive from the airport. I'll be fine. In fact, it took him most of two hours. Traffic was backed up a mile before the Bronx–Whitestone Bridge, the usual holiday exodus, but also people getting out of the city before the cold front hit. Then he took the wrong exit off the Saw Mill Parkway and only realized when he passed the cemetery. All of these streets used to be familiar to him—he had a terrific memory for directions, it was one of the binary qualities amplified or exaggerated by their marriage, Liesel got lost and Bill could always remember the way. But he disliked the rental, which was the kind of new car that didn't need a key, where you pressed a button. He came off at Palmer Road and tried to find his way back through neighborhood streets. Every time he stopped at a light, the engine turned off. At a certain point everything adds to your anxiety, traffic, getting lost, the new technology. But he found Lake Avenue and then North Broadway, and feeling a little more in control, made it to the hospital by familiar landmarks—Washington Park and City Hall. The first thing he did when he got to the hospital was take a leak.

"Have you eaten anything?" Liesel said.

"I'll eat with Judith. I'm just going to sit here for another half hour while it's quiet. I'm pretty wiped, it's no hardship sitting in that chair. I can watch TV with the sound off. At six o'clock there's a shift change, and I want to talk to whoever comes in. Then I'll go home."

When she hung up, the tree was almost finished; it glittered in the half-light. Old shoeboxes, half empty, lay on the floor, and there were piles of paper towels, which had been used to wrap the ornaments. When the kids were little, Liesel sat with them at the kitchen table, making chains of silver paper, reindeer cutouts, cardboard witches' hats sprinkled with stars, animals stuck together out of wine corks. At antique markets, she kept her eye out for baubles and trinkets—glass balls or slippers, tarnished silver birds with pincer-feet for sticking to a branch. Liesel, being German, preferred beeswax candles to Christmas lights, and Susie and Dana and Jean were placing the candleholders carefully over the barer branches of the tree, when Ben came down. He looked at his mother and said, "I want to help," and she said, "You can help us put these on," so he took a handful from the box and found a place around the tree, toward the back, by the window.

Jean told him, after he had fixed his first candle to one of the piney boughs, "You have to give it some room to burn. Here, like this," and moved it a few inches along, so the branch dipped a little, and the candle bobbed in open space. Susie, overhearing her, wished she hadn't and was almost pleased when her son, ignoring his aunt's advice, clipped another holder in place, in a thicket of needles. Jean let it go, and Susie wondered if she knew it was intentional, one of Ben's deliberate sly expressions of quiet indifference to other people's points of view. Before she could say something, Paul walked through the hallway double doors carrying a stack of dried logs in his arm, and Willy followed, holding a few gray twigs.

"I thought maybe we'd want a fire," Paul said. "Hey, kid, you want to help me build it?" But he meant Willy, and Dana, watching Cal, who was helping Liesel thread the *Kringel*, putting his finger on her knots, felt a vague pang. Susie, noticing, too, said, "He should really wash his hands if he's got a cold," and stopped what she was doing to get the bottle of Purell from the kitchen counter and give him a squirt.

"I don't like it," Cal said. "It's slimy."

"Well, it dries up pretty soon," and she squeezed some of the chemical gel onto her palm and took the boy's hands in her own. He didn't resist.

Later, after everyone had gone, for different reasons and to different places, Susie stood in the living room by herself, surveying the tree—its old-fashioned prettiness. Even without the heat of lit candles, some of the ornaments spun lightly on their strings, balls of glass turning slowly and catching the light like Granny Smiths. She stepped forward to adjust some of the candleholders, most of them clipped on by her son, and wondered if he would notice and if the argument they had been putting off having openly, whatever the root of it was, needed to be had. When Nathan called, the phone lay on the coffee table and Susie was the first to pick up. They had landed safely in Charlotte, but the plane to DFW was delayed by fifty-five minutes. At least, that's what they were saying now—ten minutes ago it was half an hour. Tell Jean. If it gets too late we'll just stay at a hotel. She shouldn't think this is her problem.

"Okay, I'll tell her," Susie said. "Nathan."

"Yes?"

She wanted to tell him about moving to England. Even when they were fighting, or not even fighting, just niggling at each other, she couldn't escape the fact that she took comfort from him, her big brother, from having her life known by him, and understood by him—to be under his purview. But instead she said, "Everybody's happy you're coming. Liesel was very upset, about Bill, too."

"Well, let's hope we get there," and he hung up.

Another day was going, the light had already started to change quality at four o'clock. Sunshine turning poignant, the sky still blue but faded. Even through the living-room windows, heavily shaded by branches and the overhanging roof, you could feel the afternoon slipping away. What had they done with the day? Not much, but at least, Susie thought, the tree was up, it was decorated, a job had been accomplished, and she got down on her hands and knees around the coffee table to gather up loose sheets of tissue and put them away into the emptied shoeboxes lying around. She would have to tell Bill, too. He didn't know about England either—another list of small jobs, things to do, was growing in her head.

The house was big enough different groups of people could be doing different things, unaware of the presence of anybody else, and she
wandered through the hallway to find Jean. It was lined with Susie's
self-portraits, various poses of unhappiness, in dark rich reds and
blues. This is how she thought of herself in college. Her skin looked
chafed by the paint, the color-tone suggested . . . a state of high alert.
She could hear the TV but there was nobody in the playroom, just
some commercial making background noise, loudly. The volume of
everything seemed to be going up, year by year, and she hunted for
the remote control to turn it off. Maybe the kids were upstairs, maybe they were in the backyard. David was still out with May, who was
probably still asleep. Sitting in noisy cafés always knocked her out,
and she might be hard to get to bed, but that wasn't *his* problem.

Over the sofa, six foot by six foot, hung her painting of the family — just the kids, Nathan and Jean and Paul, while she hovered behind them, long-faced and sad-eyed. Susie looked at it for a minute,
critically. Just schlepping it back from New Haven after graduation
was hard enough, along with everything else: rolling up the canvas,
taking apart the frame. Not her best work, and yet she also didn't
want to throw it away, out of superstition or something else. The
angles between the figures still interested her, the fact that nobody
was looking at anybody else, and only she was looking at the camera.
Actually, she *had* worked from a photograph — Liesel snapped them
on Christmas day, twenty years ago, everybody sitting on the sofa,
watching a basketball game. "*Guck mal, ihr glotzt alle.*" You're all
just staring at the TV . . . and now Susie had her own kids, three of
them, and was moving again, ending her life in one place and starting
another.

The stirrings of a thought, something that had already occurred to
her in one form or another . . . was beginning to take a more definite
shape. You become aware of these gestations after the event. One of
the things she had talked about with David, when they talked about
moving to England, was finding teaching work. Oxford, he said,

usually had plenty of short-term contracts going around. "Just so I don't feel like a mom," she told him. "So I have some kind of identity." But a permanent job was going to be hard to get, she hadn't published in years. David had a talent for offering good-natured, sweet, effusive but strictly limited support, that always somehow put her in her place.

In her own way, though, she had stopped listening, or needing it. What had occurred to her, what was taking shape, was the idea for a book, or a series of papers, to be called something like *The Invention of Family*, and maybe what she really needed wasn't teaching work but library access, so she could write it. Her field was late seventeenth-century, or used to be, when she was still producing, but she planned to start earlier, with Homer, though she could touch on *Paradise Lost* as well . . . because what she wanted to write about was the idea of family as an *escape* from history, or an insulation from it, from political forces and social pressures and cultural shifts, and the way that writers had been writing about this since they began writing. Odysseus's dog, what was his name, Argos, even the family dog was part of the picture. Robinson Crusoe had a dog, the idea of an island . . . and the lines came to her, which had been at the back of her mind all day, *With thee to go, is to stay here*. Eve promising Adam, after he's been kicked out of Paradise, to come along. *Without thee here to stay, is to go hence unwilling* . . . which always brought tears to her eyes, though the image she had, of someone to address them to, the *thee* in her thoughts, wasn't David (it suddenly struck her), but Ben. He was the one who needed to hear her say it.

Then Dana came in and saw her staring at the blank TV.

"Do we have any plans for what to feed the kids?"

"I haven't gotten that far yet," Susie said. "Have you seen Jean?"

"I think she was taking a nap, I saw her go upstairs. Paul has got everybody playing kick the can."

"Even Ben?"

"Ben, too."

"He's a good uncle," Susie said, without thinking; and Dana, quietly, felt a faint reproach.

———

Ben was one of these kids who from an early age had an idea of himself as not a physical person. A boy in his school once called him the walking brain. When he ran, he ran with a show of good-natured effort, like someone late for meeting a friend, trying to prove, as soon as he's been spotted, that he was hurrying all along by way of apology. But for some reason Paul could always get him to play games. He was a very violent uncle, who liked lifting and throwing babies, slinging kids over his back, carrying several at once, and for years he had no kids of his own to spend this energy on. Sometimes, now, he overdid it. He was strong enough to hold Ben above his head, like a weightlifter, performing the clean and jerk, and threatened Ben with something like this if he didn't join in. So Ben joined in, semi-reluctantly, because he was still loyal to the idea that Paul was his favorite uncle, even if it wasn't particularly true anymore.

Susie had said to him, the night before they flew to Austin, "I don't want you to get upset by anything that's going on with Paul and Dana."

"Why would I be upset?"

"Maybe not upset. Just don't—expect anything from them, or be surprised by it, or ask them too many questions."

"What kind of questions? You're being weird."

"Well, they're going through a kind of phase right now, which isn't easy to explain. Or understand. Even for grown-ups."

"I thought they were separated," Ben said.

When May was born, everybody switched bedrooms. It was part of Ben's compensation package (this is how David referred to it), that he got a larger room, so Susie cleared out of her study and they put a bed in it. But this also meant he was the only one sleeping on that side of the house, the town side, with a distant view of the main street, also known as Route 17, and his mom had to walk along a corridor and past the family bathroom to reach him. He was a little isolated, which he liked; but it also gave him the feeling that every night his mother paid him a visit.

Susie, sitting next to him, with her hand on his back, rubbing his shoulders under the pajamas, said, "I think that's what they are. But Dana's coming, too, for Christmas, she's bringing Cal, and I don't want you to worry about what's going on."

"I don't understand why you think I would worry," he said.

But the truth is, he *was* curious; and one of the ways this curiosity played out is that he realized he felt shy of Dana. For some reason, when he saw her for the first time, he shook her hand, he wasn't sure what else to do. A few years before she might have hugged him, but she seemed to hesitate, and he put out his hand. She took it and then kind of pulled him toward her, laying an arm on his shoulder, but she released him pretty quickly, too. Which somehow flattered him. She was obviously an unusually pretty woman—a few of the boys in his class had been given iPhones, and found a way of looking at naked women. They huddled over break, under the trees at the far side of the football field. Ben sometimes joined them, pretending to be amused. But he couldn't conceal from himself that he was always aware of Dana's presence in any room, and even when he was playing outside, with Cal and Willy and Paul, he looked over at the windows of the house to see if she was watching them. One of the reasons he let Cal tag along is because it attracted her attention.

He was interested in Paul, too. The idea of a guy not working, living the way he wants to live, and not even bound by family, but just doing what he wants, and not in a seedy way, either. If Paul had a girlfriend nobody had seen her, nobody mentioned it. But he seemed to get along with Dana, too, they were perfectly friendly, and Ben had the sense of an adult world he was still forced to look at from the outside, through the windows, where he couldn't hear what was really going on. So when Paul said, it's a sunny day, kids should be running around outside, he let himself be dragged into the game, because Cal wouldn't have joined in otherwise, and Ben liked the idea of helping out. And he ran the way he always ran, so that the grown-ups could tell he wasn't really trying, not against kids. Let Willy win; Willy always cared too much about this kind of stuff. Ben found a spot in the bamboo bushes behind the playhouse, where there was a gap in the fence that led to the neighbor's yard; and he took Cal by the hand and they hid there together, while Paul wandered back and forth, shouting. He could almost feel, like heat coming off a light bulb, the level of tension and excitement in the boy. Then, when the coast was clear, he pushed his cousin in the shoulder, and whispered, *Go, go*, and watched him run toward Paul's old CATA baseball cap, which was lying in the grass and serving as the can.

Willy made his move at the same time.

He had been hiding in the side passage behind the garage apartment. There was a little patio garden, which belonged to the apartment and was overgrown around the edges with tall spreading agave plants and rambling rose—squeezing between the leaves meant getting scratched. Rusted garden furniture, a couple of chairs, seemed to lean back with age, and were also covered with a rather pretty purplish mold. Nobody ever sat out there. The alley along the side ran between the apartment and the neighbor's fence, which was six feet tall and cast a deep shade. Willy, crouching down, felt the dust drift over his face, he could hear bugs moving in the leaves, and brushed his hand against his forehead and nose to clear away the suspicion of something tacky like cobwebs clinging to them. He wanted to win, the tension kept building inside him, and he guessed that Paul wouldn't look for him out there, but it was too far to make a sudden dash for it and trust your luck. There was also the danger of hiding so well that the game moved on without you, people forgot.

From where he sat, he could see across the backyard through gaps in the vegetation to the playhouse forty feet away and the tennis court beyond it. When Cal started running the movement caught his eye, a series of color flashes between the upright stems of the bamboo, first shady and then emerging into the light. Without thinking, he started to run, too, and knocked against one of the garden chairs on his way past, which made a clang against the pebbled concrete. A branch or tendril of the agave plant snagged briefly against one of his pulled-up socks, but he didn't care, and as his shoe touched grass the open space ahead of him in the sunshine felt like a long slide that he was rushing down.

Paul heard the clang and turned around—he had walked as far as the playhouse and would have come up on Ben and Cal from behind them if he'd gone much farther. His son was stumbling in front of him toward the cap, running with a kind of fearful hurry that was always in danger of overbalancing, his body leaning over and his legs somehow catching up, while from the other side of the yard, his nephew Willy, older and not much taller, but more muscular and compact, raced with a straight up-and-down efficiency toward the same spot. Paul, feeling the life in his legs, the kick that he still had in him, started jogging, shouting hey, hey, pretending helplessness, and let his son reach base ahead of him before he put on a late spurt and beat Willy to the cap. For reasons he couldn't have pinned down. Because he wanted Cal to beat his nephew. Because he suspected on some level that Willy wanted him to be fast, who knows.

Willy, in fact, as soon as he had caught his breath, said, "I thought I was gonna get there. Man, I thought I was gonna get there. But you were like . . ." and he made a gesture with his hand. And he turned to Cal, who hardly looked at him, and said again, "I mean, he was like . . ." and made the same gesture with his hand.

Paul, touched, feeling sad or a little guilty, recognized the tone— boys somehow were taught to admire other boys, older, bigger kids, and to tell their stories as a way of brushing off the sense of failure. He rested his palm on Willy's head and then said, "Ben, I see you, under the . . ." pointing toward the playhouse veranda, where Ben had already begun to walk carelessly out of his hiding place, with his hands up.

"You got me," he called out. "Does that mean I'm it?"

"Can we play tennis?" Willy asked.

"Do you want to hit a ball around, Cal?" Paul said, but Cal shook his head.

"I guess you're it," Paul told Ben, and the game went on.

Dana and Susie started getting supper for the kids, working together. Susie took carrots and a cucumber out of the fridge, and Dana washed and cut them into sticks.

"Is Cal happy with mac and cheese?" Susie said.

"Does Ben still eat it?"

"*I* still eat it. He's picky about some things, but not food."

Dana, apologetically, said, "I'm afraid my son's a pesto kid."

"Well, we can do that, too. I don't know when David's coming back. My breasts are killing me."

Dana, dutifully, asked her: "How often does May still feed?"

There was a cupboard next to the oven with a collection of jars in it, most of them several years old, and Susie had crouched down to see if she could find some pesto. This involved taking out cans of soup and chopped tomatoes, a jar of piccalilli, which Bill had brought back from some long-ago trip to London, packets of Miso powder, cans of cherries, etc.

"Usually just twice a day, mornings and evenings. But I let her feed more on the plane last night to keep her quiet, and now my clock is all out of . . . hers, too. Red or green?"

"Excuse me?"

"Red or green?"

"Either is fine."

Dana could do this kind of small talk among mothers, it was a part of the skill set, but she didn't like it much either, and she couldn't help feeling that she was being managed in some way. Or appealed to for some reason. Then David came in, you could hear the front door bang, and the screaming of a baby, and the noise of wheels making their progress over wooden floors. When he walked in the kitchen, still pushing the stroller, May was straining against the belts, her face was red, that peculiar rich skin color of the long-crying child, where the blood-color seems to have gone deep into the flesh, and Susie said, "Why don't you carry her?" while David, good-humoredly, kept repeating, "I'm sorry, I'm sorry. I'm sorry."

"Okay, okay," Susie said, "I hear you," and began to gather up her child.

"I gave her some water," he told her. "She's hungry not thirsty."

"She's both." Susie had begun to pull the neckline of her dress across her shoulder; May, with her mouth still open in a scream, but no sound coming, butted her nose against her mother's breast.

"Let's not start this again," David told her. "It's five o'clock. She needs dinner not milk."

"It's six o'clock East Coast time. It's almost her bedtime. You shouldn't have taken her out so long."

"She was *asleep*, sleeping . . ." and so on. At one point David looked up at Dana, with a smile, and raised his eyebrows.

"Okay," Susie told him. "You can finish making dinner. I'm going to get her changed, she's wet through."

"What am I making?"

"I can do it," Dana told him, and Susie, departing, said, "Don't let them all off the hook."

The girl was hot and damp in her arms but so insistent that Susie sat down at the top of the stairs and let her nurse. Like lots of hallways in big houses it was a strangely quiet and private space. Light from a side window fell palely across the double-height volume of the stairwell. She could see into the entrance hall, if somebody was coming home; she could see into the dining room window of their neighbor's house, but nobody was there and she didn't feel exposed or overlooked. The truth is, David was right, May didn't need to feed. It was mostly for comfort, and after a minute she stopped crying and got bored and stared up at her mother with the inscrutable calculating look of a baby. Susie was always touched by how unfrightened she appeared to be. The world must seem to her like some bizarre arthouse movie, a succession of images and everybody talking in a language she couldn't understand. But most of the time she just watched it like you watch TV, because it's on.

"What am I going to do with you?" Susie said, feeling guilty already. She shouldn't have said that to Dana, she didn't mean anything by it, she was mostly mad at David, and not for taking May out too long and bringing her back in a state, but for the other thing. Bill and Liesel's bedroom door was behind her, and for a moment she wondered where Liesel was, what she'd been doing. Sometimes her mother tried to escape the crush of people by reading in her room—what used to be their dressing room, which overlooked the backyard and had been turned into a study with a camelback sofa and a pretty desk. Her parents as they grew older had become more and more sensitive to noise. Not just noise but the . . . pressure of too many people, all their different demands and points of view, which is funny, given the fact that for much of their married life, they had kids in the house, sometimes four of them at a time, and at least a decade of dealing with babies. But you forget, or you grow out of it, and you figure, I've done my time, and Susie remembered that she hadn't told Jean about Nathan's flight.

Her sister was staying in what was sometimes called the Blue Room, because of the wall color, and sometimes Granma's room, because for the last five years of Bill's mother's life, that's where she slept, driving everybody crazy. So Susie hitched May onto her hip and walked creaking down the length of the hall, toward the front of the house, where the bathroom was, and pushed the door next to it gently open. Like most of the upstairs bedrooms, it had too much stuff in it—the built-in closets overflowed with the kids' old dresses and couldn't be closed, bookshelves were stacked two deep, there were paintings and framed posters not only hanging on the walls but leaning against them, and all the surplus antique chairs had been arranged in a circle, as if anybody would ever sit in them and socialize. Jean lay on her belly, in her Levi's, with one leg draped over the edge of the sofa bed, and her shoes kicked off beneath her. She was out cold, and her plain pretty face, like a boy's under the short hair, showed a red crease on her cheek where she must have pressed against it awkwardly before turning over.

Susie, with one baby in her arms, couldn't help feeling the connection, my baby sister . . . it was easy to forget all the adult additions to Jean's personality, when she lay like that, opinions and habits, case histories, and it was also easy to think, none of these matter very much. Maybe she should let her sleep. With Nathan's flight delayed, she still had a little time before she needed to set out for Dallas. But then a thin persistent beeping sound began, sudden and irritating, and Susie noticed the watch on her sister's wrist. Its digital face flashed on and off and Jean suddenly startled into consciousness, an unfiltered animal response. Her eyes opened, she seemed to draw back and freeze at the same time, as if she had been interrupted in the middle of a guilty act. Then, after a moment, she pressed a button on her watch and sat up.

"Shit," she said.

"You're fine. Their flight's delayed, I was coming to tell you but wasn't sure if you wanted to be woken up. By at least an hour. You're fine."

And Jean, rubbing her eyes and then putting her head in her hands, took a couple of breaths, and said, "All right, all right. I'm fine," and then looked up and said, in a different voice, "Hey baby," and reached out to touch May's fingers. Susie didn't know which way it would go, but the baby, bored of being held, made the little movement of her back and legs that meant she was ready to be released, so for a moment Jean gathered her in her arms and felt her intimate heat but had to let go again, because she wanted to play on the bed.

"I guess I had my moment," Jean said and flipped open her laptop, which lay on the coffee table—an old leather chest.

"Just watch it she doesn't fall off," Susie told her, and Jean shifted her butt around and half-reclined, resting on her elbow to form a wall. "It's two hours now," Jean said, tapping at the keyboard anyway. "Fuck. It's my fault."

"Nathan told me to tell you if it gets too late they'll get a hotel."

"Well, that's what he expressly didn't want to do. Fuck."

"Hey, Jeannie," Susie said, changing tone. "It's fine. He's a big boy," and Jean rubbed her cheeks again and pushed back her hair and lifted her shoulders and stretched out her hands. "Well, whatever it is, it's too late now."

Dinner was in progress when they came back downstairs. Dana and Paul were fighting about something, David had disappeared. Susie said, "Where is he?" and Paul told her, "I think we scared him away."

"He's not so easily frightened." But the kids were eating—Ben had mostly finished his plateful and was reading a book, and Willy was looking for something else in the fridge. Yogurt and jam. Dana, sitting down, fed Cal his pesto macaroni spoon by spoon. Paul, hovering, tried to get him to eat a piece of cucumber. From time to time, he said, "Come on, Buddy. Be a big kid now. You can do this yourself," but when Susie started fixing a high chair to the end of the table he backed away. Jean left them to it and carried her computer into Liesel's study, to check for flight updates—the WiFi in the kitchen was temperamental anyway. She also looked up tickets for a UT basketball game. Maybe Henrik would be interested. After a few minutes, she heard Dana calling her, and with a very slight delay responded, "I'm here."

"Want to get a drink?" Dana said. "Paul wants to put Cal to bed by himself. He thinks if I'm around he won't let me. So I'm being sent away."

She stood between the sliding glass doors in a jumpsuit made out of some patterned material, vaguely African-looking, but light and comfortable. It also showed off her long legs; she wore leather sandals underneath, her toenails were freshly painted. Jean thought, I'd feel embarrassed in something like that, I couldn't pull it off, and said, "I'm supposed to go get Nathan from the airport."

"When do you need to leave?"

"I don't know. His flight's delayed."

"So you can check your phone from the Spider House." And then: "Please come. I'm going a little crazy around here."

"Okay. Give me a minute to get ready." But in the end, she went out like she was, in jeans and a T-shirt, she couldn't be bothered, and slipped on a pair of sneakers at the kitchen backdoor. Dana was giving Cal another kiss; he didn't want to let go. Paul kept saying, "All right, all right, all right," and eventually she pulled herself away and they walked out together, into the early dark.

As soon as the door closed behind them, Dana felt the shift in mood. They were out of the house, a couple of women heading to a bar, on a Sunday night two days before Christmas. She looked good, it was nice to feel the softer Southern air again on your skin, after two months of New York weather, snowfall and the aftermath of snow, the grit and dirty puddles and constant cold—to wear the kind of clothes you can wear on a mild evening, to feel the grass on your toes through the sandal straps. A few blocks away, someone was having a party: music, open-air drinking sounds, a bit of low cloud cover held the noises down, she could feel the baseline in her rib cage, like a heartbeat, and her blood kicked a little, she was out on the town. When you're single, with a kid at home, you don't get many chances, and she said, "Maybe we should just follow the . . . I mean, go where *that* is," and Jean said, "I don't know. I just woke up." And then, after a minute, being honest: "I'm not very good at crashing parties."

They had to watch their step on the unlit lawn—the branches of a crepe-myrtle appeared, you felt the leaves on your face, blinking, and afterward, pushing through, had to step around the spines of an agave plant, like a mop of prickly hair spread out to dry on the grass. Jean fiddled with the back gate (someone had stuck a twig in the latch to lock it), then they stepped out onto the dead-end street. The party music suddenly got louder, while Trudy's, the frat-boy Mexican restaurant at the end of the block, was lit up by strings of colored Christmas lights in the shape of a reindeer and Santa, dangling and twinkling from the branches of a live oak. Dana could see, about thirty feet away along the empty road, a guy walking toward them with low-hanging arms. He carried in each hand a paper shopping bag and had the slightly lugubrious and deliberate gait of a young man on his own (maybe he was twenty-two years old), showing up at a party like you're supposed to do, with beer, before he turned up the front path of the house where the noise was coming from and slipped around the side past the air-conditioning units toward the backyard. The sound system was playing "Locked Out of Heaven" and Dana heard the "yeah yeah, yeah yeah yeah yeah" of the lyrics and felt a sudden nervousness at the thought of actually following him in. But Jean kept going anyway and they crossed over West 30th toward the Spider House, whose courtyard glittered with Chinese lanterns and smelled of wood smoke from a couple of outdoor braziers and was starting to fill up with people.

Dana ordered a frozen margarita; Jean had a hot chocolate. "I've got to drive all night, and I'm kind of out of it already," she said apologetically. A band was setting up at the other end of the courtyard, but they hadn't started to play. There was a woman in blue jeans and a red dress and cowboy boots messing with one of the speakers, and a guy in Stan Smiths came over and gave her a soft kick in the butt, and Jean could hear her say, "Hey." The stage area, really just a raised level of the courtyard, covered like the rest of it in patterned paving stones, was draped in colored lights, whose profusion of reds, blues and greens cast little halos that shattered against each other and seemed to spill and run. Jean felt the weirdness of the afternoon napper. She felt hollowed out and totally un-hungry at the same time, and all of these effects taken together—the lights, the jet lag, and the slightly awkward but familiar position of hanging out with her brother's ex-girlfriend—made everything seem a little more meaningful or dramatic than it otherwise might have.

"You must be excited," Dana said.

They were sitting on old garden furniture, which wobbled metallically on the stones. The smoke smell from the firepit was strong, and from time to time the wind shifted, so that you had to close your eyes and turn away.

"You mean because Henrik is coming? I guess. I don't mean that . . . in a downplaying kind of way. I'm probably more terrified than . . . that's too strong. I'm a little nervous."

But that's not what Dana had meant. She meant because Susie was moving to England, but changed tack now because this line of conversation was more intimate than the other, and she wanted to have, just for its own sake, the more intimate version of any conversation she could have at the moment with Jean. And Jean guessed as much, and decided to push through anyway, because what she actually realized, not for the first time but maybe for the first time clearly, is that she had been holding back on Dana, a little bit. Out of loyalty to Paul maybe. Pretending to be friendly but not really opening up, and she could use her nervousness about Henrik's arrival as a tool to that effect, or a unit of exchange.

"If you like him, then I'm sure he's nice," Dana said simply.

"I don't know if nice is the . . ." but Jean was touched. She hadn't always felt, for the past two years, as confident as she used to feel of being liked or trusted in a certain way, even though a lot of what she had been doing involved unusual levels of selflessness. Making nice to his kids, arranging her life around them, and also, after Henrik's diagnosis, sitting with him in hospital waiting rooms, questioning doctors, mastering complex information, making sure he showed up at his appointments and took his medicine, and communicating what needed to be communicated to the woman he was getting a divorce from, without responding to her consistent low-level sniping or angry or provocative remarks. "I like him," she said. "He's very . . . I don't know if good is the word either. I mean, he's superficially perfectly friendly and polite, he's not like an . . . but he's very straight with people. I want to say honest but I know how that comes across, given how we got together. But he basically is. He's also very open or nonjudgmental. I don't know if I mean any of this. People are hard to describe. Even when you love them. I mean, it's total bullshit—he makes lots of judgments . . ." And she closed her eyes, a gust of smoke blew into her face, and she added, "I'm not making much sense. My brain isn't really . . . I'm losing my words, as Granma used to say."

"People are hard to describe," Dana said.

The waitress brought their drinks, a red-haired woman in a surprisingly formal dress, something velvety (it was hard to tell in the light) and sneakers, Jean noticed, as she walked away—Nike running shoes. The band had started warming up. There were three of them, the girl seemed to be the singer. She held the mic and was humming along and tapping it, though she had a guitar around her neck as well. The first guy was still fiddling with his drums, and an older dude had joined them, pony-tailed, grizzle-faced, standing and plucking at a cello—they started a song and stopped, they were messing around. The girl said something and the other two laughed and Jean checked her phone to see if Nathan's flight had taken off.

Somebody said, "How're you ladies doing?" and Jean glanced up—she thought for a second it was another waiter. He wore dirty black jeans and an Antone's T-shirt and looked like he was maybe thirty years old, though it was hard to tell. He had the strong tattooed forearms and chapped broken-nailed hands of somebody who does a lot of manual labor, but his teeth weren't great and there was something sheepish or damaged about his face—a kind of habitual appeal in it, to be treated leniently. His hair was black, greasy, and uncombed but he was otherwise handsome, tall, muscular, and skinny; his belt sat on his bony hips, there wasn't any fat, and his T-shirt didn't quite cover the dark hairs of his belly.

"Can I get you ladies a drink?"

He sounded like an actual Texan, and Jean noticed he had a bottle of Shiner in one hand, which he had been holding with a touching formality behind his back, until he brought it out to take a swig. It was clear by this point to both of them that he was drunk.

"We're fine," Jean said. "We just got our drinks."

"All right, all right," he said, backing up good-humoredly, and he stumbled a little and sat down at an empty table. "I'm just gonna sit here," he said.

"What's it say?" Dana asked.

"It says fifteen minutes. But that's what it said the last time I checked as well."

"You're a good sister, to pick him up."

"Well, I don't think he really wanted to come. I kind of bullied him into it."

"Liesel will be happy."

"Yeah, well," Jean said, but she was withdrawing again, she didn't like Dana bringing their mother into it, but corrected herself and said: "I wanted him to meet Henrik. That's kind of the whole point of this trip for me."

"I'm not really sure what I'm doing here," Dana said, after a moment, into the silence. She made a face, flattening her lips and raising her eyebrows slightly.

"You're . . . I mean, Cal, it's perfectly . . ."

"I wouldn't guess y'all's from around here, am I right?" the man said, hamming it up—leaning forward now in a friendly way, with his elbows on his knees. He was five or six feet away.

"I'm sorry," Dana said. "We're trying to have a conversation."

"Now you sound to me like one of those . . . stuck-up kind of . . . I don't mean to be rude, but I mean, just like, in terms of where you come from. Like Anne Hathaway, in *Rachel Getting Married*, that's all I mean, I mean, she's a . . . she's a movie star. You kind of look like her a little bit, too."

"She asked you to leave us alone," Jean said.

"That's not really what she said. She said you were having a conversation. Now I'm having a conversation, too. We're all having a conversation."

"Okay, now *I'm* asking you to leave us alone."

"It's not really you I'm trying to . . . I mean," and he started laughing, "what I'm saying is, I don't mind if you want to . . ."

"Do you want to go?" Dana asked Jean. "We can move tables or something."

"Fuck him, why should we move. He should move."

"All right, ladies," he went on, "all right, all right. All right. I won't say anything. I'll just sit here. In my hole, in my man-hole," and he started laughing again. When he laughed you could see his teeth; there was a gap on one side, and several others looked heavily discolored—his face seemed to give way into his mouth. But there was also something phony about his laughter, something forced, which in its own way seemed sad, and almost sympathetic.

"I guess you get this a lot," Jean said. They were speaking in undertones now and had subtly shifted their positions, turning their backs on the fire and looking toward the street, where an SUV was trying to park, and somebody, a woman, stood in the road directing. Beyond them was a triangle of grass, empty one-way streets cutting through a park, and beyond that a dark slope that led through a gap in the trees to college housing and the beginnings of the university.

"Me?" Dana said. "Yeah, all the time. Pushing Cal around. I have to fight them off."

"Come on, you know what I mean."

The band by this point had started playing and they could use the noise to talk almost normally—in fact, they had to raise their voices slightly, and turned around now to listen. The girl in the red dress leaned forward and back with the microphone in hand (Jean thought, the way they all do, it's funny how conventional these gestures become), and sang, "Don't take the dogs away. Don't take the dogs away from me . . ."

"Seriously. Maybe before Cal was born. But now. I got no tits, he sucked them all dry. Some days I don't even wear a bra."

Jean, smiling, said, "I'm sure the guys hate that."

"It's not like I'm worried about it or anything. I'm fine. It's just . . ."

She shook her head, and thought, why are you talking like this, it's just a habit, but she wanted to communicate something, about her situation, she had a desire to explain herself to Jean but wasn't quite sure yet what it was she was supposed to explain. Some kind of sadness about Paul, but maybe that was just a means to an end.

"Come on," Jean said again, getting slightly annoyed. "Who are you kidding. You're obviously, in terms of female attractiveness, in the top two percent. For what it's worth, I put myself somewhere in the top forty. In our age category."

"Now you're being ridiculous," Dana said, more confident now of the tone you're supposed to take in this kind of conversation.

"I don't want to . . . it's not like I'm trying to ask for . . . I mean, it's done the job. If this . . . thing with Henrik works out, it's done the job." After a minute, when Dana didn't say anything, Jean added, "That's all you can ask of it."

"Of what?"

And Jean looked at her suddenly very sweetly, changing mode. "I don't know. Ignore me. I'm talking . . . crap."

The first song had ended, and the front woman ducked down for a minute to make an adjustment to the amp, then stepped up again and said, "In case you don't know, that song was by the Mountain Goats. Which you should know," and Dana said to Jean, "I don't know if I should tell you this, but I'm seeing somebody." Then the woman said, "All right, folks. See if you recognize this," and began singing, "Couple in the next room, bound to win a prize . . ."

For a minute, Jean and Dana listened to the music, with the firelight in their faces, not speaking, on a soft winter night in Austin, with Christmas lights glowing multicolored in their eyes, though Jean also felt the wind knocked out of her, surprisingly upset, and like she had to speak carefully and measure her words.

"I'm glad you told me," Jean said.

"Well, it's . . . early days. I don't know what it is."

"Does Paul know?"

"I don't . . . we don't really communicate about . . . anything you would expect us to be communicating about. He's . . . I mean, he made his intentions pretty clear, and acted on them, and seems to expect me to do the same."

"Is that what you're doing?"

"If you mean . . . I don't have the feeling that I'm doing what I want, no. But I can't wait around for that forever."

"Who is this guy?"

"He's a guy. He's a nice guy. He's older. He's very . . . we're both weirdly nervous about everything whenever we meet up."

"Does he know you're here?"

"You mean, with you guys? Yes, I told him. He thinks it's weird."

"I think it's a little bit weird. In a good . . . I mean, I'm glad you are." And Jean looked at Dana again, with her wide eyes. One of the things she knew how to do was make the younger sister appeal, where you show that you know that there's stuff going on that's above your head, but you prefer the action on your level, and want to make them feel that, too. "I'm just sad about . . ."

"Me, too. But I don't want it to mean anything. I mean, it's just Paul, right? It's not you or Liesel, I haven't really changed . . . I still love him, but he's . . . We're just going through a period of our . . . parenting life . . . where what we have to do is make an effort to be nice to each other, and that's fine, that's the best we can expect."

"Is it such an effort?"

"It's kind of an effort," Dana said.

When the song ended, the guy in the dirty black jeans, who had been listening, too, turned back in a friendly way toward the two women and said, "I've been thinking about . . . I've been trying to work out how you guys know each other."

"Hey, just fuck off," Jean said suddenly.

"I'm just trying . . ."

"Nobody wants to talk to you. You're drunk, you stink."

"Hey, hey," he said, in a let's-all-keep-it-down kind of way. "If I . . . have, I mean, I'm not trying to . . . I'm just trying to have a good time here."

"Well, you tried. I'm sorry, I'm not in the mood to pretend to be nice to asshole guys."

He leaned toward Dana and said, confidentially, "I'm sorry if I've offended your friend over here, who seems like she's . . . having . . ."

"Hey, waiter," Jean said, because she had seen the woman in the velvet dress bringing out a pitcher of sangria to another table. So the woman in her running shoes quietly came over—she had a way of walking like she'd been choreographed to do it, and stood at attention afterward with her feet together.

"What can I do for you?" she said.

"Can you get this guy to back off?"

"It's okay," Dana said to Jean. "Let's just go."

"I'm just trying to . . . spread a little Christmas spirit . . ." the guy said.

"Come on, Kevin," the woman said to him. "Are you getting into trouble?"

"I told her she looked like a movie star," he said. "I'm a big jerk."

"I'm sure she's heard it before." And then, making a face for Dana and Jean: "He's all right, I'll kick him into line." And she pretended to kick him, to show they were all friends, but also a little like he was a dog, and he pretended to react, like a dog might, whimpering, but he didn't make a sound.

"If we could just have the check," Dana said, feeling a little stuck-up.

"I'm sorry," Jean told the waitress, "that's not good enough. It's not like he's everybody's fun drunk, he needs to learn to react to what he's being told. We came here to have a private conversation, we made that clear to him."

"This is a bar," the woman said. "People want to—I mean, they want to interact."

"All right, whatever. Just get me the check. Please."

They had a minute of just sitting there while Kevin made a big deal out of looking the other way, and then, from time to time, glancing around and turning back, like he'd touched something hot. At least the band was playing—the music spread a layer of sound over everything, you could hide in it. Jean checked her phone again. When the bill came Dana put ten dollars on the table, and Jean added whatever else she could find, a couple of singles, a few quarters. Nathan's flight had finally taken off, it was a three-hour drive to DFW and she wanted to be there when they came out of the gate. They had to walk past Kevin on their way out, but by that point whatever tide of feeling Jean had been riding had started to recede.

———

Cal didn't eat much at dinner, and after Dana left, Paul tried to get him to eat a little more. He sat down next to him at the table and offered to do what he had complained about Dana's doing earlier: to spoon-feed him. When that didn't work, he gave him a bowl of dry Cheerios, and for a few minutes Cal sat in his chair and played around with his food, sometimes putting a handful into his mouth—gummy little Os stuck to the skin of his mouth-wet hands. "It's like he's regressing," Paul said to Susie, who made her whatever face.

"When they're ill," she said, "it's not worth fighting about this kind of thing."

Paul knew he had opened himself up to motherly advice, felt his stubbornness rising and then let it go again, an almost physical sensation, like letting something slip through your fingers; he didn't want to pick anymore fights. And the truth is, Cal's nose was streaming, his eyes looked cruddy, and he seemed to be receiving information through a kind of scum or film: there was a slight delay in all of his responses. But he also didn't want to be left out. When Ben and Willy —the "boys"—got to watch a little TV after dinner, he insisted on joining them and sitting next to Ben on the sofa. Insisting meant bursting into tears until Paul gave in.

"Where's Liesel?" Susie said. "Has anyone seen her?"

They sat in a couple of rocking chairs in the playroom, staring at the screen. May sat on Susie's lap, watching, too, while her mother rocked gently and played with her baby's fingers, rubbing them a little, each separately, as if she were cleaning them and counting them. *The Brady Bunch* was on.

"I can't believe they still show this," Paul said. "I can't believe we used to watch it."

"It's fine."

He turned around to look at the kids. Cal, glazed over, sat with his legs stuck out and his shoes on. Shoes on the sofa is the kind of thing that annoyed Bill. Paul almost said something but didn't. From time to time Cal rubbed the back of his hand against his nose, and then against his shirt. Willy had a tennis ball on his lap and was letting it run down between his thighs and then catching it at the knees. Ben occasionally said "Stop it," and then Willy would stop for a bit and then forget and let it roll. Ben didn't care that much, but he still said *Stop it*. Cal seemed very small next to his cousins, and Paul somehow felt his exclusion, even from this pointless exercise in mutual irritation. It's the stuff his childhood was made of, which Cal would probably never experience. Above the boys' heads the four painted figures of the Essinger kids looked on.

Liesel walked in and Susie said, "Where have you been?"

"I wanted a walk so I walked to Breeds." Breeds was the hardware and general store on the corner of 29th and West, opposite the bakery. "We needed light bulbs and I wanted to see if there were any little presents for the kids."

"Power drills. Chainsaws. That kind of thing," Paul said.

"Just little things." Liesel looked flushed with the exercise, happy but tired. "Where's Jean? I wanted her advice."

When Paul didn't answer, Susie said, "At the Spider House. With Dana."

"That's nice." But for some reason Liesel's heart sank. "Okay. I'm going to sit down for a moment and then make supper. We've got some tuna steak and I thought I might make a *salade niçoise.*"

Susie turned around in her chair—her mother was standing behind her, staring at the TV. "That sounds great. The kids have already eaten, right?"

"What is this show?" Liesel asked, almost angrily. "They look like plastic people. Why is everybody always smiling?"

"Because they're Americans," Paul told her, playing up to her, faintly mocking.

When the show finished, he had a hard time getting Cal off the couch. Ben wanted to watch something else, something *he* wanted to watch, which wasn't just for kiddies, but Susie had to turn the TV off to let Paul persuade his son to go to bed. In the end, Cal said, "Carry," so Paul carried him. The boy felt hot, he was sweating, you could feel the fever in him like a kind of intensity, of sensation or feeling, which communicated itself to you through the dampness of his T-shirt and the heat of his hands around your neck. Paul felt tender and loving and said (his mouth was next to Cal's ear), "You're my good boy, you're my tough kid." He could also hear, behind him, Susie telling her sons, "All right, before we do anything else, let's all wash our hands."

Cal was half-asleep by the time they got upstairs; his eyes had closed, he was breathing regularly but with a little hitch in his intake, like a bump in the road. Paul laid him on Dana's bed and undressed him there, taking his shoes off, pulling his pants down. "All right, Buddy, all right, all right," he kept saying. But he was also conscious of a slight intrusion—this was Dana's room now, not his, and he could see her clothes, including her underwear and bras, carefully folded in the open suitcase. There weren't any drawers to put them in. "Time to pee," he said.

"I don't need a pee." He was talking but his eyes were still shut.

"Well, you're going to. You gotta brush your teeth anyway."

Cal, still dopey, eventually managed to walk to the bathroom by himself. He stood naked at the low toilet, holding his penis in his right hand, patiently, and after a moment the urine streamed out, and he shifted its arc a little and waited for it to stop.

"I thought you didn't need to go," Paul said, amused or touched to see the familiar male ritual reproduced in miniature. Afterward he wet a cloth and washed the kid's face, pulling a little at the crust of snot around his nose and mouth. Cal winced but didn't much complain. Paul brushed his teeth. And this time, holding hands, they walked back to the bedroom.

But the real fight started when he tried to put him in the crib. "You said I could have a bed," Cal told him, suddenly alert.

"Let's do it tomorrow. It's late. You're not feeling great."

"But you said."

"I promise you, tomorrow."

"But you said."

Each time louder, each time more desperate—it was like a knot of irrationality you couldn't iron out, the kind of knot that as an adult you feel in your shoulder or neck, but which in children expresses itself in these moments of insistence. *You said you said you said*. It always amazed Paul, their instant access to deep unhappiness. They just have to throw out a line and that fish bites. But there were also in this case contributing circumstances. Cal's fever didn't help, the fact that it wasn't his house, that Paul was Paul and not Dana didn't help. The only thing that would help is getting him some sleep.

"Yeah, well. I say a lot of things."

Paul tried to lift him up and lay him down, but the kid was too strong and the truth was, the crib really was too small. For a moment he felt the sudden surge of his own anger, *I can make you do this*, like the flare of a match, but it died away again, leaving a kind of residual sadness behind. "All right," he said at last. "You win."

The problem was he couldn't dismantle the crib and there wasn't enough space to put a mattress on the floor unless he took it out. For a few minutes, he tried to carry the crib out of the room, but the doorway was too narrow and he ended up dragging it along and scraping the floorboards. Imagining in the back of his mind what Bill would say when he saw the scratches in the varnish, but also somehow at the same time imagining that Bill was standing there, offering advice, or maybe he *was* Bill, and saying what Bill would have said, *God damn it, God damn it*—his disproportionate despair at minor household disasters. Dana's bed was a trundle bed, which you could pull out to make a double. This is what they slept on when they started going out, when Paul took her to meet his parents. In theory Paul could lay the second mattress on the floor for Cal . . . but only if the fucking crib was out of the way. He jammed his finger trying to lift up one of the sides (there seemed to be a lever you had to push) and sat on the bed afterward, sucking at his hand. And feeling surprisingly miserable. Cal by this point appeared to be perfectly awake, hot and sick, but awake, and stared at his father with wide bright eyes. Most of what grown-ups tell you is packaged for consumption, but somehow the sense of adult raw material had gotten through to him. He was old enough to know you shouldn't swear and said, "Mommy says don't swear."

"Well, Mommy can . . ." But Paul let it go. "What am I going to do with you?" he said, looking at his son and tapping more or less deliberately into his reserves of ironic detachment. Then: "What are you going to do with me?"

"Nothing," Cal said.

"You need to go to sleep."

In the end, he put Cal down in Dana's bed and lay with him a while, on top of the sheets. With his shoes still on, he rested them against a bedpost; and then, when that got tiring, tried to kick them off, using the toe of one against the heel of the other—without shifting his body, because Cal was in his arms and beginning to close his eyes. Of course, when the shoe came off, it fell bang against the wooden floor, but Cal only gave the startle reflex and settled back and Paul knew he was asleep.

For a while as he lay there staring at the overhead fan, he worried he might fall asleep, too, and then in a kind of border state followed through some kind of fantasy logic, where Dana came in to check on Cal and saw him sleeping there with Cal in his arms. One of the things that worried him is that she couldn't get in the door, the crib still blocked the way, and he knew he had to do something about it but wanted her to see them like that, for some reason, father and son, in her bed, though what kind of point he was trying to prove, he didn't know. Before kicking off his other shoe he slowly released Cal from his side, letting his head fall lightly back against the sheet. Then, using his arm as a prop and trying not to shift the mattress too much by the shift in his weight, he rolled across his son, for a moment staring down at him, almost lying on top of him, but suspended by the elbows, before crawling like a crab over his body and out of bed.

With Cal asleep, in the quiet and the calm, it took him ten minutes to dismantle the crib. He leaned the various parts against the book-case in the hallway and pulled out the mattress from the trundle bed and laid it on the floor. Then he got sheets and pillows from the bath-room closet and made the bed. The last thing he did was transfer Cal from one bed to another, carrying him across like a forklift and low-ering him again, while resting his knees on the carpet and trying not to throw out his back. Afterward, he picked up his shoes and stood in the doorway for a moment, more or less self-consciously, marking the occasion, a job done, before closing the door.

Liesel was peeling potatoes at the sink when Dana and Jean came back. She wore her red apron. She held the potatoes under a running faucet then cut them in two on a wooden board and dropped the halves, clean as eggs, into a pot full of water. She looked happy.

"Supper will be in about an hour," she said.

Dana asked her, "Is there anything I can do?"

"You can pour yourself a glass of wine. You can open a bottle."

"I've got to go," Jean told her. "I've got to pick up Nathan."

"Which bottle?"

"Whatever you want. There may be some white wine in the fridge, otherwise look in the laundry room."

"You smell of a good fire," Liesel said to Jean, while Dana opened the fridge and stared at it for a minute and then went out. "*Du bist mein gutes Mädchen.*" You're my good girl. But then she stopped and dried her hands. Something had been worrying her and she remembered what it was (it rose to the surface again)—that Jean would fall asleep on the road. "Why don't you take Paul with you? You can keep each other company."

"There isn't room in the car. For the way back."

"So maybe Paul should go."

"Why should Paul go?"

"You just got off a plane. You already took Bill to the airport this morning. What's Paul doing? He doesn't do anything."

Jean said, "He's putting Cal to bed."

For a moment they looked at each other, and Liesel knew that if she said anything more explicit, her daughter would criticize her, but she also thought they were basically in sympathy and wanted the same thing.

"He can go afterward," she said, but she was already giving in.

"That's probably too late."

"You must be dead on your feet."

"I had a nap," Jean said. "Anyway. After what just happened, I feel totally awake."

"What happened?"

"Nothing happened, I got in a stupid . . . Dana can tell you. It's nothing, I just mean I'm awake."

Before she could go, they had an argument about the keys. Jean

insisted she had given the Volvo keys back to Liesel, in case she wanted to go shopping, but Liesel couldn't find them in her purse. This
went on for several minutes, while Jean felt increasingly anxious and
annoyed. They looked in all the ordinary places, on the counter by
the oven, on the bench in the front hall. I'm late, I'm going to be late.
In the end, they found them in Liesel's study, on her desk, which is
probably where Jean had left them, saying, *I'm giving you the keys*,
so nobody was right, nobody was wrong. This is what Liesel claimed.
"I'm not always crazy, it's not always my fault," she said, still in her
apron; her hands were red from the cold water. Jean, relenting, looked
at her. "You're not *always* crazy," she said, and Liesel followed her
out the front door, down the steps, to say goodbye.

"At least this time of year there are no mosquitoes. Wait," she said.
"Wait, let me give you some chocolate for the road. In case you get
sleepy."

"I'm not sleepy, I'm fine," but Jean waited and watched her mother
go carefully up the steps of the house, not actually hurrying but moving her arms and leaning slightly to indicate haste, and after a minute
returning, under the yellow glow of the front-porch light, with her
purse in her hand.

"This is good chocolate," she said, passing over a half-eaten tablet,
which was still carefully wrapped in the foil. "It's eighty-five percent."

"Too good for me."

"It will keep you awake." And she said again, "*Du bist mein gutes
Mädchen*. If you feel sleepy, pull over."

"Okay, whatever," Jean said. "I love you," and reversed carefully
over the dip in the drive. Liesel watched her until the car had disappeared around the bend in Wheeler Street, under the arching trees, a
winter's evening, two nights before Christmas, cold enough now that
she was glad to go back inside.

It's a boring drive to Dallas-Fort-Worth Airport, you just take I-35
the whole way. The radio was broken on the Volvo, and the tape

player had swallowed its last cassette. All you could listen to was whatever was on that tape: one of Nathan's old grad-school albums, an early Billy Bragg, *Talking with the Taxman About Poetry*, not his best. But Jean put it on anyway and knew the words well enough to sing along. Something about the tinny guitar, his voice, reminded her of Nathan's old room at Holywell Manor, Balliol's graduate student housing, just opposite the law faculty. Jean visited him there over spring break during her final year at Yale. He was going out with . . . who then? . . . the American girl, and sometimes stayed over with her, and so Jean slept on his futon. His English accent was terrible, but he liked to sing along: *Whoops, there goes another year, Whoops, there goes another pint of beer* — and the world it opened up to her again, of his goofiness and happy ambition, before the success kicked in, almost brought tears to her eyes.

When she was young, eight or nine years old, starting to read for herself, to want to follow adult conversation, Nathan was her point of access: a high-school kid, dark-skinned and wild-haired, with an unshaved mustache, too clever for his teachers and quick enough to pick fights with Bill and Liesel, too. He could always see the principles at stake in any situation, no matter how small or petty it seemed, and could push you into positions you didn't know you occupied, until you found yourself defending stuff you didn't want to defend. So you gave in or gave up and let it go. She used to practice copying his handwriting, one of those facts about the depth of her child-devotion she only mentioned to him fifteen years later. "Huh," he said; he didn't know what to say. He seemed genuinely surprised, and she realized (not for the first time) that the childhood she had lived through wasn't quite the same as her brothers' and sister's. No matter how close you are. She had reached the frontage road now and had to focus. Traffic wasn't bad, it was Sunday night, and anyway the Austin rush hour comes earlier than London's, but the ramp was short, and something about the distortions of the overhead lights and the urgent noise of tires on rough asphalt made speed and distance difficult to judge. But then she was on and that was it—a long straight ride to Dallas, almost due north, a couple hundred miles of interstate, some of it brightly lit but much of it also dark, country dark, where you had to chase the glow of your own headlamps between the lines.

She wasn't sleepy, that was one thing, at least not sleepy in any ordinary way, she felt wired and drifting and strangely emotional—just the rush of the car (she was doing seventy-five, sometimes eighty), the mild existential danger of her own speed and the pressure of the night around her, the wide empty countryside around her, and the presence of other cars, coming and going, the luck or chance of passing them like this, with their own urgent personal reasons for driving somewhere on a Sunday night, all these people, produced in her a kind of intensity of consciousness. When she stayed with Nathan that year (it was just a weeklong visit), on some level deals must have been struck inside her, decisions were being made, to come back to Oxford, because as soon as she graduated from Yale that's where she went. To follow in Nathan's footsteps, she even signed up for the same degree. Sometimes she wondered whether she had failed Susan somehow, by not directing more of her imitation-flattery at her big sister, and whether this failure involved a more general kind of failure, to grow into a normal woman—to go through not just the rites of passage but the ordinary feelings you're supposed to go through, about boys and sex and motherhood. So that now she was stuck at the age of thirty-two trying to make up for lost ground.

Paul once said to her, when she first told him about Henrik, "There's plenty of time to make your own life with someone." As if she were trying to steal someone else's. She got mad at him, but it's not always easy to tell, especially in the heat of the moment, if you're pissed off because someone's right about you or because they're wrong. And she knew that what she was doing, the reason she was thinking these thoughts through, was to prepare herself for a long conversation with Nathan. They had three hours together on the ride back. Sometimes it's easier to talk late at night, jet-lagged, in the dark, when you're both staring at something else, like the road in front of you. Of course, for the first part at least the kids would be awake, Clémence would probably sit between them in the back. But then they'd fall asleep (after ten hours in transit, it was even later East Coast time), and the noise of the road was loud enough to make it hard to hear in back. The Volvo was an old car—there was no sound protection. Even the background warmth of sleeping kids contributes to the sense of intimacy.

Well, it doesn't matter. You never have the conversations you want to anyway; almost never. Something always comes up, other people get in the way. But still she prepared herself, she wanted to get her story straight, even in her own head.

When Henrik was first diagnosed, she thought, *that's it*. Her first reaction was selfish: *that's it for me*. When shit like this happens, people don't walk out on fifteen-year marriages. One morning he woke up with an ache in his "balls area," this is how he put it. The truth is, he had felt something before, a sort of numbness, like you get when someone kicks a football into your . . . between your . . . legs. But when you're forty-seven, forty-eight, a lot of things hurt, especially when you get up in the morning. And if you pay attention to everything that hurts . . . But he was also coming down with a cold, something was going around the kids' school, everybody back after the long summer holiday, the temperature had dropped, leaves were falling, real life had begun again.

He called Jean to tell her that he wasn't coming in—an easy call to make, because she worked at the company and needed to know. In other words, one of those conversations he didn't have to conceal or disguise. Monica was almost out the door, dragging the kids to school. Emil and Freya still needed to be walked (Sasha left earlier for her cello lesson), and he had come down in his dressing-gown to make himself coffee and wave them off, before going back up to bed. For some reason it gave him pleasure to be able to speak openly to Jean, for legitimate reasons, in front of his wife. Later, around eleven o'clock, he called again, just to pass the time. "I think I found something on my . . . I think I felt something . . . on one of my testicles. It hurts a little, too."

"Have you talked to somebody about this? Does Monica know?"

"It's fine, I'm sure it's . . . I'm just lying here and feeling bored and sorry for myself."

"Go see someone," Jean said. "Go see someone today."

"I don't feel well, remember. That's why I'm in bed."

"I don't care," Jean said.

Like many practical and competent people she treated complaints as problems to be solved, but she also had a nervous tendency, she took everything seriously and had a habit of thinking in terms of worst-case scenarios. Maybe this is what he wanted from her, and he was using her anxieties as a kind of test, to see if he should be worried or not.

"I'll do it," he said. "I'll go see someone, but not today. This is nothing new." He meant, the feeling of numbness or the slight ache. "I can go tomorrow, when I don't feel like shit. I can go next week."

Ten minutes later Jean called back to say she had booked him an appointment with his GP—for three o'clock. (She had worked as his assistant for several years; it felt natural for her to take charge in this way.) So he went.

Among the various things she blamed herself for, Jean sometimes added this to the list: that she had somehow made the cancer happen to him, either because it was a kind of accretion of his guilt, something his kidneys couldn't process or whatever . . . or because she had made him go to the doctor and it was only because the doctor found something that it was actually there. He had to wait three weeks for an appointment at the clinic in UCL and then another week for the results. In other words, almost a month of keeping the lid on her anxieties, which is more or less what it felt like. She was conscious of a kind of rattle in her manner, an almost audible low-level and constant need to release internal pressure. They were carefully polite to each other, both at work and afterward, in their moments of man-ufactured alone time—sharing a taxi, for example, to a screening at Soho House. Jean couldn't tell if he was distancing himself from her, for understandable reasons, in preparation for the necessary break, or just hunkering down, or if in fact she herself was pushing him away. Selflessly or selfishly, who knows.

Still waiting for results, Monica rented a cottage in Somerset for half term and he drove down with her and the kids on Saturday morning. Jean's envy felt like a kind of poison, which makes you unrecogniz-able to yourself. One night he called her from his cell phone—their first contact in almost a week. The cottage had no reception so he had to walk about ten minutes along a B road to the nearest pub, where there was free Wi-Fi. ("I told Monica I wanted to check my email.") It was about six o'clock, the sun was setting, he would have to walk back in the dark. Already the pub was filling up, she couldn't hear him clearly, background noise of people and music, the signal quality was poor, so he stepped outside and she could feel the change in at-mosphere like a shift in weather—he was standing outside in the mild evening cold.

The clinic had called while they were having lunch at Coleridge Cottage in Nether Stowey. What he had was a stage 3 embryonal car-cinoma. It had spread to his lungs, and maybe elsewhere—he needed more tests. The good news was . . . it was . . . he wasn't very good at the terminology, yet—seminomatous, which is typical of . . . older patients. He laughed. Most of the time it's very treatable. Jean was still in the office, about to go out for the evening—she was meeting a few girlfriends at the Curzon on Shaftesbury Avenue, and took her cell phone into the bathroom, so she could listen in peace and talk to him without being overheard. Or break down if she wanted to. He said, "It's what Lance Armstrong had. But not as bad."

"Okay," she told him, as clearly as she could. "What do you want me to do?"

"Look," he said, "I've been thinking about it all day. I can't live like this and make them care for me." No, thought Jean, you can't, and knew what was coming next. But then he said, "I think we should move in together. I want to tell her."

"That's a terrible thing to do to somebody," Jean said.

Even in the bathroom she kept her voice low. The floor was tiled (a strand of wet toilet paper lay by the loo) and everything echoed. There was a smell of running drains and disinfectant. She leaned against the door, with her back against it.

"I think it's better in the long run. It is already terrible, what we're doing. But I have to . . . I have to live a life I want to live. I want to live it with you."

"What about the kids?"

"We need to get an apartment together. They can't come and visit you—in that room." (Jean rented a room from a woman near Brondesbury Park; she had access to a shared kitchen.) "You are not saying anything now. I don't know if this is something you want."

"Yes," Jean said. "I'll do whatever you want me to. I love you."

"Okay, good. Me, too. Okay," he said. "I should go back now—it's dinnertime. I'll see you Monday in the office. We can work everything out."

When the phone went dead in her ear, she didn't move for a moment. It was like lying in bed and thinking, I should get up. The pressure of conflicting feelings . . . a kind of standoff . . . but she also thought, if my life has an emotional center, a moment on which all the different forces converge, it's this, and I'm going through it now. But maybe this is just a kind of self-importance, which means you haven't digested or thought through what's actually going on. Not yet anyway. When she came out of the bathroom, she sat down at her computer again and typed "Lance Armstrong's cancer" into Google and followed the various threads until it was time for her to meet at the cinema, about a fifteen-minute walk away—across New Oxford Street, busy with buses, the lights coming on and people going home—into Soho.

For the next few days, until he came back, apart from everything else that she was worried about (and she spent much of her spare time online, looking up his diagnosis, coming to grips with the various terms, trying to understand the treatment options, and following the science and evidence-base behind recent developments), she also worried that he would change his mind. Maybe it was just the heat of the moment. He was stuck in Somerset with the kids. But his explanation when he saw her again sounded perfectly reasonable.

"I knew as soon as I heard from the clinic that I had to tell Monica. I mean, about us. You can't ask someone to care for you on this basis."

They were having lunch at one of these *bibimbap* places you find on the backstreets by the British Museum, among the secondhand bookshops and expensive ceramic stores, the tartan outlets. Hot sauce bottles sticky on the plastic table; a strangely provincial air of quiet and neglect. The staff seemed to live downstairs, where the kitchens were. There was only one other group of customers, four men, sitting in the back by the restroom door. Henrik and Jean had at least a little natural light, such as it was—falling between tall gray buildings.

"I expect there will be a certain amount of drama in the next year," he said. "Even if it is mostly very boring. And I won't ask her to feel whatever she will feel about that . . . we have not had such feelings for each other in many years . . . without telling her about you. And as soon as I tell her, our marriage will be over. I don't expect anything else."

But even then, as she lay in bed that night, too excited to sleep (not happy exactly but deeply agitated, and debating whether she should call someone—Paul, Nathan, Susie, Liesel? anyone but Bill), she remembered what he had said and wondered if it left room for doubt. As if it were still up to Monica in the end. But she never found out if that's what he meant, because it didn't matter: Henrik was right. Monica kicked him out. And for a week he stayed either on the sofa bed in the office (which they sometimes offered to "friends" in the business, other directors and producers, visiting London) or at her room in Brondesbury, while she looked for an apartment. For years she had lived, more or less, in student squalor—either in Oxford, in a shared house on Marlborough Road, near the Head of the River pub; or lodging in various rooms in northwest London. Her land-ladies were mostly divorced mothers whose children had grown up and moved out. But now she was looking for her own first grown-up flat, and they needed three bedrooms, so that Henrik's kids could stay on weekends, once all that was sorted out.

The fact is, she was having fun, and she felt guilty about that, too. And not just fun—she knew that whatever else she was doing, she was living more importantly than she had been living before. Spend-ing more money, living on a grander scale, with bigger things at stake. They looked around Kensal Green Station, because the rents were still borderline affordable and they could catch the Overground train to Euston and walk from there into Bloomsbury. It's like shopping for an imaginary life, which you then pay for and live. Here's where I'll sit and have my coffee, here's what I'll look out on from my bed. A city life, with a commuter train to catch each morning, and a home with somebody to come back to at the end of the day.

Sometimes they threw dinner parties, and she got off a stop early and walked across the park and picked up something from the deli on Chamberlayne Road on her way home—a big glass-fronted kind of chalet or hut, with antique wagons full of organic vegetables parked under the awning. Behind it, on the access road to another station, buses lingered and the pavement was lined with a fried chicken outlet, a low-budget estate agent (cheap rentals) and a betting shop. That's the kind of neighborhood it was. Gentrification had happened so rapidly that everywhere you felt and saw and heard the clash and contrast of extremes. Boutique wine shops stood next to pound stores. Semi-homeless men hung out on the public benches with cans of high-alcohol lager while young City types in their skinny suits got drunk even on cold evenings sitting around the picnic tables outside

The Chamberlayne—once a pub, now a chophouse—so they could smoke. The walk between residential streets to their apartment, on the top half of a bay-windowed Victorian on Buchanan Gardens, wasn't always totally scare-free; but she was used to that by now, and most of the time she walked home with Henrik.

On Friday nights, Euston station filled with long-haul commuters. There were trains leaving for Newcastle and Glasgow and even their own small branch line trundled past Kensal Green to places with names like Hatch End and Headstone Lane. She could indulge in the usual thoughts of the middle-class Londoner facing the homeward journey at the end of a long week. Should we move to the country? Should we just get away?

Although as the year wore on Henrik's kids began to stay over, and their Saturdays were taken up with homework and trips to swimming pools. Something else she felt guilty about, nervous, clumsily on edge, but also secretly . . . not secretly . . . but with her deeper emotions very near the surface, ready to do their duty, the work that you have them for. Emotions like love and fear, expressed among other things in trying to remember your seventh-grade math. She had to figure out what they liked to eat, and to learn how to cook it so that they didn't complain. Like every other second wife—part of what you realize is how many there are around. It's like buying a car, you begin to spot them everywhere: at the Tesco Express, and on the bus, and outside the school gate, picking up the kids with a purse full of crisps and chocolate. Even this was part of being alive, and belonging to a demographic, or whatever you want to call it. One of the types.

Not that she was quite yet a second wife. Also, you never stop forgetting, these aren't my kids. Part of the guilt is that you sometimes think, this isn't my problem, and then on Sunday night, after you hand them over, it isn't anymore.

The first time she saw Monica after the . . . they didn't have a word for it, the announcement, after Henrik had told his wife what was going on, she was sitting in a Zipcar van outside their house in Acton.

(When he first moved out, all he took with him was a duffel bag full of clothes and shoes, and a backpack with his laptop and a couple of books.) Henrik had an office in the house, with an exercise bike and a bench press—his response to middle age, as he put it, was low-key but traditional. Anyway, Monica wanted them gone. She needed the room for a lodger, a friend of hers, who could also help with the kids. "I don't care what you do with them," she said. "Just get rid of them."

"This is expensive equipment. I have nowhere . . . at least not yet," he began to say.

"Get them out! Get them out! Get them out!'

Jean heard about it all later. And now she sat in the van, in the driver's seat, not quite daring to go in. *You're a coward*, she told herself. You're a bad human being. But still she didn't move.

Their house had four or five steps to the front door; the ground floor was slightly raised up, with the kitchen in the basement, and Jean could see the entrance hall and Henrik backing out with the exercise bike in his hands. It was a heavy machine; he couldn't carry it himself, and Monica had taken the other end. Jean immediately got out of the van and moved quickly, that half-scuttle, to indicate hurry. But since Henrik was first, she started to take the weight off his hands, until Monica said, "I need a little help here, I need to put it down." So they put it down—Jean squeezed past (the front garden was narrow and unevenly paved; she had to push against the recycling and garbage bins) and reached out awkwardly to grab a pedal, but by that point the work was mostly done. Monica stood up to arch her back and rub the blood back into her hands. Jean, half-crouching, stood up, too; they looked at each other.

"I think you can take it the rest of the way," Monica said.

They had known each other a little, inevitably; Monica had always been friendly to her, if slightly condescending. She used to try to set her up with dates, and sometimes called her up last minute if they were having a dinner party and needed an extra woman. Monica liked to complain about Henrik to her—not complain exactly, but to include Jean in her wifely frustrations. "He always says yes yes I'll do it and he never does it, he isn't even listening . . ." That kind of thing, as if Jean would know what she meant. Jean used to resent these appeals, slightly; she didn't like being lumped in with the sisterhood of female patience. Although Monica herself was a busy and competent woman—she worked in PR for a film distribution company.

"I can get the other stuff, too," Jean said.

"That's fine," Monica told her, un-angrily. "I don't want you in the house." And then, matter-of-factly: "I don't want the kids seeing you."

She had passed Waco (in the dark) and was coming up to the turn-off for 35E. Many of the streetlights seemed to be out of action. Even thinking about that . . . interaction . . . made the blood concentrate in her face . . . why did she get so mad when that guy—poor Dana, and the thought of Cal, shuttling between . . . Sometimes you find yourself taking sides and you don't exactly like the side you happen to be on. Driving through the dark like this . . . up at five, with Bill on the way to his sister, and now tonight . . . She wouldn't be back until one in the morning, at the earliest. All of this looked even now like a kind of penance. The road at night went inward, too, and the landscape you were traveling through looked a lot like . . . nothing much . . . a few gas stations . . . a few half-built developments . . . tractors or cement mixers or some kind of paving machine, standing on dirt, with those bright rolls of temporary fencing, curled over and lying on the ground. And the cars kept coming at you. From time to time, you had to get out of the middle lane, move around a truck or to let someone pass. What did she want to say to Nathan about all this? What was she trying to prove? She could talk about Henrik's kids but even the thought of them, of telling Nathan about the way she had learned to . . . brought out in her own mind a tone of voice, the tone she would use, and which she wouldn't like. Anyway, he doesn't care, that's not what he cares about.

Henrik had surgery the week before Thanksgiving. Even by then

Monica had relented a little. Henrik wanted the kids to visit him, he wanted Jean's company, he wanted "all of this to start now." He meant, an acceptance of the new arrangement. He also thought, I can make use of my weakened condition, and everybody's sympathy, to force them to get along. For Emil's sake, he pretended to be a monster. He was hooked up to all these wires, there was a stent in the veins above his wrist, he looked very white. *Ooh ooh* he said, lifting his arms, like a zombie—and the graphs on his readout flared. You could see the tangle of wires, running through his sleeve and from around his waist to the monitor, which was connected to the wall by a mechanical arm. Emil said, "Stop it, I don't like it." Sasha, the oldest, politely laughed.

They took out his testicle and used keyhole surgery to remove the lesions on his lungs. For the next two months he went in for weekly chemo sessions, followed by a six-week recovery, which was followed by two more months of chemo, another recovery period, and then another round of chemo, which brought them roughly into summer, into the school holidays. He lost his hair but he didn't have much hair to begin with and there were times, when one of the kids had a cold, for example, that he wasn't supposed to be in contact, and even on his weekends to see them, they didn't come. This kind of thing had to be worked out with Monica—Jean often ended up being responsible for the arrangements.

On the whole, Henrik was a good patient. He was relatively unafraid of dying (it's hard to measure these things, as he said himself) and he had a high tolerance for physical discomfort. Boredom upset him; he didn't like not working, and Jean, when she could, made it possible for him to work at home, doing what could be usefully done by computer. During his recovery periods, and at the beginning of each treatment cycle, he also went into the office, although Jean worried a lot about what he might pick up on the train. Part of what sustained him, what sustained both of them, was that this period of his life also coincided with the open and honest committed beginning of their relationship. They were living together, playing house, could meet friends and go to the movies (when he was up for it) without any pretense or surge of guilt, and it turned out that the pleasure of living naturally more than made up for the excitement of what they had been doing before.

Henrik also got to see Jean at her best—competent, loving, and selfless. And he got to see her with his kids.

Her relationship with Emil was the simplest, he was an easy boy, very like his father, square-jawed, silent, he did what he wanted but generally didn't cause much trouble because he wanted harmless things. He played with LEGO for hours. They set up a corner in their new kitchen where the box of LEGO lived, so they could cook and talk and eat while he was occupied. And he could also be suddenly and surprisingly physically affectionate. Sometimes, when Jean was standing with her back to him, or sitting on the sofa, watching TV, he would throw himself at her—holding on to what he could, her neck if she was sitting down, her waist, and not let go. The fact that she had taken his father away didn't mean much to him; he was still too small. And also, as the youngest child, he seemed to have been born with an assurance that everybody loved him . . . one more person didn't matter.

And Sasha, the oldest, seemed to like her, too. There was a kind of pleasure she took in having this extremely adult relationship with a woman who was not her mother. She had just started secondary school at Henrietta Barnett, a grammar in north London, which meant getting a train and then a bus every morning by herself—over an hour each way. She was still at the stage where independence pleased her; you could almost see her consciously adopting what she considered to be adult poses and attitudes. Of course she was also sometimes very tired and stressed, and Jean tried to imagine her real thoughts, the thoughts of a twelve-year-old girl, getting on a train and then a bus with everyone else, the other commuters, keeping to herself, clutching her backpack on her lap if she could find a seat, and taking the same journey back at the end of the day to a home radically altered from the home she had been living in just a few months before. That's a lot of adulthood at once, Jean said to Henrik, and she made a point of reading some of the books that Sasha was reading, not just John Greene, but *The Lord of the Flies* and *The Canterbury Tales*, which is what they were studying at school. So they could talk about them on the weekends.

Only Freya was difficult, resentful and misbehaving. If a kid wants to act up, there really isn't much you can do about it. You can threaten and you can plead, but game theory isn't on your side (as Nathan put it to her, when she complained to him over the phone), especially for someone in your position. "What do you mean, my position?" she said, but she knew what he meant. She just wanted to hear how he was going to put it. Well, you're in a setup where what the kid actually wants is a breakdown of law and order. She didn't eat Jean's cooking. Jean could ask her, what do you want to eat tonight, what's your favorite thing, and she would make it, and Freya would suddenly pretend not to be hungry. If you pushed her, she'd explain, almost sweetly, I don't like it the way you make it, which was maybe even true. Well, what do you want to eat then, and the whole thing began again. She made a mess at the table, picking the middle out of a baguette, for example, rolling it around between her fingers into a ball, and flicking it at Sasha, until Sasha complained. If you told her to clean up after herself, she looked at you like, make me. And you couldn't make her. Henrik sometimes lost his temper, which made everything worse. "I hate coming here, I don't want to come . . ." and so on. All of which Jean sympathized with.

In spite of all this, it gave Jean pleasure to be in the middle of a family again, in the middle of all that, the way she used to be as a kid—caught in all the webs of intimacy even if in her case she was the least involved and could remove herself when she wanted to. But she was good at family life, too. She had spent eighteen years at the firm of Essinger & Co. training for it, and then, when they kick you out and send you to college, and later expect you to make a life on your own, all of these skills have nothing to do. And she was using them again. The density of her life had increased. And she also felt a new proximity to the big beasts, the monsters of childhood, which loom so large and seem so vivid and terrifying, until you hit your twenties and turn everything into a kind of domesticated pet, a job a love-life somewhere to live, these are the things you think about, and not death, and what it means to an eight-year-old girl to find out that your father isn't your father anymore, but somebody else, who sleeps in a bed with somebody you don't know.

By this point, she had merged onto the north fork of I-35 and was counting the exit signs for the turnoff to 121. There were actual neighborhoods, with trees and front yards and quiet streets, peeling away below her—she had entered again into conurbation, and could see the skyline of Fort Worth ahead of her, something to shoot for. Waves of sleepiness had been coming and going for the past half hour, but paying attention was good for her, and she felt like she'd emerged again, come up from under, and now lay beached and dry . . . not rested exactly, but out of danger. An incident in the road meant a buildup of yellow lights, the towtruck was just arriving as she passed by, but at this time of night, two days before Christmas, the slowdown in the remaining lanes was just a case of rubbernecking: a Mazda hatchback and some kind of throwback pickup sat parked or slewed at awkward angles to each other. There was glass in the road, glinting in the headlamps, and the weird wobbly but silent rotation of the sirens, which fattened and thinned out like a swinging water balloon. Everybody looked okay though; a woman in a man's coat sat on the barrier talking on her cell phone, she looked like she'd been there a while, and Jean kept going (the traffic flowed again) away from other people's problems.

Part of what you want to prove, part of what you want to show people (people like Nathan), is that this is now something you know how to do—to look after kids. Only she didn't have the kids around to show it with. She missed them, especially Emil, who had started climbing into their bed with a book on Sunday mornings. Jean, even if she didn't feel like it, would sit up and read to him, though her audience, as she knew full well, was also Henrik, who lay with his face in the pillow and left her to it. Sometimes you can read without even really waking up. She needed to concentrate now; there were signs for the airport, among dozens of other signs, and the highways were starting to metastasize as they approached the city, entangling and disentangling, it wasn't always clear what lane to be in. Cars thickened around her, and she felt the mass of people, like a kind of contraction, after driving at night through the empty country; this was different and you felt it in your head. Joining a line for the toll, she opened her window—and the cold December air came in, flavored by exhaust, the wide continuous noise of cars, like a fact of life, and she had to shift her butt to get her wallet out and find the change. Even two nights before Christmas it was somebody's job to sit in a booth and take her money. On an eight-hour shift how many cars went by? Then you drive home.

Right from the first his doctors were optimistic. One of them said to him, "This is a good time to get this kind of cancer. Even five years ago, you'd be looking at a very different set of outcomes." And Henrik believed in professional expertise. If the people you paid to be good at something told you something, you believed them, that's what you paid them for. Jean was more skeptical, she spent too much time online. It's like I'm having an affair with his worst-case scenarios, she said to Paul. I can't tell him about it, but this is what I do when he's not around. Henrik went through ups and downs, but they were mostly physical. When your white blood-cell count declines, you feel small, you shrink, and in fact he also lost a lot of weight; your presence changes, people around you change, but even at his lowest ebb he assumed this phase would pass, and wanted to make plans for when it did.

About the divorce, for example: if possible he hoped to arrange things so that Monica could keep the house. Really so the kids could keep their childhood home. But he also needed to get some money out of it, if they were ever going to buy a place themselves. Jean had always made it a point of pride to get by without her parents' money—except for flights home. "You have to pay to see me," she told Liesel. But the money was there, and Henrik wanted to have a reasonable conversation about what kind of apartment they could afford.

By the end of the summer, when his final round of chemo ended, he looked almost like a different person. The shape of his face had changed; he looked almost younger. He had always been a square, strong, competent Danish-sailor type, with a little fat on him, but not too much—a solid citizen. And now even the way he moved in his clothes seemed to suggest a kind of nervous energy or restlessness, you could see the shape of his skull, his face looked naked, the egg of his bald head looked like it would crack if you tapped it with a spoon. But he was very happy; they were very happy together, and the habit of the past six months had made him feel dependent and affectionate, he wanted to sit next to Jean at parties, he smiled more, and the fact was, the roles in which they had gotten to know each other, when he was married and her boss, had shifted, too.

At his three-month checkup, when the doctors gave him the all-clear, they went for a drink afterward at the Russell Hotel. He asked Jean to marry him, when the divorce came through, and she joked: "I think you're feeling emotional now because you've had good news."

"Does that mean you don't want to?"

The tone of the conversation had suddenly changed—it was like a change in temperature. "I want to, but you haven't even met my parents."

"You think they will change my mind?" Then, smiling: "You think they will change your mind?"

And she said, "I want you to meet them."

There were traffic cops working the access road to the terminal, and she joined the line of cars and taxis and tried to keep an eye out on the side of the road, for somewhere to pull in. But you could only pull in if your passengers had arrived. What a day. At six she was dropping Bill off at Austin-Bergstrom, and now she was here, sixteen hours later and two hundred miles away. What Bill would call a two-airport day. Henrik was almost certainly asleep—it was four o'clock in the morning Greenwich Mean Time, and she still had at least another three hours to drive. All these people looking for cabs and rides, college students, flying home for Christmas; young parents, crying kids. But the cops wouldn't let you linger, they kept waving everybody along. Then you went through the whole business again, pulled out of the line and onto the freeway, heading out again, into the night, into the wide country, before you doubled back. But on her second time around she saw them: Nathan, in his travel suit, by the side of the road, handsome and fidgety, after sitting on flights, waiting in airports—he was walking up and down, a big restless well-dressed man. His hair was even wilder than usual, he looked tired. Clémence and Julie leaned against each other on a bench; Margot lay on a couple of suitcases pushed together, fast asleep.

"Hey," Jean said, pulling over, lowering her window. "You made it."

Nathan had gone back into the terminal, searching for something to eat (which is why Jean missed them on her first circuit). Julie was hungry, but all he found was vending-machine food, Ritz peanut butter crackers, Fritos, bottled water, and he battled with the intake slot to accept a five-dollar bill, then kept pulling out the change to pay for the rest. Margot had fallen asleep on that second flight—he had to carry her from the airplane. She was heavy enough these days that he still felt the pressure of her weight on the crook of his arm; he was conscious also of a light sweat against the collar of his shirt. Anyway, he felt hungry, too, and when Julie turned down the crackers, he said, okay, and started eating them, pacing, he didn't like to wait and he had to suspend whatever he felt about the fact that Jean was late.

When she came, she got out of the Volvo to help, and he said to her, "Why don't you let me drive?" Julie climbed in the back, and Clémence sat in the middle, so Margot could lie with her head on her mother's lap. But the girl woke up when Nathan lifted her. She wanted to walk ("It's okay, Daddy," she said, "I can walk," with the patient enduring sweetness of a kid in transit late at night), and he picked up the suitcases instead and put them in the trunk. His brief-case, which had his computer in it, among other things, he gave to Jean—she wasn't sure why, but she took it off his hands.

"I thought you don't like driving at night," she said.

"I'll be all right if you keep talking. At least for the first shift. You've been on the road for the last three hours." And she let him— he was her big brother, and she sat in front with his briefcase on her lap until she thought, this is silly, and put it between her feet.

But she had to guide him out. The road to Austin was far from straightforward and for the first twenty minutes all they talked about was what lane to be in and when to come off. They joined the traffic into downtown Fort Worth before following signs for Waco, but the exit was a left exit, and Nathan had to cut across two lanes in order to merge. After that, it was relatively plain sailing, they could talk. Jean said to Clémence, turning her head to get her voice across (the Volvo was an old car, with poor sound insulation, and you could hear the road noise coming through in constant vibrations, through the windows and the soles of your shoes): "Do you hate me for making you come? I feel like I bullied you into it, you must have been cursing my name all day."

"Not at all," Clémence said.

She had a kind of European charm or social ease that was hard to figure out. Her mother was Canadian, and she grew up in Mon-treal, but had also lived in London for several years. With her hair tied back, undyed, streaked equally with black and white, her elegant neck, and her face, pointed and dark and pretty, but also showing her age . . . she was one of those successful women for whom this is also a show of power. I don't have to care anymore.

Jean once complained to Susie that Clémence had a way of treating her like a kid sister, and Susie said, "Well, she's Nathan's wife," as if that explained it. But in fact, Nathan was eight years younger; when they met, most of the status and influence were on her side (though he'd been catching up). She started as a print journalist before making the jump into radio and then TV. Both of which require a certain manner. In private life, too, she often came prepared with topics of conversation—even late at night, with tired kids, on a long drive from the airport. But maybe this was just a form of shyness, or what used to be shyness; she needed a script.

Anyway, what Clémence wanted to talk about now was the Christmas lights on 37th Street. One of her gigs was presenting features for *This American Life.* "My producer suggested I check them out. Since I'm going anyway." Maybe this sounded more critical or half-hearted than she meant it to, because she leaned forward to compensate, into the gap between the front seats. "What I mean is, I'm happy to be here."

She had to shout a little, over the noise of the car.

"I haven't been to see them yet," Jean said. "I only got in yesterday."

About a year before she had asked Clémence to present one of Henrik's programs, on Tunisia after the revolution. (Her father was Egyptian and she still kept in touch with relatives in Cairo—she spoke reasonable Arabic, along with fluent French). It should have been simple enough, either she wanted to or not, but somehow it turned into a favor Jean was asking and which Clémence felt some pressure to accept. So that when the dates didn't work out, which was really from Jean's point of view completely fine, there was still an aftertaste of embarrassment or apology.

"It's not really the lights," Clémence went on. "They've been looking for an angle on Austin. A surprising number of people I know want to move here."

"I get the same thing in London," Jean said. "People ask me, where are you from, so I say Austin, and they say, oh, that's like the acceptable or cool part of Texas, right? I've heard such great things . . . and so on. And part of me wants to say, you know, it's just . . . even when we were kids, it's just a nice American campus town. At least it used to be."

"Well, I think that's what we're trying to get at," Clémence said. "The way Austin is changing."

"Maybe it is, but what I mean is, the whole hippie thing gets over-blown sometimes. They were always a small part of the culture, most of my high-school friends were perfectly . . . I mean, most of the people we knew could have been living in Madison."

"Why Madison?"

"I've never actually been to Madison, but somewhere like that." The car was the wrong place to have this conversation, it was too loud, and Jean couldn't quite tell what she was arguing about anyway.

Nathan was only partly listening, though what Jean said also set off a train of thought. Whenever he came back to Texas he felt a strange elation. He could taste it in the air coming out of the airport, even on a cool December night. Something was being communicated, a different flavor of reality. Many of his Harvard colleagues were privately educated East-Coasters who had gone from prep school to Ivy-League college to law school, without at any point having to adapt to a new set of cultural norms or values, or adjust their views or manners. He liked these people, and to many of them probably seemed indistinguishable from them, after the years he had put in at Yale and Oxford, but still he liked to think . . . he liked to think of himself as somebody who didn't entirely belong.

His high-school friends were nothing like his college friends or law-school colleagues, but he kept in touch with them lovingly or conscientiously, deliberately, and every time he came home again, to Austin, made a point of hanging out and doing whatever they wanted to do. Some of them even now, in their early forties, worked part-time jobs while they tried to get a new band off the ground. One of them waited tables in a Mexican restaurant (high-end interior cuisine) and spent his free time making stuff out of metal, yard art, whatever you want to call it. Another was a nurse at St. David's but had also appeared in several independent movies as an extra. They rented apartments or still lived with their parents. A few of them had kids with women they weren't together with anymore, but still they did a lot of childcare, they were always around, they had time on their hands. They made time for Nathan, too.

When he set off for T. F. Green, he wore his conference suit, a casual Nicole Farhi, with a white shirt, open-necked, and cuff links that Judge Schuyler had given him after he finished clerking. But in the morning, in Austin, he would pull on a pair of ragged shorts and his ten-dollar discount Nikes and not care. If Texas was somewhere he had escaped from (and that's what it felt like, when he got to Yale), it was also somewhere he could escape to.

He heard Julie say, "Can you stop talking? I'm trying to sleep," and her mother say, "All right, all right, everybody sleep." Clémence leaned back, so that Julie could rest her head against her shoulder—and she closed her eyes, too, disappearing into the dark and noise of the back seat.

Jean, after a minute (feeling in spite of herself slightly rebuked), said to Nathan in an undertone, "You doing all right? I know you don't like to drive at night."

"There are some Fritos in my briefcase. Maybe if I eat something."

"I can take over if you want me to."

"I'll be fine if you get me the chips."

So that's what she did, holding them out for him to dig his hand in while he drove—she could smell the salt and the corn, and took a few herself, licking her fingers afterward to get the oil off, and drying them on her jeans. But then she had another handful, and another.

Nathan said, "You must be pretty tired yourself."

"I'm all right."

The road was even emptier now than when Jean had driven up. It was after eleven, the land was flat, unlit, the grassy verge by the highway stretched away into nothing much. All this land . . . and from time to time Nathan flashed his brights to see the lanes ahead of him, the concrete gray seemed to jump into the beams, but then he dipped them again as a pair of headlights slid through the dark, coming the other way. But the noise of the car seemed to have done the trick—in his rearview mirror he could see Julie lying with her head on Clémence's shoulder. Clémence had her eyes closed, too, it was after midnight East Coast time, and they'd had a fight on the road to Providence.

She liked spending Christmas in Cambridge, where there was a reasonable chance of snow. The rest of their lives were diluted by colleagues, work, ambition, travel. Their house was large and the law school used it (Nathan ran a series of guest lectures on international law) to host various events and prominent visitors. The kids had to deal with the fact that for six or seven nights a month their house, at least the downstairs area, the kitchen and living room, was a public space, but at Christmas, for a few days . . . She had family, too, in Montreal, but she liked to hunker down, and this wild-goose chase, which is what it seemed to her . . . which he didn't entirely disagree with, but after they had decided to come—"*you* decided"— there didn't seem any point in arguing. When they caught the flight to Charlotte, by which point, obviously, they just had to make it to Texas, Clémence shifted ground, she flipped the switch and stopped complaining, but this also made Nathan feel slightly cut off. Waiting for their bags in DFW, she suddenly leaned against him and said, "Your crazy family," but she was smiling, too, and the fight had been resolved.

"I know, I know."

"It's very sweet of Jean to come and get us. It's totally insane but it's also very sweet."

"She wanted us to come."

"I'm thinking about you, too. You need a break, too."

"Well, this is a break."

But she didn't say anything, and it's true, Nathan sometimes fought with his family, with Liesel especially, he felt an implicit . . . the status he had in other areas of his life was not always . . . the respect he received . . . this isn't the kind of thing you can explain to your brother or sisters, or expect them to . . . especially when there are other things you also need to explain. Anxieties, ambitions, if they're going to understand. But half-listening to Jean and Clémence he realized that even though they weren't arguing in this case at least he was probably on his sister's side . . . about Austin and the tone of Clémence's curiosity. It's very hard to take sides . . . you don't actually have to take sides . . . and yet, when everybody comes together, you can't help but feel the pull of different allegiances. He was starting to drift off, the road ahead of him had set up a pattern for his thoughts, or a rhythm, and in the middle of the pattern or rhythm it was difficult to tell if being conscious of it was the same thing as being awake. So he reached for another handful of Fritos and said to his sister, to keep her talking and break the pattern, *"Diga me."*

"What do you want to talk about?" Jean said.

"Anything. Just to wake me up."

"I can drive. It's fine."

"How's Henrik?"

"He's all right," she said. "He's in Pembrokeshire with the kids."

"When's he coming?"

"Boxing Day." And that's all she said.

Maybe ten minutes later, when he saw the exit for a gas station, sitting in a pool of light by the side of the road, he pulled off. "I'm sorry," he said to Jean. "You'll have to take over. I've been sleeping very badly."

He got out to fill the tank—under a huge sky, partly covered in clouds, but there were also ragged gaps full of stars, and very little light pollution. The universe seemed strangely flat over his head; tired, he also felt the chill of it and shivered. There was a kind of wide general wind with nothing to stop it or deflect it moving in no particular hurry across the landscape. Jean switched over to the driver's seat and adjusted the mirrors. When he got in the car, she said, "Why are you sleeping so badly?"

"I wake up at three. For no reason. And when I can't get back to sleep figure I may as well work."

"What are you working on?"

"Various articles. I don't want to talk about them." And then: "You must be exhausted, too."

"You mean the jet lag? I feel okay. I seem to have come through to the other side." After she pulled out onto the highway again, waiting for a pair of dots of light to pass by, she told him: "It's fine if you want to go to sleep. I'm fine."

"No," he said, "I can talk, I want to talk," but he closed his eyes, and in a few minutes Jean felt the vague shift in atmosphere in the car that you get when everyone around you is asleep. Clémence was visible in the rearview mirror. She lay with her head back and her mouth open, and looked strangely vulnerable. Less pretty, less self-conscious, with her black-and-white hair spread out against the headrest and her neck exposed. On an empty stretch of highway Jean turned around quickly to check the kids. Margot, seven years old but still the family baby, had slipped the upper part of her seatbelt and slept with her head on her mother's lap. Julie, leaning away, had tucked herself into the corner of the car, against the door. It was like spying through the window of her brother's house, where this kind of thing goes on every night.

For the next two hours she drove like that, through dark Texas, listening to the noise of the road, until she turned into the driveway at Wheeler Street, and the clank of the dip woke Nathan. Then she carried the suitcases into the house, while he and Clémence dealt with the girls. Liesel was still up, in her nightgown—she came to the door as soon as the Volvo pulled in, and stood in the doorway, in the hall-light, in her bare feet.

MONDAY

When Bill woke up, he felt a strange charge in the room, a kind of cold glow; he didn't know where he was. Usually he got up in the dark and went downstairs through the childless house to watch TV. Around five or six in the morning: sometimes the news or Sportscenter, but they also showed reruns of *American Pickers* or *Auction Hunters* at that time. Bill had a big appetite for anything about antiques. But now the curtains next to the bed, a dingy pattern (once bright and still too busy), revealed a kind of pressure of light behind them, and he remembered. God knows why he had slept so long. The bedside table was cluttered with magazines and framed photographs, but he found his wristwatch and checked the time: almost eight. And when he stood up and pulled the curtains the reason for the glow became clear. Overnight snow, the storm had come through. Everything was white; he thought, Liesel should see this. This is one of the things she misses by living in Texas—real winters.

Last night he had a fight with Judith about who should sleep in Rose's room. Not a fight exactly, but every conversation with his niece involved some kind of battle or at least lengthy explanation. She was a woman with too much time on her hands; instead of doing anything she liked to talk. When he got back from the hospital the night before he found Judith, in her own phrase, in the middle of cleaning the house. But she wasn't actually cleaning anything. She was going from room to room with a garbage bag in her hands— and not throwing much away either. Everything had to be looked at. What she really needed was an audience, and once Bill came, well ... *I mean, look at the way she lives. Every time I come home we have this fight. It's depressing. This is what happens when* ... when you live for your marriage, when you live for your daughter, Bill thought. When your husband moves out and your daughter grows up. Why should she throw anything away? What does she need the space for? But he basically agreed with his niece—it's depressing.

Also, everyone grieves or worries in her own way. It doesn't always come out as grief, or even as sympathy.

Rose's house was one of these Fifties boxes, with a little porch and a front parlor and a kitchen at the back. There were three bedrooms upstairs, but one of the bedrooms had been turned into storage. Rose, in her old age, had discovered eBay and internet shopping, and often ordered new furniture and appliances to keep up with the times. But she couldn't throw anything out. She missed the old times, too. So on top of everything else the third bedroom contained a two-seater couch, vaguely French, button-backed, with doodads carved into the wooden legs; the pink upholstery was shiny with ancient use. It used to sit in the front parlor and before that in their childhood home on Roosevelt Avenue in Port Jervis—in the grown-up living room, where the kids could only go on special occasions. To see it there, like that; Bill shook his head.

The second bedroom was also full of stuff, including an old vacuum cleaner with a thick mesh cord. A basket of sports equipment, an Apple computer from the 1980s, dusty and lying on the floor . . . a Sony turntable (Alex, her ex-husband, collected vinyl). Garbage bags full of clothes. With stuff spilling out of them, including a pair of ice skates, which almost certainly didn't fit anyone anymore. Maybe she was keeping them for her grandson; it's hard to throw these childish things away. But there was a mattress on the floor that you could access without moving anything. The other bedroom was Rose's, still with her sheets on the narrow queen-size. For some reason, Bill didn't want to sleep in his sister's bed. But Judith didn't want to either, and he gave in.

For a while they couldn't find the bedding. Judith looked all over the house—she kept up a running commentary—it was almost like something fun they could do together, it lightened the mood. (They were in the storage room, in a chest of drawers.) Bill changed the sheets himself, pulling off the old ones, which still smelled of something, Rose's perfume—he could see a bottle on her dresser, *Knowing* by Estee Lauder. His sister used to have a cleaning woman come once a week, Rosario, she was really a friend, but Rosario had retired and sent her niece instead and Rose didn't trust her. *She's a nice girl,* Rose said on the phone, *but—I don't know, there are things I don't want her to have to do. When you're that age, you don't want to . . . who wants to . . . clean up after an old woman. There are things I don't want her to have to see.* Even her clean linens had little stains on them, discolorations, like tea stains; the elastic in the fitted sheet had stretched too far, Bill had to drape it over the corners and tuck it in between the mattress and the box spring. This isn't the kind of household chore he did at home. (When he woke up the next morning, half of it had pulled away; he was lying on the yellowing artificial fabric of the mattress.)

For supper they telephoned for takeout, Chinese food—Judith called in the order. The storm hadn't blown in yet, but the wind was picking up, it was weirdly warm for the time of year. Walking outside, waiting for the guy to come, you got dust in your eyes, bits of something, debris from the road, the tarmac was cracked and gravelly, in very poor condition. The whole neighborhood looked rundown. The Chinese food wasn't great either, but still it had a kind of nostalgia value: egg rolls and fried rice, wonton soup, moo goo gai pan, the cold noodles in sesame sauce were pretty good. He ate with a fork; Judith used chopsticks. And he listened to her talk. *Once you take yourself out of the sexual market, I'm telling you, everything goes downhill. This is a medical fact. For years I've been telling her, you need to date, you need to go on dates, you need to have . . . some reason for getting changed after five o'clock in the afternoon.*

Believe me, it isn't easy, I know that. Preparing yourself every time for disappointment. The people you meet . . . I mean, what kind of a country produces these men? You should see the . . . men who can't order at a restaurant without checking five times that you don't mind. They're so worried you think they're trying to male-dominate you. Wet handshakes. Vegetarians, vegans. They can never find anything on the menu. After a meal they give you these . . . hugs, like what's just happened here, some kind of group sharing. It's gotten to the point where honestly I can't tell if somebody is gay anymore, they all sound the same. Especially, and I hate to say this, I'm talking about Jewish men. And after a while it's like you're grateful for these people, because at least they listen. Because most people don't. But that's not the . . . that's not the . . . while she was eating, some kind of echo seemed to have come back to her. They sat in the kitchen with the wind blowing the dead ivy in the window, you could hear it rattling the panes. Because what's actually difficult, she went on after a minute, she had stood up to refill her glass of water, and this is the part that takes guts, you realize eventually you're also a disappointment to them. I mean who are you kidding, right? You can see it when you show up, and that's not . . . easy to take, right? That takes a little bit of . . . and this is what she couldn't do.

Suddenly she was crying, the lower part of her face had given way, like a landslide, and she drank from her glass of water and sat down again. She turned her head against her neck so her uncle couldn't see her, she breathed through her nose. I'm sorry, she said. It's just . . . coming back here. This is not a house of happy memories for me. Laughing again, I mean, the relationship you want with your mother is not . . . I don't want to end up like that. Right? It's not even like . . . I mean, I hope she doesn't die, of course, I hope she pulls through but even if she does, is this really what she comes back to, to sit in this house? One of the . . . you know my father has been . . . since the divorce, he's been saying—he actually calls me from time to time, which is . . . Why don't you come down to Tempe? He wants Mikey to meet his kids. He wants everybody to get to know everybody. And the truth is (she was fighting off tears again), I would rather do that than come here, because the truth is, he's made at least some kind of a life for himself, even though, it's not like I have any illusions about whose side I'm on in all this.

Bill said, "I don't think, at this stage, it's a question of taking sides."

"Well, you say that," she said. "But I don't think that's how Rose would look at it."

"I think she . . . it's something we've discussed before."

"Well."

They cleared up together; afterward, it gave Bill some pleasure to wipe the kitchen table with a cloth, to make everything clean. He was pretty tired though (he said to her, it seems like my day started a long time ago), and went up to bed shortly after. Judith was trying to get the internet to work—Rose had a computer downstairs, an old-fashioned PC in the front room, and eventually Judith gave up on connecting her laptop and used that. Bill said good night. He stood in the doorway, by the stairs, and looked at his niece, who looked like his sister when she was thirty-eight, but taller and broader-shouldered. She had her father's build but her mother's face. Thick-lipped, pale-skinned, with large eyes that were bright and pretty enough when she dressed up, when she made up, though they appeared slightly exophthalmic under the lenses of her glasses, which she needed to read the screen. Apart from anything else there was a faint residual strangeness to sharing the house like this (and there was only one bathroom upstairs) with a young woman to whom he was not particularly close. In spite of . . . or maybe especially because of the . . . level of intimacy or habit of familiarity produced by the situation and their relation to each other.

"Sleep tight, Uncle Bill," she said. This is what she still called him; it almost upset him to see her so fully recovered.

In the morning, when he came down, Judith was still at the computer—as if she hadn't slept, except that she wore a thick bathrobe and a towel in her hair. The heating was set to an uncomfortably high temperature. You could hear the vents blowing and also occasionally a kind of cracking or shifting sound, the pressure of the outside world operating against an imperfectly sealed container. But the air felt dry and close, and Judith in her terry-cloth clothes contributed somehow to the bathhouse atmosphere. She was talking to somebody, and then Bill saw the image on the screen, her son, or rather the back of his head. Mikey was in a brightly lit room, sitting on a small chair in front of a large television. The kind you can hang on the wall, and the computer on his end was stationed so that Judith could see the television, too. They were watching cartoons together, and from time to time Judith said, "oh no, oh no," when something went wrong, and Mikey would turn around to look at her. "I told you," he said, while Bill stood in the background. "I *told* you."

"Do you want any breakfast?" Bill asked her.

"Say hello to Uncle Bill," Judith said in her kiddy voice, and then, demonstrating: "*Hello Uncle Bill . . .*" but Mikey had turned back to the television.

"I thought I might go to the hospital," Bill said.

"Have you looked outside?"

"It snowed."

"It snowed like . . ." and she gave him the kind of look he remembered well, from his mother and his aunts when he was a kid, from the older Jewish women in his life. Her tone of voice was the tone you use when you finish a sentence with "like a hole in the head" but she obviously couldn't think of an appropriate equivalent. It surprised Bill a little, how comfortable she seemed in her bathrobe, talking the way you do to her son, in front of him, and he was almost touched, by her trust or sense of familiarity, in spite of the fact that he basically didn't like her much, or wouldn't have liked her, apart from loyalty to his sister. Judith seemed to him a self-involved and self-important person who had made a number of obvious mistakes in life without learning from them. Somebody who blamed other people. "Like the Pope's Catholic," she finally said. "How are you going to get there? At some point today they might get around to clearing the avenues, but you still have to make it down the hill."

"I thought I might walk," he said. "What else am I going to do?" And then, because he couldn't help himself: "I don't want to sit around the house all day."

But she didn't seem to notice. "In those shoes? Is that all you brought?"

They were the old leather Rockports he liked to teach in, with a thick rubber sole. But she said, "There's three feet of snow out there. You're gonna get soaked. You're gonna freeze."

"I thought I might put plastic bags around them. This is what we used to do, for the kids."

She gave him a look but she helped him find the bags—long thin sacks, the kind they deliver the *New York Times* in, a faint translucent blue. And by the time he set off she had entered into the spirit of the adventure, more Essinger craziness, in which she took a kind of pride, even though she also liked to present it as her personal affliction. "You know the way, right?" she asked him. "If you want to go the scenic route you can take the Old Croton Trailway."

"I'll probably just stick to the roads."

"Have you got a phone? Have you got a map?"

"I made it here all right, I can make it back."

"You haven't had breakfast."

"I don't like to . . . I like to eat lunch. If I get hungry, I can pick something up at the hospital."

She was still in her bathrobe when he left, a tall large-breasted thirty-something woman, wrapped in towels. Already you could see she had some trouble with her hips, you had a sense of second-rate construction, the need for maintenance. She said, "When the cabs can make it on Ashburton Avenue, I'll come in. You can tell her that. I'm willing to walk that far." And then, in a different voice, the voice she used for serious discussion among women, "From what I saw last night she won't know the difference." She raised her eyebrows at him, surprised at herself. Sometimes just saying it brings on the emotion, and he looked at her, full in the face, he gave her the frown of sympathy. But when he walked out she called out, "Close the door, you're letting all the cold in."

The snow came up to his ankles, though it was deeper by the eaves, almost knee-deep, where sheets of ice had fallen off the roof in the morning sunshine. Cars lay tufted, trees wore wigs. White lay everywhere and the light bounced off it so vividly it was like staring too closely at a television—a bright pervasive blur that quickly induced a faint sense of headache, if not the thing itself. But it didn't feel too cold, at least at first. After a few blocks the bags on his feet stretched and tore, the wet came through, and he eventually abandoned them, or rather, pulled them off and carried them dripping in his hand until he could find a garbage can. When he crossed Yonkers Avenue, he saw the entrance to the Old Croton Trailway Park and decided to take it. From what he could tell, the path was tarmacked, and no worse than the sidewalks. Going was still hard, you had to pull your leg out of the drift at every step, and the wet snow slipped a little underfoot, so that by the time he'd been walking ten minutes he felt the sweat and the heat of the sweat building up in his armpits, under his shirt, his sweater and his L.L. Bean winter coat—rising into his neck. His glasses fogged, his beard dripped. But the roads were empty, the parked cars looked abandoned. It was a bright sunny winter morning, he saw someone walking his dog, he saw kids riding sleds down the middle of a steep road. People talked to each other, he didn't mind walking, it gave him something to do. Yesterday he was cooped up in the plane all day, and then sitting in traffic. He wasn't unhappy.

———

D ana was up half the night with Cal. She went to bed early, a little after ten o'clock. Paul and Susie and David were in the TV room, flipping channels (Paul had the remote control). Then Liesel came in and wanted to watch the headlines. Dana as it happens was sitting in her chair, the wooden rocker with the loose armrest and the cushion that Liesel always placed on the floor before sitting down. "I'm going to bed anyway," Dana said. No, don't bother . . . but Liesel accepted the chair and removed the cushion and sat down heavily, with an end-of-day sigh. "*Na du.*" She had an orange in her hand, with a bowl and a knife, and began peeling. It gave Dana pleasure to understand the routines, to *not* get in the way—to show Paul. Two car bombs in Damascus, coordinated attacks. Outside government buildings, thirty-seven confirmed dead, though the figure would probably rise. Hundreds wounded. Dana, standing in the doorway, said, "Too depressing for me. Good night." But she had got the tone slightly wrong, and felt it, as she left them there and retreated along the darkened corridor. Paul was reaching for a piece of orange from his mother, but he said good night, too, like everybody else.

Cal was still deeply asleep when she looked in their room. It bothered her that she wouldn't be able to read in bed, because after brushing her teeth and changing in the bathroom, she felt suddenly awake—tired but superconscious. If she left the door to the hallway open a wedge of light fell across her lap but not enough to read by. And she wanted the door closed; she wanted to feel shut in. Lying down, climbing under the sheets, she could make out the blades of the ceiling fan above her. Wooden blinds over the windows facing the street revealed in thin lines that the front porch lamp was on. Liesel had said she was going to wait up for Nathan and Jean (and Clémence and the kids, Dana thought). At dinner Paul and Susie had argued about what was a reasonable time to expect them. One in the morning, two in the morning. For some reason even this kind of conversation could become a source of heated disagreement, but Dana could see it from Paul's point of view, too, because really what Susie was saying is, *you should have gone.* And maybe Susie was right. But the reason she couldn't say it explicitly and why Paul couldn't defend himself was because the subtext was that Susie and everyone else wanted him to spend time with . . . She must have drifted off because the next thing she heard was Cal whimpering.

He was still asleep, or mostly asleep, but every breath now seemed to involve his speaking voice, as if he were saying, *ow ow ow*. For a while Dana just listened to him, but then she got out of bed to check. He lay on his mattress on the floor, and when she kneeled beside him, he must have felt the pressure of her weight, because his eyes opened, though it still wasn't clear if he was awake. Snot crusted his nose and apart from anything else he had trouble breathing — his chest lifted with the strain, and she could hear a catch in his nose or throat, like a loose screw rolling around. "Hey Buddy, hey Cally," she said, and stroked the hair off his forehead, partly to feel his temperature. But also because she couldn't help herself, she was glad to see him and thought or felt something like, *it's just you and me, right? and all these crazy people*. But he felt hot, too, he felt too hot, as if his brain were working overtime, dreaming hard, giving off a kind of engine heat. It was like touching a radiator.

Maybe this woke him up; he began to cry properly and after that she couldn't get him back to sleep. Probably he'd have woken up anyway. She had to blow his nose. There was a tissue in the pocket of her jeans, but she couldn't find them on the chair for almost a minute, by which point he was borderline screaming. His cousins' bedroom lay just across the hall and she felt the panic of an intruder when an alarm goes off. Who knows how late it was. Everyone was probably asleep. But she found the tissue and wiped his nose and threw it somewhere on the floor, who cares, and lay down next to him. He called her Daddy, and eventually she realized what he was saying: *I don't want you, Daddy. Go away*. So she picked him up in her arms and rolled on to her back. He lay on his belly on her belly, with his head on her breasts, while she told him, into his ear, "It's Mommy, it's okay," feeling at the same time a kind of pang of disloyalty and some vague sense of being in the lead.

After that she was stuck. Four years old, long-limbed, he was too heavy for her to sleep like that, with his weight on her chest, but every time she tried to lay him down he woke up again, and the whimpering began. When she heard the clank of the Volvo in the drive and the front door open, she couldn't tell if she'd been lying awake the whole time or whether the noise had woken her. Cal by this point seemed deeply asleep, still hot but quiet, and she listened to the sound in the front hall, which was just below her bedroom, Liesel saying something and Jean saying something and Nathan talking, though she couldn't make out the words, just tone and rhythm, and something else, a kind of efficient affection or familiarity. Then she heard the noise of footsteps in the hallway running to the back of the house, heavier because of the weight, of kids or suitcases. It was an old house, both creaky and echoey, high-ceilinged and wide-halled, and Clémence's voice, in its vivid friendliness and lively hushed politeness carried, too, until it disappeared into the kitchen and was replaced by someone climbing the stairs, either Jean or Liesel, going to bed.

When she woke up again it was already light and late—bright slats of winter sunshine lay like the lines on a piece of paper across the floor. Cal said to her (he was squeezed into her armpit now and looking up), "It hurts."

"What hurts, sweetie?"

"I told you!' he said, angrily.

"You didn't tell me," but it was pointless arguing so she stopped. "My ear!' he said eventually. Which ear, and so on.

She had some Children's Tylenol in her toiletry bag, but it was another fight to make him sit up and take a spoonful. Meanwhile some dream or half-memory of the night before came back to her, lying in bed and listening for the front door, because it meant that Paul was leaving, driving to Wimberley alone and in the dark, and leaving her in the house with the rest of his family. And she wondered if Cal knew that his father wasn't there, but the truth is he didn't ask or seem to care. After the Tylenol kicked in, she managed to get him dressed, she managed to get herself dressed, and came down to breakfast carrying her camera (a Leica M, black with a leather strap), with the slightly shifty and guilty feeling of the late-riser.

Susie sat over her coffee and an empty bowl of cereal, reading the *New York Times*. Ben and Willy were watching TV next door, and Cal without asking went to join them, and Dana let him go.

"Where is everybody?" Dana asked.

"In bed. Liesel stayed up last night, till they got in."

"What time did they get in?"

"One-thirty. I couldn't sleep."

"I'm sorry," Dana said, "that's probably my fault. Cal had one of those nights."

"It's not your fault," Susie told her, which annoyed Dana. "I'm not sleeping very well at the moment anyway. There's coffee in the pot if you don't mind heating it up."

And so, obediently, Dana went to pour herself a cup of coffee and took it to the laundry room in the hallway, where the microwave lived. While the turntable spun and hummed, Dana looked in on the playroom and felt something of the pleasure Cal must have been feeling, to be included among the boys. Though she also noticed his nose was running again, the skin at the tip seemed blistery, and there was a slick crust over his upper lip. His eyes had a kind of intensity of blankness, a feverish shine, and when she went over to wipe his nose ("just so you look as beautiful as you are"), the microwave beeped. He shrugged her off, but she took a photograph anyway, framing the boys on the couch against the background of Susie's family portrait, which hung over their heads.

Nobody blinked; they were watching *Scooby Doo*. It surprised her a little, that Ben didn't consider it beneath him. But maybe even at his age . . . kids are still kids. At least, some of the time. "When this is over," she said to Cal, "I want you to come have breakfast," but she left them alone and walked down the hallway to the laundry room. The body of the mug was too hot to touch so she carried it carefully by the handle into the kitchen.

"Is that a new camera?" Susie said, looking up from her newspaper.

"Secondhand new. It was a sort of present to . . ." but Dana let the answer drift away and instead took a picture, which included Susie, who made a deprecatory frown. Like, this is not what my face is useful for anymore. She looked like Anne Frank, pretty and ordinary, at fifteen, but somehow as she grew older Susie's face hadn't changed but what it meant or suggested . . . Her brown eyes were still too big but they looked sensible now, or worried, instead of amused. In the photo afterward (Dana, that night, uploaded the images onto her computer, and while Cal slept in the dark of their bedroom, went over them one by one), Dana felt, as she often did, real affection for the way people are exposed by the camera. It was clear from her expression that Susie did not want to be photographed: that faint awkwardness had been preserved.

For all their family self-obsession, the Essingers were not picture-takers in any consistent way. But for the rest of the day, Dana kept taking their pictures. She wanted something to do besides hanging around the house, trying to help out and getting in the way, while the Essinger family business carried on, clearing up, shopping, getting ready for Christmas dinner, all the competitive preparations of mealtime. Also, she wanted to make an album for Liesel, to thank her for the visit afterward. There was a company you could send the digital images to, and they turned them into books, hardbound, with glossy pages and captions (if you provided them) under each photo ("Cal tries his first beef rib!"). It had become a mild obsession for her, making these albums, a time-occupier and creative outlet, and she used birthdays and thank-yous as an excuse to indulge it.

Dana had been tinkering with photography since her (very brief) career as a model, when she was nineteen or twenty years old and using the money to help pay her way through Amherst. And then, when she dropped out and married Michael (her first husband, an old rich not-quite-dead white male, as he called himself), she kept it up a little longer but without any real . . . ambition or . . . It was mostly just another thing she didn't want to quit because of him. But it embarrassed her, too, the fact that when she invited some of the other girls back to her apartment, they saw how she lived. The grandeur and expense . . . not because they would judge her or think her odd but almost the opposite, because it seemed so in keeping with the world she was moving in, the pretty women and the older men who paid for their lives.

Most of her modeling gigs were for mail-order catalogs; she once appeared (this was the highlight of her career) in a De Beers ad. Her look was WASPy handsome, but in a kind of anonymous, almost approachable way. People wanted to imagine her as their daughter, the one they had brought up well and sent to boarding school, who could ride a horse. Even at the time she was dimly aware of something bland and maybe even sad about the way she looked in these magazines: a typical example of her class. Almost in protest, she took a camera along on shoots and photographed the locations or the set or the dressing rooms or even the photographers themselves, as a way of turning the tables and insisting on some kind of status. I'm really a college girl, this is just a means to an end. Though she also had to overcome a certain amount of embarrassment. The camera drew attention, and she basically didn't like attention. But she persisted, as she often did, against the grain of her nature, or even the occasion . . .

She poured herself a bowl of Grape Nuts and said to Susie, "Do you know where you're going to live yet? I mean, in England."

"I've got some . . . you can imagine, I spend a certain amount of time on websites. The college is very generous with home loans. But I don't want to rush into anything. I mean, part of me wants to just make every decision at once. But I'm trying to resist the temptation." And she laughed, turning back to her newspaper.

The truth is, she didn't really want to confide in Dana or even talk seriously about her own life. There was some impediment there, related to Paul, some kind of resentment . . . Then Clémence came in with the girls, clattering through the backdoor, letting the screen door slam behind them, letting in the cold air. They were sleeping in the garage apartment out back: you had to go outside (across the patio) to reach the main house. Nathan had stayed in bed; he was working (Clémence made a face), and Susie went next door to turn off the TV, so that the cousins didn't spend all morning *glotzing*—staring at the box.

"It's cold," Clémence said. "I always forget that this place has actual seasons."

She wore silk pajamas and bright Moroccan babouche slippers, in red, green, and gold. Everything seemed busy and fun after she arrived—she started making eggs for the girls ("and anyone else"), raiding the fridge and bringing out onions, tomatoes, Gruyère and goat cheese, red peppers and olives (in a tall cloudy plastic container— Susie said, "I don't know how long that's been there"), whatever she could find. Including a yellowing bunch of cilantro from the vegetable drawer, a little slimy maybe, but she cut off what she needed, and cracked chopped sprinkled, made a mess. The spice cupboard hung to the side of the oven—you couldn't take anything out without scattering bright powders and dried brown leaves. When Liesel came down, in her dressing gown, sleepy-faced, she shuffled over to the coffee maker and looked suspiciously at the pot. She said to Clémence, noticing, "You have such elegant pajamas," and Dana, stupidly, felt a pang of something, jealousy.

As the morning wore on, she retreated more and more behind her camera. Stephen had given her the Leica on her birthday. He took her out to eat at a restaurant in Chinatown, which is where he handed it over, and she remembered how touched he was that it was her *actual* birthday, a Wednesday night in October—that she had given him priority. Part of what appealed to him is the sense he must have had, which he couldn't entirely conceal, that there was something a little lonely or sad about the fact that a beautiful young woman like Dana should have nobody she preferred to spend her birthday with than a guy like him. Given that their relationship was in its early days, and that his attractions, such as they were, were of the solid kind. Tasteful and affectionate companionship, a shared curiosity and detachment about life. She almost felt like she had to apologize to him, or explain herself in some way, so she said that Paul had just flown back on Sunday, after spending a week in town to hang out with Cal, and she was so—she was always so . . . just discombobulated by these visits, that she could never see past the . . . or make plans for anything afterward. So when he called and wanted to take her out, she was very . . . but he said, *You don't have to apologize, I mean you've got nothing to . . .*

This is how they talked to each other, kindly.

He was very supportive generally of her photography and encouraged her, for example, to take classes at the New School. At their summer exhibition, he said obviously intelligent and perceptive things not just about her own work but some of the other pieces, which he took seriously. His daughter worked for Carl Kwon, who had shot covers for *Vogue*, but Stephen also belonged to the generation of New Yorkers who grew up listening to talks at the Aperture Gallery and later going to shows at Howard Greenberg in the Eighties. Photography for people like him, especially for people with a background in documentary TV, was really *the* art form of the twentieth century. This is the kind of thing he said. His apartment on Third Avenue was only a few blocks over from the Whitney, and he had a Nan Goldin in the entrance hall (*Misty in Sheridan Square*) and a Winogrand over the living-room sofa—a fat boy and his ugly dog, standing in front of rows of chain-link fencing, animal pens, all brightly lit. He's drinking a Coke. So for someone like that, with his air of authority or experience or culture, to say, you should pursue this, you have a real talent for this, made a big difference to her, had a real effect, given how, in the rest of her life, she had this sense of helplessly drifting.

Paul used to treat all her photography . . . stuff . . . as a kind of useful hobby, something to keep yourself busy with, while you figure out what you really want to do. Which coming from a guy who played tennis for a living . . . but that was part of the problem. He had gotten to a point where he really didn't have any respect for any human endeavor. So it was a relief to talk to someone like Stephen, whose enthusiasms were so important to him.

Maybe this is why she brought the camera to Texas, as a kind of coded reminder that her real life was ongoing and didn't depend on Essinger approval. At the same time she planned to take a lot of pictures of the family in action. Because she wanted Cal to know his cousins. And something about the *busyness* of their family life . . . the constant coming and going and reconfigurations of people, the endless plans and arguments, the quantities of food consumed and information produced (Susie moving to England, Bill's updates about his sister in Yonkers, Liesel's stories) seemed so different from her own childhood, her sisterless and brotherless relations with her parents, their occasional friends, the house you had to take your shoes off in. There was something exotic about the Essingers she wanted to capture on film. They seemed interesting to her, artistically. This is the kind of thing she told herself.

And then, at night, in bed, going over the images in the dark, it was like experimenting on yourself . . . with needles. What does this make you feel, what do you feel about this. Cal trying to eat baked eggs, which kept slipping off his fork. (He wasn't hungry anyway, but wanted to fit in.) Jean, kicking out a leg—she came down for breakfast in pajamas, a hooded top, and cowboy boots, because the kitchen floor was splintery and she forgot to bring slippers. Dana photographed her pretending to barn dance. Clémence with her hands full of eggshells; she made an expression ("the harassed chef"), she was used to being on camera. Julie and Ben started arguing from the beginning—whether, for example, *Scooby Doo* was feminist or sexist, because Velma is supposed to be the brains ("You know why we know that," Julie said, "because she wears glasses! A woman in glasses! She must be smart, because otherwise . . ."—"Come on," Ben said, "the whole point of the show is that Shaggy is an idiot. I mean, if that's what you're arguing . . . I mean, his *dog* is smarter than him."). It was hard, on film, to capture the sense of *noise*: everyone talking at once, and not just talking, but emoting, putting expression into what they said, feelings of anger or sarcasm or conciliation, which didn't always show up on their faces, because there was no need, that's what the *talk* was for.

Julie didn't want to be photographed—she put her hand over her face and closed her eyes, and Dana, not really thinking, took her picture like that, feeling her heart go out to her.

Something had happened to Julie in the last year, a growth spurt, which made her a half-head taller than Ben, but she also looked like a different kind of person—someone a guy could almost be excused for hitting on. Her response to all this was resistance. She kept her hair short and dressed deliberately like someone who didn't care how she dressed. Her self-consciousness had extended to her physical movements, which were somewhat mechanical. She was as tall as Jean and when her aunt first hugged her, Jean made a face like, what happened to you. Dana had a picture of that, too. Nathan came in, dressed in ragged shorts and old basketball shoes and some kind of parka—his hair stuck out from the hood. He acknowledged everyone, including (briefly) Dana, whom he hadn't seen, then went out to buy some coffee from one of the food trucks in the Spider House parking lot. Liesel said, "There's coffee in the pot," and he told her, "Yeah, I don't drink that shit"—a ritual of disagreement. He offered to buy Dana some real coffee, and Dana, subtly taking sides, said, "Okay, yes, thank you."

"I always get a cappuccino with a double shot of espresso."

"Okay, I'll have that," and she thought for a moment that he was flirting with her, or she was flirting with him, she couldn't tell. Then David came down, fresh from the shower, and May looking red in the face.

"How long did you leave her for?" Susie asked.

"I don't know. She was asleep and when I came back from the bathroom, she was awake," and May reached out for her mother and started crying again. Susie, in her ordinary voice, "I know, I know, tell me about it," and took her in her arms.

"I'm going to get some coffee," David announced.

Jean said, "Nathan has already gone, you can catch him up. Has anyone spoken to Bill?"

"I hear you're fleeing these benighted shores." Clémence was talking to Susie—David was at the backdoor and waited a second to hear what his wife would say. "You can take me with you," she added, but he gave up and walked out.

"The deal was," Susie explained, "that if Romney won, I said we could go. I said, in that case . . . but then somehow I ended up agreeing anyway."

"I spoke to him, very briefly, this morning." Liesel sat in her chair at the head of the table, with her back to the kitchen cabinets, and was laying out, from a small tin of Altoids Curiously Strong Mints, her morning pills. "Everything's fine. He was just about to go in to see Rose. The streets were . . . he was going to walk, he couldn't get the car out. He called me to tell me about the snow."

Some of the pills were large and lozenge-like, with painful-looking ridges; some were shaped like M&Ms. The colors were these peculiarly powdery pharmaceutical colors, a kind of off-gray or faint peach. Jean, watching her mother, a little anxiously, said, "Nathan said he wanted to cook. I don't know what his plans are." And then: "I'm supposed to be in charge of dessert."

This is how the morning wore on—family as information-producing machine . . . decision-requiring machine . . . argument-creating machine . . . catering company and cleaning service . . . child-care and school. Willy, as soon as he had finished his waffles, said in the voice you use when you want to get what you want, "May I please be excused?" and went outside, leaving the main door ajar and letting the screen slam behind him, clatter and tap. "Close the door," Susie called out, but he was gone. Cold air flowed in. Then Margot said, "Me, too . . ." and followed him, Clémence chasing her down to put on her cardigan. When Nathan came back with David and the coffees, he had brought pastries, too, a bag of Mexican *conchas* ("which are probably disgustingly sweet," he said, "but there was a guy selling them"), and half the people sat down to start again.

Paul showed up around eleven o'clock. On the long drive over from Wimberley he always felt a kind of insatiable eagerness to arrive, the way he used to feel after school, running into the backyard after Bill picked him up . . . he didn't want to miss out, there were people having fun or just hanging out, but then as he got nearer his eagerness always turned into something else, it seemed to thicken into a kind of reluctance. The pressure of all these intimacies. "Hello?" he called out, letting himself in, but nobody answered and he walked past the living-room doors and down the hallway listening for signs of life. Susie was still in the kitchen, with May in a high chair and her hands full of paint—she had a piece of white paper she was smearing them across. Liesel sat there, too, with a cold cup of coffee on the table. She was reading the *New York Times*, taking a few minutes, preparing herself for a day of activity. The first job on her list was going shopping, but Nathan hadn't told her yet what to buy.

"Where is everybody?" Paul asked.

"Hello to you, too," Susie said. Then Dana walked in the back-door, carrying Cal, who was crying. It wasn't easy opening the screen with the big kid in her arms, she had to use her butt to prop it, and then somehow turn the handle of the main door with her arms full.

"What's wrong with him?" Paul asked.

"Nothing. He fell over."

"Hey, Buddy." But Cal put his face in his mother's neck.

"He's not very well," she said. "He's got a fever."

"So what's he doing running around outside?"

"He's—that's what he wanted—*you* look after him," she said, pushing past.

"Okay. Fine with me." But Dana had gone; she was taking him upstairs—to get out of the crowd and give him more Tylenol. Just to get away from everybody and spend a half hour on her own, with her son, behind a closed door.

"Where is everybody?" he said again. There were some pastries left in a basket on the table, which had only been partly cleared. Paul took one and ate. His fingers grew sticky with powder, which also dusted the cloth. "These are semi-disgusting," he said, taking another. He had run just after sunrise, at seven-thirty, and always around eleven hit a sugar low.

"Ben is reading. Willy and Margot are playing in the yard. Clémence has taken Julie for a walk—I think they're going to the bookshop. Nathan is working. David is talking to his mother, at least he was. Is that everybody? Have I missed anyone out?"

"What's wrong with Cal?"

"He's sick," Susie said. For some reason it annoyed her the way he walked in like that, expecting her to fill in the details, which were really his business. It didn't help that Nathan was lying in bed with the computer on his lap, and David had spent the last half hour on the phone while she sat around with May picking things off the floor.

Paul could have gone upstairs to check on Dana, and part of him figured that's probably what he *should* do, even though he also guessed that Dana wanted to be left alone. But there was really nothing else for him to do. This wasn't his house anymore, it's not where he lived, so he could sit around while May spread paint on the tablecloth or he could read the newspaper or watch TV, but instead he went outside into the mild cold overcast Texan winter day to see what Willy was up to. Because already a slight . . . not reliance or relation . . . had been formed, but a realization, on Paul's part, that he could appeal to the kid in a way that he was particularly skilled at, that the kid responded to. They weren't in the backyard, so far as he could tell, but then he saw that the playhouse door was open, about fifty feet away, and he walked taking his time across the sharp damp grass, past the gazebo and the silent fountain, toward the little white shed with a blue trim and a small veranda under the pecan tree.

Jean was there, too, sitting inside on a kid's chair with a slight-ly warped Seventies-style veneer coffee table up against her knees, on which she had placed cans of tomato soup and kidney beans and baked beans and tuna fish and even a tall glass jar of hot dogs. She had stuck Post-it notes with prices on most of the cans, and she had a pad of the Post-it notes on her lap, and Willy and Margo were picking over a bowl full of real loose change, which included a lot of foreign currency, to see what they could buy.

"Have you come to relieve me?" Jean said.

"What happened to Cal?"

"He's just . . . he was just feeling a little sorry for himself. He seems to be having one of those mornings where everything hurts."

The playhouse got used as a furniture dumping ground. It was very dusty inside and even colder than the backyard, because of the shade of the pecan tree, which meant the windows didn't receive much light. The smell was the smell of a storeroom, the chill inside had a slightly neglected or refrigerated quality, and Jean, if she wanted, could breathe so she could see her breath. Part of her had wanted to show off how good she was with kids, but the problem was you never really had an audience for that kind of thing because as soon as you were occupying them their parents had a tendency to disappear. Unless you count the kids as audience, which made her think, my motives aren't exactly strictly honorable, and almost as a kind of penance she kept the shopping game going, even when in normal conditions her patience for it might have run out.

"You get back all right last night?" Paul said.

"It was fine."

The kids were still looking through the bowl, holding up coins from time to time and saying, *How much is that worth*? Margot said, "Is this real money?" and Jean took it and turned it over between thumb and forefinger: silver, slight, with an eagle on the back and *1 DEUTSCHE MARK 1991* stippled on the other side.

"It's real," she said, giving it back.

"Can we—can we buy something with it?"

"What do you want to buy?"

"I mean, something real?"

"Not with that," Jean said, "not anymore."

"Why not?"

"It's a little complicated. People don't use that kind of money now."

Paul listened to this for a while and then he said to Jean, "You're a good auntie."

"I don't know."

"You're a good sister," and she looked up at him, with a kind of deprecating frown that seemed to Paul to suggest a certain amount of real emotion surprisingly near the surface.

"Why do we have . . . this money if it doesn't work?" Margot asked.

"It used to work, it's just . . ." and Paul turned to Willy and said, "You want to play tennis?"

Willy looked up quickly and said, "Okay."

"Can I play, too?" Margot asked.

"Everybody can play."

"But you don't know how to play," Willy said to his cousin.

"You don't either."

"I do. I played yesterday. Ask Uncle Paul . . ." and this kept going while they all walked back to the house to get rackets and balls. On the patio they ran into Nathan, still dressed in shorts and cheap running shoes and his old green parka, stepping out of his room, whose sliding glass door overlooked the backyard, and Nathan said to Paul, "What are you doing right now?"

"I was going to play tennis with the kids."

"Come shopping with me."

"Nice to see you, too," Paul said.

"He just promised to play tennis," Jean said.

"Well, the kids can come, too. Come on, Margot. I want to show you the supermarket, it's a famous supermarket." But in the end, neither of them wanted to go and Paul and Nathan set off alone. Liesel gave them a list.

*

Whenever Nathan came back to Austin, he felt a burst of restlessness—he couldn't tell exactly if it was happy or not, the restlessness of excitement or something else. He borrowed the Volvo keys from Liesel and even though Paul lived in Texas and had his own car, Nathan assumed they would take the Volvo and that he would drive. He got behind the wheel, and Paul, without saying anything or even minding, sat in the passenger seat.

"I love this car, this is a great car," Nathan said, looking over his shoulder and pulling out. Across the road, Dodie, the old lady who had been living in the neighborhood since the Essingers moved in, stood in her front yard, doing nothing much but wearing gardening gloves and Nathan, as he turned the car in the road, lowered his window and waved to her. She acknowledged him without waving back, a short bone-skinny figure, with a face you couldn't easily read behind her thick glasses.

Nathan, when he saw her, was reminded of how much he liked Austin, that it could produce such people—independent, dignified, unobtrusive, free-thinking . . . Around election time she always stuck a simple blue-and-white *Lloyd Doggett US Congress* sign in her front yard. Nathan once interviewed her for a high-school project, and she sat with him for half an hour on her screen porch. She gave him a cup of tea, and she answered his questions politely and he couldn't help thinking that there was something about him that she didn't entirely trust—something flashy or intellectual, which upset him only slightly at the time and didn't really dent his opinion of her, or change the way he wanted to think about her as an example of something important about his hometown. One of his moods was a kind of genuine but also semi-deliberate enthusiasm, for life and everyone, and he felt a surge of this now, as he drove up Wheeler Street, under the arch of its trees, past its grand but still idiosyncratic upper-middle class houses, with their yellowing wintry front yards, and richly watered potted plants, and rusting yard art, toward 32nd Street and then the traffic of Guadalupe.

Paul said, "It can go from zero to sixty in less than two minutes."

But Nathan couldn't remember what they were talking about. Part of his burst of enthusiasm was just a kind of revving the engine, testing it out, getting ready to go; he felt it was his job while he was around to address certain family problems, to think about them and make other people think about them, and on this holiday those problems included Paul. His brother looked almost painfully skinny. The muscle mass of his tennis-playing days, the forearm strength and core stability, weren't necessary to him anymore; all he did was run and bike, and what was left of him now after a year of retirement looked not only lean but almost eager and hungry—underfed. His T-shirt looked like it was hanging on a coat hanger; when he smiled you could imagine the skull. Nathan was merging now into the median lane, preparing to turn, and he said to Paul, not looking at him but waiting for a break in the traffic, "Talk to me now. What's going on with you and Dana."

"There's nothing . . . *ongoing*. Liesel for some reason . . . Liesel invited her to come for Christmas. Without asking me. As far as I'm concerned . . ." but he didn't want to say it.

"As far as you're concerned what?"

"Well it's not like we were ever married."

"That's neither here nor . . . I mean . . . that's just a total . . ."

"Well, we had a disagreement. About how we wanted to live. And I didn't see that there was any way of splitting the difference."

"How do you want to live?" With his eye on the road it was easier to ask these questions, but part of him was also taking in Flamingo Automotive, where Bill got his car serviced—a Fifties brick and glass box, classy in a rundown kind of way, next to the ice-cream parlor where he briefly worked in high school. On either side of the five-lane road were storefronts and cafés, most of them changed since he was a kid, but the feel was the same, car culture, wide skies. Then the light turned and he turned with it onto 38th Street.

"I don't know," Paul said, in a different tone. "Maybe I mean where we wanted to live, but that's just part of it. It seemed like we stopped getting along and then it was like we didn't really want to anymore."

It's a five-minute drive from Wheeler Street to Central Market. Nathan pulled into the parking lot and started looking for a space—he had to circle up and down the aisles, the last-minute Christmas crush had arrived, and he waited for a guy in a Nissan Qashqai to back out before taking his spot. The guy had his window open and they could hear the beeping of the video monitor as he reversed. Paul said, "Honestly it seemed like it was easier for both of us when we just . . . I don't know . . . left each other alone. I mean, it's been easier with Cal, too."

"That's unlikely to be true," Nathan said.

After that they went shopping. Central Market was one of these recent Austin developments, a high-end incarnation of an old local chain, arranged not in columns and rows but in a kind of snakes-and-ladders setup that forced you to follow the path from beginning to end: past bands of fresh-color, imported apples (Fuji, Lady Alice, Northern Spy), Texas grapefruits and oranges, watermelons, canta-loupes, honey dew, then squash, pumpkins, potatoes, radishes, car-rots, lettuces of every variety and shade, from pale underbelly green to cabbagey purple, everything laid out like an art installation. Even the fish counter seemed color-coordinated, like a pharmacy shelf, salmon steaks grading to swordfish, and they pushed past illustrated maps of cheese, where each country sported its own toothpick flag. This is the kind of thing yuppies do well, there's no point pretend-ing otherwise, but it was stressful, too, in the late Christmas rush, trying to find everything, doubling back along secret cut-throughs, trying to locate this or that in all the plenty. Paul said to him, holding up what looked like a carton of cream cheese, "Are we the kind of people who spend $9.98 on rendered duck fat?" And Nathan said, "These are the questions you ask yourself," but took it anyway and put it back in the cart—for roast potatoes. Feeling mildly annoyed. There was an old family argument about the way Nathan lived, his suits and wines, but he didn't want to get into it now. At the checkout Paul let his brother pay.

Afterward, Nathan suggested that they get a cup of coffee from Houndstooth, the hipster coffee shop across the road (glass walls, concrete floors), and they loaded the shopping bags into the Volvo and waited for a gap in the traffic then jogged across. Paul didn't drink coffee but sat outside at one of the tables and waited for Nathan while he ordered, and then waited for him to drink it, too. The weather was changing, like it had the day before, and a cold white cloudy morning was giving way to a clear mild blue and yellow afternoon. Cars moved past on 38th Street, but you get used to them. It's a kind of life like anything else, like birds flying past in V-formations . . . and sitting on the sidewalk, by the parking lot, watching the traffic, you felt like someone sitting on the docks, watching the boats come in.

"Maybe we should all move back," Nathan said. "This is good coffee."

"A lot of fancy beards."

"Well, that's the price you pay."

For some reason it annoyed Paul, his brother's enthusiasm, even though Paul *had* moved back, and at various points had tried to persuade other people to come along. But when Nathan's in this mood of life appreciation you can't really win. There's nothing you can say (apart from agreeing all the time) that doesn't sound churlish, and anyway it's nice enough feeling the temperature rise and taking off your sweatshirt, feeling cold but also feeling the sun on your skin and the little hairs along your forearms uncurling. But what he said was: "We should probably get back. Dana's had Cal all morning."

"Are you guys seeing other people?"

"I don't know. She might be. We don't really . . . we don't really talk about it."

"And you?"

"Who would I see? You know where I live; there's nothing there. I go running, I go biking, I read. Sometimes I drive over to see Bill and Liesel. That's pretty much it."

"These are all choices, right. They can be chosen different."

Paul didn't look at his brother but felt that something was being asserted, something he was basically grateful for, a role or a wisdom or whatever, and part of what he was grateful for is that it gave him a chance to say the kind of thing he had on his mind, the sort of explanation or formulation he had practiced or polished to himself, on long runs, in the shower afterward, at night when he couldn't sleep, alone in his house watching TV, and which you never in ordinary life get to say. So he said it.

"Maybe they can, but it's gotten to the point where I don't even know what you're supposed to want from them anymore."

"What do you mean, *them*?"

"Women, pretty girls."

Nathan, trying to kid him out of it: "I think you know what people want."

"I'm not," but he didn't want to be kidded, he was trying to explain himself, these were conversations he had with himself all the time, and after a while you can't tell if they make sense. "I'm not talking about . . . I'm not talking about anything crude. But there's a whole—I mean, there's a whole kind of esteem or pleasure, which you're supposed to get from these interactions, right? I mean, that's the system, isn't it, it's almost like we're trained to want . . . But it's like I can't remember why I'm supposed to try to make them like me. I don't understand what it's supposed to prove. I mean, why these people? Why pretty girls? Of all the people, whose . . . approval or understanding. . . I'm aware that I'm not really . . ."

"No, I get it, it's a . . . I understand." But he didn't know what to say, and after a minute Paul said, "Should we go?"

For the rest of the day, while Nathan put away the shopping and then had lunch, while he prepared the kitchen afterward for cooking Christmas dinner, and then retired to his room and lay in bed, napping and working until it was time to put the bird in the oven; while he chopped boiled glazed roasted, taking over the counter space, filling the sink with dirty pots, which Jean mostly cleaned up as they went along; while he ate dinner, selecting different wines for each course, pouring and drinking, and later still when they transferred to the living room and gave out presents (everybody let the kids stay up late), and he fell asleep on the couch, in front of the fire, aware of the conversations around him, and Clémence telling him, *go to bed*, and Liesel joining in, he had this conversation on the back of his mind. He had been presented with an argument and needed to find the counter-argument, it was important that he . . . but that's not really what was on his mind. Seeing Paul like that, with his skinny face, and a kind of almost . . . evangelical intensity . . .

Though by the time they carried in the shopping together, Paul seemed fine. He said to Jean, who was in the kitchen, "We went to Houndstooth, and it's almost like—I mean, you can't actually exaggerate the extent to which . . ."

"What are we talking about?" she said.

"Beards and boots, the whole . . ."

"It's just as bad in London."

"As if these people think that drinking coffee is some kind of avant-garde activity. Baristas annoy me, too, I mean the word, it's like they don't think that any English word can possibly do justice to the complexity of . . . And of course all of these places basically look the same, that's the other thing."

Nathan said, "They look like your house, Paul. That's what they look like."

"What are you talking about?"

"Concrete and glass. These are your people. Don't kid yourself otherwise."

Nathan went out to get another round of bags. Afterward he walked across the road to Dodie's house, to say hello. But what he also thought of, what was also on his mind, is the summer before he left for college, when he flew to the Dominican Republic with a kind of Peace Corps program, and came back looking like Paul looked now, skinny and . . . crazy, with pent-up thoughts and carefully worked out positions and arguments, which . . . meant he argued with Liesel, off and on, for the last few weeks of childhood, until he caught the flight to New Haven.

He had bought a bottle of Promised Land Eggnog at Central Market, for no particular reason, and he took it with him now to give Dodie. It seemed like a neighborly sort of thing to do. Except she wasn't in or wasn't answering, and he stood outside her door for a minute, feeling phony or foolish. Her house was in bad shape, paint had blistered off the clapboard, and the screen mesh had given way in many places on the front porch. There were splintery little pockets or explosions of loose wires that would let mosquitoes in. The parlor window had an air-conditioning unit propping up the sash—most houses in the neighborhood had centralized systems, but Dodie's little cottage was a holdover from earlier times, a little bungalow on a modest plot of land. Maybe she was one of these people who didn't answer the door unless she knew you were coming over. And after a minute he walked back.

———

The flight to Santo Domingo stopped first in Atlanta and later at JFK—it took thirteen hours, door to door. All he had with him was the army-green Patagonia duffel bag, which he still owned. (Clémence had used it to pack the kids' clothes.) It was the first time he had traveled without his family, and as the plane lifted above Austin, the flat parking lot of the airport diminishing below him, the lakes scattered between the trees and highways, the suddenly childish-looking architecture of the houses, like so many colored blocks, he felt an onrush of anxiety. A few other Austin kids were on the program (they were joining more in Atlanta and New York), and he knew them slightly from their preparation classes, the first-aid course and form-filling sessions. One of them, Karen Heinz, he had a slight crush on. Her parents were divorced; her mother was an endocrinologist at Seton Medical Center. This was her second time flying out (she had been to Ecuador the summer before), and she had the charm and confidence of experience. They argued from the beginning, about Dukakis, about Tiananmen Square, she had red hair and an angular handsome rather than pretty face; she was big-boned, too, tall and still skinny in those days, but still somehow physically awkward or uncomfortable in a way that only contributed to the force of her personality.

Nathan had never had a girlfriend; he had never kissed a girl, and part of what he planned for that summer was to make a start on all that before he left for college. He was naturally self-assured and already had the sense, as a tall man, that tall women liked him for it, especially older women, teachers, for example, and other people's parents—his height made him acceptable on some level. In other respects, though, he was careless in his appearance. He wore Air Jordan high-tops and cheap blue jeans and the T-shirts he picked up from his part-time jobs and extracurricular clubs, like the *Summer Research Academy* at UT. At that point, he still wanted to be a physicist. With his dark skin and long uncut hair, he looked a little like an Iranian terrorist. He had started shaving, too, but only occasionally, and he normally wore the shadow of a mustache on his upper lip, which somehow contributed to his guerilla revolutionary/high-school nerd appearance. Bill and Liesel both brought him to the airport, their oldest child. She was in tears when he filed down the narrow gate, and he thought, with a rush of blood, *Here we go*, until the plane took off and he felt the faint faint snapping of the kite string that had, for the past seventeen years of his life, held him in place.

They stayed the first night at a dormitory in Santo Domingo and spent the next morning receiving equipment containers and final instructions from one of the local coordinators. Then, after lunch, they split into groups and at different times were loaded on to one of the *guaguas*, or private buses, that Dominicans use to get around the country. Karen was in his group; her Spanish was better than Nathan's, which was lucky, because they had to change at Constanza and somehow locate the next *guagua* to take them to their village in the mountains a hundred miles to the west on the Haitian border. When they got there, it was already dark—and cool in the night altitude, and they still had to pitch their tents and find a place to pitch them. There were four of them in the group, two boys and two girls, and they each shared a tent. Nathan, tired as he was that first night, imagined some future when they might organize themselves in couples instead of by gender and hoped in some childish way he was already embarrassed by to pair off with Karen.

After a few weeks, locals took them in, which often involved extended families moving in together so they could vacate the tin-walled shacks they usually slept in, four or five in a single room. The volunteers tried to refuse but eventually realized they were insulting their hosts and accepted.

Nathan had never seen such poverty. He could not have imagined it without having seen it, and already, after a few days, all social and sexual thoughts of his own—the summer camp vibrations—seemed to have disappeared. Everybody was too tired, for one thing. It was their job to dig latrines and to teach the locals how to maintain them. You dug a hole at least 20 feet from the house, and downhill and at least 100 feet from any water source. You also had to work out how deep to dig, where the water table was, what the floodplain looked like, and construct a cheap wooden hut around the ditch for privacy, but also to keep out animals and flies—especially flies, which lay their eggs in excreta and spread disease. So the entrance to the shack had to be sealable, and it was important to keep all the surfaces clean. These are the things you had to explain, in second-rate Spanish, to people who had been living in these mountains for generations.

They were also much better at working hard than he was, especially the old guys—who adopted a nice easy rhythm for any task, which they could maintain hour after hour, while he spent himself in the first ten minutes. Afterward, they ate with their hosts, rice and beans. He was ill at first, with diarrhea, for which he dosed himself from the medical kit, with Imodium and salt tablets. They boiled all their water or added halazone tablets. By the time he flew back to Austin he had lost twenty pounds. They walked for miles every day, across mountain country, to neighboring villages, carrying equipment, shovels, hammers, covering as much ground as possible, digging as many latrines as possible, talking to as many people . . . Everyone welcomed them, nobody complained, the children played in the dirt roads, he never heard anyone lose their temper.

When a boy in his village cut himself on a baseball bat (they often used old planks with rusted nails), the cut became infected; Nathan, noticing, cleaned the wound and treated it with antiseptic. The medical kits they had been given in Santo Domingo included hydrogen peroxide, in solution, iodine pills, aspirin, and basic antibiotics—penicillin tablets, along with gauze bandages, needles and suture thread. The wound healed. After that, people started coming to Nathan with other problems.

Some of them were treatable. They had been told not to play doctor, but what could you do. A woman came to him complaining of stomach pains—she had seen him preparing his drinking water with those powders. But it was clear that what she suffered from was something else. There was blood in her stool, she looked bone thin, gray in her dark face, she couldn't eat, she didn't want to. Karen thought she probably had bowel cancer. He gave her salt tablets, he figured they couldn't do much harm; she thanked him with such faith, he tried to tell her, you need a doctor. You are the doctor, she said. *El medico . . . no medico, no medico. Medico en . . .* and he tried to think of the nearest town with a clinic or a hospital . . . *en San Juan.* But she was too ill to travel—her husband had carried her to Nathan's house in his arms. Every day for the next two weeks he went to visit her—he tried to make her eat, or drink clean water, and she drank a little. But she died anyway, and her husband apologized to him, with gratitude for all he had done and tears in his eyes; Nathan was seventeen years old.

This is why they tell you not to play doctor. Other people came for help, from other villages. Somehow it didn't matter that the woman had died. And still, no one complained, nobody seemed unhappy. He liked walking through the mountains in the morning, toward the next village, with a job to do. He had brought with him a copy of Hemingway's short stories and *The Road to Wigan Pier*. At night, in his sleeping bag, in the glow of a flashlight, he read. He went to bed early and woke up early; in spite of the weight loss, he felt strong and well. His Spanish improved; he turned out to be good at making himself understood, at getting his way. He turned out to be competent in other respects, and Karen and the two other volunteers relied on him to work out how deep the water table was and where to dig. He was good with his hands, too, and could build a doorframe so the door stayed shut when you closed it.

At the end of six weeks, they all met up in Santo Domingo again. He got drunk for the first time, on *mamajuana*; they went dancing, Nathan sat at a table and watched. Nobody went to bed—the rum kept him awake, but he never lost control, he felt lucid, but also awkward, left out, miserable, and very young. Karen, it turned out, liked dancing, and men kept approaching her; the music was mostly American, synthetic-sounding, *Shakedown, Nothing's Gonna Stop Us Now*, the kind of music he thought she wouldn't like. The dance floor was outside, under the stars. It seemed like a kind of violence, the level of noise. He could see the beach and the black-and-blue waters beyond it; sexual jealousy irritated him like a rash. At four in the morning he ate *mangu*, smashed plantain, and *queso frito* and drank coffee. (He had started drinking coffee in the mountains.) By that point he was fine—people just wanted to sit around and talk.

The next day they flew to JFK and separated. Some of the volunteers flew on to Atlanta, where they separated again. On the flight to Austin, only he and Karen remained, like survivors. They hadn't slept in thirty-six hours, they had been talking for the last five, and half-asleep, sharing an armrest, as the plane needled through night skies and the flat grids of human habitation showed their strings of lights, nuzzled a little and kissed. He felt like he was giving in to something, that she knew what she was doing and he didn't, and that she knew she could make him respond, but he responded anyway.

Bill and Liesel met him at the airport, and Bill said, "You look like a concentration camp survivor," and in spite of himself, for some reason, Nathan felt ashamed.

For the next two weeks all they did was fight, Nathan and Liesel. He couldn't understand Bill's short temper—the way he blew up about inconsequential things. When Jeannie left the milk out after breakfast and it spoiled. Everything had to be an argument. Just the level of . . . luxury, and more or less constant dissatisfaction with the luxury, the levels of daily unhappiness. Why should they live like that? Why should people be frustrated with their jobs? Bill often complained about university appointments, but for some reason Nathan took his anger out on his mother. Bill had the sense to leave him alone, but Liesel took him seriously, she wanted to correct him, she wanted to say: When you escape one set of difficulties, very basic difficulties, like the problems of sanitation and shelter, having enough food to eat or clean water to drink, or even . . . or even the difficulties of war, you don't escape . . . the human capacity for difficulty . . . which is a good thing . . . you don't escape . . . the problems of other kinds of desire, which are also, in their way, perfectly reasonable desires . . . Why do you argue with him, Bill said to her, at night, when they lay in bed. Just let him be . . . he's going through a period of . . . Because I worry about him. He will make for himself a lot of unhappiness this way.

Nathan met up with Karen a couple of times, they saw a movie at the Waterloo Ice House (she picked him up in her car—he couldn't drive), but he was glad of the movie because it meant they didn't have to talk. He felt there was something embarrassing about identifying with somebody because of a shared experience, it was demeaning.

The second time they ate ice cream at the ice-cream parlor where he used to work, next to Flamingo Automotive; he was perfectly polite, even charming. She was flying out to Pomona in a few days; he was going to Yale. And after a few months at Yale, he adapted or adjusted again. He started going out with an English major, someone he met in seminar—he asked her out for coffee afterward, he took the lead. Because the one real lesson he had learned in the DR, the only lesson he could use back in America, was that women could be attracted to him; he didn't have to worry about it, he was going to be okay, on that front. But obviously if Paul was going through something like this he hadn't come out yet on the other side.

Susie was making lunch for the kids when he came back in. Just something simple, pasta and pesto. Clémence laid the table, Julie and Margot were going to have some, too. David and Jean sat at the far end, toward the backdoor, staring at Jean's computer. She was checking out property websites, looking at houses for sale in Oxford (Jericho and Summertown and off the Cowley Road) and the surrounding villages (Botley and Marston, Beckley, and Noke). For a moment Jean had to lift up her laptop so that Clémence could spread the tablecloth underneath. "Susie," David called out. "Look at this." But Susie was carrying the pot to the sink, pouring macaroni into the colander and couldn't come—she didn't want to come anyway, she was still resisting. Ben wandered in from the TV room and asked his father, "What's that?"

"Can we do this later?" Susie said.

"A house."

"It looks like a barn."

"It used to be a barn."

And Clémence came over, with a carrot in her mouth, peering over Jean's shoulder. "Look at the garden," Jean said, and clicked.

"Nice garden." A lawn, covered in fall leaves, with a kind of balustrade at one end, old stone steps. There were trees and fields in the distance, everything seemed sketched out in pencil, a little blurry, under a gray sky. It was funny to think this was somebody's actual home, another family's. Jean, staring at the screen, missed Henrik, and short English afternoons—the kind that get dark at four o'clock.

"Is that where we're going to live?"

"I said can we do this later," Susie called out, mixing the pesto in and bringing the pot to the table. "Watch out, this is hot. Can somebody get a . . . can somebody get a . . ."

"Trivet," Julie said.

"Well, can you get one?"

"I don't know where they are."

Jean said, "I think you should look at this."

"Look at this, look at this," David said, in his jollying-along voice; his accent, even after twenty years in America, was perfectly English. (Susie sometimes said it was like listening to the radio.) He wore what he called his "peasant trousers," loose jeans, and a short-sleeved floral shirt that showed off his strong forearms and barrel chest. Susie came over, still carrying the pot in her hands, and he said, "Peach Melba sofas. Linoleum kitchen floor. Isn't it great."

"You know what I see when I see a house like this?" Susie said.

"We'll take them all out," David told her. "We'll put in Essinger-grade uncomfortable Shaker furniture."

"I see recently divorced."

"Damn," Jean said. "She got you."

"She got me."

"Can somebody get a trivet? Can everybody sit down? Where's Liesel? Ben, go and get Liesel."

"Is Cal gonna eat?" Paul said.

"He's watching TV."

"Well, he can stop watching TV."

"Every time I turn it off," Dana told him, "he cries."

The table wasn't big enough for everybody, unless two of the kids sat together at the end—but Margot wanted to sit next to May, who was perched in one of these Swedish contraptions, a high chair strapped to the table, and Julie didn't think it was fair that as the oldest child . . . but Nathan said, "You can sit at the end."

"There *is* room, if Jean moves the computer."

"I'm moving, I'm moving," and she snapped it shut and stood up.

Paul went to check on Cal. There was a narrow sliding door to the playroom, and unless it was closed you could hear the TV blaring away while you ate, the static quality of a five-year-old set. (Bill always liked to keep the sound turned up; his hearing was going, and the kids left it like that, because everyone was always talking around them.) Cal sat back on the couch, staring, his cheeks looked red and his fair fine hair lay stuck to his forehead. He didn't complain when Paul turned the volume down. His eyes flickered with the movement of the lights on the screen, and when Paul walked across the rug and sat down next to him, Cal shifted slightly so that he could rest his head against his father's arm.

"What are we watching?" Paul said, but Cal didn't answer; one of those flea-market bargain shows, God knows what he sees in it, not that he cares, it's just TV. The phone rang next door and Susie looked into the room.

"Does Cal want any pasta?" she asked, in the quiet direct voice you use to communicate intimacy. She was also a mother talking to another parent, with a sick kid.

"Can somebody get that?" Liesel called from the hallway. You could hear her moving across the wooden boards, her show of hurry. The ringing stopped and Dana said, "Essinger residence," and Paul in spite of himself felt a flare-up of some faint emotion.

"I don't know, you hungry, Buddy?" but the boy didn't answer and Paul said, "Give us a minute and we'll come in."

"I'm just wondering because I'm wondering how much to give everybody. There isn't exactly an excess amount . . ."

"It's fine," Jean shouted, invisibly, from the kitchen. "Everybody's happy, everybody's got plenty!'

"Well . . ."

"I'm heating up some Vietnamese," she called out.

"How old is that?" Nathan asked her.

"Not old. It's from last night."

"Last night you were picking us up."

"From two nights ago then, it's fine."

"You can probably count us out," Paul said to Susie.

"There's enough, I just want to get a sense . . ."

"I don't know, just give me a minute. I just want to sit here for a minute."

"Are you okay?" Susie asked, but he was watching TV.

When he came back in, Liesel was still on the phone, talking to Bill. She was dressed now, in one of her smocks; her gray hair looked wet, and she sat on the chair by the window, under the telephone base, which was mounted on the wall.

Dana said in an undertone, "Does he want to eat something?"

Paul shook his head. And then, looking her full in the face, which he didn't usually do: "Should we take him to the doctor?"

"Will they be open on Christmas Eve?"

"I'll ask Liesel when she gets off the phone. Otherwise we can always go to the emergency room . . ." and Jean said, "It's exciting, looking at houses. It's like shopping for a new life."

"I don't want a new life," Susie said.

"Who doesn't want a new life?"

"You're worrying me," Dana said.

"He's fine, I just thought, if the drugs will help, let's get him some drugs."

"The deal was, that if Romney won, I said we could go, but then Obama won and somehow, anyway," but Susie knew she was repeating herself, and stopped.

"I want a rectory," David said.

"Why do you want a rectory?"

"What's a rectory?" Margot asked.

"We're just renting," Susie said. "Until we work out—"

"I don't care what we do but it's the way we talk about it together that leaves room for improvement." Sometimes David used her family to say the things he wanted to say in private, but so Susie couldn't respond without picking a public fight. "I want to be able to . . . even just in the realms of make-believe, we should be able to make plans or show some of the usual human emotions . . ."

"It's where a rector lives," Julie said. "It's a house."

"What's a rector?"

"Do you really want to talk about this now?"

"Yes," David said, "because Jean is here. She can protect me."

"I'm here." Even at thirty-two she could play the kid sister. With her short hair and boyish face . . . she blushed, easily, too.

"These *are* my usual human emotions," Susie said.

Nathan, standing at the kitchen counter, was fixing himself a plate of fish curry and rice. He ate from the serving spoon, he tried everything out. After a meal, the tablecloth was always dirty around him. "It's not a good time to buy property in England. Prices there are historically overinflated."

Jean, indignantly: "You don't know what you're talking about. You make that stuff up."

"A rector is a priest," Clémence said. "What's wrong with your carrots?"

Margot had a code, according to which . . . "They've got pesto on them," and her mother tried to spoon them apart. She had come late to motherhood, after years of watching her friends . . . playing the role, adopting new personalities and habits. So this kind of thing bothered her less than it might have. Even the ordinary battles had a certain charm.

"These are fine, you can eat these."

"I've seen the figures," Nathan said. "The relationship between median income and house price—"

Liesel, still on the phone, lifted her hand in the air. "Is Judith there now? Yes . . . when . . . Can everyone be quiet? I can't hear."

And Bill, from his sister's hospital room, watching her sleep while the monitor over the bed recorded her data—in constantly shifting lines and charts, with an electronic pulse that seemed to fade in and out, expanding and contracting in the form of a number, 57 55 58—tried not to raise his voice. He didn't want to wake her (Rose had been awake earlier, and semiconscious), but he could hear in the background the noise around the kitchen table, not all the words but everybody's tone, and thought, *Oh Nathan, let it go.*

———

Judith had come at lunchtime with a foot-long Subway sandwich—she had managed to get a cab after all. (There was a Subway concession in the hospital food court.) "I can't eat all this anyway, Uncle Bill. I figured you might want some." Bill stood up to let her take the lounger—he borrowed a folding chair from one of the nurses, and in fact, when she offered him half of her sandwich, he accepted it. He hadn't eaten all day. "Would you believe some of the houses around here," Judith said, comfortably. "When I came last night it was dark. Gables, wraparound porches. Turrets. Who lives in these places—they must cost, what. A million bucks. Two million."

While they talked, his sister slept, with her mouth open but color in her cheeks. Cold winter sunshine, ten stories up, poured into the room, as white and clinical as the hospital walls. Rose's room had a view of the river and the bare bluffs of the Palisades State Park on the other side, covered in white, looking like an unexplored, unsettled continent, while the wide flat slow-moving Hudson drifted by. Only the traffic on Warburton below and the rusted railroad tracks beyond it reminded you of human occupation.

Bill said, "Is Mikey all right? It must have been hard, leaving him behind. Especially at this time of year."

And this set her off again.

"He's fine, you know, my mother-and-law and I—I guess I won't be able to call her *that* much longer. What *do* you call her? We have an understanding, and part of that understanding is that, as women, who have spent our lives putting up with Jewish men . . . Of course, she takes her son's side but she also feels like . . . she's getting him back. The first thing he did when all of this started is move home. I can understand it for a couple of months, but . . . he's not even *looking* for an apartment. He says he needs the help with childcare, when Mikey stays over. Okay, so his mother helps. But she would also help him at the Park Evanston, believe me. The truth is, he *wanted* to move home, he's happier at home. So I say, let him be happier. Who am I to stand in his way. It's like I'm saying to Leah, you win. She won. But what bugs me is that Mikey has no sense of Christmas. When I was a kid, we used to go to the movies, it was a nice day. We never had a tree or anything like that, but Rose always wanted me to think it was a nice day—she didn't want me to feel left out. Half the kids I knew in school came back after the holidays with . . . I don't know what. Stuff. Atari *this*, Atari *that*. This is one of the things I've promised myself, this is one of the deals you make, when you get divorced. To get you through it. That next year Mikey will know what Christmas *is* . . ."

And sitting there, listening (he didn't have to ask many questions), Bill couldn't help feeling comfortable, too. He admired Judith, almost in spite of himself, and recognized that there was something cheerful and patient in her complaints. It touched him, also, the easy intimacy she showed around her uncle, whom she had seen, God knows, maybe half a dozen times in the last ten years. Maybe she talked like this to everyone, maybe she talked like this to the cab driver on the way over. But he didn't think so. And Rose, in her mechanical bed, knocked out, drugged up, hooked up, but she was a presence, too—part of the intimacy. Apart from anything else it astonished Bill how un-distressed her daughter seemed. She was already making plans to fly back to Chicago as soon as the airports cleared.

There was a limit, of course, to how long she wanted to leave Mikey. "I guess it's just you and me for Christmas," she said to Bill.

Maybe the day after, she could fly back. Rose seemed stable, there was no point in sitting around all day, staring at her like this. When she needed help was when she moved back home, right? And she didn't want Mikey to see his grandmother in this condition. It bugs me anyway, the . . . the difference between the way . . . her and Leah . . . Because how can Mom compete? She lives in New York, we're in Chicago. Maybe at some future point we can move back home, but that's going to be difficult, depending on the terms of custody, and the fact is, I don't really have a home to move to. Manhattan is too expensive and if I move in with Rose . . . you can see for yourself. It's depressing, right? And all we do is fight anyway. I figure at my age I have a very narrow window to meet somebody—very narrow. And to make a new home for myself. Otherwise, what am I looking at, what kind of future? I have to be realistic. We're going to have to sell the house. Gabe says it's too big for two people anyway. Which is *of course* (and he knows this perfectly well) just another one of his reproaches. He wanted a lot of kids . . . Well, he can make them with somebody else."

And she laughed, and Bill thought, I listen to all this for her, because when we were kids . . . I was Billy and she was—running the show.

But he saw the resemblance, too. He couldn't help seeing it, with Rose lying there and Judith sitting in the armchair. The heavy lips, and their coloring, rose on pale, a constant sort of uneven flush on her cheeks, not healthy-looking, but vivid and showing a certain . . . energy of character . . . in spite of other indications, physical sloppiness, laziness. When Judith stood up, she pushed up with her hands. As a tall woman, she wore flat comfortable shoes, and she moved, in her layers of clothing, a little like she was dragging something behind. Whenever she sat down, she had to adjust herself. Her shoulder bag contained multitudes. She drank a lot of bottled water and applied herself obsessively to the Purell dispenser, mounted against the wall behind her. Bill disliked the chemical quality of the gel, which evaporates but never entirely and leaves a definite smell. Judith's hands were starting to look a little raw.

After lunch the doctor came in—always a different doctor, and Bill, who was squeamish, tried to make himself pay attention to the medical details. This one looked in her forties, short but not unattractive, with curly hair. She was obviously Jewish: Dr. Kleinman. Her accent was the accent of people he grew up with. She wore a wedding ring. Judith couldn't help herself, she needed to impress these people, and show them that she had spent two years in medical school. She referred to this fact again and again. "I've got a lot of respect for doctors, because I couldn't make it. Two years at Pritzker was enough for me." And he could hear in his niece's voice her own conviction, that she was endearing herself by confessing this failure—that this was one of her likable qualities. Maybe it *was*, who knows. The fact that Pritzker was an elite institution, very difficult to get into . . . of course, that was also part of the confession.

But Dr. Kleinman had an easy, businesslike manner, natural without being personal. What Rose had picked up was a kind of CRE, almost certainly during or after her hip operation. She was lucky to come in when she did—a little later . . . the infection had spread to the blood, there was a danger of sepsis. Sometimes with these bugs some of the older antibiotics turn out to be relatively effective, but they can really knock you out. She also had some fluid on the lungs, which they needed to keep an eye on. And so on. Has she been conscious at all since you've been here?

Bill said, "She woke up a little around eleven o'clock. I've been here since ten."

"And how did she seem?"

"She knew who I was, she didn't seem surprised to see me. But she was also very tired, she seemed a little underwater. I asked her if she wanted to watch TV and she said, okay, so I flipped through the channels. *The Price is Right* was on and she wanted to watch that. But she fell asleep again pretty soon."

"Well, she's fighting, she's a fighter . . ." But Dr. Kleinman had already made her notes. "Her numbers are in the . . . she seems to be responding to the drugs." And she looked at Bill, rather than Judith. It was a human look—this was also part of the job, the last thing on her list. "Don't be afraid to call if something worries you. That's why we're here."

"When will she . . ." Bill began to say, he didn't want her to leave. "I mean, at what point can we expect . . ."

"That's hard to . . . these bugs are very unpredictable. Your sister has had a significant event. But she seems to be responding well. I'm a little worried about the pneumonia, but like I say, we'll keep an eye on it." She was starting to repeat herself, and Bill let her go.

Judith had brought along her iPad. She was looking at real-estate websites, partly to find out what their house in West Ridge would go for. The market had recovered slightly but not enough to make a difference—they'd be lucky to get what they bought it for six years ago. "It's the kind of house that realtors call *cute*," she said. Real estate was one of the things she was thinking of going into. You can't just sit around the house all day when the kid goes to school. Dinah, the woman who sold it to them originally, had mentioned . . . when Judith got in touch a few months ago . . . it's funny how these people become figures in your life. But she was also looking at rentals, somewhere she and Mikey could move to afterward. Whatever she did seemed to involve a lot of interruptions. Messages of one kind or another would ping through, and she'd react semipublicly to these interruptions (laughing or making noncommittal noises), and then turn around to Bill and try to explain her reaction: "My friend Sharon is in the process of hiring an au pair . . ."

He said, "I'm going to call home," and she offered to let him use her phone, but he said, "I need to stretch my legs anyway." He needed a break anyway. Also, he wanted to use up the calling card.

There was a telephone in the waiting room, really just a kind of lobby or unused cubicle near reception—a few toys in a corner in a box, a couple of wipe-down fake-leather armchairs, a coffee table with old magazines (*Homes and Gardens, People, Sports Illustrated*). The television on the wall showed CNN: an American contractor had been shot and killed at police headquarters in Kabul . . . the shooter was an Afghan policewoman, who had been on the job for two years. It took him several minutes to get a ringtone, he had to battle a lot of numbers, and then Dana picked up and gave the phone to Liesel, but it was hard for her to hear. Everyone was just sitting down to lunch (Texas is an hour earlier), there was a lot of noise . . . and Liesel, across all the miles, said, "Is Judith there now?" and he started trying to describe her, the way she was taking it all, but stopped, because it wasn't the kind of thing you could explain without meanness, and he didn't want to.

———

After lunch, Paul said to Liesel, "Do you think we can see a doctor today? I wanted to get Cal checked out."

"Don't you have a doctor?"

"This is not one of the things I've dealt with yet."

She stood up from the table. Clémence was already clearing up, and Nathan had started making some counter space for himself. He had complicated plans that required a lot of room; his cooking was always something of an operation. Ben and Julie were old enough by this point they were expected to bring their dishes to the dishwasher, but they needed chivvying, Ben especially. Clémence said, "I don't know what to keep and what to throw away, I don't know the Essinger algorithm."

"Bill's not here," Paul said. "Throw everything away."

"I'll deal with it." Susie was shifting containers in the fridge. "My kids like rice, it's an easy meal."

Willy and Margot had run into the yard.

Liesel said, "Come to my study. I need to look up the number." And Paul followed her.

"*Armes Kind. Wo tut es weh?*" she asked, making her way slowly through the house, out of the kitchen and into the corridor, past the stairs and through the living room, where the winter sunshine, broken up by pyracantha leaves, left footprints on the rug. *Poor kid, where does it hurt?* She opened the sliding doors to her study and sat down at her desk, which faced the back of the yard. Willy was running in the grass, under the mild blue skies. He carried something in his hand, and Margot followed him in an attitude of complaint or protest, dragging her feet and waiting for him to stop. He stopped and then she started toward him, and Liesel lifted the lid of her computer. She pushed the mouse around, with an impatient and strangely touching gesture, to wake it up, and Willy ran away.

"He says his ear. I figure we may as well get it checked out."

"I think I left my glasses in the kitchen. On the windowsill over the sink, maybe. Bill always tells me to put them in the same place." And Paul went to get them, feeling childish.

For a moment, when she looked at the screen, she remembered the work she needed to get done, one of her jobs for the day: transcribing the rest of the letters her brother had sent her. Mostly from her parents to each other, when they were separated toward the end of the war. Her mother took the kids to Berlin, to an uncle's apartment, while her father stayed at the front in Gotenhafen—now Gdynia, waiting for the Russian assault. But she was thinking about her brother for other reasons. His wife had died; he was living alone, and the last time she saw him, in July (every summer Liesel returned to her childhood home in northern Germany), he looked very thin. He looked, in fact, like Paul, and for some reason the resemblance struck Liesel with particular force as Paul came back and said, "They weren't on the windowsill. I found them in the big bowl with all the other crap."

"Somebody must have moved them there," Liesel said, putting them on.

She searched her desktop for the folder containing contact details and other necessary information, peering through bifocals at a certain comfortable distance from the screen. Liesel had never learned to type, and Paul felt, watching her, what he sometimes felt with Cal— that he had to be deliberately patient. She tapped one finger at a time and used the arrows to move the cursor up and down, but she found the number in the end and took up the phone on her desk to dial it. The clinic had an office on Far West Boulevard that was open till eight. It's pretty quiet today if you just want to show up. Shouldn't have to wait more than half an hour.

"Do you know where that is?" she asked.

"I can find it. We'll go now."

Dana was still rinsing dishes when Paul came into the kitchen, but she was almost done, and Paul went into the TV room to get Cal. "Come on, Buddy," he said, "we're gonna get you checked out," and when he bent down to lift his son from the sofa, Cal didn't resist. But his neck felt hot against Paul's neck, as he carried him to the car. Dana took along a sippy cup of water and a few books. Both of them felt a sense of occupying familiar roles, and a kind of shyness or uncertainty about resuming them.

Paul was parked in the road; it wasn't easy getting the key out of his pocket, with the boy in his arms, but he managed to squeeze a free hand into his jeans. Dana opened the backseat door, and Paul, carefully, bent over to deposit his son in the car seat.

"Where are we going?" Cal asked.

"To the doctor."

"Can we park there?" he said.

"There's plenty of parking."

Dana wanted to climb in back, to sit next to her son and make him drink a little water, but Paul said, "He's fine, he's used to it," and for some reason she gave in. There's never any traffic on Wheeler Street, just the odd car, and driving along is like driving into a postcard of a residential American neighborhood, under the arch of trees and the winter sky, everything quiet, everything happening behind closed doors. At the same time Paul was aware of Dana's legs. She was a woman who could still get away with wearing shorts, and in Texas, on her weird Christmas holiday, in the sunshine . . . she let herself show off a little bit. Partly just for something to say, Paul asked her: "Have you heard from your parents?"

"What do you mean?"

"I mean, how are they?"

"My mother has discovered Instagram," Dana said. This was a line she had recently used with friends, on the phone and in person, half a complaint and partly a confession, to describe what her relationship with her mother was like. It surprised her now that she was using it on Paul, but she kept going anyway. "She takes pictures of restaurant food, because that's pretty much all she eats. If you ask me how she is I can tell you what she had for dinner last night."

"I thought they were on a cruise."

"They're on a cruise that has like seven different restaurants. She thinks . . . she thinks this is a way of communicating with me, because, you know, *I* do photography, too."

Paul, driving, slightly distracted, was turning on to 35th Street and passing the clinic where he used to get allergy shots as a teenager. There was a bridge over the road, a passageway between two Eighties office blocks, clad in that synthetic material that looks like cardboard for grown-ups. Its windows were tinted brown. Whenever he drove underneath it some voice in his head, maybe Bill's, maybe his own younger voice, making a joke for Bill, said *Bridge of Sighs*. It was Bill who took him each week to get his shots, sat with him in the waiting room and then in the nurse's office and watched the needle go in. Just one of those stupid things you endure as a kid, and now his own kid was in the back seat, on his way to the doctor. "How are the photographs?" he asked, to keep the conversation going.

"I don't know, she eats a lot of fancy salad. Sometimes I get to see what my dad eats, too. Mostly steak, and . . . manly seafood, the stuff you have to kind of break into. He was always trying to get me to eat that stuff growing up. For some reason, it was like a big deal to him, and because I was Daddy's little girl, I always . . . I don't know. Learned how to use a lobster cracker. You know what my parents are like, they're conventional people. I don't mean that in a . . . because of course they're actually fairly weird and don't even know it. Or maybe they know it. Maybe that's what . . . conventional probably isn't the right word, people who belong to the kind of social class where you don't have to worry if you belong or not."

"They must think it's pretty weird your . . ."

"I don't know what they think, about any of this. But you cannot underestimate their capacity to accept everything as normal. Especially my mother's. You know what she said when I dropped out of Amherst."

"I know what she said."

"She said, where are you going to live, you're not living with us. So I told her, Michael's apartment, you know, 83rd and Central Park West, and she said . . ."

"That's a good address."

"Right, so in this case . . . I don't know what she thinks." But she was losing steam and wanted to keep it going, whatever vein of intimacy she had tapped ran deeper than this. Though she also realized there was something impersonal about it, her tone of voice, she could have used it with any of her girlfriends, and so she said, changing tack, "It's good to get out of the house. Everybody just kind of sits around." But maybe this sounded more critical than she meant it to, and she added before he could respond, "I think Henrik has asked Jean to marry him."

He was merging onto Mopac, rising along the access ramp and turning the corner, joining the flow of cars. There were neighborhoods receding below him on one side, and on the other Camp Mabry rolled along—the old Air Force base, part of which had been turned into a museum. Airplanes parked along an open green, old tanks and rocket launchers, and he said, without thinking, "Cal would probably like that, we could take him if you . . . I don't know when it opens after Christmas."

"What?"

"Camp Mabry. You get to climb on airplanes. That kind of thing. I can't remember how long you're around for."

"I fly back on the twenty-eighth."

"In that case, I can take him after . . ." but he let the thought drift away. Mopac runs through west Austin, and the view of the city it offers is spaced-out and suburban, especially as you go farther north. The treescape from the streets below rises to the level of the freeway, it's like driving through clouds or skimming a forest, but there are also malls and office buildings on the high side, blue-glass-fronted, computer-generated. Shopping plazas, new apartments. The wide grassy verge has a half-constructed feel, piles of dirt and pebble line the roadside, orange cones, dump trucks. Traffic is never too bad, there seems no danger of running out of room, and Paul always kind of liked taking Mopac (the only highway Liesel was still willing to navigate). It gave you a sense of Austin as a place where history is not particularly a burden. He was looking out for the exit sign, Far West Blvd., and said to Dana, "Did she say something to you?"

"Who? What?"

"Jean, about Henrik."

"In so many words. We went for a drink last night, and she . . . gave me the impression that . . ."

"They're not getting married," Paul said, signaling and pulling onto the exit ramp.

"Why not?"

"This is not how we do things. She would tell me . . . but anyway, this is not how we do things."

He drove, braking gradually up to the bridge, and signaled again.

"I think you're making some kind of judgment about her, which I don't understand." Dana's voice had changed, her tone was different, she was annoyed but also dimly aware that a layer of friendliness like skin had broken, and that what lay underneath counted more.

The light turned, and Paul turned with it, crossing over the highway and getting a glimpse of the old train line underneath, which the highway had been built along, tracks rusting in rising grass, and Austin itself spreading into the distance, flat and green, a map of roads like veins across a hand, people with places to go, taking their cars to get there, and he entered the relative quiet on the other side, business developments and parking lots, and wide empty streets circling and cutting through them. When he pulled into the clinic, there were only a few other cars in the lot, and Paul turned around in his seat to say, "Nothing to worry about," but Cal was asleep. Dana said she'd wait with him until he woke up or the doctor was ready to see him, so Paul got out of the car and closed the door quietly. Dana, surprisingly angry, calmed down by looking at her son.

It was almost hot, sunshine reflected off the pale asphalt of the parking lot, and Paul felt the sweat in his armpits as he walked into the clinic. A beige and brown Seventies building, single-storied, with automatic glass doors that didn't seem to work, he had to push them open. The wide empty lobby was paved in marble tiles; there were chairs arranged along one of the walls, and a little Christmas tree, about three feet high, draped in spangles and lights, standing on a side table. Someone had pinned a wreath of plastic mistletoe to the ceiling, which was made up of those dimpled and gritted squares of material you stare at from the dentist's chair. A few other people sat around, waiting, including a middle-aged couple with their teenage son. He had blond hair and braces; his mother was reading something on her phone, while the dad, in a Members Only jacket, watched the tree lights blinking on and off. So the long day wore on. A few seats away, a mother and her daughter spoke quietly in Spanish; the daughter had a baby on her lap. Paul went up to reception and gave his name and Cal's name. The woman at the desk handed him a clipboard with some forms to fill out and, turning around, said to a guy sitting down and changing his shoes at the back, "If she does that again, this is what you should do . . . no wait, I'm *serious*, this is what you do . . ."

but she was laughing. Paul retreated to one of the empty chairs. There was a clock on the wall that showed a quarter to three. He wrote his name and Cal's name and took out his wallet to check the insurance details, and wrote them down and felt fine.

Something had loosened in him, after talking to Nathan. Just saying what he said had produced a reaction, a movement away from whatever point he had been trying to get across. Nothing seems very true after you say it, and when Dana came in, a few minutes later, holding Cal's hand—he seemed okay, he looked pink and unhappy but not floppy or weak—Paul took out a quarter from his wallet and hid it in his palm.

"Hey, Buddy," he said. "Which hand?"

Dana said, "I haven't locked the car."

"That one."

And Paul opened his palm and showed the silver coin.

"I was right."

"You were right. It doesn't matter. Nobody's here, nobody's going to take it."

"I just thought I'd say."

"Should I do it again?" Paul asked.

"I've also brought your books along. Do you want to read one of your books?" and Dana sat down and pulled Cal onto her lap, and that's what they did. Paul got up to return the forms and when he came back, he said, "So what did she say?"

But Dana was reading. "Whose mouse are you?" she read. Cal looked at the picture and turned the page.

"Nobody's mouse," he said.

"Where is your mother?"

"Inside the cat," and he turned the page again. It was a game they played, but Dana was also showing off. She didn't know if Paul knew he could do this. While he was in Texas, doing whatever he did, she was watching this—making it happen.

"So what did Jean say?" he asked, when they were finished.

"About what?"

"About Henrik, about getting married."

"It wasn't exactly what she said, it was more like . . . She said she was good-looking enough."

"What does that mean?"

"She said, it's done the job, or something like that. Like she didn't need it anymore, it's done the job."

"What has?"

"Her attractiveness or whatever. That's why I thought, because, if Henrik has asked her . . . at least, that's how I interpreted it."

"I don't really know what you're talking about."

"There was this guy there, giving us a hard time. He was just stupid and drunk, and Jean, anyway, she really turned on him. She really got mad. Which kind of put an end to the conversation." But she was also aware of keeping something back, something else they were talking about, and for the first time making the connection in her thoughts (why Jean got mad, what she was upset about, what Dana had told her), she felt a sudden softening, too, toward Paul—almost for Jean's sake. The way the whole family expected . . . or wanted . . . for each other . . . To be included in that network of anxieties and affections had always been something she kicked against and felt comforted by at the same time. So that when Paul said, "Maybe it's better if she marries him, maybe it makes the whole thing more justifiable," she realized he was giving in to her, a little, acknowledging Dana's right to have an opinion, maybe even asking her for it. Though at the same time, the terms he used, the way he phrased the thought, got on her nerves . . . Essinger legal language, applied to actual personal life, the life that people are actually living . . . so she didn't know what to say. And Paul himself, aware that talking about Jean and Henrik had some connection to their own situation, a man walking out on a marriage, even if the circumstances were totally different, even if he hadn't really walked out, it's just that she didn't follow, or whatever . . .

"I don't think she needs to justify herself," Dana said. And Paul

looked at her suddenly and couldn't tell if she was offering something, forgiveness or something, when the receptionist called out
Cal's name.

——

L iesel sat at her desk, reading her father's letters from the front.
Sometimes her own name came up. "I'm thinking of Liesel today.
We had a strawberry tort, in mess, and I remember the first time
she ate strawberries. Ennie let her pick them, her dress was covered in
juice, and afterward you scolded her . . ." Ennie was her first nanny.
With the laptop in front of her, and a copy of her last book serving
as a coaster for cold tea, in the study of her big old Southern Colonial, Liesel worked out that she was seven years old when he wrote
this. How deeply involved they had been in each other's lives . . . and
where had all that involvement gone? What had it come to? Most
of them were dead and she herself was living so far away from these
scenes that they seemed as scaled-down and unreachable as a photograph in a snow globe.

Klaus told her when he sent the letters, "Perhaps I should have
edited them a little, the odd word or phrase confounds us when we
come upon it. But it is better to be honest—such were the times." Her
parents spent fifteen months apart; the first winter was particularly
bad. Her father wrote: "I do not believe we will win, but I do what
I can toward victory. If we don't drive the Russians out of Ober-
schlesien by March, all kinds of materials will run out. We can hold
out that long. When will I see you again? The dinner table is very
jolly—last night we ate *Königsberger Klopse*! Things are looking up . . .
they shot two deserters, and since then, discipline has improved. But
I believe, as before, the decisive stroke won't fall here. Has it fallen
elsewhere? God grant the end is sufferable."

While Liesel sat reading, various things ran through her mind. The
sunshine moving across her desk, between the slats of the blinds,

which she had lowered because, as the sun descended—the strong level light filled her eyes . . . winter warmth, a feeling of . . . having somehow landed on a benign shore, away from—all that. She could hear someone moving next door, probably Nathan, to get a bottle of wine from the armoire. Jean called after him. More and more she found that little things distracted her—the present moment or . . . Sometimes her father's letters were hard to follow. They required a knowledge of recent conversations and events, which, even if you could work out the context, seemed to have lost some of their meaning or narrative drive . . . even though, at the time, these are exactly the kinds of thing . . . poor Klaus. The last time she spoke to him on the phone they had a fight. Even at this distance (five thousand miles!) they could still get on each other's nerves. His wife had died three years ago, one of those women who serves as a kind of corrective or promissory note of her husband's qualities, because if she, whom everyone loved, loved him . . .

Since her death he had begun to retreat . . . or maybe it's truer to say that there was nothing or no one to shake him out of bad habits, which he had always had, impatience, distrust, shortness of temper, all of them consistent with other qualities, generosity, selflessness, honesty. Also, a capacity for taking small pleasures. Music, for example, cake . . . at certain hours of the day, looking out of windows, sitting in the sun . . . In one of her father's letters, he mentioned hearing a news item on the radio about a market in Flensburg where they used to go shopping together. "I almost danced," he wrote, "with surprise." Klaus had a little apartment in Hamburg, overlooking a courtyard. His daughter lived in Paris, which is where his wife came from. Why don't you move to Paris? she asked him. What would I do in Paris? he said, getting angry. Who would look after the house? He meant the house in Flensburg, which was still in the family. Several times a year he drove a few hours north to spend a week or two by the sea, and often complained about the state in which he found it. All the work he put in, while you . . . while I am here in Texas.

It's important to insulate yourself from loneliness, especially in old age. Though there is also something comforting in the thought of fighting with your brother, after all these years, as if . . . especially since you have the feeling that, over the course of your lives, that you . . . which is why, when you're young, you should make as many people as you can. Because, children . . . but she had lost her train of thought. How many more years will we come together like this, at Christmas? Nathan and Susie and Paul and Jean. And their kids . . . and husbands and wives. Or ex-wives. Can I count them on one or two hands? And when I'm dead, what will Bill do with the house? Because in some ways the house is what you have made of your life, it's the family museum. And after Bill . . . if the house is sold . . . where will they come together? Nobody will want to sell the house; nobody will want to live in it. Maybe Paul, if he has nothing else to do. But you can't live like that, in a museum. Just because it's where you grew up. You have to escape that, too, which is what I did.

There was a particularly charming letter her father sent for Klaus's birthday. He hoped it would arrive on time, and that the watch (there was a package, it was wrapped in cotton balls) had not been damaged. "You must explain to him," her father wrote (Klaus was nine years old), "that he has to wind it at night before going to bed. Tell him that since he has a watch now, it's up to him to make it to school on time." Her brother was seventy-six now, retired from the law, he had nothing to do and nowhere to go, no reason to get up in the morning. To read this letter . . . it was like stepping on a gravestone, and she remembered anyway that she still had some wrapping to do before dinner. Just a few silly presents—half the pleasure for the children was opening them, and she could hear the front door opening, and Paul and Dana coming back with Cal.

Nathan and Jean were in the kitchen, having an argument about potatoes. Giblet stock was simmering in the pot, the window over the sink had steamed up, and the room smelled of bay and juniper berry.

A heavily salted goose lay ready in the roasting pan, the oven was already going, making a kind of revving noise like a car in overdrive, but Dana (walking into the kitchen) had a funny brief feeling that the bird looked cold, in its pink skin, lying there. With half an orange sticking out of its . . . Nathan wanted to wait until the goose fat rendered to make roast potatoes—Jean had been planning on "going Dauphinoise." Otherwise, what am I doing here she said. This is your show.

"Is there anything I can do to help?" Dana asked.

"Ask the boss," Jean said.

"We're fine. What did the doctor say?"

Cal had an ear infection. It was probably viral, which meant that giving him antibiotics wouldn't do any good, but they say that every time, Dana said, and every time you give them the pills and twelve hours later they stop complaining. So she persuaded the doctor to write a prescription.

Paul, in fact, had the little white paper bag in his hand and put it on the kitchen counter. "What do you want to do," he said. "Should we give it to him in front of the TV?"

He noticed that he was deferring to Dana, but this didn't bother him. The old competitive urge to insist on his fatherly expertise had abated somewhat, he wanted to show her that he wanted to please her, that he was willing to follow her lead, especially in front of his brother, so that Nathan could see what was going on and make his own inferences. Somehow in the car, on the trip to Far West Boulevard, in the waiting room at the clinic, his sense of allegiance had shifted—the fact that Jean was there, too, that she had trusted Dana with inside information, made a difference, too.

"Do you have any strong opinions about potatoes?" Jean asked.

"Make both," and Paul said, "Come on, Buddy. You can watch a little TV."

"Is it the nice kind or the not nice?"

"Is what?"

"The medicine."

"It's the good kind," Paul said, "it makes you better," and together with Dana, walking the way you walk when you're lagging behind with a tired kid, but letting him make his own way, on his own two feet, they trailed him out of the kitchen and into the playroom.

Nathan put the bird in the oven and told Jean, "I'm going to lie down, if that's all right. I'm pretty tired. Do you mind turning down the heat after half an hour?"

"What do you want it at?"

"350."

And he walked out the backdoor onto the patio with the sun in his eyes. It lay seeming to rest on top of the treeline at the end of the long backyard. Over the tennis court, in the far corner, a billboard advertising Jose Cuervo stood at an angle—its base was planted in the patch of graveled wasteland behind the apartment building next door. Sunlight glanced off it now, the color of the tequila in the bottle, and Nathan could feel the sunlight on his skin, too, and the presence of the city around him. He was still wearing shorts and a T-shirt and stepped barefooted across the pebbled concrete to the apartment at the back. Kids were running through the yard, he could hear them and some of them were probably his—messing around in the bamboo hedge and playing in the shed, but he pulled open the sliding door and went inside. Clémence sat typing at the table under the window. She had the blinds down; the room was dark.

"Are the girls outside?" he asked her.

"I put Julie in charge, I'll go check in a minute."

He took his computer out of the suitcase and lay down on the bed. At home in Cambridge they lived in four thousand square feet, but in Austin their only private space was his old high-school bedroom, and what they called the "library" next door, which had a pool table sitting in the middle. The girls slept on mattresses under the bookshelves. Every time you walked anywhere you had to find stepping-stones of empty carpet, because everything they took with them, books, clothes, suitcases, stuffed animals, lay spread across the floor. So what you did instead was withdraw a little inside your own head. Clémence without turning around said, "It's amazing how makeshift all these local affiliates are. I'm trying to arrange for a couple of crew, but at this time of year . . ."

Nathan, while he listened, was aware of the onset of what Clémence sometimes called his dissociative episodes, which he had learned (with her help) to recognize, the way people who suffer from migraines spot the early-warning signs . . . thickness of vision, difficulty reading. But dissociative wasn't really the word. He went inward and got stuck and had a hard time climbing out. That stupid argument with Jean about the potatoes, which was really an argument about something else. But it bugged him when she called him boss. She had also sniped at him earlier when he asked Paul to come shopping. Yesterday she drove six hours to pick him up from DFW, but sometimes, when you do something nice for somebody, afterward . . . or maybe she regretted bullying him into coming and felt bad about that, too. She wanted him to meet Henrik, so he could give his approval, so he could say okay, that's fine, go ahead, but at the same time resented needing it and so she . . . Or maybe she worried that he wasn't going to give it. When these feelings struck him the world appeared slightly out of proportion, or weirdly close and distant at the same time, like images at the wrong end of a telescope, and one of the symptoms, at least this is how it felt, was a kind of super-acuity of motive perceptions—which had the effect of making him suspicious of everyone, even people he loved.

The code they had worked out between them was that he said to Clémence, *I'm feeling pretty tired, do you mind if I lie down for a minute*, and she let him opt out of the normal obligations of the household, whatever they happened to be, looking after kids, putting the shopping away, entertaining guests. One of the comforts of their marriage lay in the age difference between them—because Clémence at forty-nine was old enough to mother him a little. She turned around now and said, "Maybe you should take a nap, we got in pretty late last night."

"So did you."

"This is a vacation for me."

"You're working, too."

"I get to be the guest. You have to be . . ." But she didn't say what he had to be. "Do you want me to leave you alone?"

"Lie down with me for a minute then leave me alone," he said. So she joined him in bed, and he thought it strange, that even after all these years, where he lay in high school night after night, now she . . . With the blinds down it looked like they might be doing anything, but they both had their shoes on and she rubbed his forehead, pressing and smoothing the skin away from his brow between thumb and middle finger. Drawing the hair out of his eyes. On his back, he looked up at the ceiling fan. There was something pleasant about lying in a dark room with a sunny day outside. Though the sunlight was going, too, changing color, the planet was cooling, and eventually she said, "I'll go check on the kids. You should take a nap," but he didn't want her to leave but he let her anyway.

"I've just got an email to write," he said.

"I'm sure it can wait."

To get out of the room, you had to pull open the door and push through the blinds, which was like walking through ferns or rustling leaves, and then they settled again behind you as you closed the door. For a minute he lay there doing nothing, but then he sat up in bed and opened his computer.

Nathan had been positioning himself for the past few years to take Judge Mannheim's place on the First Circuit Court of Appeals. Now Mannheim had announced his retirement. He'd been waiting for the election results to come in, and when Obama won, he thought, okay, I can go. He was seventy-three years old, he had a house in Wellfleet. From Nathan's point of view, his timing was good. Elizabeth Warren, whom he knew pretty well from her Harvard days, was currently the senior senator from Massachusetts. Her recommendation to the president was likely to carry weight. If Ted Kennedy hadn't died, there was no way Nathan would be in the running, but he got along well with Senator Warren, who used to teach at Texas and looked out for him when he came to Cambridge. She was an old friend of Bill's old friend Judge Kirkendoll—another thing for Nathan to think about, making an appearance at the Judge's Boxing Day party, which nobody else in the family would want to go to.

Someone from the Justice Department had already gotten in touch. A guy named Michael Labro, whom he used to clerk with. They spent a summer fifteen years ago running through their *per diems* at various high-end Manhattan restaurants, but at this stage in their careers these conversations acquire a formal quality—it's amazing the way you learn to talk. It doesn't even involve a special effort. Nathan took the phone call at home, in his Cambridge study, which looked out on the yard (the wooden swing set had leaves stuck to the seat; the grass had grown too long and was now too wet to mow), and answered calmly and afterward went down to tell Clémence. She was in the kitchen. His method of expressing strong emotion was to speak matter-of-factly, and he told her, "Look, I don't want anyone to know, not even Bill and Liesel." It was still early days, they were at the vetting stage, and the next thing he did was return to his study and draft a letter explaining his medical situation. He worked into the dark, concentrating completely in the small arc of the desk-lamp light, and in the morning showed it to his dean, who was aware of his condition.

Two and a half years ago, Nathan had suffered an attack of optic neuritis, an inflammation of the optic nerve. Basically, he woke up blind one morning. There was also numbness in his legs, and his doctor sent him for an MRI. The results were good, in the top ten, fifteen percent of expectation, and at the moment he was still operating under a diagnosis of what they called CIS—a clinically isolated syndrome, which is almost always a precursor or in fact the first instance

of the onset of multiple sclerosis. Since then, on the advice of experts
at the Mellen Center in Cleveland, he had been taking preventative
medication, Avonex, which he or Clémence injected into his thigh
once a week. There had been no relapse. At least, nothing symptom-
atic, but this is partly why he didn't like driving at night or putting
himself through any unusual stress, of the avoidable kind.

He hesitated for twenty-four hours whether to send the email and
then sent it. He might have printed and mailed it in but decided that
it was wiser to leave an electronic trail, in case at any point in the
future questions arose about full disclosure. So he pressed send and
eventually received a courteous response. Now he was just waiting.
Presumably there were people checking his background, interview-
ing old colleagues and professors (his doctors, too, probably), reading his articles and even, where they could get their hands on them,
his student essays. Nobody talked to him about any of this; he didn't
talk to anybody else. It was like trying to ignore a mosquito in the
room, and get some sleep . . .

Meanwhile, he wanted to stay out of trouble. Some of his students
had written a petition about Sandy Hook, and asked him to sign it.
This was the email he was supposed to respond to, which he'd been
putting off. *Dear Professor Essinger, Please find attached* . . . The
petition contained various legal arguments about the right to bear
arms, and Nathan was reluctant to get his name in the papers, fighting
a fight that seemed to him almost completely hopeless, and therefore
pointless, when he might have his own fights to fight at the Senate
nomination in a few months' time. Also, he felt uncomfortable putting other people's words in his mouth, petitions are a clumsy form
of argument. But several of his colleagues had already signed, it might
look awkward for Nathan to refuse. He had a good relationship with
his students; he didn't want to spoil that either. Because there was
also a danger in pissing off the left, he didn't like either of his options, and so, like Buridan's ass, he sat up in bed and did nothing, he
scrolled through his emails.

There'd been another attack in Afghanistan. An editor from the *New York Times* had gotten in touch, to ask him if he wanted to write an Op-ed about it. His message included a link to the story on CNN. Somehow Nathan had become the go-to guy for talking about the line between state and non-state actors in conflict zones. One of his articles had been cited by the Obama administration to justify its use of drone strikes against US citizens abroad without judicial process. This was something else he worried about, in the confirmation hearings. Nathan's own views were much more equivocal, but he had argued that the law, and not just the law, but legal culture, the long-established and complicated traditions of the law, the kind of formal training lawyers have to go through, which is still regulated, controlled by academics, defended by tenure . . . remained the best defense against abuses of state power. It's a question of what kind of people get to make the decisions, which also means, counterintuitively, that lawyers have to be willing to get their hands dirty, they have to be willing to get serious and involved—otherwise you surrender the field to CIA-types, private contractors and ex-military . . . but he didn't want to go over his arguments, as he listened to someone crying in the backyard.

In general, whenever possible, his policy had been to push his public pronouncements as far to the right as he was intellectually willing to. Or rather, to pick his topics carefully. Only Clémence knew his reasons, she was the only one he talked to about the fact that in the long run . . . what he was building toward . . . he felt foolish even articulating such ambitions, which somehow sound childish, like wanting to be president, and partly because . . . If you're going to play this game, you have to play it. You can't write something and not believe it, and if you believe it, what's there to confess? Or who should he confess to? Bill? But it also meant that his marriage had a kind of privileged intimacy, which made him feel more dependent on Clémence, in a way that he basically liked and approved of, because it meant . . . but it also cut him off from other people. These arguments, which he had almost daily with himself, the kind of arguments you have in your head to prepare for the moment when you have them with other people, were now overlaid with other reflections. Paul, and what he said about girls . . . Jean and Henrik . . . the arguments you have to win with other people, which it's your job to win, as their brother. At the same time, he remembered walking over the mountains in the DR, from one village to the next, eating what people cooked, but now because a woman had shot a man in Kabul, at Police Headquarters, after two years of US-sponsored training, he was supposed to have an intelligent opinion, and the reason he needed this opinion was so that he could defend his other intelligent opinions.

The man was a civilian contractor, who worked for SimCorp, one of these hybrid outfits, a private company doing government work — over ninety percent of their revenues came from taxpayer money, and their boards were filled with former Department of Defense officials. Among other things, they supplied and operated drones for American crop-spraying programs in Ecuador (part of the war on drugs), where Karen Heinz had spent the summer a year before he met her. Farmers had filed a class action suit against them, alleging widespread medical "collateral damage" — ten years later the case was still ongoing. Public and private interests had become almost impossible to disentangle. CNN didn't say much about the shooter, except that she was forty years old. The dead man came from Mansfield, Georgia. "A woman who answered the phone at his house said she had no comment," and for some reason this line suggested instead a phone continuing to ring . . . and when he woke up Jean was standing in the dark room.

It was the noise of shifting blinds that woke him, and Jean said, looking at him tenderly, "I've strained off the goose fat but I figured you probably had some idea about what you want to do with it." And then, after a moment, "Clémence said it was okay to get you. They've all gone to look at the lights."

"So it's just you and me," Nathan said, sitting up.

—

Dana put Cal in his stroller and figured, if he falls asleep, that's fine, he can sleep. She would have put him to bed but it was Christmas Eve, when the Essingers gave out presents, and she didn't want him to miss out. For much of her childhood she ate Christmas dinner alone with her parents and Granma Mamie, her mother's mother, who was divorced—Grampa Jack had remarried shortly after and nobody got along with his second wife. Her father had more or less lost contact with his own family. His parents lived in Annapolis and sometimes sent her a birthday card. There was also an uncle in LA but they never saw him. She wanted Cal for once at least to feel part of a crowd—maybe it was his last chance.

The house had a little portico outside the entrance, with four or five steps leading to the driveway. Paul offered to carry the stroller but she bumped it down slowly and even before they reached the sidewalk Cal had shut his eyes and turned his head against the little triangle of rayon or plastic or whatever it was called between the upright and horizontal bars of the Maclaren. She bent over and tucked the blanket around his neck. It always surprised her when the sun went down, how cold it got in Texas, especially on a clear night. The stars seemed close and the sky didn't offer much protection—if Paul had put his arm around her, for warmth, she wouldn't have minded, but he was walking the way he usually walked in his old neighborhood, in the middle of the road because the streets were quiet enough it didn't matter.

Wheeler Street T-junctioned at a park, or really just a field with a creek cutting through it, and the kids crossed over and ran through the grass toward the water. "Don't go too close," Susie said. There was a drop of five feet from the field to the creek bed; limestone walls had been built to hold it in. Sometimes, in summer, during a flash flood, the water level rose two or three feet an hour, but now on a cold night after a dry December the current was more like a long thin irregular puddle edged with slime and reeds. Ben had the two younger kids in tow and was telling jokes or stories while Julie slightly resentfully and feeling left out went over in the dark to hold her mother's hand.

Clémence gave her a squeeze of vague sympathy. She had been thinking, maybe I should knock on a few doors tonight and talk to a few people, just to get a sense of what I'm talking about. But she didn't want to annoy Liesel, with whom she had a friendly but also slightly formal relationship. She was aware of Liesel as someone who held strong and not always entirely consistent opinions—you could never tell what she might find annoying. In general, Clémence got along well with her in-laws and genuinely liked them, too, though at the same time she felt that their level of interdependence was not entirely a source of comfort and joy to Nathan. He seemed to bear more of the responsibility and receive less of the sympathy than the others, so that when he came home and entered again into all of these slightly intense relationships . . .

Of course, her family had its own craziness. Her mother and sister lived on the same street in Montreal, which meant that most of what she heard from each of them was complaints about the other. Her theory was, listen to everybody but don't pay too much attention. She said to Nathan, not all of these problems are your problems anymore. But that's how he took it. While for her it was easy enough to treat the Essingers as what they basically were, nice, interesting people, who, if you met them at a party . . . so that's how she treated them.

Liesel said, "*Es tut mir Leid, Kinder*," and then, in English, "I'm sorry, I can't keep up. I don't see so well in the dark," and Susie, who was walking with May asleep on her breast, strapped in the Baby-Björn, slowed down and took her arm. Clémence fell back, too, and Liesel said to Julie, "What did you to today? I sit at my desk and don't get anything done, and I don't even see anybody, I just sit there."

"We played in the playhouse," Julie said.

They had come to the end of the park, and the road passed dark-ly between two large houses—there was no sidewalk and everyone walked on the asphalt, including Dana, pushing the stroller, while David went ahead to catch up with Paul. The house on the other side of the road had boarded-up windows. It used to be very grand and still had an air of faded good times, cocktail parties and piano lessons, the sort of house where the girls in the family learn to ride, whitewashed brick, peaked roof, a large plot of lawn, and Paul said, "Susie's best friend lived there, Chantal Breuer. She was the only other Jewish kid in the neighborhood. When I was seven they used to make me pass notes between them—I mean, between the houses. They called me the Messenger, I think they even dressed me up. May-be I was a little older."

"You have obviously suffered a great deal," David said.

"I rode my bike."

"Did you read the notes?"

"No, they were just . . . I'm pretty sure they were just . . . that wasn't really the point. But I didn't read them."

"Do you know what the playhouse was originally?" Liesel asked Julie.

"A playhouse?"

Liesel couldn't read her tone, whether she wanted to hear or not, but went on anyway. "The old lady who sold us the house was a widow—she had been living alone for a long time. It was her servant who lived in the playhouse. His name was Mosby, I don't know his first name."

"Why didn't he live in the house?" Julie asked.

"He was . . . this is a difficult question to answer. He was black, and the old lady . . ."

"I don't understand."

"The truth is, I don't really understand it myself. But at that time, in Texas . . ."

"What does it matter, if he was black?"

"It doesn't matter to me, but at that time . . . it's possible he wouldn't have wanted to sleep in the house. He might not have felt comfortable."

"Of course he wanted to sleep in the house," Julie said. "I mean, the playhouse, it's like . . . there's no water . . . there's no—he must have been cold."

"You forget that in Texas for most of the year it's too hot."

"Then he would have been too hot."

"But in those days nobody had air-conditioning anyway. And the playhouse was always very cool. It has the pecan tree standing over it, and a room that size, if you open the windows and the door . . ."

"I'm sorry, Liesel, but this is . . . I don't even think you believe what you're saying."

She was almost as tall as her grandmother now, and with her short hair, in the dark, she looked like a woman, too. Her voice had changed, you could still hear her father in it, but somehow that mattered less—it didn't seem like an imitation anymore. After a while, after you grow up, it doesn't matter what the influences are, you're stuck with them. And Liesel could have the same fights with her that she had with Nathan.

"There are other reasons he might have felt uncomfortable. I mean, for his sake, too. Because if people knew that he was living in the house with a white woman, it could have made his life very difficult."

"But that's what I mean. That's what I'm saying."

"What interests me, about all this, is the way that people, in spite of terrible . . . somehow at the same time they manage to maintain . . . When she died, I mean the old woman—I never knew her of course, because we bought the house only afterward. But Dodie, the lady across the road, knew her, she used to tell me stories. When she died he was sitting with her. She had bowel cancer, which is also what my mother died of, and it can be very painful toward the end, the doctors give you morphine, mostly you just sleep, you don't really know what's going on. But he sat with her anyway. The doctor had told him she might not last the night and . . ."

"Of course he sat with her. That's what she paid him to do."

"I don't think she paid him very much."

"Liesel, you're not making any sense. Are you trying to say that he was like her slave and so . . ."

"You have to understand that when I first came here, I mean to Texas, all of this was strange to me. None of it made sense. I could see that something terrible had been happening for a long time. But eventually I also learned, that in spite of everything, people as human beings sometimes . . ."

"I don't think I can have this conversation with you," Julie said, and Clémence told her, "Enough, okay? That's not the tone you take with your grandmother."

"I'm not taking a tone, I'm making an argument."

"Your argument has a tone."

"I'm sorry if you don't like the way I *sound*." And she walked off in the direction of her uncles, who were talking quietly in the middle of the road.

"And I suppose eventually," David said, "you developed a terrific crush on Chantal Breuer. This was the real point of the game."

"You think that was the point? I don't know. For me I just liked . . . you know, being made use of, when you're a little kid, by older kids. It's hard for me to exaggerate the excitement of getting on my bike with an actual message. Also, I liked doing stuff for Susie, she was a good big sister. But I liked Chantal, too. She had red hair, I guess she was a little heavy, she was pretty, too. Maybe I did, I don't know."

"*Mais où sont les* Chantal Breuers *d'antan*?"

"Portland, I think. Susie would know."

"What are you talking about?" Julie asked, coming up behind them.

"Girls," one of them said, and Julie felt a little shadow of exclusion fall across her, or something else maybe, as if she was being included in a conversation she didn't want to be included in, as a certain kind of outsider to it, which was maybe the same thing. Or disappointment, that even in her family . . . but it had taken her a modest dose

of courage to leave one conversation, the way she had, especially after her mother's intervention, and enter another with two grown-up
men. She didn't want to pick another fight so didn't say anything.

They turned right on 34th Street and then left on one of those little
side alleys that still exist in Austin, in spite of all the overdevelopment,
just a narrow track of broken asphalt bordered by backyards and
chain-link fences. There were houses people had been living in since
before the property boom—with peeling clapboard, sunken roofs,
furniture in the yard and air-conditioning units bulging and dripping
from the windows. At the corner lights started to appear, strung from
balcony to doorway, and lining the trees, and even stretched across
the surfaces of unused cars, sitting in the driveway with garbage cans.
Someone had threaded little bulbs in and out of the wheels and frame
of a bicycle, which rested like any bicycle on the front porch, underneath the front window, but also looked like a constellation of a
bicycle, a geometric arrangement of stars. Susie caught up with Dana
and said, "I guess we got two sleepers," and Dana, turning around,
glanced at May, at the awkward angle of her head as it lay against her
mother's breast (or the bony space beneath her clavicle), the cheeks
squished, that look of concentrated sleep, and said, "Yours keeps you
warm at least."

"How's he doing?"

And Paul, walking back toward them now, his face visible in the
reflected glitter, said to Dana, "It's like the Fourth of July out here,"
and she knew what he meant. The whole length of 37th Street, from
Home Lane to Guadalupe, was decked out in lights. You could almost hear the kilowatts ticking over and the bills running up. When
they first started going out, about five months into their relationship,
Dana got invited to the big Fourth of July party at Condé Nast—
in one of those skyscrapers rising out of the mess of Times Square,
above the fray. Paul had just come back from Wimbledon, where he
had lost in the first round, and was still feeling jet-lagged and anti-
social. Making plans around tournament time was always difficult,

you never knew how long you'd be out of action, so he tended to require the girlfriends in his life, if he was at all serious about them, to be willing to shut down their social calendars at the same time he did. But it was early days with Dana and when he lost she managed to get him another ticket to the party, which he didn't want. They had a fight at her apartment, while he waited for her to get dressed, and kept it going in the taxi afterward, but she felt it somehow important at this stage to maintain at least the surface obligations of her own life, because in the past, when she got caught up with some guy, she had a tendency to . . . but the truth is, she didn't really want to go either.

There was a line at security as they waited to get in, and then another outside the elevator, and the whole time Paul, in actually kind of a friendly voice, kept saying, "Let's just get out of here, I'm hungry. Let's get some pizza," and Dana answered, "We're here now, let's just . . ." and he said, "What's here, we're waiting in a line . . ." but the line moved on, and they were pulled along with it, into the elevator and up.

Waitresses in little black dresses handed them champagne as they stepped out, and Dana said, "Look, isn't this . . ." and drank and felt the bubbles rising in her nose, the heat of people, the noise, the view around them of the floor-to-ceiling windows, all of this got her blood racing, because she looked good and didn't mind feeling the effects of it once in a while. But the whole time Paul stood around waiting for her to finish her conversations. He didn't know anyone there, and trying to get him to join in was like pulling teeth . . . so whereas before she felt mildly sympathetic and ambivalent herself, after ten or fifteen minutes something cool and polished in her personality, which she had access to and had probably inherited from her mother, took over, and she started to enjoy herself. I mean, fuck him. So that when the fireworks started (even at that height, you could hear the faint percussion) and bloomed against the windows, with Manhattan itself lit up around her, and spread out underneath, the dark stain of Central Park, the ridiculous neon traffic-jam of Times Square, she let her natural appetite for glamour and extravagance and . . . feeling like, this is where the action is, this is where people want to be, here, living like this . . . express itself in her reactions, until he said, "Oh for God's sake you don't have to pretend to like it just to piss me off . . ." And because part of what she wanted was to be there with him, the tears in her eyes changed meaning almost instantly, though what he meant by referring to this now, years later, if by way of apology or something else, she couldn't tell. But she said anyway, just to show she got the reference, "Isn't it the most beautiful thing you've ever seen . . ." and felt like she was giving in to him again.

Jean and Nathan worked hard to get the dinner ready before everyone came back. Liesel had already set the table—Paul carried the trestles in from the garage apartment, to extend it, and they laid two cloths over the whole thing, which was almost ten feet long now and could seat twelve people comfortably enough, with two kids at each end. This was fine, so long as May didn't eat (her high chair took up a lot of room) and Cal stayed asleep or sat on somebody's lap. The good china lived in the armoire next to Liesel's study, where they also kept the wine. It was a wedding present and part of what Liesel thought about every time she brought it out was how her tastes had changed, because this is what she had asked for from her mother forty-odd years ago: a set of Royal Bavarian Hutschenreuther dinnerware, birds and flowers on pale white porcelain, with a blue rim. None of her kids would want to inherit it, but still she brought it out on special occasions.

The goose was done and sitting in its tray, draining fat, and Nathan had turned up the heat on the roast potatoes. Jean kept running back and forth to the garage apartment, which Nathan and his family were sleeping in. It had its own kitchen and another oven, where her Dauphinoise potatoes had started to brown nicely. (As soon as he woke up, she put them in.) She didn't want the cream to split, but it was an old oven and the temperature was hard to predict or control. Jean was also in charge of the vegetarian stuffing and every time she carried something from one kitchen to the other, she had to go through the sliding door and into the cool night air, under the starry sky, then up the back steps and past the screen (pulling at it with a loose finger, propping it open with her butt) and through the backdoor . . . Her face had gone red with concentration and worry, she kept drying her hands on her apron, and the flesh around her fingernails looked scuffed or abraded. In general she was a high-frequency Purell-using kind of girl, and since Henrik's illness, keeping her hands germ-free had become a mild obsession. When she cooked she washed them constantly.

She had seven or eight things on her mind, she was running back and forth, but there were also moments when they both just stood around in the kitchen waiting for the next bell to ding. In one of them Nathan said to her, "When's Henrik getting in?" and she said, "Boxing Day. He's taking the BA flight, which gets in around four. He's asked me to marry him, when the divorce comes through."

"What did you say?"

"I said, let's wait until you meet my family."

"Are you trying to put him off?" Nathan said.

For the past hour, ever since Jean woke him up, he had felt vaguely underwater, in the depths of something, or the grips of something, but this pulled him to the surface. He needed to concentrate; he needed to think this through.

"I don't know. Maybe. I want him to . . . maybe I'm looking for a second opinion. It still feels like . . . I'm thirty-two years old, but it still feels like . . . I need a note from home to skip school."

"This isn't skipping school."

"I know what it is," she said.

"What's going to happen with his kids?"

"Nothing different. The current arrangement is Wednesdays and every other weekend. That's what we've been doing."

"Does he want more kids? Is that something you want? Is that something you've talked about?"

"We've talked about it. My answer is yes. His answer isn't exactly . . . definitive, at least not yet. He says it's something he's willing to think about."

"Because in my experience that's something he needs to think about now."

"Of course he thinks about it. Of course we talk about it, Nathan. I mean, but give the guy a break, right. I'm not exactly in a position to push him. He's just gone through chemo, he's just coming through a divorce . . ."

"That's exactly the position you're in."

"Sometimes if you push these things you make people give you a definite answer when the answer isn't really definite."

They could hear the front door opening, down the hall, somebody running up the stairs, and Susie calling out, "My kids at least need to wash their hands." Nathan bent down to check on the potatoes—he could feel the blast of heat against his face, then lifted the pan out using a couple of dish towels and set it at an angle across the burners. The smell of garlic and rosemary filled the kitchen, and he took a wooden spatula and scraped at the potatoes to loosen them from the metal.

"You're hoping for something that you basically know isn't going to happen."

"I'm hoping," she said, and turned off the oven, "but I don't know," and Liesel came in, with her eyes bright from the exercise. "*Sag mal, Kinder, dass sieht Klasse aus . . .*" and then, in English, "Do I have time to get changed?"

"I have time to get changed," Nathan told her, "but I don't know if you do."

"Well, I'll be quick," she said, and Jean added, "I have to take the other potatoes out anyway."

She followed her brother out the backdoor and he said to her, "Look, I'm not trying to give you a hard time."

"So don't give me a hard time." She left the sliding door open behind her and walked past him into the library to the kitchen at the other end. Then she took the stuffing out and came back. "This'll take two trips," she said.

"You're letting the cold air in."

"Well, then, you can take the other potatoes over. I want to make myself look pretty anyway."

"You are pretty," he said, but it was a stupid thing to say, and he knew it, though it didn't matter much. They looked at each other for a moment, as she stood in the doorway with the dish in her hands. "I'm Marilyn Monroe," she said and when she left he pulled the door closed.

Susie wore her wedding dress, which she could still fit into. It wasn't anything fancy or white, but just the kind of pretty dress you wear to a party, though more expensive—from Saks Fifth Avenue. She said to David, when they were working out wedding details, I'm going to get the dress from Saks and you're not going to ask me how much it cost. But her tastes were modest, and what she wanted was something she could continue to wear, so that afterward what she ended up concealing from him was how reasonable the price was . . . and she thought, the secrets of marriage.

Jean put on something Henrik had given her, a sheath dress covered in little spangles, squares of metal, the kind of thing she would never have worn before they started going out. She felt self-conscious in it, too tightly wrapped, on display, but it was an act of loyalty to wear it, and everybody made nice noises. Very London, Dana said, when she came down. "What does that mean?" Jean asked her, bristling slightly. "It means classy, it means fun," Dana said. "I always think, when I go to London, they're not so serious, they know how to have a good time." Dana herself wore black jeans and a simple sleeveless black top. She looked unornamented but at the same time almost stupidly lovely, long-limbed, like an athlete of prettiness, her face only faintly made-up, a bit of lipstick, to prove that she had made an effort. Nathan walked in in his suit and tie, dark suit, paisley tie, the expression on his face an expression that went with the suit, conscientious and charming, social but also a little formal, which he couldn't help. He had a part to play, especially with Bill out of the house, and began carving the goose, standing at the kitchen counter after pinning his tie between two buttons of his shirt.

Julie was the only kid who dressed up, in one of Bill's mother's dresses, conservative Jewish middle-class finery, which now looked quaint and somehow like the kind of thing a kid would wear, putting on old-lady clothes, except that Julie didn't look like a kid anymore. Underneath she had on black Doc Martens. There was a tenderness Nathan felt for her, because of their clothes and the sense of occasion, so that when she passed him in the kitchen he bent down to kiss her short hair and she leaned against him, feeling a little foolish. It was a step for her, putting on a dress; she did it to please him. Paul wore what he had been wearing all day, sneakers and jeans and a T-shirt, it wasn't his house anymore and he didn't have anything to change into.

"I didn't realize we were doing this."

"Doing what?"

"Dressing up."

"It's on a volunteer basis," Jean said.

David, big-chested, open-necked, had put on a jacket. Liesel wore her complicated silver necklace, which had many layers and strands that fell across her linen smock. Bill gave it to her, after she saw it in a market and decided she didn't deserve it, because of the price . . . but a few months later, at her birthday . . . another one of the secrets of marriage. Clémence had wrapped herself in a shawl of some kind, a vivid Moroccan blue, over a low-necked gown, which showed her dark skin. Her hair, tied back, was white and black, her face, with the forehead exposed, looked eager and pleasant. Everybody sat down. Susie lit candles and turned off the overhead light. The table, crowded with food, and the rose patterns on their grandmother's Royal Bavarian plates, the pale blue singing birds inside them, Liesel's old fine-stemmed glasses, filled with red wine (Nathan had decanted a bottle of Malbec earlier in the afternoon), tumblers of Coca-Cola for the kids, to keep them up late . . . Paul felt subtly excluded from whatever ritual was being performed, partly because of the way he was dressed, but it wasn't just that, and the feeling only grew stronger as the night wore on. He stopped drinking after one glass of wine, because he still had to make the drive back to Wimberley, and even though Jean didn't drink much either, even though Susie was still breastfeeding, a sense of constraint had crept into his relations with all of them, and Dana, somehow, seemed to be included in that constraint . . . he couldn't quite reach her.

Julie still wanted to talk about the playhouse—she couldn't believe somebody used to live in it, it made her feel . . . it made her feel like . . . "What I am, I guess. A spoiled little rich kid. A spoiled little rich *white* kid."

"None of this is your fault."

"At Granma's house, when I was little," she was doing a voice, faintly sing-song, pretending to be older and looking back, "I used to play in the shack where the slave used to live. It was *fun*."

"He wasn't a slave, he was . . ."

"I want to sleep there tonight," Julie said.

"Why do you want to sleep there?"

"I don't know, I just do. I want to see what it's like."

"I bet it's *fun*," Ben said.

"Stop it, both of you." Susie was trying to eat with May on her lap—she kept giving her spoonfuls of mashed potato and sneaking in pieces of goose. May had become suspicious, she was testing the food on her tongue, and Jean said, "She's on to you," while Susie went on, "Nobody's sleeping in the playhouse."

But Nathan disliked it when people intervened with his kids. "She can sleep in the playhouse if she wants to. It might be good for her."

"It might be cold for her," Clémence said.

"I don't want to do it because it's *good* for me."

And so on . . . Clémence tried to change the topic. She had knocked on a few doors on 37th Street, to ask about the lights, but only one woman answered, saying, "Personally I don't understand how any-body can get to sleep." It wasn't her house, she was babysitting for her daughter. "It's like living on Broadway." People walked right into the front yard, they left bottles of beer on the bench. "They ring your doorbell," she said, and looked at Clémence, but added, "I'm sorry, I'm feeling kind of pissy right now. Somebody gave my dog nuts to eat, and he hasn't been able to (*excuse me*) shit all day." She had straight gray hair and a longish face; she was wearing a TCU T-shirt with the slogan, *Fear the Frog*. "You realize something about people," she said, "when you have a dog. Other people are idiots."

"What did you say to her?" Jean asked.

"What could I say? I ran away."

Eventually they agreed that Julie could sleep in the playhouse but not tonight—it was going to get too late anyway and nobody wanted to carry a mattress out there in the dark. "I'll do it," she said but had lost steam.

When the phone rang, Liesel responded instantly, "That's Bill," and struggled to push her chair out. She had been waiting for him to call all day. She wanted to hear about Rose, but it also surprised her sometimes, when the kids came home, and brought *their* kids, and the whole house was taken over, how much she felt the need of Bill as a kind of ally, or not exactly that, but somebody who was in the same boat—putting up with all the noise and disorder, and not just the noise, but the pressure on your attention, and even on your sympa-thies, which you have to somehow distribute evenly, not just to your own children but the grandkids, too . . . Otherwise, you get blamed for it. Meanwhile, your own life is basically on hold, which nobody seems to notice. But when she reached the phone, it wasn't Bill, and for a minute she couldn't work out who it was, a voice kept saying *Hallo, Hallo?* in some confusion, almost as if she had called him, and then she realized her brother was on the line.

"*Sag mal,*" he said, almost angrily, "*ich hör garnichts, ihr seid alle zu laut.*" I can't hear a thing, you're all too loud, and Liesel turned toward the table and made a gesture with her hand. "*Seid ruhig,*" she said, channeling her brother, his tone and impatience. Be quiet. And then, in English, for the in-laws: "I can't hear."

Klaus had just gone to Midnight Mass, for Mutti's sake—to Sankt Johannis, the big gothic church in Altona, where he lived. Once a year he went, and always at Christmas, and always it was full of people. Who knew there were so many people who want to go to church; the organ is new, it makes a wonderful—noise, and since he can't hear anything anymore . . . But I can hear that. They played Haydn, the *Nikolaimesse*, Schnabel's *Transemus*, and of course Franz Gruber. All these people . . . children, too, even a few babies, but when he got home he found he couldn't sleep. It was one in the morning, and across five thousand miles of phone lines, or really much farther (they bounced the signal into the skies), Liesel could hear the loneliness in his voice, like the echo on marble tiles of a hospital corridor.

May had started spitting food on the floor and Jean got up to fetch a cloth. Cal still slept. He lay in his stroller in the doorway to the TV room, and Dana, every time she looked over to check, felt something like guilt or anxiety, about what she was doing to him, keeping him up like that, when he was ill, but also . . . Maybe she should wake him, because he was missing out, and the whole point of coming here was so that . . . Nathan said to Julie that if she wanted to knock on Dodie's door tomorrow, he would go with her. Dodie could probably tell her something about Mosby, but Susie broke in, somehow taking her son's side, that you can't knock on somebody's door on Christmas Day. Of course you can, he said, she's a lonely woman . . . She has a daughter . . . Well, there was nobody there today . . . and Clémence said in an undertone to David, who was sitting next to her, "I don't think I've said congratulations."

"You mean because I managed to drag her away from all this?"

"I mean because of the job."

Paul looked at Dana, he wanted to catch her eye, but she was saying to Ben, "The longer you can put off . . . I mean, that's something everybody always tells you, isn't it . . ." But he didn't know what they were talking about and felt a strange pang, of jealousy or . . . Because why should Ben get to sit there like that, next to her, and listen to her . . . but Willy was trying to get his attention. He said, "Uncle Paul, Uncle Paul," the repetitions of children, which never change tone, or only slightly. Even when he talked to you he kept interrupting himself to say your name. "I was—like this, and then—Dad—*Uncle Paul*—and then . . ." He was trying to say something about tennis, about playing tennis and hitting the ball, but—instead of hitting it on the front of the racket, where he was trying to hit it, he missed but on the—he couldn't explain himself—after he swung and missed, he accidentally, Uncle Paul . . . and Paul said, "That's funny," but Willy kept going anyway, he hadn't finished his story. I hit it *backward . . . behind* me and Paul said again, "That's funny," while Liesel looked on, feeling the crowded table, the noise of her life, and said to her brother, "I've been reading Father's letters . . ." because at the same time, in her brother's loneliness, she felt a kind of release or escape, a slightly cooler air communicated down the phone line, as if she sat in a draft in a stuffy room.

After supper they left the table to be cleared up later and went into the living room, where Paul lit the fire—Willy helped him. He had started to follow his uncle around and once, for example, while watching TV saw a commercial that advertised the brand of tennis racket they had been using in the backyard. It had the same logo, which he pointed out to Paul, extremely excited. *Look*, he said, *the Dunlop*—a black D squeezed into the head of an arrow. Just Dunlop, Paul corrected him, not the. It was a golf club commercial, which is maybe why Willy felt surprised, but Paul also heard in his nephew's excitement something else, that stage of childhood where you want only to please and have no real consciousness yet of failing to please . . . no real sense that something you say might be embarrassing, that you have to watch out. Though probably he got embarrassed all the time at school, and what Paul was actually hearing, almost unmediated, was the way that Willy, among his friends, might try to appeal to them and join in—as if

Paul were one of them, but somehow safer, and . . . you do what you can to teach them to protect themselves, and the rest of the time, at home . . . Anyway, he let Willy light the fire. He gave him the matches and told him where to touch the newspaper, and afterward, before the flame reached his nephew's fingers, blew it out.

Dana wheeled Cal into the living room like an invalid, or an old man. He just sat there, being present—fast asleep. Then she remembered her camera and went back to the breakfast room to get it. For the rest of the evening, when her hands were free and she wasn't singing, she took photographs, and later that night, in the dark of their room, while Cal was finally asleep in his bed, she looked them over in the glow of the digital light. Including the pictures she took of Paul, wondering what she felt about him.

Susie and Jean and Clémence lit the Christmas tree lights (*click-flash!*), because the Essingers, like good Germans, used real beeswax candles. A bucket of water stood under the tree, with a wet towel draped over the side. It always seemed to Dana a kind of craziness, to light dozens of little fires in the middle of a pine tree in the middle of your living room, but it also made her feel like her own family traditions, such as they were, grew out of shallow soil. When they were finished, Susie turned the lights off. The fire was burning brightly now, and the tree itself cast an immensely complex and strangely moving glow, made up of overlapping shadows and arcs of light, faint halos of unclarity around the candles themselves, slight movements, as the branches shifted under the changing weight of the melting wax.

Liesel in every room of the house had certain chairs she always sat in, and which were always ceded to her, whenever she walked in. In the living room, she occupied the bentwood rocker and fidgeted it around to face the tree. Ben liked to look at the fire; he sat on a stool in front of it. Susie and the rest of the kids squeezed together on the sofa. Julie wanted to sit next to May, who lay on Susie's lap, and Willy and Margot piled around them. Jean, in her spangled dress, sat up straight and uncomfortably on the fauteuil armchair, which Bill had bought in a market in Berlin and shipped over. Some of the spangles were a little loose—she didn't want the kids to jump on her.

"Should we sing?" Liesel asked, and Susie said, "Let's start with the Hanukah songs." For Bill's sake, in the spirit of raising a glass to absent friends.

By this point, even the in-laws knew many of the words, though not always what they meant. They sang *Mi Y'malel* and *Maoz Tzur* and for the kids *I have a Little Dredel* and *Hanukkah oh Hanukkah*. Dana actually had the best voice among them. She had spent five years in the choir at Sidwell Friends (the uniform was a surprisingly short brown sleeveless dress; the girls felt safety in numbers but also enjoyed the attention) and Paul was reminded listening to her that there always seemed to be something impersonal about her talents, and even her looks. Singing was just another thing she could do well, with expression and range—but you couldn't tell whether she liked it or not. Even at parties, as soon as they entered a roomful of people, he sensed her . . . not distraction exactly, but a kind of glaze would cover the surface of her face, so that he felt a little removed from her, or rather, just like any of the other guys at the party, trying to catch her eye. But he liked watching her sing.

David also joined in loudly . . . *Who can retell the things that befell us, who—can—count—them?* . . . in his slightly comic church-hall baritone. Every year in the village he grew up in the Christmas concert at St. Nicholas was the big-ticket cultural event. His mother, at the age of seventy-nine, still sang for the Brockenhurst Choir, which was practically semiprofessional. They went on tours and their conductor was Royal College-trained and, in civilian life, the Director of Music at King Edward's. One of the many ways he had disappointed his parents, he liked to say, was dropping out of the school choir. But the truth is, he enjoyed singing, and the Jewish songs moved him. Partly because of . . . various things, including the fact that both of his parents struck him as garden-variety anti-Semites, the kind of people who believe that Jews talk only about money, and to see his own children humming along to the *Maoz Tzur* . . . he put an arm around his wife.

After *Hanukkah, Oh Hanukkah*, Susie suggested *Auf dem Berge da wehet der Wind* (shrugging him off very slightly) and the singing shifted without any pause or transition into the Christmas songs of Liesel's German childhood: *Schneh Flöckchen, weiss Röckchen* and even the famous Franz Gruber . . . *The wind blows on the mountain . . . little snowflake in the little white frock . . . silent night . . .* while the candles flickered and grew still, and Liesel, listening, thought of her brother and his cold apartment, coming home after Midnight Mass. While I am surrounded, and she remembered something her mother once said, shortly before she died, when everyone came to visit her, that you should make as many people as you can, who love you. But then the kids started opening their presents and Liesel had toward the whole business the reaction she usually had but which somehow always managed to surprise her. Such excess, such wastefulness, her mother would have thought. And the way they just take it for granted . . . It also annoyed her that Dana kept taking pictures.

Jean got up in her stiff dress to turn on the overhead lamp and Nathan and Paul pinched out the candle flames. Susie let May sit on the carpet and tear at her pile of presents, which were heaped under a corner of the coffee table, and eventually Liesel pushed herself out of the bentwood chair to get a garbage bag from the laundry room. It wasn't so much an opening as an excavation. Susie tried to rescue some of the prettier paper from her daughter's clutches, smoothing it out and laying it down in a separate pile for reuse. But May was tired, it was several hours past her bedtime, and another hour later because of the time difference. There were lots of little battles being fought, and it got to the point where . . . even if you gave in to her it wasn't enough, her feelings of frustration and reproach had become too general.

Until Nathan said, "I think we need to speed things up," and Susie, still faintly in conflict with him for reasons she couldn't have articulated, responded: "In that case somebody else can deal with her," because she had been carrying May around since . . . God knows where David is . . . you would have thought, maybe, he wanted to see his . . . while she got down on hands and knees to retrieve torn sheets of wrapping paper from under the table. Clémence picked up the little girl (to compensate for Nathan's tone) and said, without total conviction, "I miss having babies in my life." But then May started crying and butting her head against her, she tore at the shawl around her neck, to pull it away. "It's no good," Clémence told her, standing up and jigging from side to side, "I haven't got any milk," in a pillow-talk kind of voice but also for public consumption, until Paul offered to take the baby off her hands. "Can I try," he said, "I never get to see her," for which she was almost grateful although she also felt like some kind of judgment had been made, especially when, against the heat of her uncle's chest, May fell asleep. Paul sang to her, the way he used to sing to Cal, in an undertone, *Who can retell the things that befell us—who—can—count—them* . . . while Dana watched and David came back from the bathroom, drying his hands on the seat of his pants.

The kids got their presents first, in order of age, so it was Cal's turn next and Dana said to Paul, "I don't want Cal to miss the whole thing," and he said, "Well, what do you want to do?"—but softer than usual, less insistent. "I want him to at least open his eyes and see it . . . I want him to have some kind of memory," and Paul, still circling, in a slow rhythm, with his face in May's soft hair, said "I've kind of got my hands full." She went over to the stroller and lifted him out. "Hey, Buddy, it's present time." "Isn't it always?" Jean said, and Cal looked out through fever-dreams and sat on Dana's lap happily enough but was otherwise unresponsive . . . so that his mother unwrapped the presents for him, and said thank you for him, and then it was Willy's turn. Paul had given him a tennis racket, and Dana thought, *But that's what you just gave Cal*, and Willy ran up to his uncle who turned his back slightly to protect the baby so that Willy ended up holding him by the leg. "We can hit around tomorrow," Paul said. And then, turning to Dana, because he sensed or felt something of what she was feeling: "Maybe one night before you go . . . maybe you and Cal could stay with me." Dana didn't answer and Paul went on: "I mean, there are plenty of bedrooms."

After the presents, in a softened mood, Liesel asked whoever was listening if they wanted to look at her father's letters, and Paul (still holding the baby) followed Susie into the study. Then Susie called to David, because she thought they might interest him and she wanted to make up, while Dana, feeling left out but also glad of the excuse to get away, put Cal to bed upstairs. (For a few minutes, in the dark, while he settled, she sat on her bed and wondered if she could call or text Stephen in New York. In the end she took out her phone and checked email but didn't call.) It was about ten o'clock, Clémence had started on the dishes in the kitchen, and Jean was making custard, while Nathan carried the Christmas pudding to the microwave in the laundry room. David put on his glasses and bent over the desk, and Susie translated on the spot: *The dinner table is very jolly—last night we ate Königsberger Klopse! Things are looking up . . . they shot two deserters, and since then, discipline has improved.*

They waited until Dana came down before Nathan poured brandy on the pudding and set it alight—the blue flame was the ghost of a flame, and Dana had time to take several pictures before it disappeared—and after he finished his portion Paul said he had a long drive back to Wimberley. He still had May in his arms (eating had involved leaning awkwardly to the side), but Susie took her away, and after that he sat for a minute on the sofa feeling like . . . well, I said I was going to go. So he left—Liesel looked at him with wet eyes. There was something strangely formal and deliberate about his leaving, almost fake or somehow staged, which he felt, too. They could see him from the living room walking down the steps of the front porch and past the Volvo along the drive. "I think that's my cue," Susie announced, breaking the spell. "I don't mind doing the dishes in the morning, but right now I'm going to bed." And she carried May, still fast asleep, toward the staircase, with Willy trailing behind.

The big kids were allowed to stay up as late as they wanted. Julie was reading her Kindle, she had been given a fifty-dollar voucher, and Ben lay on his back in front of the fire playing games on Susie's phone. On Christmas Eve, for once, she let him have it. Nathan took Margot in his arms (she had been sleeping on the sofa for the past hour), and carried her through the house and out the backdoor, backing out carefully so the screen door didn't wake her, and then walking across the patio—Liesel had draped white blankets over the potted plants, there was going to be a freeze, they looked like furniture in a house shut up for the season—to the apartment where they all slept. She woke up anyway when he pulled at the sliding door, so he set her down ("It's cold, it's cold," she said, meaning her feet on the concrete), and since she was up, he made her change into pajamas and brush her teeth and pee before crawling into bed. Then he sat next to her on the mattress on the floor in the shadow of the pool table, not thinking much, until she was gonzo, but at the same time realizing that some decision he had been putting off had somehow been made.

Clémence went into the kitchen to finish the dishes, and when Jean joined her and offered to help, she said, "That's all right, you did all the cooking. The truth is, I kind of like . . . making everything . . . cleaning up," and Jean, feeling a little as if she had been turned away, turned away. While Clémence, in Liesel's apron, soaked the plates. She didn't think there was enough there, in the story about the lights on 37th Street, because . . . there were too many things going on. The couple who started the whole thing moved out about six years ago, though maybe it would be worth tracking them down. One of the landlords who owned three houses on the block had been holding out for ridiculous rents, which left them unoccupied. But the thing she was trying to get across would be hard to pin down, the way neighbors used to come and go but whoever came in somehow

. . . there was continuity, they worked together on something, even when they didn't always get along, whereas now . . . some part of the natural process had broken down. Several of the houses were rented out to students, who had become much more conventional, but she was also thinking about Paul, who seemed a little quiet all night, and imagined him driving back along the empty roads to an empty house.

Her relationship with him had always been . . . in some ways he was very like Nathan, but easier, the kid-brother version, so that she could . . . also, she had never really trusted Dana, who struck her as a slightly below-room-temperature human being, though at the same time it took guts to come here, at Christmas, and stay here while . . . She had said to Nathan that afternoon, it can't be easy on Paul either. And he looked at her surprised. It's funny sometimes the things brothers don't think about each other. He can come and go whenever he wants, and she said, but she's always here and he isn't. She has Cal.

Jean went to check on the fire before going to bed, and saw that Liesel was still up, sitting at her desk and peering, tapping at her computer in the study next door. So she went in to say good night, it was only eleven o'clock, but she had been moving through fogs of jet lag all night, in and out, though now felt mildly alert.

"You should go to bed, too," she said, and Liesel looked up at her.

"I wonder why Bill didn't call. But it's too late now, isn't it."

"I think so. He'll call tomorrow."

"I heard Paul say to Dana, why don't you come with Cal one night and sleep at the house."

"He wouldn't say that."

"I heard it," Liesel said. With her brown wrinkled face and gray hair, she was still capable of childish expressions of pleasure.

"What did Dana say?"

"I don't know. But she didn't say no."

"I don't think they're getting back together."

"Why not? Why would she come here otherwise?"

"Because you invited her."

"I invited her because I didn't think she would come. She's a very . . . I think she's essentially a very lonely person."

"You're not making any sense, Mom."

"She's the kind of person whose parents go on cruises, when their daughter—"

"I'm sure they asked her to come."

"She lives alone with a small child. She can't go out unless she gets a babysitter."

"What's that got to do with anything?"

"I want you to remember that this was my idea. Inviting her here . . . this was my idea."

"Nobody else is going to claim it," Jean said. But she didn't feel like joking and also thought, I need to tell her what Dana told me, that she's seeing somebody else. But she didn't tell her, she stood looking at her mother in the glow of the desk lamp (the room was otherwise dark), and said, "You should go to bed, too."

"I want to talk to Bill. He thought I was crazy, too. I want to tell him what happened."

"Nothing happened," Jean said, feeling suddenly tired and unhappy. "It's an hour later in New York, everybody's asleep. I'm going to sleep." And then, after a moment, when Liesel didn't answer, Jean added, "It was a nice Christmas. Everybody was well-behaved." She put her hand on her mother's shoulder and rubbed it a little, between the neck and the shoulder blade. Her mother's back was always like a piece of wood.

"It was a nice Christmas," Liesel repeated.

On the drive home, Paul thought about Marcello, his first agent and coach, who had died a little over a year ago. A few nights before, Paul woke up from a dream, thinking, *I owe him a phone call*—because they hadn't spoken in a while. But what he felt when he remembered wasn't particularly sad, it was nice to think that your subconscious at least didn't pay much attention to death. Marcello had always been a phone-caller, not an emailer; he never learned to use a computer. But even after their formal relationship ended (Marcello had semiretired, and looked after only his big-name clients, which didn't include Paul—one of his former assistants had started his own agency, and they represented him), once every few months the phone would ring, and when you picked up, Marcello's voice on the other end would say, "Well?" Because Paul had won a match the night before, or maybe because he had lost.

It was Marcello who first suggested that Paul could make a living as a professional, after he saw him play at the UT summer camp. He had flown in to give a talk, and watch the kids play a tournament, and hand out the trophy at the end—a short fat slightly implausible figure, like the Wizard of Oz, stepping out from behind the curtain. Paul finished runner-up, and Marcello gave him his card and told him (Paul was thirteen years old) that his parents should call him. So Bill called, and after that they began a kind of relationship—whenever he came to Austin he had dinner at their house. Because to Liesel's great surprise she liked him (he always brought a bottle of Cortese di Gavi, my native wine, he said, and dressed like a professor, in slacks and cashmere), even though she didn't like what he was trying to do to her son: persuade him to become a tennis player.

For a year it seemed every night the family had some kind of argument about whether or not Paul should move to Bradenton. There was an academy there, run by the agency Marcello worked for. Even Nathan weighed in. But Liesel eventually got her way, partly because, the truth is, Paul didn't fight hard enough. Marcello flew with him down to Bradenton one weekend (he was fourteen at the time) to play in their spring break tournament, and for three nights he slept at the facility with all the other kids—most of them boarders, who went to high school at the academy, too, and had homework and curfews and guidance counselors to deal with. Paul, shy, younger than most, still coming to terms with puberty, had never been so miserable in his life. A whole world of people like him, healthy, sun-browned, relentlessly competitive, whereas before, in his Austin life . . . Most of them knew each other, too, they knew the same coaches and sponsors, and the games they played, the arguments they got into, had a ritual element that was very hard for an outsider to participate in. But he didn't want to participate. He wanted to run away. Because eventually you always lose, somebody is always better—probably somebody you don't like much, because when you're better you show it, you talk about it, and so everybody there had to put up with the constant sense of being measured, and not just measured, but valued, according to how hard he could hit a topspin forehand or . . .

He reached the third round before losing to a kid from Philadelphia, whose mother sat in the stands (there were only two or three rows of bleachers on court), and shouted *Jam him, jam him*, before every second serve. *No mercy*, that was something else she called out . . . *no mercy*, when the kid put away a volley at the net, and Paul could imagine Liesel listening and shaking her head. She wore Bradenton Tennis Academy gear, a purple fleece, even on a humid afternoon, and from time to time her son looked over at her with an expression on his face that Paul couldn't read. Of dependence or annoyance or something else. But you're not supposed to notice these things, and afterward, after he lost, he could tell that Marcello had been disappointed—that he had expected him to do better. This was extraordinarily painful to realize. On Sunday night, Marcello drove him to the airport. He said, "Talk to your mother about it, if it's what you want." Somehow that "if" seemed a new development, too. It had never seemed in question before. "I'll call her on Monday," Marcello promised. It was the first time Paul had flown alone. Bill picked him up at the other end, and even though he was deeply relieved, even happy, to be among family again, Paul hardly said a word on the drive home. He didn't want to disappoint his father, too.

Somehow after that weekend the conversation about sending him to Florida lost its urgency, and he wondered if Marcello might have said something to his mother. Even now, twenty years later, Paul remembered one of the shots he missed against that kid from Philadelphia. After working him from side to side, he tried to put away a cross-court forehand that caught the tape and rolled back. Break point against; shortly after, he lost the first set. Sometimes when he couldn't sleep things like this came back to him, he had to watch it all again. In the last match of his career, against Borisov at the US Open . . . but also the way Willy called him *Uncle Paul, Uncle Paul*, while Cal slept on Dana's lap . . . He was passing Dripping Springs, and entering again the deep wide Texas dark, out on Route 12, past Driftwood, before the lights of Wimberley appeared, such as they were. There's a case you can make, there's a case you have to make against her, to her . . . It's possible to live a different kind of life, with the kids, especially when they're kids . . . because they don't . . . they don't care about anything, apart from what we teach them to care about.

After a tough first set, where he couldn't get his rally shots deep enough and Borisov used the angles and even started coming to net, he managed to stay on serve in the second, and pulled out the tiebreak, too, when Borisov had a run of overhitting his forehand, until in the third . . . at break point against, and three-all, he hit a drop shot that bounced up, and Borisov, gliding in, whipped it cross court, but Paul had guessed right, he was already moving . . . and the net was open, all he had to do was . . . using the pace of the ball . . . all he had to do was get it over, and down the line, but for some reason he . . . maybe he jumped on it early, just because he wasn't expecting it to sit up like that for him . . . and even a year and a half later had to watch himself dump it into the net, over and over and over again. Even in the fourth set, Paul had his chances, but by that point . . .

Sometimes in the middle of a game, you get the feeling that you're not gonna win, and it's not even a feeling anymore, it's like a kind of knowledge, in the same way that, when you *are* going to win, you know that, too . . . so that this point or that doesn't matter much either way, because whatever happens is going to happen. Marcello always told him, *You have to fight that feeling,* because it's part of the problem, but you could tell he believed in it, too. Everybody believed in it . . . partly because it's the reason . . . you play, to have some kind of insight into . . . or feel some kind of relation to . . . what's happening to you right now . . . but he couldn't tell if, as he crossed the empty riverbed on Red Hawk Road, over the level concrete, and switched on his brights (so that brown grass and juniper seemed to jump out of the night) whether Dana, when he asked her to stay over with Cal, was going to stay or not . . . or even if it was a good idea or if he wanted her to.

David woke Susie when he came into the room, trying to find his way in the dark. He often stayed up after she went to sleep, and he'd been sitting with the kids, messing around online, while they . . . but she said, "What time is it?" and he said, "A little after one o'clock." "You woke me up," she said, and then, because she was only now waking up (saying it made it so), asked him if Ben had gone to bed yet. "Not yet," David told her, taking off his clothes and leaving them on the floor, before he climbed in next to her—his hands and feet were cold, and he tried to warm them on her until she pushed him off. "I've had an idea for a book," she said.

TUESDAY

TARZAN

The reason Bill didn't call was that he decided to take Judith to the movies. He figured she could use a break, but the next morning, Christmas Day, he phoned Wheeler Street and told Liesel the plot. Judith wanted to see *This Is 40*, because who am I kidding, right, I'm practically the target audience, although she's only thirty-eight. Bill, somewhat to his surprise, liked the movie, even though they exaggerated certain elements for comic effect. For example, it didn't seem plausible to him that the husband, I can't remember the actor's name, but I believe he's Jewish, would have lied to his wife about playing fantasy baseball. But much of it was also well observed.

They went to the Showcase Cinema in Ridge Hill, which meant getting in the car. By this point most of the roads had been successfully cleared, certainly the avenues and highways, but they were almost late for the previews because . . . because he couldn't get the damn thing to start. The rental had one of these keys without a key, one of these keys you just have to press a button, and then you—I don't know where you put it, Judith says you can just put it in your pocket—but he couldn't figure out how to turn the engine on. You just turn it on, she said. They sat there in the cold (because of course without the engine running he couldn't turn the heating on; the windshield was starting to fog up) pressing buttons while nothing happened. He put his foot on the brake, he took it off again, he shifted gears, and none of it made the least bit of difference, until Judith said let me try, so he got out of the car and she got into the driver's seat and sat down. And for her it started. She doesn't know why, but she didn't want to drive so left it in neutral and I got out again and she got out and then we both got back in.

But she was very—she was very good-natured about it, and Bill, talking to Liesel, remembered letting himself go on the drive to Ridge Hill, complaining about the fucking car, what's wrong with a key you can stick in the ignition, but Judith somehow let it wash over her and by the end . . . Of course, what really pissed him off wasn't the car, it was his sister lying there in the hospital bed, connected to tubes, breathing through a ventilator, it was listening to Judith all day, and then driving out to Ridge Hill on Christmas Eve to watch a movie, but by the end . . . The fact is, he had a good time, Judith was tolerant company and very interested in small things. She said, I'm telling you what you already know, Uncle Bill, it's a generation thing. I'm basically on your side, but I see the way Mikey is growing up. They call them digital natives, if you leave him alone on the computer for five minutes . . . I mean, he's six years old but afterward you have to ask him to unblock or . . . and she was off again, boasting but also exposing herself, which is really the same thing, while he paid attention to the road and let the traffic overtake him, because on a cold night, after a sunny day, after snowfall, you have to watch out for black ice.

What you realize, what he had forgotten . . . but after a few days of spending really whole days with Judith . . . there are certain people you need to be continuously present in their lives to understand why they are interesting and sympathetic, because their opportunities for self-expression are made up entirely of local and daily problems and their solutions, and you can't understand what matters to them without involving yourself completely . . . while Liesel, listening, heard also in Bill's voice the deeper presence of his family. His mother, for example, who always asked for recipes at every meal, even if she didn't like the food, because she had been taught that asking for recipes was polite—a cultured and well-mannered thing to do. It showed an interest in your hosts, though she was tone-deaf to any attempt at changing the conversation and would force you to explain from scratch, and repeat yourself if she didn't understand . . . so that discussions about the food could take up most of the meal, and you never had to talk about anything else, politics, culture, art, because they might cause disagreement, which she considered inappropriate.

Afterward, would you believe it, Bill said, the whole thing happened again. It must have been five minutes they sat in the cold car at the Cineplex parking lot while he fiddled with whatever there was to fiddle with until the damn thing finally kicked into life. From where he was sitting, in Rose's front parlor, he could see the snow piled up by the side of the road against the chain-link fence of the park opposite her house, still white, still clean in the drifts. Judith was still sleeping, it was half past eight in the morning, and the skies were overcast today. Low clouds seemed to hang over the baseball field not much higher than the trees. Well, he said, this is paradise if you like this kind of thing, and Liesel said, "How's Rose?"

Last night they kicked us out after dinner, but she was . . . measurably better, he said. She was somebody you could recognize, I mean, as herself. She was conscious, she talked (when they unhooked the ventilator) and sat up in bed, she asked me to watch whatever I wanted to watch, sports, it didn't matter, she couldn't concentrate anyway. So I turned on one of the Bowl Games. But we also had a conversation about what was happening to her, she knew where she was, she had some awareness of the sequence of events that had . . . at least, she remembered breaking her hip and going into surgery, where they put her under, she remembers coming home again though after that . . . everything else has been wiped clean. But she was capable of surprise, that seemed to me a good sign, that she's taking on information. They're pumping her full of steroids, which make you hungry, and she asked last night for a little ice cream, so Judith, she can't help herself, she has to step in . . . because Rose is borderline diabetic, and the steroids . . . but I don't think it would have mattered. For some reason the diabetic ice cream the hospital serves is Cherry Garcia, which Rose doesn't like. But they brought it to her anyway, and she picked at it with her spoon, until Judith reacted. She said you're worse than Mikey. This is how they interact.

The doctor says he's satisfied, Bill said. It's good to see her breathing on her own. Though after we left, they put the mask on again. I guess we'll both go back when Judith wakes up.

I don't know when I'm coming home. How was Christmas?

Already it surprised him, how distant he felt from scenes in Texas, and Liesel, hearing it in his voice, decided not to say anything about Paul. Do you want me to go to the Kirkendolls' party, she asked? Maybe, without knowing why, trying to involve him again in their daily lives. Judge Kirkendoll used to be one of his colleagues at the university, and every year on Boxing Day he threw a party. Bill and he had a peculiar relationship. Years ago Bill loaned him a significant amount of money to buy a piece of ranchland outside Brenham. This was before the judge got married, when he was still a young academic. Ever since then, on the basis of that money, some kind of deeper trust had evolved, even though, in other respects, their personalities offered few points of contact. Kirkendoll came from an old Texas military family. His father was a famous senator, who dropped out of West Point to become a teacher, and later a lawyer, before turning to government. He did a lot for liberal causes when the Southern block still voted Democratic and was the only Texan in either House to support the Civil Rights Act in 1964. A complicated but basically honorable figure. And Kirk (as everybody called him) had the manner of someone who knew people and kept secrets.

His wife was the granddaughter of Jimmy Bayreuth, the construction millionaire—one of the men who could reasonably claim to have built Texas, including the Miller Dam outside Austin, and the old Gregory Gym. In fact, they still lived in the Bayreuth mansion in Pemberton Heights, which was, as Jean liked to say, only modestly grand. In those days millionaires lived like everyone else. But the Kirkendolls had style. His parties were full of congressmen and other local celebrities, prominent journalists, even television presenters, and ever since they were kids the Essinger children had dreaded going to them.

"Nathan can go," Bill said.

"Why should he go?"

"Well, he minds it less than everybody else."

"Paul asked Dana to stay over at his house," she said. You make these resolutions and then you break them. They don't even last five minutes.

"What does that mean?"

"I don't know, but he asked her last night."

She still lay in bed—Bill's phone call woke her though this was usually when she got up anyway—and could tell, from the vague white glow of the curtains, that another mild overcast morning was in the cards. Their bedroom opened on to a dressing room, which twenty years ago they had turned into a study. A little Art Deco settee, covered in frayed green velvet, stood next to an old desk, though nobody ever worked there. It looked like a room her own mother might have sat in, paid bills in, retired to, to escape her children, nothing had changed . . . and when Liesel put on her glasses she could see it, and the gap in the curtains, and a branch of the crepe myrtle tree, waving outside.

"I still don't understand what that means," Bill said. "What did she say?"

"I couldn't hear, the kids were all talking. Jean says I'm making it up but I heard it." She added, "Henrik's coming tomorrow." All of these things were happening, and he was away, but then, in the background, in the three-dimensional space suggested by the depth or static quality of the telephone line, the heat of the earpiece against her ear, she heard Judith's voice, saying something, she could only make out the tone, a good-morning voice, and Bill, from the front parlor turned around to see Judith walking down the stairs, in her thick terry-cloth bathrobe, with her hair unwashed, her glasses on, her face unmade up, and she said, "You see me as I really am, Uncle Bill."

"I should go," he said. "Judith is here and I want to get to the hospital."

"Give Rose my love," and he hung up.

But it took Judith an hour to get ready and he sat around waiting.

First she made coffee and carried it up to her bedroom, she showered and dressed, then when she finally came down she wanted breakfast. She didn't seem to feel any hurry, any urgency, and called her mother-in-law in Chicago to see if Mikey could Skype. Her one concession was to eat her bowl of cereal in front of the computer, but her idea of communicating in this way was simply to leave the computer on and go about her business while he lived in the background—Mikey was watching TV, sitting on a white leather sofa. Most of the light in the room came from the television, and you could see his face in the glow of changing images.

Meanwhile Judith decided to clean out her mother's fridge. The opened milk was sour, there was half a carton of slightly fizzy juice, restaurant leftovers in stained containers, she started throwing them all out and couldn't find another garbage bag. Occasionally she looked at her son, she tried to get his attention. "Guess who I'm going to see today. Granma—Granma Rose. I want something to tell her about you. She likes hearing stuff about you, it cheers her up. Hey, Mikey. She likes hearing news. You guys doing something fun?" But he seemed happy enough staring at the box and Judith had to break through to her mother-in-law: "Leah? Leah?" All of this went on an unbelievable length of time. When Leah came (her face a gray blotch, she didn't know where the camera was), Judith couldn't help herself. "How much TV is he watching?" she asked. "Is Gabe around? I mean, it's Christmas, right? The clinic is closed?" And so on.

Bill said, touching her on the shoulder, "I'm gonna walk around the block. Maybe we can go when I get back."

So he put on his coat and walked out—into the cold air, one of the mornings of his childhood, snow on the ground, blue skies, the kind of neighborhood he grew up in. His breath was visible and he walked in the middle of the road. Most people hadn't cleared the sidewalks yet, snow and ice, the neighborhood was getting older, and he followed the ridges of car tracks carefully beside the park. There wasn't any traffic on the road. Christmas Day.

When he came back in, after stamping his feet on the porch (his toes had frozen, he couldn't feel them), Judith said, "I turned the sound off on my phone last night in the movie theater and forgot to plug it in when we got home. The map function uses a lot of battery, it's dead."

"Are you ready to go?"

"I want to see if I have any calls."

"Can't you check in the car?"

"I just want to charge it first."

"Can't you charge it at the hospital?"

"They don't like you using phones in the hospital." But in the end, she gave in—both of them a little bad-tempered as they climbed in the car. Which was a shame; they had been getting along pretty well. But maybe this was a part of that, too. Affectionate friction. At least the car started and the roads were almost completely empty; it's funny how quickly certain journeys become routine. He took Ashburton and Broadway, he liked driving through Yonkers and avoided the Parkway, it gave him some pleasure to see the simple brick houses, the fire escapes, even the discount stores and rundown pharmacies, the Chinese restaurants, beauty salons, and graffitied store-front grilles, the *For Rent* signs, and plants in the upstairs windows, signs of life. And then on Broadway itself the big apartment buildings with their unused balconies, maybe a few bicycles or laundry racks, plastic toys, exposed to the weather, the tall leafless trees, the public basket-ball courts, and later on, closer to the hospital, the grander houses on plots of sloping lawn that Judith liked to fantasize about. Some of them were probably split into apartments. Even the parking garage, the entrance to the hospital, the corridors you take, the elevators, these quickly become familiar, too.

Except that Rose wasn't in her old room and the nurse at reception didn't know who they were talking about. She had been off all week, her shift started at six a.m. Patients with MRSA get their own rooms. The hallway is separated from the rest of the wing by locked double doors, you need to get buzzed in, and often there's nobody at the desk so that you stand there waiting for several minutes until someone lets you through. All of which meant that Judith was moderately annoyed even before the duty nurse told her she didn't know where Mrs. Weintraub was—Rose had kept her married name after the divorce.

"I thought that's what computers were for," Judith said. "Look her up."

But the system had crashed that morning, they were coming back online right now. If you want to wait in the waiting area I'll come find you when . . .

"I used to work in a hospital," Judith said. "This is not . . . The first thing that goes when things are going wrong is the paperwork."

Bill stood beside her, not saying much. Sometimes, he knew, it helps to raise a stink, but at the same time, he was basically nonconfrontational outside of family life. These people are doing a job, it's not a job that he would want to do. And you end up in the same place anyway, sitting on the fake leather chairs, staring at the television, which was still tuned to CNN.

One of these financial roundup shows was on—an end-of-year thing, people talking about stock market picks, the best and worst of 2012. Everybody was in good spirits. There was a Christmas tree in the studio, but instead of ornaments, lights, and candy canes, various S&P 500 listings hung off it, with arrow signs going up or down, and the hosts walked over to the tree and untangled the signs from the branches (it was a real tree, and there was something strangely unrehearsed or authentic about the way these signs got caught up among the complicated needles and had to be extracted, by people who at the same time were concentrating on what they were saying, stuff like "If you bought in July, which was when I told you to buy, and sold up now . . .") and either threw away the ornament afterward— accompanied by sound effects, noises like leaking balloons or breaking glass—or hung it higher on the tree.

Bill, almost in spite of himself, found himself paying attention: Radian Group stocks did well, a company called Lumber Liquidators, Stratasys . . . meanwhile Judith was looking for a socket to plug her phone into. An Indian-looking man, balding, in an itchy wool sweater, sat with his hands in his lap and a composed expression on his face, while the television emitted at a low volume (almost too quiet for Bill to hear, although the general mood of the show came across anyway) its conversational atmosphere, which contrasted strongly with the fact that nobody in the waiting room was talking.

Then Judith said, "Gabe called me," and Bill said, "What did he want," and she said, "I don't know, he called me twice last night but didn't leave a message," when the doctor walked in. In her white coat, with a blue mask hung around her neck.

"I don't know if you remember me," she said. "I'm Dr. Kleinman, I was one of the doctors looking after Rose."

"Yes, I remember."

Bill struggled to his feet, it wasn't easy getting out of the soft upholstery.

"I'm sorry to have to tell you, she died last night. I want to say that now so that there's no . . ."

Bill said, "When we left last night she seemed to be . . ."

"Sometimes with pneumonia, it can be unpredictable."

"I thought she was doing better."

"Her temperature started spiking; we couldn't bring it down. She was in a very weakened state. These things happen fast, but I can assure you that everything that could be done, we tried. She was unconscious the whole time, she wouldn't have felt . . ."

"I don't care what she felt," Bill said, but then, correcting himself, "I mean, I want her to . . ." But he couldn't explain what he meant, he couldn't think.

And Judith, whom he had briefly forgotten, couldn't stand up without putting aside her phone. The cord was caught in the shoulder bag, which was still hanging on her neck.

"This is not how you inform people," she said, pulling her bag off, the phone, the whole mess, leaving it on the chair. "You said she was doing better. You said there was nothing to worry about."

Dr. Kleinman looked at her. "I wouldn't have said that."

"Somebody said that."

"What are we supposed to do now?" Bill asked.

"You can look at her; it often helps to say goodbye. There are some papers to sign, and you can collect her things. Someone from the hospital is going to talk to you about organ procurement."

"I don't want her *things*," Judith said, still angry—her face red and thick, her lip stubborn, her eyes staring. "Last night, when we left, she was fine. And today nobody knows where she is." The staff changes over, Dr. Kleinman began to explain, it's not . . . but Judith interrupted her. "Then you come in and tell us in front of everybody." The Indian man looked away, and she went on: "Nobody calls us. This is not how things should be done in a well-run hospital. I don't know why I wasn't called. I have a phone. The number is on her contact sheet. We could have come at any time. My uncle and I have made considerable sacrifices to be here. When . . . what's the point. We're ten minutes away in the car. I don't understand why she had to die alone. I don't understand that."

"It happened very quickly." The doctor was starting to repeat herself. "She wasn't in any pain."

"Don't give me that crap about pain," Judith said. "That's just one of those things that everybody says. I know because I used to say it, too."

"Do you want to see . . ."

"Yes, I want to see her," Judith said. "She's my mother." And Bill felt a flare-up of admiration. But it didn't last long, Judith's anger—it was quickly replaced by something else.

In fact, it was Bill who descended the elevator to the mortuary, into the windowless depths; Judith couldn't face it. His sister lay on her back, her cheeks swollen and pale, her hair brushed thinly across her scalp.

Afterward, they had to wait around to talk to someone from the OPO—the organ donation people. Judith sipped from a can of Diet Coke among the rows of chairs lined up in front of another reception desk, in another windowless room. Everything takes time, whole days seemed to pass without sunlight. Her face in the energy-efficient glare had an oily sheen, a layer of something unhealthy on the surface. She looked like an unhappy teenager, except middle-aged, thick around the waist—in a sulk. There was no public element to her expression, all the meaning was withheld or turned inward. Who could blame her, Bill thought. She had been cast adrift. With what? With him, among a few other people.

Sitting down again, he put an arm around her. "We can probably go." But she responded by hiding her face against his shirt. For a moment it was like he held his sister in his arms again, he was doing her bidding, looking after Judith but also somehow . . . consoling her for her own death.

Then the woman from the OPO found them. Middle-aged, she had short hair—dyed black. A slight cold; her nose looked red, it was that time of year. But her manner was efficient and practical, she kept emotional appeals to a minimum. Bill had the conversation with her but Judith signed the papers; she was next of kin.

By this point it was almost one o'clock, and Bill rarely ate breakfast. He didn't want to drive home without something in his system; he felt weak and jittery and also strangely reluctant to leave the hospital. Because once they left, they had no reason to come back. The reason had gone. So they got lunch at the food court, Chinese food, and he even made a joke about Jewish traditions. But the taste of lo mein and fried rice stayed in his mouth for the rest of the afternoon; the food sat on his stomach, too, the sugar and fat content was high. A growth of sharp nail was also bugging him—it kept catching on fabric, he even scratched himself.

After lunch, he left Judith eating dessert, key lime pie (she was a comfort eater), and went up to the isolation wing to collect whatever belongings Rose had left behind. There wasn't much, but he stood outside the locked doors again and waited for someone to buzz him in. Dr. Kleinman came through reception while he was talking to one of the nurses, and he tried to thank her, or apologize, he wasn't sure which—but he wanted some kind of continuing contact with her, because contact with her meant . . . nothing much anymore.

"I'm sorry about my niece," he said, and the doctor responded, perfectly reasonably, "It's understandable."

Her shift was almost over, she had the unaffected quality of real tiredness, and for some reason he tried to keep the conversation going. On Christmas Day nobody wants to be here. Not you either, I guess, though maybe . . .

"My husband is Jewish," she said, "I'm not," and he couldn't tell if offense was taken, or she was just stating facts. For maybe half an hour this uncertainty bugged him. His sister had just died, but still this slightly awkward personal interaction with an attractive middle-aged woman occupied some of his mental space. Because you're a foolish person, he thought, beating himself up—visibly shaking his head.

It was after three when they got home and Bill went straight to the downstairs bathroom. Usually he liked to play cards on the pot, solitaire, but his cards were upstairs so he looked at the stack of magazines under the sink, slipping against themselves on the small tiles. Rose had a subscription to Martha Stewart. What do you want with this stuff, he thought, flicking through the glossy pages. The kind of life she's selling. Afterward he washed his hands thoroughly and dried them on the bathroom towel, which hadn't been changed, probably, in several weeks. Rose had dried her hands against it.

Judith sat at the desk in the parlor, talking to somebody on Skype. You could hear her voice all over the house—he heard it from the bathroom. Part of what he was doing while he wiped his ass was trying to work out who she was talking to. Not Mikey, it didn't sound like her kiddy voice. Maybe one of her girlfriends, she had the air of a woman confidently enlisting sympathy. But in fact it was Gabe, her ex-husband. He didn't say much; Bill could see him in the background of the computer screen, looking slightly veiled or protected by the low resolution. His face was generally hard to read. He was a person to whom facial expressions don't come naturally. Judith was saying, "The trouble with emergency rooms is nobody goes shopping for where they end up. Otherwise they'd be better run. If people had a choice . . ." But she was losing steam. "When's Mikey coming back?"

And Gabe said, "Do you want me to tell him?"

"I don't want to upset him."

"He won't be upset."

"*Of course* he will, she's his . . ." but Bill interrupted her quietly.

"I'm going to make a few phone calls in the kitchen," he said. "In case you need the phone." But she shook her head.

For the next hour he sat at the kitchen table dialing numbers. The handset grew hot against his ear. The first person he called was Liesel, and left a message. "Hey, it's me. Rose died last night. I'm okay. Maybe I'll try one of the kids' cells if I can find the number." But the next person he called was Alex, Rose's ex-husband. He could see his phone number written on the fridge. Alex lived in Arizona, his wife was Catholic. It was two hours earlier, and they were still sitting down to Christmas dinner. Bill got the feeling that Alex was happy to walk out of the room—he was one of those guys who wore his cell phone on his hip, even on weekends. Even on Christmas Day.

"What's on your mind?" Alex said.

They always got along easily enough. Bill could hear the background noise of small children, plates, somebody moving around the kitchen. His wife's family was local—she had a lot of relatives.

"Rose died last night," Bill told him.

He was aware of repeating himself and the slight diminishment of meaning. He was going to have to say it again and again. Diminishment of meaning was part of the job. You can't be too sensitive or squeamish about it.

"Hey, jeez," Alex said. "Oh shit. Poor kid, I'm sorry. You really hit me in the solar plexus. She's really had a pretty shitty ride."

"Well, I wanted to call you. I thought you should know."

"I appreciate that, Bill." His accent hadn't changed at all, he was still a Jewish guy from New Jersey. If anything, it had frozen in time. Sometimes Alex liked to appeal to Bill, as another Jewish guy who had married a shiksa, and lived in the sunny Southwest. "Does Judith want to talk to me?" he asked. "Is she still there?"

"She's talking to Gabe right now. I'll tell her to call you."

"Maybe she will, maybe she won't. Okay . . ." But the way he said it, he was stalling for time, he wanted to keep talking. Maybe he didn't want to go back to Christmas dinner.

But in fact as he stayed on the phone Bill figured out the reason. Something was bothering Alex about Rose's estate. It turned out that after the divorce Rose couldn't afford to buy out his share of the house. So he ended up loaning her the money. She was supposed to pay interest on the loan, but that was one of those things . . . the truth is, he let it slide. For various reasons. Guilt being one of them. "Now I guess the house will be sold. I don't know what it's worth these days, but whatever it sells for the interest is going to have to come out of it. I expect this'll be another argument with Judith."

Alex wanted Bill to help explain his point of view. He figured Bill was probably the executor of the estate. "Look," he said, "I know it's not the time nor place. But in my experience there is no time or place, I wouldn't be having this conversation at all except for the kids." He meant the twins, the girls he had by his second wife, who were coming up to six years old.

Bill said, "I think all of this is a little premature. But consider it noted."

He got off the phone when he could and called Nathan. Nathan was the son he turned to when anything of this nature came up—when what you had come into contact with was reality at this level of moral and technical detail. "Listen," he said, "can you talk?"

Nathan, who disliked having a cell phone, but nevertheless kept it around and reachable on his person, said, "I'm sitting over the road. At Dodie's house. Julie's talking to her for a school project."

"I'm sorry, son. To interrupt. Rose died last night," and Nathan said, "Let me walk outside."

Bill could hear him making his excuses. He could hear Julie saying something, and then the screen door closing behind. After that Bill explained himself and Nathan listened. His immediate concern was to get through whatever came next without permanently alienating Judith and her father. Much of the trouble was likely in the future, but he wanted to lay the groundwork now, and if there were little things, like the funeral, decisions he could make now ... "Part of me of course is also pissed off at the guy and always has been. But I'm trying not to act on those feelings. There are other complications."

Over the years, Bill had loaned his sister a considerable amount of money. He wasn't good at keeping records, but probably he had a list somewhere. Or several lists. Their understanding, for tax reasons, is that these weren't gifts, in which case they had to be charged interest at the minimum legal rate, but as Nathan knew, the rate went up and down, and given the state of his records ... Why this mattered, though, is that he didn't see any reason that Alex should claim as *his* share of Rose's estate money that properly belonged to Bill, and which he could otherwise dispose of as he wished. By helping out Judith, for example, who was trying to buy an apartment. Or even setting up a trust for Mikey.

Nathan, standing on Dodie's porch, in the mild pleasant yellow-grass pale-skies sunniness of a Texas December day, could hear in his father's voice something else, a kind of outpouring, which expressed itself in Bill's case as anxiety, or not even anxiety, as an appetite for practical steps and details. A way of deferring. "Don't worry about this now," he said. "Not right now. I can't call anyone today, it's Christmas. But tomorrow I'll get on the phone to Beverley Lang . . ." and afterward, after Nathan hung up, Bill was still in Rose's kitchen, and going through numbers. He called Liesel again, and when she picked up, he said again, "Listen, there's been some bad news. Rose died last night." And when she hung up he called Paul.

———

Julie had been in a mood all morning. Mostly she was just tired. The kids were allowed to stay up as late as they liked on Christmas Eve, and Julie didn't get to bed until one. When she left, Ben was still sitting in front of the dead fire, playing on Susie's phone. For some reason she felt like she was in some kind of competition with him. Everybody thought that he was struggling or misbehaving or going through some kind of hard time. Whereas from Julie's point of view ... even Margot kept tagging after him ... he always got his way. This was one of the ways that parents basically didn't understand what was going on. They all felt sorry for him, because he was moving to England. But where am I going? Nowhere.

But sometimes it was helpful to be in a bad mood. It helped you get your way. In the morning, after breakfast, Nathan carried her mattress across the backyard and leaned it against the side of the little hut. They had to take some of the crap out to make room— the kitchen set, and the old edge trimmer, which didn't work anymore but lay in a pile of its own coils on the wooden floor. Nathan dragged it through the doorway, thinking, if Bill were here, he'd complain that you can't leave it outside, it's going to rust. It doesn't work anyway. You haven't used it in years. It just needs a new fuse, or something like that. And so on. So even without Bill he had the conversation in his head, but set it under the window on the porch, where unless it rained horizontally the trimmer would be perfectly fine.

Clémence came out with a broom and helped Julie sweep—she cleared the cobwebs out of the corners and off the ceiling. It was very dusty. There were no curtains. "You sure you want to do this," her mother said. "Nobody will blame you if you change your mind. I'll be relieved."

"I already said . . ." Somehow she found it difficult to accept help graciously from her parents. Ben stood around, watching—his glasses made him look innocent and interested. Willy was hitting balls on the court behind. Margot wandered between them. It was all very public.

"You're not going to sleep out there," Ben said. "I don't believe it."

"Of course I am."

"You're so predictable," he said. "It's so easy to get you to do stuff. I don't even think you really want to."

"If I didn't want to, I wouldn't do it."

"I don't think you're going to anyway."

Whatever she did or said, Ben twisted it around, so it looked like she was giving in to him or proving him right. Nathan, listening, put his hand on Julie's shoulder and pulled her toward him a little. "You'll be fine, it'll be fun," he said. It occurred to her that he wanted her to win—that she was fighting *his* battles, too. Against Susie or whomever. This cheered her up.

So after lunch when her father suggested going over to Dodie's house she pretended that this is what she wanted to do. The skies had cleared again, the temperature was rising, and they walked together down the driveway and across the street. Her house had a little sunporch (with a swinging bench inside, a side table with plants on it, there were jars of dead cacti on the floor, next to a box of garden chemicals, ant poison, bug spray, etc.) and you had to pick your way through to knock on her door. Nathan carried in his hand the bottle of Promised Land Eggnog, which he had failed to give her the day before. Julie waited on the step outside and hoped that Dodie wouldn't answer.

But she did and invited them in. The old woman wore thick brown sunglasses, which must have pinched a little, because she shifted them constantly. Her face was skinny and wrinkled. Julie found it hard to look at her. One of her hands was swollen, but she held it out anyway, in a kind of gesture of greeting, and Nathan gripped it lightly from above and let go.

She offered to make them tea then thought better of it and poured out the eggnog in three glasses on the kitchen counter, which served as a barrier between the kitchen and the living room. It was a very small house—they were sitting in the living room, under the fan, and could see her struggling with the lid. Then she put the glasses on a tray and carried them over. The kind of Seventies water glasses with colorful patterns painted on. (The paint had begun to peel away, they didn't look clean.) Julie took a sip and set it down on the chest in front of her feet and didn't touch it again for the rest of the visit.

"Did your daughter come down?" Nathan asked.

No, she was in Denver with *her* son's family. They just had a baby and didn't want to travel. "My great granddaughter, would you believe it. Of course, they invited me, too, but I don't like flying anymore. It's fifteen hours in the car. I'm fine. I've had a lot of Christmases. I don't mind being on my own; I'm used to it."

Even in high school, Nathan got the feeling that she didn't like him much—that something about him got on her nerves, his manner or air of considerate behavior. But he could usually rely on this manner to help him ignore it. Her house always pleased him, it was very Old Austin. The air-conditioning unit in the window, its tidy clutter, the potted plants, carefully looked after, her framed photographs, mostly of roads in landscape, hanging on the narrow spaces of wall between the windowpanes. (Her husband was an amateur photographer; he had been dead for thirty years.) Even the modest kitchen, with its linoleum counter and wooden drying rack.

He said, "Julie wants to sleep in the little house in our backyard tonight. As a kind of protest. I told her you could probably tell her some stories about Mr. Mosby."

"It's not a protest . . . that makes it sound. I mean, who am I protesting against? It's just something I want to do."

"You want to suggest . . . or at least, you want to know what it feels like . . ."

But they were talking to each other; it was a performance.

"I remember there was some bad feeling when your parents let him go," Dodie said. She was looking at Julie, maybe she was more confused than she first appeared. "Because what's he supposed to do? Where's he gonna go? But the whole neighborhood was changing. When we bought this house, in 1951, everybody got along. You saw a lot of black faces. The Tylers had a live-in maid. The Gormans—all of their children had black nannies. Everybody knew each other, they worked hard, nobody had any problems. But that's all changed. How many black people live in Hemphill Park today? Nobody. If you see somebody now you reach for the phone."

And this is how it went on.

"I voted for Obama, too, the first time around," she said. "But not again. It's getting so you can't even talk about anything anymore. Without everybody getting excited. I tried to explain to your mother when they moved in, this is how it works. For a few years I gave him little gardening jobs, when I could. He mowed the lawn. But just getting here on the bus from Govalle . . . I think that's where he lived. He was already pretty old, not as old as I am now but old. His brother ran an auto shop over there. But I said to him once, I'm not sure who's doing the favor. He liked coming but it's a long way. I don't know what happened to him."

Nathan's cell phone rang while she was talking. He said it might be Bill, who had flown to New York to see his sister, who was in the hospital. "I'm sorry," he said, "I should probably take it," and walked out the front door onto the sunporch—Julie could see him through the screen window.

"Now your mother counts as one of the old-timers, like me," Dodie said. Julie didn't correct her. "That's what happens, I guess," Dodie went on, and then she laughed. "This is what you get for outstaying your welcome. You're probably sitting there, thinking . . .

I don't know what you're thinking. If my daughter were around, she'd tell you—she'd tell me . . . Mom, she'd say. Cut it out. What? What? Sometimes I act like I don't know what she means, but I know. Some things you don't say. But that doesn't mean people don't feel them."

"I think it's better to say everything," Julie said, at last.

"I don't get much opportunity," Dodie told her. She was really a very small woman. She wore blue jeans and house slippers and a sweater that was much too big—gardening clothes. But on her hard dining-room chair, she sat up straight. (Julie occupied the two-seater couch.) Her gray hair was pulled up in a bun, which she must have pinned herself. There were only a few stray curls. And yet the main impression you got of her face was a certain vagueness, almost as if what she actually used to look like didn't matter anymore, it didn't count. Those sunglasses covered up a lot. Her lips were thin and colored like the rest of her face, an old woman's tan.

"Can I get you something else?" she asked. "I don't think you like that eggnog much. Neither do I."

"A glass of water. I can get it."

"Sit down." And then, coming back, with the water glass in her hand, "I got a lot of good neighbors, I've been lucky. Liesel sometimes asks me if I need anything. She's no spring chicken either. Bill brings over the *New York Times* when he's finished with it. I read the headlines, that's all I can still see. The headlines are usually bad enough. I was no great fan of Mitt Romney, but I voted for him anyway. I liked his father. My daughter tells me I talk too much. You probably just want to go home."

"Did you have a nice Christmas?"

"I got a phone call in the morning, which is all I wanted. I talked to my daughter. I talked to my grandson. I heard the baby crying."

There was a silence—they could both hear Nathan on the porch. He was pacing, too, among the clutter of plants and furniture. The screen mesh gave him a faint sepia blurriness. Tall and wild-haired, in his Austin clothes: crappy shorts, crappy T-shirt, cheap sneakers. Then he hung up and walked back in, and the feeling in the room changed again, Julie felt less exposed.

"I'm sorry," he said again. "That was Bill. His sister just died. We should probably go."

"Aunt Rose?" Julie asked, instantly and almost to her surprise on the edge of tears.

"Yes, last night."

Julie stood up; she held her hands in front of her and carefully aligned her Doc Martens so that the edges touched. Clémence used to make her do ballet, before she got too big, and Julie still found some comfort in standing like that with her feet together. She didn't know if Dodie would shake her hand, or hug her, but she managed to make it outside without any kind of physical contact. Leaving her water glass on the wooden chest, where it might make a ring. Dodie followed them into the front yard in her slippers.

"You wanted to hear stories about Earl Mosby," she said.

"That's okay."

"I guess you'll have to come back." And Julie said thank you.

It was only thirty feet from Dodie's house to their front door, but even though she thought that what she should be thinking about was Rose's death, what worried her was something else. Though maybe the feeling of guilt she had, like a black smudge in her vision, the kind you get looking through binoculars before you focus properly, was intensified or exaggerated by her sense that she should cry about Rose, or show some kind of appropriate response. Dodie had said racist things and Julie hadn't corrected her. She had sat there politely instead and accepted a glass of water. In fact, the only thing she said was something like, it's okay to say these things, or it's better to say what you feel, which is the opposite of condemning or challenging her opinions, and she felt angry at Nathan for leaving her alone with that old woman.

"You made me sit there for ages," she said, pulling at his arm as they walked, because in spite of feeling angry she wanted his forgiveness, but he seemed to be thinking about something else.

—

Cal had spent most of the day in a passive state of illness acceptance. He didn't seem to be in pain, but he didn't have much energy either, and Paul and Dana couldn't get him to eat. His tummy hurt; it's probably the antibiotics, Dana said. She kept filling his water bottle with fresh water and putting it to his lips. They let him watch a lot of TV, and Paul sometimes sat with him on the low couch, under Susie's family painting, with his arm around the kid. Feeling the heat coming off him, staring at some dumb show—*Jake and the Never Land Pirates*, which always ended with a couple of guys wearing pirate beards, singing and playing guitar. Paul wondered if they were happy, the actors, youngish men, approaching thirty; if they were having fun, if they thought, this is a stepping-stone to something else.

Dana came in after clearing the lunch away and looked at them: father and son, blank-eyed. "Make him drink something," she said, and Paul lifted the bottle to his mouth. Cal didn't react and Dana left them to it. They were sitting there comfortably enough, she didn't mean to get involved.

At some point in the afternoon she tried to make Cal take a nap. This was the only time he showed any resistance. Eventually she gave up and retreated downstairs again, carrying him in her arms. She didn't want him to be mad at her. It's stupid, you withdraw until they cry, and then step in again, rewarding yourself with their affection.

Paul said, "I don't think it matters much. He'll sleep when he wants to."

He was sitting at the kitchen table, teaching Willy how to play gin rummy. Liesel and Susie were mixing something in a metal bowl— Dana could smell cinnamon and ginger.

"You must be tired," Liesel said to her. "Why don't you go lie down. I'm going to take a nap in a minute."

And Susie said, "We can look after Cal."

"I'm fine. I'm not really doing anything." And then, in case this sounded like a criticism, "It's very relaxing here." But in fact Dana didn't want to be pushed to the margins; she wanted to hang out with Paul and Cal, she wanted to worry about their son together. "Maybe we can take a walk," she said. "Maybe Cal will go to sleep in the stroller."

"Okay, let me just finish this game," Paul told her.

But when it was over, Willy wanted to play tennis with his uncle, and Cal overheard them and wanted to go outside. "He's sick, he's got a fever," Dana said, but when she felt his forehead, it was cool enough. "He hasn't eaten anything all day," she objected, "he gets very clumsy when he's like this, this is when he hurts himself." Somehow she knew she had already given in, and Paul got the rackets and balls from the TV room and took the boys outside.

"He's a good uncle," Susie said, by way of apology maybe, but instantly regretted it—she heard an echo somewhere and wondered if she had said this before. Dana didn't answer and watched them through the breakfast-room windows, moving across the lawn, toward the playhouse at the back, and the tennis court behind it, another sunshiny winter afternoon, and felt weirdly helpless, or like something was slipping through her fingers.

"What are you making?" she asked. "Can I do anything?"

"A gingerbread house. Every year we do it, and every year it sits there for weeks getting stale."

"Smells good."

"It would be good, if we ate it now."

After they put it in the oven, Liesel lay down in her study for a nap; and Susie heard the crackle of the monitor—May was waking up. She went upstairs to get her daughter (David was working at the Starbucks on Guadalupe), and for two or three minutes, Dana hung around the kitchen, checking on the gingerbread and waiting to pull it out. What am I doing here, she thought. Paul doesn't need me, really he just wants Cal. Nobody loves me here, everybody's nice, but it's not like I'm anyone's first choice. Even Cal just wants to run around with his cousins.

She wanted to call Stephen, but he always spent Christmas Day with his daughter and first wife. They had a place in Connecticut, and Stephen got along fine with the new husband, who by this point wasn't particularly new anymore, and in fact they sometimes complained together about . . . anyway, it was a good thing, it was one of the things in his life he hadn't screwed up. Everybody still got along, and so on Christmas . . . Dana didn't want to interrupt him. His daughter had had a little baby, his first grandchild. You're dating a grampa, he said. She opened the oven door and felt the heat on her face (a real blast; she turned her head away for a moment) and stuck a knife in the gingerbread and pulled it out again. Fine, it looked fine to her (but what do I care—by the time they eat it I'll be gone), and she put on the oven mitts and lifted the pans out carefully, and set them on the stove.

When Susie came down, carrying May in her arms, freshly changed, smelling of Desitin, she said, "Fuck this, right?" She meant the baking and babies. "Let's go shopping," and she started looking through the house for Jean and Clémence, to see if they wanted to come along.

Dana went outside to tell Paul. She found him on the court behind the playhouse; Cal looked happier than he had looked all day. He was running after the tennis balls that Willy hit. Paul kept saying, "Give it to me," but while Dana was watching Cal threw the ball at Willy himself, who scuffed his racket, trying to swat it on the ground, and Paul had to scramble among the stones and weeds.

"Susie and I are going shopping," Dana told him.

"Buy yourself a nice dress," he said, in his father's voice, like a game show host. He meant, you've earned it, for putting up with us.

At least, that's what she understood. Her mood had lifted, Cal was improving, that's really all it was, you can't be happy when they're not. But still she called out, because she couldn't help herself, or maybe because she felt happy, and intimate and normal, "Make sure he drinks."

He didn't respond at first (she regretted it instantly). Then he shouted after her, "It's Christmas, everything will be closed," and so she walked back to the house to tell the others.

Susie and Jean were out front, strapping May into her car seat. "I don't know where Clémence is," Susie said. "I couldn't find her."

"It's Christmas," Dana told her. "Everything will be closed."

"Of course it will."

"It's confusing in this weather," Dana said.

And for a minute they just stood in the driveway. May was buckled in and Jean was teasing her with her English house keys—holding them just out of reach and then giving in. They made a tinkling sound, May tried to put them in her mouth.

"Let's do something, let's go somewhere," Jean said, taking them away, and suggested they get a hot chocolate at the Driskill Hotel.

So that's what they did, or tried to do. They managed to park downtown, but the restaurant itself was fully booked, and Susie didn't really want to bring a baby into the bar. People are paying for an upmarket experience, they don't want . . . "I don't care what people are paying for," Jean said, but Susie told her, "I won't have a good time." And in the end, they drove out to Zilker Park to look at the tree. By this point it was almost four o'clock. The sun was starting to descend behind the cone of lights, and the pale clear blue of the sky had darkened like a glaze. It was getting chilly, too, and Susie felt glad of May, whom she covered with her jacket and held against her breast.

"This is nice," she said. Other people were there, it was a communal experience. An Austin thing.

But Jean said, "It's fine, but it's another . . ."

"What?"

"It's something you do with kids. It's fine. I thought Dana could use . . ."

"Don't worry about me."

Susie offered: "We can go back to the Driskill and I'll drop you off."

"I'm okay."

"You can get a cab home."

"It's fine, this is nice," Jean said.

"We should probably go back anyway," Dana told them. "I'm worried about Cal."

"I'm sure he's fine. Paul's there."

But they went back, and when they got home, Liesel met them at the door. Her hair looked uncombed after her nap; she was in a state of agitation, not tearful at all, but full of a kind of emotional energy, which she didn't know what to do with. "Bill called," she said, as they walked up the steps. She must have heard their car, or been looking out for it. "Rose died."

Conversation about Rose took up most of the rest of the day. Nathan was worried about Bill. He's going to get caught up in the argument between Judith and her father. This is what happens to families, especially when their affairs are badly managed. And Rose lived a very disorganized life. She owed money, she was generous, too, and made promises she couldn't deliver on. My sense is, for example, that Judith expects the house money, or most of it, to go to her. She's maybe even depending on it. And when she finds out it isn't, the person she gets mad at is going to be the person she's still communicating with. In this case, Bill.

Only Susie cried. Her tears were very near the surface, but she tried to suppress them because, as she said to Liesel, "May ends up feeling whatever I feel, I don't want to upset her." And the kids still had to be fed (Clémence, quietly, started making dinner), while Susie sat in the living room nursing May. Jean sat with her for a few minutes.

"From Yonkers to Durham is less than two hours in the car," Susie said. "Every Thanksgiving we called her, we said, come to us. The boys can share a room if she wants to stay over, it's no trouble. I called her almost every year. She came *once*. David actually liked her. I mean, he's good at that kind of thing, he likes talking to old ladies. He grew up in an English village, this is what you learn. But the way she lived . . . I can't even imagine. What did she do all day? And you hear about these people and you think, who let it happen. *We* let it happen. It's an hour and thirty, an hour and forty minutes in the car . . ."

And Jean listened, partly feeling, Susie represents something, or has a point of view in which she stands for a part of society, and its obligations . . . while May sucked at her breast. She wore the kind of shirt you can just pull up. Whereas Jean . . . for some reason she imagined Paul dead. To feel what she would feel. But this was different, because there were always the others, Nathan and Susie, while Bill—for him, everybody was dead. Everybody connected to his childhood. Maybe because Paul lives alone, because he's divorced. But he's still stuck there, in Rose's house, in New York, where he grew up, while the rest of his family, in Texas . . . her thoughts went back and forth.

Dana went looking for Cal when they got in, and found him watching TV again, sitting on the sofa next to Paul. Paul had a bowl of dry Cheerios on his lap. He put some in his hand and Cal took them out of his hand. Cal's eyes were glazed, he had red cheeks. Willy and Ben and Margot were on the sofa, too.

"He looks hot," Dana said.

"He's all right."

"I told you not to let him overdo it."

"It's just that time of day."

And Dana, feeling helpless, corrected what she was going to say next. "I'm sorry about Rose," she said. "Has he got any water?"

"It needs filling up," Paul said and held out the bottle.

When Dana came back, there was nowhere for her to sit, but she leaned over and gave him a sip of water. Cal shifted his head—she was in his way.

Ben said, "I can't see." His voice was . . . it was like she was a stranger at a movie theater.

"Deal with it," Paul told him.

"Do you know when the funeral is?" she asked, standing up.

"I haven't really talked to anybody."

"Because I could go . . . if you wanted me to. If Bill wanted it. I assume I'll be back by then."

Paul looked up at her for the first time. "I'll ask him when I talk to him," he said.

Kids and grown-ups ate together. There were several days of leftovers to get through, cold goose and potatoes, and curry and rice from the Vietnamese place, which Clémence had heated up. Everything was laid out on the kitchen counter—you just came and took. (Susie had also decided to boil some pasta, as a kind of filler, in case any of the kids wanted something simple, pasta and cheese, but most of it went uneaten, and after the meal Susie found herself picking at sticky bits of macaroni while clearing the table and doing the dishes, until she emptied the pot into the trash with a feeling of . . . for once, let it go.)

Dana and Paul went up to put Cal to bed. Paul said, "Don't wait."

And then, at dinner, Liesel and Jean got in a stupid argument about Rose.

Liesel was very fond of Rose, and not just fond but full of admiration for her. She was a very uncomplaining woman, when she had many things to complain about. Liesel felt grateful, too, because Rose in spite of everything showed up at their wedding, when nobody else from Bill's family would come. And for Liesel's family it was too far to travel. But Rose took the bus from New York, against her parents' wishes. She got all dressed up, as if she thought . . . but they got married at the registry, with a couple of friends to sign the papers. Rose was very disappointed, and maybe even felt, which wasn't totally inaccurate, that she was really in the way. She kept getting the tone wrong, she didn't know what to talk about, she tried to make polite conversation.

Her whole life was a little like this. Her life was like one of those days where you can't decide what to do, you argue about whether to go out or stay in, and then it starts raining when you finally leave the house, and the restaurant is closed, so you try somewhere else, which turns out to be a disappointment. And nothing turns out the way you want it to.

"That's ridiculous," Jean told her. "That's a ridiculous thing to say. You can't say that kind of thing about people." And then: "You could say that about me."

"I would never say that about you." Liesel was genuinely hurt. "Your life is a good life," she said, indignantly.

"I'm thirty-two years old. I'm going out with my boss, who is getting a divorce because of me. The only reason we can afford where I live is because of him, and because you lend us money."

"Please, I don't care about the money. The money is yours, it's mine, it doesn't matter."

"I'm just saying that someone like Rose, the difference between her life and mine, is cushioning . . . it's privilege, it's because I'm spoiled. You spoil me."

"Listen, don't talk like this. You don't even believe it." Her face, under the gray hair, was going red; her eyes were shining, her accent, under the pressure of feeling, began to sound foreign. "Rose was in many ways an impressive woman, but she had no self-discipline. She sat in that house all day, she put on weight. She didn't have a job."

"That's just a generational thing."

"Who are you saying this to?" Liesel asked. "What generation do you think I belong to?"

"Yes, but you . . . nothing gets to you. Everything bounces off."

"I don't know what that means." But Liesel had heard it before. "And if we're talking about money," she added, "Bill gave Rose money, too. Tens of thousands, hundreds of thousands. It's not a question of money." And so on.

Really what bugged Jean is the way Liesel talked about Rose— her tone, as if Rose's death were an occasion for working out what you really felt about her. An interesting test of the affections. As if that's what mattered. And five minutes later Liesel asked Nathan if he thought she needed to go to the funeral. By Jewish law Rose was supposed to be buried as early as possible, within twenty-four hours, though Rose was not particularly observant, and with her grandson in Chicago, nothing was likely to happen before Friday.

"I don't want to go," she said. "Everybody's here." And then, to placate Jean: "Henrik is coming, I want to meet him."

Jean raised her eyes at this, but she wasn't really mad. She was upset but also anxious about other things, which both of them knew.

"Talk to Bill," Nathan told his mother. "I don't think he'll care."

"Of course he cares," Susie said. "He's alone out there, he's got to deal with everything himself. I don't expect Judith will help much."

"Judith won't help at all. But it's not the short-term aggravation I'm worried about. What happens will happen, Rose is dead, there's not much they can really get wrong, as far as she's concerned. None of this is fun for Bill, I get that—it's the opposite of fun. But in a few days it will be over. The long-term fallout is what worries me more. Judith and Alex are going to argue about money and Bill is going to be caught in the middle of it."

"It's not a question of," Susie said, "it's not a question of getting it right or wrong. There are some things you do even if it doesn't make a difference. Somebody from our family, I mean other than Bill, should be there. Somebody should be there for Bill."

"So go."

"May is ten months old. I'm still nursing her twice a day. I'd love to go but I don't think . . ."

"So don't go. Nobody's making you."

David gave Clémence a look across the table, from which she turned away. She didn't like being roped in like that, as if they were laughing at the Essingers together. Also, it annoyed her the way everybody relied on Nathan to make certain decisions, to deal with certain aspects of family business, and then blamed him for sounding unemotional or disinterested.

He seemed to feel something similar because he changed the subject. "Why don't you tell us what Dodie said to you about Earl Mosby?" he asked Julie. "We knocked on her door this afternoon, and Dodie said . . ."

But Julie didn't want to; she was embarrassed. What she had told her father was a kind of confession—she still felt bad about it. About not correcting Dodie or objecting when she said . . . but it was hard to remember exactly what she *had* said. "Her basic point, though," Julie in spite of herself was trying to explain, "her point was something like, in the Fifties and Sixties, when they first moved here, everybody got along much better than they do now, black people and white people, even if the black people were all basically servants, everybody kind of knew their place. Whereas now—"

And Nathan interrupted her. "I thought she also said that these days there really aren't any African Americans in the neighborhood at all—that there's no interaction."

"I think that's what she said." And she looked at Liesel. "She said that people were upset when you didn't let Mosby stay."

"She can't have said that. There was never really any question. I mean, by the time we bought the house . . . we never met him. You must have misunderstood her."

"Are you excited about sleeping out in the playhouse tonight?" Jean asked her.

"Isn't it a little late for that?" Susie said. It was almost eight o'clock, and a cold night after a clear afternoon. The curtains were drawn and the heating was on. Liesel had already draped blankets over the patio plants.

"What do you mean?"

"I just thought that, given what's happened, we could leave it be."

But Nathan was quick to sense interference. "What's Rose got to do with it? We spent all morning setting up."

Ben said, "I don't think she wants to do it anymore."

"What do you mean?"

Nathan looked at his nephew, who had kept a straight face and sounded sympathetic. He looked like his father, but thinner: an English schoolboy, with little round glasses and a pale complexion.

"I don't think she wants to. She's—"

"I'm not scared."

"I didn't say you were. I just think you changed your mind."

"What are you talking about? I haven't said anything."

"Well, it's what I think."

"Of course she wants to," Nathan said. "It's all set up."

But Ben was right and her father was wrong. This is what upset her, and why she had to stick up for her father now, she couldn't help it. And so after dinner while the table was being cleared she got ready for sleeping in the cold—and put on socks and a sweater over her pajamas. Even Clémence was against the idea and at one point took Nathan aside. "Have you talked to her about this?" she said.

"Of course I've talked to her."

"I mean have you talked to her again?"

"I don't know what that means. We've been talking about it all day."

"Well, she says one thing to you and another to me."

"Then what difference will it make if I talk to her some *more*?" he asked, reasonably enough, and Julie herself (they were in the back apartment) intervened.

"It's fine, Mom. I want to do it."

Liesel was only dimly aware of these undercurrents—Paul and Dana still hadn't come down to dinner. In spite of everything else that was going on, she noticed. A point in her favor, a little chalk mark on the right side of the ledger. At nine o'clock, with the kitchen cleared, she put her head around the door of the TV room and said, "I'm going to bed."

"Good night, Mom. Good night, Liesel. Good night."

Paul was there now, lying on the carpet with his head on a pillow. They were watching a basketball game. Jean, David, and Ben sat on the sofa.

"Where's Dana?" she asked.

"She's gone to bed, too."

"Is Cal okay?"

"He's fine, he's just sort of clingy. And Dana was tired anyway."

"She's a good girl," Liesel said, but Paul didn't answer.

In her old slippers, Liesel had to be careful on the wooden floors, which were very smooth, especially the stairs. She went up slowly, holding the bannister. From her dressing room, with its window overlooking the backyard, she could see a light in the playhouse window. Or thought she could see it, under the billboard advertising Jose Cuervo, which was also lit up. Poor Julie, Liesel thought, in her little cabin. But she was thinking of Nathan, too—like father like daughter.

After brushing her teeth, she sat on her bed and called Bill in Yonkers. He didn't have a cell phone; she had to look up Rose's number in her address book.

He picked up on the first ring. "Judith's sleeping," he said. "I should keep my voice down."

"How are you doing?"

"I'm okay, I'm fine. I'm just sorry I didn't get to the hospital earlier. I was waiting for Judith, she wanted to talk to Mikey, but everything with her takes twice as long as it should."

"I thought Rose died in the night."

"Yes."

"It wouldn't have made a difference."

"Probably not. Listen, at some point, we're going to have to go through all these clothes. I don't know if there's anything you or the girls might want."

"They wouldn't fit, would they?"

"Well, there are things like shoes, there are coats. Some of them are basically still in the box. She bought these things online and never wore them."

"What about Judith?"

"Right now, she says she doesn't want anything. She associates all this stuff with . . . she's still in the middle of this fight with her mother. She doesn't realize yet that the fight is over. But I don't want to just throw it all away. Some of it looks pretty expensive. Some of the shoes. I don't know what size the girls are."

"I'll ask them tomorrow," Liesel said, and they talked like this for another few minutes before hanging up. Bill, sitting on Rose's bed, with the heating on full, and the snow in the park opposite Rose's house visible under the streetlamps.

Nathan sat with Julie for a minute after she turned off her light. Still in his shorts, he felt the hairs on his legs uncurling in the night air. The room smelled damp, like an old sofa, it was very dusty, too. Not a nice place to sleep. The darkness seemed very present somehow, it seemed to come right up to the window. He could also hear party noises from the alley behind their backyard, maybe one of the bars was open.

"If at any point in the night you want to come back to the house," he said. "Nobody's going to judge you for it. Even if you just need to pee."

"Ben will make fun of me."

"I don't care what Ben says. You can use the bathroom and just get into bed."

Julie said, "I feel bad I didn't say anything to Dodie."

She felt childish, sleeping on a mattress on the floor. Her father sat above her, on a kids' chair, with his knees up.

"What could you have said?" he asked.

"I don't know. I could have challenged her."

She couldn't really see his face in the dark. Just the shape of his head, framed by long hair, which he rarely combed, and a patch of indistinctness around his mouth—he hadn't shaved in several days.

Eventually he said, "She's an old woman. She's been here a long time. It's not unreasonable for you to think about what kind of information she might have for you, before you correct her."

"I just feel bad. I feel like, I talk a lot about this kind of stuff, but then when I actually have a chance to . . . say something . . . I just . . . I didn't want to be impolite."

"That's a normal thing not to want. This stuff isn't easy." And then: "I'm in a similar position right now."

"What do you mean?"

He started to explain himself carefully. Part of what she loved about her father is that he had these conversations with her, even though they made her nervous, too, she felt almost shy, because she didn't want to disappoint him. One of his students had emailed him about a petition they were drawing up in reaction to the shooting at Sandy Hook Elementary School. It was about gun control and contained a certain amount of highly abbreviated constitutional arguments on the right to bear arms. Anyway, they hoped he would sign it, several of his colleagues already had. This put him in a difficult position.

"Why?" she said. "I mean, don't you think . . . I just assumed . . ."

"Look. The gun laws in this country are ridiculous. What happened in Sandy Hook was unspeakable. There's no question about that. But I'm used to making my own legal arguments. Certain points in the petition have been simplified more than I'm really comfortable with. I can come back at them with suggestions but that's not what they want from me. They want me to sign it."

"So don't sign it."

"That's not so simple either. It looks like a statement if I refuse. It seems to put me on the wrong side. There's also the fact that I have a good relationship with these students—they think of me as one of the good guys."

"But that's not a reason . . . to do something you don't believe in. That's like doing something because it makes you popular."

Nathan didn't say anything for a minute, and Julie could hear the music on Fruth Street—the bass sounds, distorted by the speakers. She was worried about what she would feel when Nathan left. The playhouse was really very small. And the door didn't lock, it didn't even close properly. The screen door just had a little hook, the kind you use in bathrooms. Between the playhouse and the main house was about eighty or a hundred feet of dark lawn; she was closer to the back gate. Anybody could wander in, but there was no reason to. She was being ridiculous.

"There's something else," her father said at last. "Another reason I don't want to sign the petition. If I hope at any point to become a federal judge, and it's a possibility I'd like to keep open, this is the kind of thing that can make life difficult at the confirmation hearings. The gun control lobby is very powerful."

"That doesn't seem like a good reason," Julie said.

"You don't think so?"

"I mean, because you're scared what people might say about you."

"Well, it's more complicated than that. Part of why I'd like to become a judge is so that I can . . . implement justice. According to the law and my own best sense of whatever justice the law permits. But to get to a position where you can do that involves some compromises. Signing this letter or not signing it won't really make any difference to anybody, but I think I could be a good judge." He added, a little ashamed of himself now: "I know what you mean though."

"Are you going to sign it?" Julie asked.

"What do you think I should do?"

"What would you want *me* to do?"

Nathan looked at his daughter. He could see her eyes in the dark, looking up at him. "What do you think I'd want you to do?"

She thought. "I think you'd want me to sign it."

"Yes," he said, and sat there for another minute before bending down on his knees to kiss her good night. He was really very cold by this point, almost shivery, and feeling strangely vulnerable or emotional, which sometimes happened to him when he got too cold. Julie, when the screen door closed behind him, slid out of bed to put it on the hook and then scrambled back in with dusty feet, and lay under the duvet, listening to the music, which seemed to get louder when she closed her eyes.

—

When he woke up he could see his mother. She lay on her belly with her head to the side, breathing heavily. The outside light cast rays through their bedroom window, which was directly above it. Shadows from the French blinds lay like the steps of a ladder against the ceiling. Cal felt fine, he felt wide awake, he needed to pee. For most of the day, he had drifted in and out of vagueness and clarity, but now he felt hungry, he felt normal. Liesel had given him a pair of slippers for Christmas, more like woolly boots than shoes, and he sat on the edge of his mattress and put them on.

The bathroom was at the end of the hall. Under the old rug, the floorboards seemed to ache when you stepped on them. There was a table against the wall, with a bowl and a pitcher on it, and whenever Cal ran along the corridor Liesel told him to watch out for the bowl. If the rug slipped out from underneath him . . . It was very old; it cost lots of money. So he walked carefully. When he shut the bathroom door, it swung and banged against the frame. Everything sounded loud in the night. Even the noise of his pee against the water in the toilet, so he tried to pee on the porcelain instead. But it was nice to pee; he peed and peed, and afterward washed his hands but didn't flush. He didn't want to make more noise.

He was walking back to his room, when a door opened suddenly, and Ben came out in his pajamas. "Jesus," he said. "You gave me a shock." He was carrying a pair of shoes in his hand. "You should be in bed."

"I had to pee."

"Go back to bed."

Cal just stood there. "What are you doing?" he asked, in his normal voice.

"Nothing. Go to bed."

But he wouldn't go, and in the end there was nothing Ben could do but take him along. They crept together down the stairs. Cal asked him, "Where are we going?" and Ben eventually realized it was better not to answer. If you answered, he kept talking.

Liesel always left one of the downstairs lights on when she went to bed, the light over the oven, which cast a dim artificial colorless glow, but it was bright enough to show them the kitchen doorway. After that, it didn't matter how much noise they made; all the bedrooms were upstairs.

"What are we doing?" Cal asked again, and Ben finally told him.

"We're waking up Julie."

"Is she coming, too?" he said.

"No, she's not coming. I just want to scare her, a little." And then, "It's just . . . we're having some fun."

The backdoor was always unlocked, in case Nathan or one of his family needed to get into the main house from their apartment. A light shone on the concrete patio; the outside air felt warmer than Ben expected. Cloud cover had blown in, there was a low sky, and in the distance, over the trees and the tennis court, the Jose Cuervo sign lit up the telephone wires. It all seemed very . . . undark, as if the night were only 60 or 65 percent night. But he warned Cal to be quiet again, because Nathan and Clémence lay sleeping just ten feet away, on the other side of those sliding doors.

He sat on the back steps and put on his shoes. Cal wore his thick slippers, but his pajamas were really for a two- or three-year-old. The pants fit like shorts, the shirt was like a T-shirt, but Cal wouldn't let Dana throw them away, and for the past several nights she had put him to bed in them, because he felt so hot. But the fever had passed, and he was vividly awake now and almost totally consumed by excitement, which brought its own kind of stillness or concentration, because he stopped asking questions.

As they walked across the stones in the grass toward the back of the yard, Ben had no clear idea what he wanted to do. Maybe just look at her, and maybe if Cal hadn't come along, he would have looked at her and left her alone. That would have allowed him . . . a kind of feeling of power that might have been enough . . . a secret, something he could tease her with, what she looked like when she was sleeping in the playhouse. Or maybe he didn't even have to tease her. Just the fact that he could have done something if he wanted to, and nobody knew.

Julie had been getting on his nerves since they came to Austin—her Doc Martens, for example, which looked like clown shoes, and which she wore because she was somehow embarrassed about growing up, and having breasts, or whatever, and looking like a woman, so she tried to look ugly instead, and cut her hair off, so that nobody could make fun of her for trying to look like a pretty woman, or something like that. Also, she turned everything into an argument. As if she were the only one who ever thought about racism or inequality or sexism, and even if you were just making a dumb joke, even if it was dumb, it was also a joke, and you didn't have to take it so seriously. But the thought of her lying there woke in him protective feelings, too, a twelve-year-old girl in her pajamas, and something harder to pin down, an appetite for intimacy or closeness, which they used to have as children but was being withdrawn.

It was darker under the shade of the old pecan, the wet grass reached his ankles, he wasn't wearing socks. Maybe it had rained earlier, maybe that's what woke him up. The lights of the main house glowed eighty feet behind them. Nobody could hear them, except Julie.

Cal reached up for Ben's hand, and Ben let him take it. They walked around the side of the playhouse to the back window—ducking under a tree, Ben felt the leaves brush his face. Julie lay on the mattress on the floor, but it was hard to see her . . . the screen was dirty, and the broken metal mesh produced an impression of light sketching, as if she were drawn in pencil strokes. But he thought there was something awkward about the way she lay, half on her side, with her T-shirt pulled out of shape. Her foot had come out at the end of the duvet. It looked like she was wearing a sock, maybe she got cold in the night, and Ben dragged Cal away from the window, toward the tennis court, which had a border of smooth stones. He picked up a handful and threw them onto the roof of the small house.

He thought they might sound like heavy rain or something like that—it seemed relatively harmless. The roof was covered in old asphalt shingles, but there was also a layer of leaves, nuts and twigs lying on top, which scattered when the stones hit them and made a scratching noise. He threw another handful. One of the pebbles struck the metal gutter that ran around the edge of the roof and clanged.

For the first time Ben felt a pulse of fear, maybe because he thought they'd get caught. But also out of a kind of sympathy for Julie: he was imagining what it must feel like to lie there, listening. The yard spread around them, large and gloomy under the trees, the main house looked far away, and the back gate led to an almost unused alley, a dead end, where anybody could be sleeping or lurking.

Cal picked up a stone and threw it against the side of the house. There was a sharp crack, and then they heard something else, the door opening (which they couldn't see; it was on the other side), the screen door clappering behind, and footsteps running through the ivy.

"I think you broke the window," Ben said.

"I did what you did."

"I threw it against the roof. It doesn't matter." And then: "It's not your fault."

He went to check, but it was hard to see in the dark. Maybe it wasn't broken, maybe the cracking sound was just the noise of stone on glass. There was a screen in front anyway but the screen was damaged. He said to Cal, "She really didn't mess around, I mean, she was gone," and he thought he might be able to laugh at her about it in the morning. But he also felt like, I didn't even get to see her, something was missing, a confrontation, but also like, for maybe a minute or two, Jesus, she must have been scared, while she lay there awake and wondered whether to run, before she ran. I guess that's what I wanted, and Cal said, "She just . . . she just ran," and waited for Ben

to laugh before he laughed, too. Ben laughed and said, "She was like
. . . gone."

Cal laughed and Ben felt sad or stupid or dissatisfied, because they
were standing at two o'clock in the morning at the back of the yard
outside an empty shed and had to walk through the wet grass to go
to bed.

"Don't tell anybody, okay," Ben said.

"I won't."

"If we have to say something, I'll say it."

He took his cousin's hand again as they walked around the hut
and under the pecan tree toward the house. Ahead of them, sixty or
seventy feet away, somebody stepped into the patio light that shone
over the backdoor—a man, it must have been Nathan, barefoot and
moving gingerly over the pebbled concrete. Ben stopped, he pulled
Cal back a little, they were still in the shade of the tree.

Nathan stood on the edge of the patio and looked at them, or looked
at the playhouse behind them, and Ben couldn't tell if he could see
them or not, but after a minute he turned away and disappeared again
behind the side of the apartment.

"Let's just wait here," Ben said. "Are you scared?"

"No."

"Are you feeling better?"

"I'm okay."

"You're a tough kid," Ben said, and thought, this is dumb, we can't
stand out here all night, and started walking back through the grass.

When they reached the patio (Nathan and Clémence slept behind
glass doors; the curtains had been drawn when they set out, and Ben
peered around the side of the apartment to see if their lights were
on; they weren't), he whispered something to Cal, and they snuck
along the far edge of the patio, by the bamboo hedge that bordered
the neighbor's yard, and then along the side of the main house to the
backdoor. There were four steps and he opened the screen door for
Cal, and held it with one hand while Cal stepped under his arm. Then

he opened the main door and Cal went in while Ben carefully let the screen door close against the weight of his shoulder, and turned the handle of the house door so it didn't make a sound.

WEDNESDAY

Margot and Willy both woke up with temperatures. They had caught Cal's cold, and Nathan in particular slept badly, with Julie in bed beside him—she was too scared at first to sleep on her own after coming inside. Then Margot cried out with an earache at four in the morning. Julie ended up retreating to her mattress on the floor, next to the pool table, while Margot slipped in between Nathan and Clémence. But that was another argument. It's not fair, Julie kept complaining, loudly in the dark, I'm lying here on my own, it's creepy, until Nathan gave up and got up and crawled on to the mattress beside her. It was like old times, musical beds, the first intense years of parenthood. Vague hours before dawn, warm shifting interchangeable bodies, half-states of consciousness, somewhere between dream and anxiety.

Susie had a rough night, too. Willy started whimpering when Ben crept into their room at 2 a.m., took off his shoes and slid silently under the covers. He pretended to sleep when Susie came in to check on them. For several minutes, he listened to her trying to keep Willy quiet, lying in bed with him and whispering "Sh, sh, sh, you'll wake your brother." Feeling ashamed but also somehow hidden or protected by his sense of shame.

Only Cal slept late. Dana woke up at eight and rolled over to look at him. He lay with his head flung back off the side of the mattress, and his mouth wide open. His color was good, his breathing sounded comfortable, he was out cold, and Dana lay for a while listening to him before she got bored and went down to breakfast without him.

Nathan and Susie were arguing when she walked in. Susie said, "Look, this is the kind of thing that happens. I thought it was a dumb idea from the beginning. People get drunk over the holidays, they wander into other people's backyards, we're just lucky that's all it was."

"You don't walk in and throw stones at somebody's garden shed. That's not a thing that a reasonable person should have to game plan for."

"I told you last night I thought it was inappropriate. I told you so last night."

"You're conflating things, Susie. You're not making sense. You sound like Liesel."

"What did I do?" Liesel asked, and Julie walked in the backdoor with Clémence behind her. Ben, who was eating waffles, didn't look up.

"Hey, Julie," Susie said, in a different voice. "I hear you had a bit of an experience."

"I don't know what I had. Maybe I'm crazy, maybe I made it all up."

But Nathan before breakfast had checked on the playhouse. (In his socks; they were still wet from the grass and had tracked footprints into the breakfast room.) The window at the back was cracked, and there were stones lying in the dirt underneath it.

"She's a brave girl," her mother said, who had her arms around Julie. "She got the hell out."

"I don't feel so brave," Julie said.

The rest of the argument was about whether or not to call the police. Susie thought you should absolutely call the police, but Julie didn't want to. She seemed softened by something, more childish. She kept her left hand on Clémence's lap, and Nathan poured the milk for her cereal.

"Maybe it was broken already," Julie said. "I don't know. I don't really have anything to say. I mean, it's like, dumb kid sleeps in the garden shed and gets scared. That's not really a crime scene."

"I saw the stones." But Julie told her father, "Those stones get everywhere," which was true.

"Look," Nathan said. "I'm not going to force you to do anything. It's up to you how you want to respond to this. If you think that nothing happened, and the right thing to do is let it go, that's what we'll do. But if you think that somebody was out there, who might have been a danger to you or to somebody else, and should be reported . . ."

"Let it be," Clémence broke in. "She's said what she wants to do. This isn't one of your moral questions."

"Excuse me, but that's exactly what it is . . ." and so *they* were fighting now.

Susie stayed quiet and Dana thought, I should stay out of it, too. Everybody looked tired, and somehow hungover, sensitive to noises and slights, and probably upset about Rose, though that's not the kind of reason or motive that Nathan would ever admit to. When she said this kind of thing to Paul (trying to help him understand his moods) he always told her, that has nothing to do with it, you're imputing to me your own emotional reactions, and so she learned not to offer these explanations. Essinger men liked to believe that they weren't motivated by feelings. Cal would probably be like that, too.

David came in, dressed and showered, fat, good-natured, social, and offered to buy everyone coffee. "Where's Willy?" he asked.

"I let him watch TV," Susie said. "He didn't want any breakfast." And then: "Apparently Margot's got it, too."

"I'm sorry, it's all my fault," Dana said.

"What is?"

"For bringing disease into this house."

"Don't be silly," Clémence told her, but nobody else said anything.

When David came back with the coffees, Susie handed him the baby. "I'm going up to shower," she told him, and Ben followed his mother out of the kitchen.

"I want to talk to you," he said.

"Can it wait? I didn't sleep much and I just want five minutes to myself."

"Please."

"Okay, so talk." But he didn't want to talk in the hallway and in the end they went into Liesel's study, where Ben shut the sliding doors behind them. Susie sat down in the desk chair and faced her son.

"Okay, so talk," she said again.

"Do you think they're going to call the police?"

"It's up to them. It's up to Julie. I think they should, if only because I think Julie should learn that if this kind of thing happens, you report it, you tell people, you make a stink, even if it doesn't do any good. This is what she should learn. But it's not up to me."

Ben said, "I want to tell you something, but after that I don't want to talk about it. I mean, you can get mad, you can shout at me, that's fine, but after that I don't want to talk about it."

Susie stared at him. He stood on Liesel's old rug under the ceiling fan and still looked like what he was, a twelve-year-old boy. Other kids, some of his friends, seemed to be going through growth spurts; their mothers complained about how much they ate, and other things, which Susie hadn't had to deal with yet. In any case, that was David's department. There must be some benefits, she liked to joke, to marrying a man who had gone to an English public school. They learn to deal with certain facts without embarrassment, and she wondered if Ben was leading up to something like this.

"Okay," she said.

"I don't want to talk about it with Dad either. Whatever you want to say to me about it, I want you to say it now."

She waited. "I'm listening," she said eventually.

"It was me who threw stones at the playhouse."

"What do you mean?"

"I just wanted to scare Julie a little. It kind of annoyed me the way she was acting, like . . . There was no good reason."

"What time was this?"

"I don't know, maybe two o'clock. I woke up and everybody was asleep. I thought it might be funny just to see her there."

"Did you set your alarm? I don't understand. Was this a plan? Did you plan this?"

"There was no plan. I just thought it would be funny." There was a silence, which he broke. "Are they going to call the police?" he asked again.

His voice was changing, he sounded like Willy, like a kid.

"They're not going to call the police."

"Are you going to tell them?"

"I have to tell them. Otherwise they might call the police."

"Can't you get them not to without telling them?"

Susie held her hands between her legs (they felt cold) and leaned forward slightly in her mother's chair. She thought, I have to be careful what I say.

"I have to tell them."

"Just so you know, I didn't break the window."

But this set her off. "Don't lie to me, Ben, on top of everything else."

"I'm not lying, it's true!"

"Who broke it then?"

He hesitated. "I think it was already broken."

"Ben . . ."

"It was! I didn't do it." He was crying now, or trying to, and took off his glasses. "You have to believe me."

"I don't want to believe any of this," Susie said. "None of this makes any sense. But if you're going to tell the truth, you should just get it over with."

"I am telling the truth. Why don't you believe me?"

She didn't say anything, she just looked at him.

"You have to believe me," he said.

"I don't really care if you broke the window or not. That's not the point."

He had stopped crying now. His throat hurt, it didn't feel natural, and Ben put on his glasses again. From where he stood, he could see Liesel in the backyard, hanging out clothes on the washing line. There was a brown tub at her feet. She bent down slowly and straightened up again.

"When are we going home?"

"After New Year. You know that—in about a week."

"I don't think I can be in this house with everybody. I'm too ashamed."

Susie asked, "Why did you do it?" Her tone was not in her control. "I don't understand why you would do something like that."

"I don't know. I just wanted to. I don't know."

"You have to be in this house. This is my family. We can't run away just because . . ."

"I'm your family, too. I don't think I can face them."

"Who can't you face? Julie? She'll just think it's a stupid . . ."

"Uncle Nathan. I don't want to talk to Nathan about it."

"I don't much want to talk to Nathan about it either," Susie said, with something like returning humor.

"I'm sorry, Mom. What do you want me to do?"

"What do you mean?"

"Should I go to my room?"

"There is no punishment. For this kind of thing . . . there is no punishment."

"I can't talk to Nathan about it. After . . ." and he paused. For almost the first time in his life he was conscious of saying something intimate, something painful and secret that had happened to him, which he could communicate. "After Julie ran inside, I walked back to the house, and Nathan was standing on the patio. He couldn't see me, I was standing under the tree, but I was . . . scared of him."

"How do you think Julie felt?"

He didn't answer, and then he asked, "Is there anything else you want to say to me?"

"Not right now."

"Please don't talk to me about it again. You promised."

"I'll do my best," Susie said and went up to shower.

*

Bowl by plate by glass the table was cleared, cartons of juice and milk were squeezed precariously into the crowded fridge, boxes of cereal and jars of jam, honey, and golden raisins put back in the cupboards under the kitchen counter. Various sections of the *New York Times*, which arrived every morning, wandered from the counter to the table to the TV room. Some were occasionally removed from circulation, read in the bathroom, refolded and returned, slightly damp.

In the after-breakfast period of hanging around, an argument broke out about who in the family should represent the Essingers at the annual Kirkendoll Boxing Day brunch. Nathan said somebody had to go. He was willing to go on his own but he didn't see why . . . and he would like Clémence to come with him, but that meant either bringing the kids (and Julie interrupted here, "I don't think I'm up to it."), or somebody staying behind to look after them.

"I'll stay," Clémence said. Her dark pretty narrow face conveyed a certain amount of cheerful force. Nathan tried to argue with her but got nowhere. "I'm not leaving Julie after last night. I'm staying right here," and Julie, who was almost as tall as her mother, let herself be pulled against her side.

David was happy to come, he liked a party, and he wanted to see the Bayreuth mansion, but he didn't know what Susie's plans were—she was in the shower. He was sensitive to emotional undercurrents but not always insightful or accurate about what caused them, and felt there was some conflict being played out, between Nathan and Clémence, which he didn't understand, something marital he wanted to steer clear of.

Liesel asked, "Does it look bad do you think if I stay behind?"

"I think you should come," Nathan said, while at the same time Jean told her, "It's fine."

Jean herself was just killing time until she had to pick up Henrik from the airport. His flight went via Chicago, and Nathan said, "Never fly through Chicago," and Jean said, "I told him that . . .

I told him that. It's even worse, he's got like an hour and a half for the connection, but if all goes well, which it won't, he should be landing a little after four. I don't particularly want to go to the Kirkendolls but I honestly can't say that I have anything else to do, unless someone needs me to look after their kids."

Dana said, "Cal's still asleep, but I don't want to leave him and I don't really want to take him along."

"I'd like your company." Nathan was still trying to win the argument with Clémence. He spoke in his private voice, a kind of urgent undertone, the voice he used to say, I have strong feelings on the subject but I understand if you don't share them. Clémence shook her head. "We can talk about this later." Liesel was always relieved to see Nathan's wife stand up to him—it was one of her consolations that she thought they had a very healthy marriage.

"Anyway," she said, "I have to shower, I have to get dressed, I want to call Bill. Nothing's going to happen in the next hour, is it?"

But it was already after ten o'clock and Nathan's disappointment was turning into impatience. Jean said, "Go shower, make yourself beautiful," and Liesel on her way out of the kitchen put her hand against the pot of coffee under the machine, which was already cool, and poured herself a cold cup, which she took upstairs with her.

"Has anyone called Paul?" Jean asked, and Dana felt and not for the last time a flush of shame.

In the end only the men went, Nathan and David and Paul, in Paul's car—he showed up at the house a half hour later. Cal was awake, he looked like himself again, and Paul lifted the boy wriggling above his head, pinning his back to the kitchen ceiling. Dana said to him, "Please, he's only just . . ." but Paul said, "It's just nice to see him like . . ." and Dana said, "I know. You don't realize until afterward. It's like I can breathe again." They ended up having another argument about going to the party, and Julie said to her uncle, "You're just exactly and totally like my dad."

Clémence stepped in and said "the girls" would do something to-gether—knowing the phrase would annoy Nathan, but teasing him about it, too. He was freshly shaved, ready to go, in suit and tie. They were just waiting for Susie . . . who appeared eventually, with her wet hair drawn back in a ponytail, so that her face and neck seemed somehow exposed and vulnerable, though it also made her look a little severe. Her Quaker look, David called it. Everybody had to go over everything again, making plans. Nathan said, "I don't like it. I've said what I wanted. I want you to come," but Clémence didn't budge and eventually the men drove off.

It was warm enough to leave the window open—Nathan felt the breeze against his face. His wife at the last minute had tried to comb his hair down, using her fingers, but he shrugged her off; it stuck out anyway. For various reasons he was in a complicated mood.

Nathan had always been closer to Judge Kirkendoll than the other Essinger children. This was sometimes embarrassing, because you don't want to admit to liking somebody your brother and sisters have lumped together with all the other adults you try to avoid at dinner parties. But Nathan was old enough to remember some of the earlier stages of his father's friendship with the judge, when Bill and Kirk were still junior faculty who met occasionally to play pool or watch a ball game (Nathan as a four-year-old boy sometimes watched them play, or watched them watch) . . . before the other children took over Bill's social life, and he drifted away from his colleagues. As Nathan got older, Kirk sometimes talked to him about Bill—about the fact that he wouldn't play the games you need to play if you want to climb the ladder. It didn't need to be said that Kirk was teaching Nathan what these games were, so that he when he grew up Nathan would not repeat his father's mistakes.

Which is why he still felt embarrassed by their relationship. It looked to the rest of the family (or so he figured it to himself) like he was taking sides against their father. Kirk used to buy him ties or IZOD shirts for his birthday, the kind of expensive and conservative clothes his own parents would never spend money on. They shared a sense of style, but Nathan had also in his own way tried to distance himself from the judge.

In law school, he brought his girlfriend back to Austin and introduced him to the Kirkendolls; they went to dinner at the Bayreuth mansion. The next summer, while he was interning in Manhattan with Sullivan and Cromwell, Kirk, who had helped him get the job, took him out to lunch at the Century Club. He said how much he enjoyed meeting Jenny (that was the name of the girlfriend). One of the pleasures of youth, he said, is that you get to meet a lot of nice girls, smart, interesting girls, it's one of the ways a young man gets to know the world. Nathan understood what was meant and didn't react or contradict him, which he was afterward ashamed of, but he also fought harder than he otherwise might have when his relationship to Jenny naturally came to an end. After law school, she went home to work for Bakers and Hostetler, and when he tried to find a job in Seattle, too, she put a stop to it. Who are we kidding, she said. This is not where your life is.

Kirkendoll, as it happens, approved of Clémence. He thought she was a good thing, and told Bill, who told Nathan. This irritated him but not enough to keep him from showing up at the judge's Boxing Day party. Apart from anything else, Kirk had friends in Congress, including Elizabeth Warren and various members of the Texas delegation to the House. He had friends across the aisle, too, and there was even a chance that Kaye Bailey Hutchinson would come down from Dallas. Nathan if he wanted to be a federal judge needed to get his name in front of these people. Kirk could help him do that, or maybe this is the kind of thing you tell yourself, when you want something you don't know how to get, or where the decision is really in other people's hands.

Paul waited at the slow lights by the old Schwinn bicycle shop, where all of the Essinger kids got their first bikes, then crossed over North

Lamar and the Shoal Creek greenbelt, before rising up West 29th into
Pemberton Heights. Trees spread over the gritty asphalt. They passed
what Liesel always called the ship house, an old Art Deco mansion
built against the slope, with white walls and curved metal windows,
balconies overlooking the creek, a terraced garden, and a *For Sale* sign
stuck in the driveway.

"Why didn't you buy that?" Nathan said. "Why didn't you move
there?"

"Too urban."

Paul was only partly joking. David sat in back and listened to
them, feeling like one of the kids and slightly fed up. When they got
in Paul's car Nathan automatically took the passenger seat. Maybe he
was a couple of inches taller, but David was also aware, this is a power
play. Or maybe Nathan genuinely didn't notice or care. They were
brothers, after all, it was their town, and for one week of Christmas
David understood that he was just tagging along; but he was also
quietly glad to be taking Susie away from all this. Individually, he
liked most of the family (especially Bill and Jean), and even though
his relationship with Nathan wasn't straightforward, he could appreciate his virtues and charms. But collectively . . . there was a kind of
self-involvement or self-importance that struck him as bad form—
and like most bad form, makes you unhappy.

Pemberton Heights counted as old Austin, though most of it was
developed in the Thirties or later. There were the usual colonials,
painted white and gray, with pillared porticos and fenced-in yards,
but also a few stranger constructions, ivied castles and contempor-
ary faux-moderns that looked like parts of supermarkets. When the
Bayreuth mansion was built, the land was mostly farmland, and you
still had a sense of grassy spaciousness from the wide front lawns. Tall
trees let through a lot of light—the cloudy morning was giving way
to another mild curiously dead and pleasant sunny afternoon. Paul
felt hungry and light-headed; he hadn't eaten much after his eight-
mile run, but he parked where he could (a few blocks past the house;

the curb was crowded) and they got out and walked back to the party.

The judge's home had a faint New Orleans feel to it, with French windows and fretwork metal balconies on every floor—Christmas lights had been strung through the railings and glittered and blinked. Two women in black aprons stood next to the pillars at the end of the brick front path and one of them had a tray in her hand, with glasses of champagne.

David decided to get drunk. He didn't know anybody but he didn't want to hang around Paul and Nathan and was perfectly happy talking to strangers. The hall was already full of people, most of them in their sixties, and the doors on either side, to the library or living room, and then to the kitchen and dining room at the back, were hard to pass through—people had a tendency to get stuck. David with his farmer's shoulders and businessman's belly took up a lot of room, but he could use his accent to get him through most tight spaces and he pushed his way into the library, where there was a fire going. The trick (David had found) in a party like this where you don't know anybody is to start by talking to the photographer, who is usually standing alone and happy to have a little conversation. In this case she turned out to be a friend of the judge's younger daughter, a woman in her twenties named Ilyana or Alana or Elaine (it was too loud to hear), who was working on a master's in Mexican-American studies at the university. She was really just doing a favor, though she couldn't quite tell who was helping out *whom*—they were paying her pretty well.

"I've just walked in from the street," David said. "Maybe you can tell me who everyone is."

"I don't really know either . . ." but she knew enough.

Paul said to Nathan, "I really need to eat something. I don't know why I'm here."

More women in black aprons circulated with trays of food, but the going for everybody was pretty slow, and Paul found a buffet of breads and cheeses laid out on the dining-room table. Nathan ran into somebody from the law school and got lost on the way, so Paul stood by himself and spread brie over a piece of baguette and ate and felt the calories make their way into his bloodstream. He hated this kind of thing, this is exactly the kind of thing that made him want to get out of New York in the first place. But for some reason Nathan wanted him to come along so he came. Most of the people there were people with money but nobody you had any reason to recognize, lawyers and businessmen and their wives. One of the judge's neighbors presented the six o'clock news on KXAN, the local Austin affiliate of NBC. On air she had a very natural presence, her blonde hair was untied and she looked pretty in a perfectly appropriate and PTA kind of way, but when he saw her she looked exactly the way she looked on TV but somehow the effect was more like a kind of confection and you noticed her human strangeness. Still, she's what counted for a celebrity, and the pockets of people moved around her accordingly, so he ate and watched.

The Kirkendolls had three kids, the oldest was roughly Paul's age. At family get-togethers (which didn't happen often; they were much more social than the Essingers), there was a kind of expectation that Paul and this girl would interact. Her name was Elsa, after the judge's grandmother. She went to St. Stephens, which was private, instead of McCallum High, where Paul went, and he always found contact with her embarrassing in a teenage way that had somehow survived their childhoods on the few subsequent occasions when they had met. They were now thirty-five, and he saw her talking to a woman with a kind of hairnet until she excused herself and joined him at the buffet table.

"I sometimes see you running through Stacy Park, but you're going so fast I don't dare to say hello."

He remembered something he had forgotten, which is that she flirted with you almost out of good manners—the way little girls are taught to say please and thank you. She was always complimentary.

"Maybe it's someone else. I don't usually run along there. I live out near Wimberley now."

"No, it was you, but maybe you were on your bike. I think there was a group of you."

"That's possible," he said.

Elsa had put on weight but she carried herself like an attractive woman, and in fact she was still reasonably pretty. Her eyes were large and clear, and she used them—Paul often found himself looking away, partly because she wore too much makeup (Dana hardly needed any). One of the things he always liked about Elsa as a kid is that she liked to eat, and he watched her fill one of the paper plates with bean salad, guacamole, and French bread. She worked in arts administration, whatever that means, and was on the board of the Blanton Museum, among other things. His impression of her was that she went to a lot of openings and parties, though he had also heard that she wasn't married.

"Is that where you live?" he asked.

"I'm sort of house-sitting right now. A friend of mine has moved to Buenos Aires, she's got one of these residency things, so I'm staying in her apartment in Travis Heights."

This wasn't what he expected, and he didn't understand it. The Kirkendolls had a lot of money. Elsa leaned over and said, "My father is very excited. Guess who said she might come?"

"I don't know. What do you mean? To the party?"

"Sandra Bullock. She's selling her house in Barton Creek and wants to look around Pemberton Heights."

"I didn't know . . ." but someone had pulled Elsa away, and she made an excuse-me face, and let herself be pulled. He looked around for Nathan but couldn't find him, so he looked around for David and saw him talking to a woman with a camera around her neck. For some reason he didn't want to interrupt. If he had to guess he would have said she was in her early twenties, she had a pleasant young-person's face. While they talked, she kept taking pictures, but David seemed to be making her laugh. And something like envy, or not even envy, just a realization of what he was actually like began to settle on Paul.

Everyone else at the party had dressed for the occasion. The women wore jewelry, some of the men wore ties. Paul, who hadn't expected to be showing up at any social functions when he set off for Wheeler Street, was still in his jeans and sneakers, and the Wheatsville Co-op T-shirt he bought for Dana once, and which she didn't want. When the waitresses came by with their trays of food, he tried to joke with them. "Keep 'em coming," he said. "I'm the guy you can rely on to empty the tray," but the woman he said this to didn't react and only waited patiently for him to put his toothpick back.

He walked outside, into the yard. A few people were smoking on the grass, and he found himself checking the faces for Elsa, not because he was particularly attracted to her but because she was somebody he knew and could talk to. But also maybe because he found her attractive. It was hard to say, he was in a state of preoccupation. He was also aware of one of the waitresses, a light-skinned black woman, very tall and thin, who somehow reminded him of Dana and sometimes lifted her tray over the heads of the guests as she squeezed between them . . . the fact that he paid her attention made him unhappy. So far they hadn't made eye contact, and he felt somehow like the hungry male, eating food and looking at women, and not talking, a phrase he had heard one of Dana's friends use to describe that guy at the party who . . . just kind of stands there, and it had stuck with him.

Almost as a relief from these feelings he tried to think about Elsa. The judge had a ranch house near Brenham, and once or twice when they were kids the Essingers got invited out there for lunch on a Saturday afternoon. The Kirkendolls smoked their own brisket and sausage. There was a lake on the property, and on one of these occasions the judge suggested to Elsa that Paul might be interested in going for a row. He was about fourteen years old. What was embarrassing was just the careful way nobody teased them (not even Nathan or Susie) as Elsa offered to walk out to the lake and show him the boat. It was after lunch, still light, but pretty late in the year — November maybe. The grass looked like the grass looked now, pale and dead.

Elsa let him take the oars, even though it was her boat, and praised the way he handled them. She said something like, "It's so nice just to sit back and let someone row you around." Paul felt like he was being condescended to, or not exactly that . . . pleasantly managed, just because he was a boy, which disconcerted him but he also found himself responding in predictable ways. He tried very hard not to splash her.

From these thin memories . . . maybe four or five of them of equal quality, a relationship that had lasted almost thirty years was constructed. It didn't add up to much.

Nathan with a glass of champagne in each hand passed him on the veranda and then stopped. Large bright pots of plants stood against the brick wall, between the windows. He said, "I've been assuming you're willing to drive."

"I don't mind driving," Paul said. "I'm pretty much ready to go right now."

"Where's David?"

"Flirting with some . . . I don't know. I don't know why I said that."

"You all right?"

"I don't know," Paul said. "I seem to be going through a period where I'm annoying to waiters and . . . other kinds of service personnel. I don't know if it's an indication of anything."

"Are you nice to them or are you a jerk?"

"I'm extra nice, that seems to be the problem."

"Listen," Nathan said, "I'm supposed to deliver these," (he held up the champagne flutes) "but I want to talk to you. Give me a minute, okay. Don't go anywhere."

Paul waited a minute, then he saw Elsa coming out of the French doors leading a small group of people, including the woman from KXAN and Sandra Bullock. She had a sensible handsome famous face, though partly she just looked familiar, like one of his sister's friends.

He walked up to them and Elsa introduced him. "This is Paul Essinger, who I grew up with. He's a famous tennis player."

"Oh really?"

Sandra was wearing high heels; she seemed somehow delicately poised.

"I wasn't very good," Paul said. "And then I retired from not being good a couple of years ago."

"What do you do now?"

"Nothing much. Am I right in thinking your mother is German?"

"Yes." Her manner was the manner of someone who is always polite. She tolerated conversation but you didn't get through.

"Me, too. We speak a kind of mishmash at home. At least, we did when we were kids."

"Pass the *Apfelmus*," she said, and he thought for a second, maybe . . .

Elsa touched him on the elbow. "I'm just giving a little tour of the grounds. My dad is very proud of what he calls his English garden."

"I didn't know you could grow an English garden in Texas."

"You can't. Come join us."

Paul said, "I'm just waiting here for somebody, I'll find you," and he let them go. Feeling for reasons he couldn't totally understand an intense sense of foolishness. Either because he was the kind of person who chose not to walk around an English garden with Sandra Bullock . . . but if he had, and left Nathan in the lurch, just to hang out with a group of people that included somebody famous and beautiful, he would have felt . . . but if you turn this kind of thing down, you should just turn it down, and not mind. If you want to stand on principle. But either way he knew he would have felt like a jerk. This had happened to him before, but the intensity itself is kind of useful, eventually it burns itself out. He waited by one of the potted plants for his brother.

The judge had been talking to a woman in a wheelchair, when he saw Nathan. "Nathan," he called out, "Come here, I'd like you to meet . . . Texas royalty. This is Carrie-Anne Jennings," he said.

Nathan reached out his hand, but he had to bend down and Mrs. Jennings had folded a wool blanket or a kind of poncho over her lap, from which she had to extricate herself. It was an awkward beginning, and the judge himself looked bright and lively but uncomfortably thin. You felt in his presence that you were refraining from asking the obvious questions, and Nathan remembered that Bill had told him something, three or four months ago. He tried to remember what. Lung trouble, maybe; in any case he had a kind of post-op brittleness. Kirkendoll was never a big guy, he had the natural upright dignity of small men, but now for the first time he looked elderly. He held a glass of champagne and the glass trembled. Part of what surprised Nathan is that he found himself feeling actual sympathy for him, when the judge had always been a figure in his life that you faintly resented, like a fact.

"This is a grand affair," Nathan said. His intercourse with Kirkendoll involved a certain amount of young fogy-ism. Nathan saw it as a form of politeness or respect, and their small talk included discussions of wines and watches, handmade shoes and tailored suits.

"I don't go to parties anymore," Mrs. Jennings said, "unless it's one of Kirk's."

"Ask her to tell you stories about her father," the judge said and excused himself, but after he had gone, she told Nathan, "Push me outside. I want to smoke."

This required some careful maneuvering—they were stuck behind the grand piano. But he got her out in the end, through the French doors, and wheeled her to a quiet spot on the veranda. The porch ran all the way along the house, and Nathan said, "Tell me about your father."

Mrs. Jennings was trying to light her cigarette—her matchbook had slipped out of her hand. Then she found it and lit it and sucked in, and said, "We don't have to go into all that." But that's what they did, Nathan was good at getting old ladies to talk. Her father was Bishop Kimball, presiding bishop of the Episcopal Church and one of the

founders of St. Stephen's school. She herself still sat on the board.
For the first few years ("We're talking about the Fifties now."), they
didn't have any classrooms to teach in. Students and staff built much
of the housing themselves; they lived in cabins. It was also the first
boarding school in the South to integrate. She was nine years old at
the time. Her father got death threats, and a man in a suit started
walking with their nanny, who was of course black, to drop them off
and pick them up from school. "We lived in Westlake Hills. In those
days, there wasn't anything there. Now to make that walk you'd have
to fly over the highway."

"There's a little shed, which we called the playhouse, in our backyard. My parents bought the house in something like seventy-five,
the old woman who lived in it had died, and her servant lived in that
shed."

Nathan felt bad about using his kids for conversational purposes
but he did it anyway. She said, "Yes. Yes." Her voice was deep but
had a quaver in it.

"Last night my daughter wanted to sleep in the shed. Out of indig-
nation, I suppose you would call it."

"And did she do it?"

"She lasted about half the night." And then, changing the subject:
"The judge looks well."

"They're going to have to try harder than that to kill him."

She had a large, unlovely, unembarrassed face. Nathan liked her;
it was difficult to imagine what she might have looked like when she
was young. Soft and glamorous, maybe, that was the style of the day.
Then a woman said, "Carrie-Anne!" and bent over to kiss her, and
Nathan offered to get them both champagne—the waitresses didn't
seem to be making the rounds outside. He ran into Paul on his way
back, then he delivered the drinks. The judge was standing on the
other side of the French windows and watching them.

Nathan stepped inside. "It's a wonderful house," he said. "I'm glad
I got to see you. You look well," and the judge frowned at him.

"I'm half the man I was." He meant this literally—they had taken out one of his lungs. "I don't like to stand around in their smoke, but then when I'm around they don't want to smoke."

"Are you enjoying the party?"

"I like to see people have fun." You had to lean in to hear him (his accent was gently Southern), and somehow the tone of the conversation had shifted. His frailness itself produced a kind of intimacy, and changed the footing.

"How's Bill?" the judge asked.

"I don't know if you know, but Rose, his sister, died. She went into the hospital just before Christmas and he flew out to see her—she lived in Yonkers. Now he's sticking around to arrange the funeral."

"I didn't know. He calls me on the phone maybe once a month. More since my operation, but I've gotten slack about returning people's calls. You assume they're all well-wishes."

"That's all right, he's all right. You know my father. He spends his life expecting some kind of disaster, so when it comes . . . at least he's prepared for it. But I'm worried about what happens next." Nathan had said all this before, to other people; but still it felt like a confession or offering, part of the price you pay for this kind of relationship. "Rose was divorced. Her ex-husband has remarried and has a couple of young kids, and I think there's going to be an argument about the money. I don't want Bill to get caught up in it."

"If there's anything I can do, you'll let me know."

"I will," Nathan said, and then, after a moment: "Right now, I'm wrestling with my own stupid problem. Some of my students have put out a statement on gun control, in response to Sandy Hook. They're looking for signatures. I approve of the sentiment but some of the legal reasonings have given me pause. These petitions are very clumsy expressions of whatever you want to say. I don't like signing them."

"I agree," the judge said.

"You heard that Mannheim's retiring."

"Yes, I heard."

"Someone from the DOJ has been in touch. I'm sure they're looking at several people."

"You'd be a strong candidate."

"I don't like putting anything on record that I haven't written myself."

"I think that's wise."

In spite of himself, and his real opinion of Kirkendoll, he felt something of the disquiet you feel after the confessional—which can only be relieved by more confession. But other people were joining them, greeting the judge, introducing their wives. Nathan said, "Let me know if you want to come Boston. We'd love to have you talk at the law school."

"I've cut back on all of that recently. But the new year is a new year." Then he put out his hand, their time was up.

Nathan looked pleased by something when he finally returned.

"I'm sorry," he said. In his green Armani suit, with a linen shirt and a pale blue tie . . . he spent money on clothes, but there was also something about the way he walked or stood that made his shirt come out of his pants and his tie hang crooked. Fine things couldn't contain him. "The judge introduced me to the kind of person you can't easily escape. But I wanted to talk to you. I'm worried about you."

"I'm okay. I just want to go home."

"Give us a minute. It's easier to talk here than at home." And then: "The champagne is better."

"You're more charmed by all this than I am."

"Oh, fuck you," Nathan said.

Paul didn't answer. He had been waiting by the potted plants for about ten minutes.

"Listen, I want to talk to you, but I don't want to talk like this."

"Like what?"

"This isn't an argument about lifestyle. And I don't want to turn it into a conversation about me."

"Who does?" Paul asked.

"But I don't know how worried about you we should be."

"I'm fine. Not at all. Let's go home."

"I don't think you're fine. And I don't think you're in a position or emotional state to assess your own position or emotional state."

"Well then what's the point of talking to me about it?"

Nathan looked at his brother with a certain amount of amusement.

"All right. Let's get out of here."

"Look," Paul said, not moving. "You get something out of this kind of thing that I don't get anymore. I don't want anything from these people."

"What people are these? I said leave me out of it."

"Okay."

"Some of the people here are serious people. You underestimate . . . what it takes to be a person of influence."

"Okay," Paul said. He knew that he had somehow turned the conversation around and forced his brother to explain himself.

"All of us were born into enormous privilege."

"I'm aware of that."

"I'm not sure you are. We're in a position," Nathan began, and then he said: "We have the chance to live unusually good lives."

"I don't know what that means."

"Because you haven't thought about it. It means material comfort, it means having available to you a range of experiences, like travel, like art, like seeing your kids as they grow up. It means playing a role in public affairs, it means doing actual and significant good."

"Not everybody wants to be Judge Kirkendoll."

"Because they don't want to do what you have to do."

"Because they don't want it," Paul said.

"Well maybe they should. Because if we're not going to do it, who will?"

Nathan's phone rang. Normally he wouldn't answer it, but he was angry or upset enough to take it out, and Paul told him, "I'm going to find David," and left him to it.

Clémence was on the line. "I wanted to talk to you before you got home."

"What's wrong?"

"Nothing's wrong, I just wanted to warn you. Susie had a conversation with Ben about the playhouse. He says he threw the stones."

"I don't understand."

"It was supposed to be a joke, I think. It got out of hand." And then, when he didn't say anything, she said: "You're not saying anything."

"I'm trying to think it through."

"You don't have to think it through. Susie said Ben's very upset, he knows what he did and she doesn't want us to talk to him about it. She's going to talk to David and they're going to figure it out."

"That's fine but that's not our problem."

"Nathan."

"Does Julie know?"

"Yes, I told her."

"How is she?"

"Basically relieved. Before she thought something had happened that was genuinely scary, now she's just mad."

"Is she allowed to say something to him?"

"We're all allowed. Susie asked me as a favor. I said okay."

"That's fine, you can do what you want."

"Nathan. If you want to get mad at somebody, get mad at me."

"I'm not mad at you."

"We've got three days left here and then we can go home."

"That's not how I think about it," he said.

David was a little drunk as they walked to the car. He smelled of cigarettes, he'd had a good time. He said, "I don't mind sitting in the back," and Nathan said, "That's good, because you're sitting in the back."

Paul felt cheerful again, something had shifted. Nathan still looked like he was pissed off about something so Paul could be the guy who didn't mind. The car was parked three or four blocks away, there weren't any sidewalks, so they walked in the road, in the sunshine, with dry bits of leaf in the asphalt crackling underfoot. He said to his brother, "I passed up my chance with Sandra Bullock waiting for you."

"Then you're an idiot," Nathan said.

When they got home, Susie was feeding May in the living room rocking chair. She could see them walk up (one of the side windows overlooked the front steps) and she half-called out to David when she heard their voices in the hall.

May kept falling asleep on her breast; it was more or less time for her afternoon nap. She hadn't finished feeding, and Susie thought, I should wake her up, but she liked feeling her weight and it was a hassle to do what you had to do: shake her a little, pinch her until she opened her eyes and sucked for a few seconds and fell back asleep . . . then you had to go through the whole thing again. So she let her lie there for a minute. Her eyes were closed with what seemed like an intense muscular effort.

When David came in, Susie said, "Close the doors."

He could tell that his wife was in a particular kind of mood. The baby on her breast gave her a sense of authority, and she said, "I want to talk to you about something. Don't make me shout."

She meant, come closer, so he sat down beside her on the bentwood armchair, and inched it around. The truth is, he liked to see her nursing. She wore old canvas shoes and loose blue jeans (because she hadn't yet lost the baby weight) and a thin cotton blouse, which was covered in some kind of Indian pattern and easy to pull off the shoulder. She looked in other words like an American mother of a certain class, upper-middle, vaguely hippieish, but at the same time financially comfortable and modestly old-fashioned. So that what had survived from hippiedom was really just an aesthetic sensibility, which David had always found attractive, and which mapped pretty well onto his own mother's English and small-c conservative tastes and preferences—for tea served in a teapot, for homemade jam, for bright comfortable clothes. He had been married to Susie for thirteen years, and whenever she had a baby, for the first ten or twelve months afterward (while she was still nursing, and before she began her diets) he noticed in himself a spike or renewal in his sexual interest, which wasn't often reciprocated.

She said, "I don't know if you heard what happened last night."

"Someone threw stones at the playhouse."

"Yes, well." And in spite of herself, she couldn't keep out of her voice the tone of someone sharing bad news: "It was Ben."

"Why the hell would he do that?"

"He says it was a joke. He just wanted to scare Julie a little bit."

"Well," David said. "I guess he succeeded."

"Please. I'm extremely upset by this." May was still fast asleep; they were speaking quietly.

"Of course, we'll pay for the window."

"Nobody cares about the window," she said. "Ben says it was broken already. I don't know what to think, I'm not sure I trust him anymore. I feel like I'm losing . . . contact. I didn't know what to say to him."

"I hope you told him to apologize."

"He was extremely upset, too. He knows that something's going wrong."

"Let's not exaggerate any of this. It's schoolboy stuff. When I was at school . . ."

"I don't want to hear about what you did at school."

"I did much worse, when I was his age. He's a twelve-year-old boy."

"You act like this is happy behavior. This is not happy behavior. Sneaking out at two in the morning to throw stones at a window is not happy behavior. Trying to scare the . . . out of your cousin, and taking pleasure from that, is not happy behavior."

"It's a prank, Susie. It's a stupid prank, but that's all it is."

He was still a little drunk from the Kirkendolls' party and not yet willing to come down. Nathan had pissed him off on the car ride home (the way he threw his weight around generally annoyed him), but David's response to irritation was to retreat into amusement. He had a few more days to get through, mostly he just needed to be patient. But he was also aware that it wasn't just a question of patience; that being amused and patient was a way of defending himself, against Susie, too.

"The Essingers turn everything into a moral dilemma," he said.

"What he did was evil. It's not a big deal, it's not the worst thing in the world, but it was evil."

"Susie," he said, more gently. "He's your son. He's Ben."

She turned to look at him; May shifted a little against her chest. "I've been imagining what it's like to stand out there in the middle of the night and throw stones at that house and imagine what Julie is feeling while she lies there listening. I don't see how you can want someone to feel those things."

"He's a boy. It was a joke. He just wants attention."

"Believe me, he has my attention," Susie said, and David stood up. "What do you want me to do about it? Do you want me to talk to him?"

"He doesn't want to talk to you. He asked me to ask you not to."

Almost in spite of himself he felt a kind of sugar rush of hurt— everything seemed to be happening on their turf, he felt left out. But this was only a short-term problem. In a few days they were flying back to Connecticut. "Let me know if you change your mind," he said, walking out. There's no point in fighting about it now, when you know perfectly well what she's upset about. Moving to England, and that's not an argument you have to win, because it's happening anyway.

———

Jean had been checking her computer throughout the morning for updates on Henrik's flight. In fact, for the past few days she had been tracking the weather forecasts in Chicago. Temperatures all week hovered around freezing, but so far there hadn't been anything worse than a light rain, and Wednesday dawned clear and sunny. There was a Bowl game in Detroit that night, and she walked into the TV room after lunch while David and Willy were watching some pregame roundup on ESPN. The reporters outside Ford Field stood in mittens and heavy coats—snow fell silently behind them, and Jean felt her heart stop and her hands start to sweat. But it was stupid, Detroit is five hours to the east, and the storm system was traveling south along the I-69 corridor toward Tennessee. Anyway, Henrik was probably already in the air.

Willy sat with his head in his father's armpit. He was still in pajamas. "Is he all right?" Jean said.

"He's all right." And then, to his son, in a hokey American accent: "You're a tough guy, right?"

"Let me know if I can get you anything," and David looked up at her.

"Thank you," he said, in his own voice. "We're just zoning out."

Around 3:30 she set off for the airport. It was much too early but she couldn't help herself. Liesel met her in the entrance hall. "Are you going now?" She must have been watching out for her, she had put off her nap.

"I don't know what the traffic will be like after Christmas."

"*Ich bin sehr gespannt,*" her mother told her. *I'm very excited,* but the German word in Jean's ears also had an overtone of something else. It could mean tension, too, something stretched between two points. "Is there anything he would like for supper?" Liesel asked. "I was going to make potato soup. I thought, something simple after a flight, but maybe he just wants to go to bed."

Jean almost blushed. "Potato soup would be great," and she walked out the door.

In fact, the roads were mostly empty, and she rolled under the highway toward East Austin and turned onto Airport Boulevard, stopping only for the lights. Some of the shops were open. There were

Christmas trees twinkling in display windows, in the bright sunshine, and Santa hats or red and white scarves draped over billboards advertising fried chicken and 99-cent chalupas. The mild pulse of holiday traffic had a soothing quality. Nobody seemed in much of a hurry, and the blue sky spread out over the raised junction with 183 like the backdrop in a photographer's studio: *Still Life with Intersection*. But the mountain cedar by the side of the road looked scratchy and gray; the grass was dirty, and Jean found herself narrating the past three or four days of family life for Henrik's benefit, telling it to him the way she wanted to tell it, practicing.

She was early enough at the airport that she could park in the lot and walk out to meet him at the baggage carousel. He said he wasn't checking any bags but that's where you came out anyway. For his sake, she had put on a dress, with ankle boots and tights. She wore the bracelet he gave her for her birthday. Even in December the air-conditioned terminal was cold enough that she felt goose bumps rise along her forearms, so that she crossed them and worried that she looked defensive. It was a little after half past four—he was probably stuck in immigration. She walked outside again, into the shadow of the underpass, where passengers kicked their heels along the curb, smoking or sitting on luggage and waiting for their rides. The light was already declining over the flat countryside and gleamed yellow and red against the garage opposite. Trees grew out of limestone beds along the side of it, taxis waited in a line. She went back in.

Whenever he saw her again, after an absence, she seemed smaller than he remembered . . . younger, too, probably. Her boyish face, under the short hair, had filled out a little as she got older, but she still looked like the kid in school who was concentrating, who wanted to be good. He saw her before she saw him; she stood in the colorless artificial light on the marble tiles by the automatic doors. Her dress was a little too snug, she didn't look comfortable in it, and with her hand on her backside tried to adjust it lower, working the hem down against the resistance of her tights. He was coming down the escalator with his backpack over one shoulder and in that state of heightened but still weirdly calm sensitivity to impressions that sleeplessness, long-haul flights, and airports produced in him. He felt curious about what her reaction would be, and then when he saw it, moved. She smiled with real happiness, the kind you have to hold back or keep down, and walked toward him.

"I probably stink a little," he said.

"I don't care."

She kissed him. It occurred to him that for a second she hadn't recognized him—he looked like every other traveler, middle-aged and tired.

In London, at Heathrow, when he got out of the taxi, it was lamp-lit and dark, raining, the windshield wipers of the taxi squeaked against the glass, he got wet paying the driver, dawn seemed hours away. But now when they stepped outside, and crossed over the walkway toward the parking lot, he felt the soft December air, smelled car fumes in sunshine, and felt something of the generic traveler's joy that being on location always gave him, and which was one of the reasons he liked his job. He liked new cities, he liked new climates, he liked finding his way and making decisions about what he liked and didn't like in foreign places. The landscape was very flat around him, the skies were blue and pale and somehow thin-looking, as if they barely covered what was out there, and a Marriott hotel rose out of nothing amid the glitter of parked cars. Jean found her father's Volvo, which looked twenty years old. All of this he found pleasant. He was interested in her family car.

"You know the joke about the old VW bug?" she said. "Zero to sixty? Yes! Well, maybe downhill."

The tape deck didn't work; the only thing it played was something funny and English, in a Cockney accent. *A rainy afternoon/ Spent in the warmest room . . .* Jean lowered the windows as they pulled on to the highway, and mild air flowed through the car. Yesterday afternoon, after Christmas lunch with the kids, Henrik cleaned up the cottage and packed up the car and drove five hours to London, so he could drop them off at their mother's house, which was also the house he had lived in for fifteen years. It took them six hours; even on Christmas Day the M4 was a car park around Newport and the Second Severn Crossing looked like an architect's model of a bridge, with model cars going nowhere. The white suspension cables were like the strings of harps; there had been an accident at the M5 junction.

"I don't see why we have to spend Christmas Day in the car," Freya said.

"I don't see why you should either," he had told her. "If your father had arranged his life better, you wouldn't have to."

"That's such a . . . you always say things like that. That's not an excuse."

"I don't know what I should say. I don't want to fight with you, when you're right." And so on. This is how he argued with them.

They had supper at the Welcome Break in Membury. By this point it was already nine o'clock. Sasha had become a vegetarian and ate a pesto salad from Waitrose, with a plastic fork, sitting at the odd little table in the forecourt, with coffee stains and a fake linoleum grain, and looking unhappy and uncomplaining. The other two ate fries and burgers from Burger King. Sasha picked at their fries, and they had an argument about that, how many she had taken from each, and Henrik stood up and used the men's room and waited in front of the mirror until he thought it might have resolved itself. And when he came back it had. His policy with the children after the separation was not to get angry—he let their mother do that—and it worked pretty well. He could keep his patience for a few hours on Wednesday, for twenty-four hours on Saturday, and for a few days in the holidays.

It was almost eleven by the time they pulled up at the house in Acton. Their mother had only just arrived from Bristol. It would have been easier for him to drop the kids off there but Monica had decided that one week with her parents was enough. You make these crazy arrangements because people are crazy. You can fight the craziness or go along with it, and most of the time it was easier to go along. She helped them carry their bags in—it was raining hard, and he had to park a few doors down. By this point their working relationship was perfectly functional. In fact, she let him spend the night on the sofa. His flight left at eight in the morning; he had to get a taxi at five, there was no point in going back to their cold apartment in Kensal Green. Was he packed? Yes, he was packed, so long as he could leave a few things at the house—he had a short connection in Chicago and didn't want to check any bags. Of course, that's fine, just leave them somewhere out of the way.

He set his alarm for four-thirty so he could shower. At five o'clock Monica came downstairs in her bathrobe. The taxi was waiting in the street; he was finishing his tea. She said, "You're meeting her family, right?" The shutters were closed; his backpack lay in the hall. You could hear the heating coming on—the flow and drip of water in the radiators.

"Yes, her parents and her brothers and sister."

"Have you met them before?"

"No. This is the first time." He hesitated, then he said: "It's not important to me, but since it's important to her, I'm happy to do it. I'm even a little curious."

"They must love the sound of you."

"I expect not."

She didn't hug him or kiss him, but she stood in the doorway as he walked, ducking his head in the rain, to the taxi, and she waited until they drove away before closing the door. He hadn't yet decided whether to mention to Jean that he had spent the night there. It was a matter of convenience for him, completely insignificant, but sometimes this is hard to communicate.

They were entering Austin now, what looked like the suburbs of a city. Recent developments were advertised by the side of the road, some of them half-built, and Henrik noticed rows of shops and restaurants between the gas stations. They had to stop at traffic lights. Jean had been talking most of the time; she had been telling him news.

"I feel like we haven't talked all week," she said. "By the way, you suck on the phone."

"This is what people say."

"I went for a drink with Dana, and she got hassled by some guy. Which isn't her fault but it annoys me a little that she acts surprised by it. Anyway, she told me that she's seeing somebody in New York. I don't think Paul knows. And Liesel has this idea that she can bring them back together. That's what all this is about. I want to tell her but I don't think it's my thing to tell."

This is how she talked, a little nervously maybe, or not nervously but confidentially. She was a competent driver. Part of her attention was also occupied by the road. Everything looked to Henrik very makeshift, like a kind of encampment; houses here or there, front yards growing into the sidewalk, or neighborhood streets without sidewalks passing you by at odd angles. Chain-link fences. The shops set back behind their parking lots looked like they had been built in a day. Like a stage set, but a stage set would be more convincing, there would be a façade. It was very green, though the grass had faded with winter; there were many trees.

"Does Paul want to—I mean, get back together with Dana?"

"I don't know what Paul wants. He's sort of post-wanting. I'm worried about him." She waited at a light, and then she turned, and they crossed tramlines or tracks of some kind, and she said, "Maybe you can talk to him. You might have some kind of insight."

"What do you mean?"

"Into what he's going through. Leaving his wife. Living apart from his son."

She looked at him; he couldn't read her look, but then she turned back to the road.

"It's possible."

"I'm sort of kidding," she said. "Only sorta. In case you can't tell I'm a little bit nervous."

"Should I be nervous, too?"

"I'm just upset that Bill's not here—we don't know yet when he's coming back. Everybody thinks that he's the hard-ass but Liesel is much scarier."

"It sounds like you think I should be nervous."

"She's making you potato soup. I'm not really nervous, I'm just happy."

There was a park with a creek, and Jean turned right along the stretch of grass. The houses had large front yards, they crossed over a limestone bridge (into a strong sunset, like swimming against the current), and then an arch of trees shaded the asphalt, the road curved. In the middle of the bend, she pulled into an empty driveway; the back of the Volvo clanked at the dip in the concrete. A hedge with red berries hid the screened-in porch, but there were pillars rising up beside it, a few tiled steps, and you could sense the rest of the house through the leaves, with its blue and white trim and tall windows. Henrik stepped out of the car, stretching his back after sitting down. A gray-haired woman had opened the door and stood in the doorway. This is what he always liked, arriving somewhere to a new situation and figuring out how to make his way.

Liesel had just woken up from her nap; she felt internally disheveled, she felt like she looked old. She didn't know whether to walk out or wait for them, but Henrik didn't have any luggage, just a backpack, so she waited in the doorway, and he followed Jean up the steps and then shook her hand. He had strong hands; he was wearing a short-sleeved shirt that showed off his forearms. Jean stood smiling on the little tiled portico—she looked like she was trying not to smile. Liesel said, "It's nice to meet you," conscious of sounding formal, and a little German. Her first impressions were okay. He was a middle-aged man, bald, with a clean scalp, attractive but not handsome and like he didn't care much either way. He looked competent and tired.

"It's very nice to be here," he said. And then, in a rough Danish accent, *"Wir können auch Deutsch sprechen."* We can speak German, too. But this was probably a mistake, it was a little too soon, and Liesel answered in English, "If you like."

She had to go back inside to let them through, she had to start cooking, and for the next half hour, as she peeled and sliced potatoes at the kitchen sink, chopped onions, opened and heated up a carton of stock, she was dimly aware of things going on around her. Some of the kids were in the TV room next door—Willy and Margot had spent much of the afternoon in front of the box, *glotzing*, as her father would say. Staring at the screen. Meanwhile everyone else came in and out. Jean was introducing Henrik, Liesel thought she sounded louder than usual, just a little, as if she were presenting something in public. She heard her say, "What are you guys watching?" And then, "Okay, okay," good-humoredly, as the kids shooed them out.

Nathan walked through the kitchen and said, "What are we eating?"

"Potato soup. There's some sausage in the fridge, to go with it."

"Fantastic." And then, "How old is the sausage?"

Henrik and Jean were standing around, too. Nathan was laughing; he was talking to Jean, but for Henrik's benefit. He was showing off somehow but Liesel couldn't figure out how.

"If you don't want to eat it," she said, "you don't have to eat it."

At dinner there were fifteen people sitting down. Only Bill was absent. They had to bring in the extra table from the shed—Paul carried it, and set it down heavily against the back window. If you were stuck on the far side, just to go to the toilet, you had to scrape past the chairs against the wall and escape through the TV room.

She missed Bill. He rarely talked much at dinner but he balanced things out; he was a counterweight and put Liesel somewhere in the middle between him and the kids. Also she could never understand what anyone was talking about. She needed a lot of explanation. Her hearing was poor, and with fifteen people at the table, many of them speaking at once, some of them children, she found it difficult to follow the conversation. This made her indignant. And Bill would have been somebody she could talk to about Henrik later, when the meal was over and cleared away, pots dripping on the tiled kitchen counter. She could have shared impressions.

At one point the question came up of whether people wanted to go out afterward and where they should go. Liesel finally intervened. "Henrik must be exhausted, it's two o'clock in the morning in England. He should go to bed."

"He can go to bed if he wants to go to bed," Paul said.

And Jean rubbed her boyfriend's neck. "I like him when he's like this. He's too tired to talk back."

Henrik looked at Liesel. "I am okay. I slept on the plane and if I want to close my eyes, I will close my eyes."

Almost to her surprise, she liked him. She thought, he's like my brothers; he seemed somehow familiar. They were all good travelers, curious, competent, good with their hands, opinionated but also reserved. He was recognizably Northern European—in his looks, too. She had seen his face in old Dutch paintings, farmers in the field or peasants drinking beer or fishers steering their skiff to shore. But she also thought, he's hard to read, too. He is somebody who will do what he wants.

Jean said, "We have to go to Mike's Donuts."

"Why?" Henrik asked. "Are they very delicious?"

"Not particularly."

"Is it a nice place to sit?"

"It is the opposite of a nice place to sit."

"So why should we go?"

"Because they're always open," Jean said, "and you can walk there from here."

And, in fact, after supper, a certain subset made arrangements to go out. Liesel said to Henrik, "*Sag mal. Dies ist verrückt. Du musst ins Bett.*" This is crazy, you have to go to bed. For some reason, she couldn't figure out why, the idea of dragging this tired, middle-aged man along upset her. She wanted to say, I'm on your side, against these children (my children included). It was a concession, speaking to him in German. But he responded: "I am really very happy to be here. I am happy to see your daughter, and I am very good at sleeping sitting down. This is something I have learned."

"Well, I'm going to bed," she told him, in English, but she poured herself a glass of wine and hung around.

Her children cleared up, mostly Jean and Paul. Susie and David had an argument about going out. It was eight o'clock at night and past May's bedtime. She had eaten a little potato soup, testing it first on her tongue, and Susie liked to sit at dinner with a baby on her lap. She wanted May to feel like part of the family, in spite of the age gap, to participate in . . . whatever was going on, but now it was bedtime and David had asked her for a "pink slip." This was his phrase for it, a hall pass; he wanted to join the others at Mike's and then wherever else they ended up.

Susie said, "I've had the kids all day. You went out for brunch already and got drunk."

"I don't think I . . ." but he changed tack. "*You* go out, I'll put the kids to bed."

"You can't put May to bed, she won't go down. I have to nurse her."

"What can I do about that?"

"Nothing, there's nothing you can do."

"It's your family, you see them one week a year. You should go out."

"I don't want to go out, I want to go to bed."

"So let me go out," David said, and Susie said, "Fine, just go."

Liesel sat with her glass of wine in the TV room, watching the NewsHour with Jim Lehrer. She could hear some of what was going on but not all of it. Nathan and Clémence had disappeared into the back apartment. When she came into the kitchen, to put away her glass of wine, Dana was there, filling a sippy cup with water at the sink.

"He looks much better," Liesel said.

"He is much better. He had a nice day."

"Are you going out?"

"I'm tired, I'm going to put him to bed and then probably go to bed myself."

"I can put him to bed, if you want me to," Paul said. He had been reading to Cal in the living room and walked in with the boy in his arms—Cal had his hands around his father's neck, he was long enough to rest against his hip.

"You go," Dana said. "Jean wants to see you. She wants you to spend time with Henrik."

"We can put him to bed and then both of us can go. Liesel can listen out for him."

"I don't mind," Liesel offered. She could sense the delicacy of these negotiations, and the tenderness behind the delicacy. Where there has been miscommunication and hurt, it's sometimes a good idea to be polite, even at the risk of being formal. "I can put him to bed, too. I've done it before. He doesn't mind."

"That's sweet of you, but I'm really very happy to stay in."

Then Jean came down, wearing her old suede jacket over her dress. Henrik was with her, he looked a little pale. "Come on, let's go," Jean said. "I don't know how long this guy's going to last."

"He should go to bed." Liesel was still indignant.

"Mom, he's a grown-up. He goes to bed when he wants to."

"He wants to go to bed."

And Henrik smiled at her. "I want to eat bad donuts in an unpleasant place," he said. Then David came in, cheerfully, with a brown wooly sweater rumpled up against his belly. "Are we going?" he said. "Let's go," and Clémence walked in from the backyard, the screen door clattered behind her. She had put on a long brown raincoat, with a wool trim, the kind with a belt that you tie around your waist. My sons' wives are very fashionable, Liesel thought. Clémence wore a scarf or shawl loosely around her head. It was getting colder, you could feel the cold air blowing in when she opened the door. Nathan isn't coming, she said, he wants to stay with the kids; and they all went out through the back, into the yard, into the dark, Jean and Paul, Henrik, David, and Clémence. Liesel watched them go.

Afterward she walked through the quiet house to her study and sat at her desk. She opened the computer and started to read over the day's work. There wasn't much, Liesel wrote slowly, a few sentences an hour. She had the sense she was putting something off or waiting for something. It's not that she couldn't concentrate, but her attention had a way of spreading out . . . maybe she couldn't concentrate.

Susie appeared in her nightgown in the doorway. She said, "I don't know if you heard what happened last night."

"About what?"

"About Julie."

"She thought someone was throwing stones at the playhouse, so she ran inside."

"It was Ben, Ben threw the stones. He wanted to scare her."

"*Ich versteh nicht.*" I don't understand.

"He said to me it was just a joke."

Liesel didn't say anything for a moment. Susie was always a worrier. As a little girl, she felt things strongly, and because she felt them, you had to feel them, too—she wanted you to feel them. And so you started putting up a little resistance, against what she felt, just to get by. It was too tiring not to. You pretended to listen to her but she sensed this and suffered more and more, until you gave in. This is how it happened, how she got her way. Liesel always thought, it's not good for her, it makes her need to feel, it's like a drug.

She was saying: "He is turning into somebody who is mean, and I don't know how to stop it. I've been arguing with him like this for over a year."

"He's not mean. He's just a twelve-year-old boy."

"This is what David says, he thinks it's just schoolboy stuff. But that's because he's English, he went to boarding school, he thinks it's normal for kids to do this kind of thing. It's not normal."

"David is probably right. I think sometimes in this family we worry too much about right and wrong."

"Of course we worry," Susie said, "but I don't know what to do." She didn't move, she wasn't talked out yet. "I think it's my fault."

"For going to England?"

"Maybe he sees too much of me, I'm at home too much. I've been trying to talk to David about finding me some teaching at Oxford. He says that's not how it works, you have to get there first. You can't ask for things as an outsider, you can't turn it into an official conversation. But when you're on the inside, people offer them, you don't even have to ask. This is how he puts me off. So I'm expected to follow him there and wait for something to turn up. I don't know."

"Maybe David is right," Liesel said.

"I feel like I'm fighting all the time with him, too. I feel like Ben is just acting out this fight."

"Not everything is your fault."

"No, it's mostly David's fault," she said and laughed, like a woman among women. "He does what he wants, he's always done what he wants. He's friendly and everybody likes him and he does what he wants. He's sly and Ben is turning into his father."

"He's a twelve-year-old boy."

"We were mean to each other when we were kids but we were never mean like that."

"I don't know, I don't remember. Everybody loved each other so it didn't matter."

"I feel like some kind of breach has been made," Susie said.

Liesel sat with her hands on her lap. Her chair could swivel, and she had turned to face her daughter. Her desk lamp was behind her, and so her back blocked some of its glow—Susie was partly in shadow. There was the concentration of intimacy you feel in a dark room around the source of light. "I think tonight I should turn on the heating for an hour," she said. "It must be cold upstairs."

"It's a little cold."

"Is Willy all right?"

"I gave him some Nyquil. He's old enough now I can give him the stuff that works."

"What's Ben doing?"

"I said he could read in my bed until I came up. I should probably go."

"It's not easy, these visits, on anyone," Liesel said. "I remember when you guys were kids and we went to Flensburg in the summer."

"Yes."

"I fought with Mutti, I fought with Bill. Everyone annoyed me. Nathan and my brother got into arguments, which I found upsetting. It doesn't always mean very much."

"Yes."

They were talked out now, Liesel knew it. Susie had made her confession; she might feel better. They could talk a little about something else.

"What do you think of Henrik?"

"Very Danish," Susie said. "Jean seems happy."

"I thought she looked very happy, she was very natural. He seems very fond of her."

"He seems very jet-lagged. Have you talked to Bill?"

"No. Is it too late to call?"

"They're an hour ahead. Maybe it's a little too late."

After Susie left, Liesel turned on the heating—the switch was in the hall, next to the stairs. Then she went back to her desk and stared at the sentences on her computer. What she thought was, the power comes from fertility. Her great-grandmother had five children, her grandmother had four. She had four herself. Susie had the boys and she had May; she would be okay. If you look down the family tree, the power comes from fertility. Some of the children make money, they buy houses and land, the land passes on, and the next generation grows up with certain expectations. But she worried about Jean.

Henrik had children already, he was almost fifty . . . stepmothering is hard work, I don't want it to replace . . . She worried about Cal, too. An only child concentrates a lot of anxiety. It puts pressure on them later, when their parents get old.

Jean would say, *of course* if you look at the family tree, what you're testing for is fertility, it doesn't mean anything. If that's how you want to measure . . . whatever it is that matters, you should have lots of kids. But it's tautological, you're arguing in circles. Her children sometimes looked down on her, they grew exasperated. She wanted to say: I know it's circular, that's what I mean, these things get passed on.

Bill called before she went to bed. There was a phone on her bedside table, and it rang very loudly. "What time is it by you?" she asked.

"I don't know, eleven o'clock." Then he said: "Eleven thirty."

Judith's ex-husband had decided not to fly in. He had too much work, he couldn't get away from the hospital. So Mikey wasn't coming—Judith was very upset. Anyway, it meant that the funeral could be held on Thursday. The graveside service was scheduled for twelve o'clock. There was no point delaying it. Judith wanted to get back to her son, she would fly to Chicago on Friday afternoon. They could drive to the airport together; Bill had booked his flight, too. He might have to come back again to deal with the house but for now there was nothing to do. He could go home.

"Oh, I'm pleased," Liesel said. "Everyone will be pleased. Especially Jean—you can meet Henrik."

"What's he like?"

"Susie says he's very Danish. They're out now, with Paul and some of the others. I told him to go to bed, but Jean wanted to go out. He seems very fond of her. She seems very happy, she seems like herself."

"Who else should she be like? Rita Hayworth?"

"How are you doing?" Liesel asked.

"It's a little depressing, staying in this house. I'm okay."

Turning off her bedside light, Liesel thought, when we were little, in the summer, we used to go down to the sea early in the morning. We collected jellyfish from the water and laid them along the beach, and covered them in sand. So that anyone walking past would step on them; the jellyfish made a mess against their shoes. We used to tie string to pieces of money, then hide in the bushes and leave the money on the path. When somebody bent down to pick up a coin, we pulled it away. But she didn't know if what Ben had done was like any of those things.

—

The clouds were low in the sky, you could hear the wind in the trees. Henrik was grateful for the cold, because it kept him awake. He had only a dim sense of what was around him. The yard, in the dark; a patio and picnic table, the back of a white clapboard house, then stiff grass underfoot and the shade of a large tree. Jean held his hand and he let her for a while and then let go. He didn't want the others to feel embarrassed. Paul was next to them and pushed open a gate. They were in the street and walked in the middle of the tarmac.

They stopped first at the Spider House and sat outside, in spite of the cold. Big fires were lit, burning logs on metal bowls, which gave off more smoke than heat, but they huddled their chairs around the fire and turned their heads away when the wind blew the smoke in their faces. Jean had a hot chocolate; Henrik had a beer. David bummed a cigarette from a group of twenty-something girls who were sitting at the next table. He seemed determined to enjoy himself; maybe this was a sign of unhappiness. Henrik was aware of experiencing time in a slightly random way, he moved in and out of focus, he was really very tired, and then lucid, and then tired again. It was really too cold; Jean leaned against him, awkwardly, with her arm around him.

"I thought I was coming to Texas?" Henrik said.

The courtyard was full of mismatched metal furniture, some of it rusty, with peeling paint. Christmas lights had been strung between trees and fences, the music from the bar leaked out. David said to Clémence, "I think Susie wants me to apologize, on behalf of the family," and Henrik heard the whole story, which Paul didn't know anything about. Clémence kept checking her phone, and a few minutes later somebody joined them—a producer from KUT, the local affiliate of NPR. He was Canadian originally, clean-shaven, fair-haired, youngish, named Kurt. He smoked, too, and Clémence turned down a cigarette. They were supposed to interview someone in the morning. Henrik tried to listen.

But the girls at the next table were talking loudly. One of them said, "So I called my dad, and he said, okay, where are you, I'm coming to get you . . . and I was like, hold on, let me check my phone. I mean, I had no idea . . ."

Paul said, "What did Nathan say?"

"My phone just kept loading and I was like, I'm a bubble in the middle of a grid, that's where I am, I'm kind of pulsing, if that helps . . . and then my phone went dead."

The girls were laughing, and Clémence said, "Susie doesn't want us to talk to Ben. She says he feels very ashamed," and David laughed, too.

"I think maybe the sense of shame has been a little overdeveloped in the family." His handsome face, under the stubble, looked like a fat boy's; the cigarette glowed in his mouth.

"Is this your idea of an apology?" Jean asked him.

Against the background of all this Henrik was aware of his ex-wife and children, whom he had left that morning in the house they once shared to enter these new scenes . . . and he felt now not exactly adrift at three a.m. Greenwich Mean Time (they would all be asleep in bed), but unanchored or even free of all that, in a way that made his life slightly less meaningful than before. But maybe that wasn't true, he was too tired to think, and Jean was there, who was happy *he* was there, so this landscape (the Canadian producer smoking, the wood in the firepit smoking, blazing, resettling, and shedding sparks, the Christmas lights strung between the leafless trees, the broken stones of the courtyard, the laughing twenty-something girls, the accent of their waitress, the pale slightly tasteless beer) wasn't entirely foreign ground, where he was a tourist, but somewhere . . . he couldn't finish the thought. It was connected to her, and her life, it was information, but that's all, and when they flew back home after New Year to their flat in Kensal Green, it wouldn't really matter. But he was here now, he was really here.

"You should see this development," Kurt said. "Near Kyle, off I-35."

"That's on the road to Wimberley. That's not far from me."

"There's a kind of gatehouse, with a tower and a bell, which doesn't work. And a security booth, where a guy sits watching CCTV. The swimming pool has some insurance issues, I don't know what they are. Anyway, it exists but it hasn't been functional in two years. Other than that, there's a little playground area, next to the highway. That's really the only communal space."

"What are we talking about?" Paul asked.

"Where the guy . . . where one of the guys . . ."

"Who started the lights on 37th Street moved to," Clémence said.

But it really was too cold to sit outside (though one of the girls wore nothing but a halter top, a skirt, and cowboy boots), and after half an hour they paid the bill and walked up the road to Mike's Donuts. "I've heard about this place but never been," Kurt said. "It is not supposed to be very good," Henrik told him. He was joining in where he could. David said to Clémence, "All of this is not really about Ben and Julie, it's about Susie and Nathan."

"Julie was very upset," Clémence said.

"Of course she was, he was trying to scare her."

"That doesn't seem important to you?"

"It was a stupid prank, that's all; he wanted attention."

To get to Mike's you have to cross a four-lane intersection. There are pedestrian lights, but Jean ignored them . . . the traffic wasn't bad at ten o'clock, though Henrik couldn't tell where the cars were coming from. He followed Jean, who ran or half-ran in her ankle boots across the road. All of the stores had parking lots in front; there was a gas station on the other side, the red of taillights diminished ahead of them, the white lights approached, slowed down.

"I told you it was open," Jean said. She was breathing a little heavily, you could see her breath.

The bakery was lit by harsh fluorescent lights; one of them flickered. The floor was dirty white tiles, and behind the counter, at an angle, you could see two or three long metal tables, like hospital carts on wheels, where the ovens were. Formica table-and-chair combinations stood in the wide front window, which overlooked the four-lane road. An Asian guy worked the cash register, but otherwise the store was empty. Behind him, lined up on plastic trays, which were stacked in a glass box or refrigeration unit, lay shelf after shelf of donuts (plain glazed, chocolate glazed, chocolate cake, blueberry cake, chocolate sprinkles, multicolored sprinkles) and donut holes and samosas.

"I feel like you're trying to enlist me in a conversation I don't particularly want to be a part of," Clémence said. "Especially since last night Julie felt so scared she had to sleep in our bed."

"I'm sorry about that but it was silly to let her sleep there."

"In our bed?"

"In the playhouse."

"You think it's her fault?"

"Of course not, but you didn't want her to either. This is just Nathan and Susie egging each other on."

"I don't see what that has to do with Ben."

"The kids get caught up in it, too."

"You're not making sense. Let's talk about something else."

"Why are you interested in this guy?" Paul asked, so Kurt told him. Joel Beigott used to live on 37th Street but then moved out to Manzano Lane (that was the name of the development) after his mother's dementia began to require full-time care. He needed the money. So what you have in this story, Kurt said, is all kinds of things coming together, a historic and unique community tradition, which was the 37th Street lights, slowly dying out because of lots of other things that are going wrong with this country, urban creep, healthcare . . .

"Where are you from?" Paul asked.

"Vancouver Island. At least, that's where my mother lives."

There was a blackboard next to the counter with a question scribbled onto it in pink chalk: "What movie did Roy Scheider drop out of, which is why Universal Pictures could force him into making *Jaws 2*?"

"If you know the answer, they'll give you a free donut." Jean was warming her hands in the pockets of Henrik's cardigan, leaning against him from behind, with her head on his shoulder.

"*Airport '77*," he guessed, but the guy shook his head.

"*Star Wars*," Jean said, but he only smiled.

"How much is a donut anyway?" Henrik asked and ended up insisting on paying for them. Like the grown-up here, like the old man, he said, which made Clémence pretend to protest. He bought a samosa, too, which he ate standing up; middle-of-the-night hunger had kicked in, and the fat and sugar were doing him good. As they walked outside, he said to Jean, "What should we do now?" because he felt happy, his girlfriend was somebody who so far as he knew and against the odds hadn't suffered any damage at his hands, and they were in the middle of nowhere, in Texas, with occasional cars going past on the wide roads. Ahead of him, he could see the lights of restaurants or bars. Under a streetlamp, against a breeze-block wall, someone had written *LOVE GOAT* in cartoon letters.

But Clémence was tired, she wanted to go home. Kurt said, "Should I pick you up tomorrow? There's no point in taking two cars." He offered to walk with her back to Wheeler Street, but she turned him down, and the rest of them set off toward the Drag.

They ended up at a place called the Ace in the Hole—a neon *OPEN* sign blinked in the window. The glass was plastered with posters and personal ads, everything had a makeshift feel. Inside, the walls were painted black, the music was country metal, and as they walked through the door a voice on the sound system sang out angrily or peevishly "What did I ever see in you?" But there was a pool table at the back, and a TV showing the football game. Western Kentucky led Central Michigan 21–17 as they came out of the commercial break. Snow had piled up by the side of the field, you could see how cold it was under the lights, but it wasn't snowing anymore. A couple of college-age kids were playing pool.

David bought a round of drinks, and Paul put a stack of quarters on the table.

"I don't know how it works," he said. "Is this how it works?"

"How what works?" But it turns out one of the guys needed a piss anyway, and the other guy was going home.

Paul racked up. They played some kind of straight pool, where three people could play at the same time—you were defending a run of balls, Paul explained to Henrik, who let Jean play instead. David was used to English tables, he'd had a misspent youth, but the fact is it didn't really matter, because Paul always won. He said, "Obsessive repetitive precision is what I do. I mean this is basically what I spent my life on." People stood up and sat down and Henrik watched them. He watched the football game, too. It was called the Little Caesars Pizza Bowl.

He said, "Imagine a world where that's a normal thing."

"You don't have to imagine it," Jean said. "I like it when you're like this."

"Like what?"

"Dopey."

He tried talking to Kurt, who sat with his elbows on his knees and his hand on his phone, thumbing the screen. But he glanced up when spoken to; he returned eye contact. His pale fresh skin looked blotchy under the harsh light. Maybe he had a reaction to alcohol where it made him red-faced.

Henrik guessed he was late twenties, Kurt was happy to answer questions about himself. He moved to Austin for grad school, because he wanted to be a writer, but he never finished his degree. Even at McGill he spent a lot of time volunteering at CKUT, the student radio station, so when he got to Austin he managed to get part-time work at KUT, which turned into something full-time. He was really very excited to be working with Clémence. This was a big deal for him. She's a real pro, he said. He said this a couple of times.

David and Jean were in the middle of a conversation. David said, "Susie and Ben have been fighting like this all year. She thinks the problem is he doesn't feel bad about anything. I think that's the opposite of the problem. He's a twelve-year-old boy, he feels bad about everything."

Paul finally missed so she stood up to shoot. When she sat down again, she asked, "Why drag Clémence into it?"

"I don't know. Nathan and Susie wind each other up. There are always higher principles at stake . . . nobody can live up to them." He felt drunk, for the second time that day. "And Julie and Ben are just the same. It was a silly thing to do, he shouldn't have done it, but it's hardly the end of the world."

"Boys will be boys," Jean said.

Paul won the first two games, then he let the others play doubles, Kurt and David against Henrik and Jean. Jean was pretty good; she grew up with a table at home and moved confidently with the cue in her hand, but also with an air of hamming it up. Henrik wasn't bad either, but he didn't care much. He had bought himself another beer when nobody else wanted one and sat down between shots, drinking it steadily.

"You've had a hell of a year," Paul said.

"I didn't think at the end of it I would be sitting here."

"Are you glad you are?"

"I am glad I am not dead." He was saying what occurred to him. "I am glad to live openly with Jean. But you know something about that."

"I don't know what I know."

Jean watched them from the pool table but couldn't hear; it gave her pleasure to see them talking intimately.

"A friend of mine," Henrik said, "who was married for twenty years calls it palliative sex. It doesn't cure the problem, which is that you want to sleep with other people—and not just sleep with other people, but open yourself to other experiences, instead of the same experiences again and again, which is why people in a family get on each other's nerves. Especially when you have teenage girls. But your wife if she is sensible will continue to sleep with you, even if she doesn't particularly want to, because she knows it helps."

"That's not what . . ." Paul began to say. "I mean, that has nothing to do with . . ." But it was Henrik's turn to shoot, and he stood up carefully and drunkenly and lined up his cue. He made a shot and then he made another and then he missed and sat down again next to Paul, who went on: "My problem is that I really don't want any of it anymore. I mean, the other experiences."

"I want to make clear that my situation was not the same as my friend's," Henrik said. "When I thought I was dying I thought, *What do you want*? Something I know about myself is that I don't find it hard to be selfish. It is not difficult for me. But I have also learned my selfishness is okay. It's not too bad, it's not too greedy. Jean is an exceptional person. I am not so stupid I don't know that. Sometimes I think it is also wrong, when good things happen, to say no. I don't know if this makes sense."

"It makes sense," Paul said.

The college kid had come back; he put some quarters on the table and looked at Paul. "Is this what we're doing?" he said. "Is this the system?" But his friend had gone home, he was happy to play whomever. So Paul played him and lost. Jean for some reason hated to watch him lose. Paul never talked much when he was playing, he never looked particularly happy. When it wasn't his turn, he stood to the side and pretended to watch the football game. The kid was taking it pretty seriously, too, he kept chalking his cue. Afterward, they shook hands, which Paul initiated—it was like he felt there should be some formal gesture. But he didn't like losing, it pushed him inward.

"You want a rematch?" the kid said.

He was a long-haired guy, a little overweight, but well-built. He filled out his T-shirt, which was sort of peach-colored. He wore a charm around his neck on a brown string. Jean thought Paul would take him on and was strangely disappointed when her brother said, "I think most of these guys are ready to go home. This guy just got off a plane. It's like five in the morning for him."

So they walked out into the fresh air, into the cold night.

Kurt said, "*The Deer Hunter*, that's what it was. I looked it up."

"Do you want a free donut?" Jean asked him. Her ears were ringing.

"They're probably closed."

Jean said, "They never close," but nobody could be bothered, and Kurt lit a cigarette instead. They crossed Guadalupe in the middle of the road and walked the backstreets toward Hemphill Park, passing a row of recently constructed campus apartments, with bikes on the balconies and a few lights on. Paul said to Henrik, "Listen, I know what it's like upstairs." Jean's bedroom was next to Susie and David's, and the two boys'. They were sleeping on a foldout sofa, with a lot of old furniture squeezed in around them—armchairs and bookshelves with nowhere else to go. French doors separated their room from Susie's, the glass was covered by thin curtains. "If at any point you guys want a night away . . . I mean, I'd be happy to stay at Wheeler Street. You could sleep at my house."

"Right now I don't care where I sleep. I could sleep on the grass."

"Not now, I mean, but later."

"I know what you mean. Thank you."

Kurt peeled off at the Spider House, where he had parked. "I guess I'll see you in the morning," he said, a little sheepishly, and Jean felt something like pity, watching him get in his car. He rented a room in Hyde Park; his housemates were students. Then they walked the long way round, by the creek. She put her arms around Henrik, it was really very cold. Clouds covered the treetops, the wind was busy, but the creek bed was dry, it was mostly moss and reeds. At Wheeler Street, she gave her brother a hug, transferring her physical affection from her boyfriend.

"Why don't you crash here," she said. "You had too much to drink."

"I had two beers in three hours. I'm fine."

"It's a long drive."

"I'm used to it."

"I don't like you going home alone."

"I'm used to that, too," Paul said.

Liesel had left the light on in the front hall, and the rest of them went up the steps into the house. Henrik took off his shoes at the bottom of the stairs; the floor creaked. They let David use the bathroom first, so he could creep through their bedroom without waking the boys. (He had taken off his sweater and his pants and carried them with the belt still in its loops. His extra-large T-shirt sloped outward like a lampshade; he had strong legs and tiptoed heavily, smiling.) But Willy lay with Susie under the duvet. He felt hot to the touch, his cheeks were flushed; they were both fast asleep. So David went into the boys' room next door and climbed into Willy's bed under the window. He thought, I shouldn't talk so much, but he didn't really care, he was ready to go home.

Henrik and Jean used the bathroom together. He splashed water on his face, he brushed his teeth. He whispered to Jean, "Maybe it's too late now, for me to sleep. It feels like the morning," but when he lay down on the sofa bed, he felt cleaned out. The distance traveled, the cramped airplane seat, the endless noise, his ex-wife coming down in her nightgown to say goodbye, none of it mattered, and Jean pushed herself against his armpit and stayed there, even after he fell asleep.

THURSDAY

The cold front blowing through had littered the grass with leaves. Fat sycamore leaves that fell all winter and lay on their backs collecting wet. Liesel thought, looking out her bathroom window, if Bill were here, he'd put on his sweatshirt and rake them up. Maybe the kids can do it. But they had other things to do, it wasn't really their problem anymore.

Bill called before she went down to breakfast. He didn't have much to report—that's what he said. The funeral was in Port Jervis; Rose wanted to be buried with their parents. "I don't expect anybody will come." But they were having a reception at her house this afternoon, which meant an hour and a half each way in the car. It was all a little crazy. In a few minutes he planned to walk over to Polanka's, the deli on Nepperhan Avenue where Rose once took him to lunch, to buy some food. It's a twenty-minute walk, maybe a little more in the snow, but he wanted to get out of the house, and he didn't want to drive. He wasn't sure about parking. The roads were mostly clear, but there was still snow piled up by the curb where you wanted to park. Liesel listened to him talk—he could have been talking to anyone. At least, his tone made no differentiation, but what mattered was to let him get off his chest these practical details. They occupied the part of his brain dedicated to grieving.

She said to him after a few minutes, "Henrik is here," but she had told him last night, she didn't have any fresh impressions.

"What's everybody doing today?"

"I don't know. I haven't gone downstairs. Willy and Margot have caught Cal's cold. Dana's leaving tomorrow."

"Is Paul around?"

"He usually comes after breakfast."

But she didn't tell him about Ben and Julie, or Susie coming to her study late at night. She didn't want to upset him, and he tended to overreact to childish misbehavior. He thought it was more important than it was.

Dana was making coffee when she came downstairs. She was fiddling with the coffee maker by the sink, dressed in some of the clothes she had arrived in almost a week before: her tweed skirt and red turtleneck, slate-gray tights and the kind of clumpy leather dress shoes Liesel associated with provincial lawyers. She looked like someone who didn't want to make a mess or get her clothes dirty. Liesel found her as always difficult to read. It seemed early in the morning to be capable of so much self-presentation—a little after eight o'clock. Of course, she wasn't really at home here, this wasn't her home. She had to self-present, because Paul wasn't around to do it for her. But maybe also she was retreating a little, she was getting ready to go.

Liesel said, "Is Cal up? How's he feeling?"

"He's up, he's not only up, he's running around the yard."

"It's cold today. I've turned on the heating."

"I spent most of this morning trying to talk him out of wearing shorts. But I guess he's got pent-up energy, it's like he needs to make up for lost time."

"I like the cold. I'm jealous of Bill—he looks out the window and sees snow."

This was an odd thing to say, and Liesel knew it. Bill's sister had died, he was stuck in her old house, making funeral arrangements. But somehow it opened up the conversation, because Dana said, laughing, "Well, I persuaded him to put on a coat. Shorts and a coat. Small victories," and then she said, "He loves the backyard. In New York we have to—someone has to take him to the park. He's very happy here. I'm grateful for that."

"It can't be easy, leaving him behind."

"You get used to most things." But Liesel couldn't tell if this was a confession or an evasion. Then Dana's phone rang—it was lying on the breakfast table, and she let it ring.

For the next hour people came in and sat down, they made breakfast and coffee, they cleared their plates and set the table again. Ben had waffles. Cal clattered in and ate a second breakfast—he had waffles, too. Clémence walked in the backdoor, in a pantsuit, ready for work. Margot was still asleep; she'd had a bad night. Her fever spiked at two or three a.m. She was very worried about something, she kept saying, *Nobody has my shoes.* But she was sleeping now so they were letting her sleep. Nathan wanted to get a little work done, he was giving that talk at the law school in a few days. Maybe he was sleeping, too. Julie was . . . Julie had discovered the bathroom. I don't know what she does in it—she reads, she takes her iPad in there. God knows when she's coming out.

Henrik and Jean eventually appeared. Jean was still in her pajamas, Henrik had showered and dressed. His clean bald head had little indentations. He was very undemanding. Liesel offered him lukewarm filter coffee, which had been sitting in the pot for an hour, and he said thank you, even when David proposed to bring back drinks and pastries from the food truck at the back of the Spider House. So David went out into the cold—it was a different kind of cold from previous mornings, thicker or deeper, north-flavored, the real thing— and everybody sat around making plans for the day, or talking about plans. You have to go through all of the options, Jean said, and after that you have to wait for Nathan to decide.

His wife made a face at her.

The doorbell rang and Liesel went to open the door. A pale young man in a pale cashmere sweater and pink collared shirt stood outside.

"Is Clémence around?" he asked. "I'm supposed to pick her up."

So Kurt came in, was offered coffee, politely declined, and waited around embarrassed for a few minutes, leaning against the kitchen counter, while Clémence went out to tell Nathan she was going. Jean said, "I've been thinking about it. Roy Scheider's an idiot. *The Deer Hunter*'s a pretty good movie."

"The first half is," David said.

Liesel thought, I don't understand anything that's going on. But in a few more days everybody would be gone, the house would be quiet again, and all of this activity or inactivity and the complicated relationships that produced it would happen offstage or be suspended entirely until they met up again next Christmas. In a few more days, she'd sit down to breakfast alone, unless Bill would sit with her, which he sometimes did.

Dana didn't check her messages till after the table was cleared and the boys were watching TV. She watched them watching from the doorway and listened to her voicemail. Stephen had called from Manhattan. His daughter and her husband and the new baby were staying with him for a couple of nights—they had driven down from Connecticut together.

"Hi," he said, "hey. Listen," but there were noises off and he seemed to be walking or shifting the phone around because a few seconds later he continued, in a slightly different voice. "I miss you. I've been thinking of you. I've been thinking generally, and feel like there are certain things we should probably clear up. Because I'm not completely sure where we are right now, or what we're doing." He laughed. "All right, all right, just say it. I want you to know that whatever your hesitations might be—and there may be many—I don't want you to think that having more babies should be one of them. This may be totally premature but I want you to know that's not an issue for me. I'm happy to go through it all again." There was a pause and he said, "Feel free to ignore any of the above. Give me a call . . . or not. Merry Christmas," and hung up.

She didn't want to call him back in front of the kids, so she wandered down the hall and into the living room but Liesel was in her study. She could phone him from the porch but it was really too cold, and she might have felt exposed in other ways—anybody could see her talking. So she went upstairs, into her room, and closed the door and sat on her bed. For a second while listening to his message she thought that Stephen was trying to break it off, and she had this physical reaction, which surprised her, so part of what she felt afterward was just relief. She called his home number and he picked up almost immediately.

"Hey, I'm glad you called. I didn't think you would, I couldn't tell how crazy I sounded."

"You didn't sound crazy."

"They've gone out, they're taking the baby for a walk." Alexis, his daughter, had always been vaguely friendly with Dana. If they ran into each other at a party, both of them said, let's get together and meant it but not enough afterward to make the effort. Then she married and got pregnant and her husband took a job in D.C. "The thing is," Stephen said, "I like her husband, I like him fine, he's a good guy, he appreciates her, but when he's around it's like, there's this kind of dust or Teflon coating on my daughter. It's like she's wearing this weird veil of pleasantness. I can't get through and I start to feel . . . it's kind of this intense kind of loneliness, because even though it's my apartment, the family unit is really her and her husband, and this baby, and I'm just . . . I'm a ghost, I'm a piece of furniture. Every night they go to bed around nine o'clock and retreat into their bedroom, or whatever, and I just hang around watching TV or something. Anyway, I've had a lot of time to think."

"I don't feel like I get any. There are always all these people around. Everybody wants to know your opinion, and if you don't have an opinion . . ."

"About what?"

"About anything, it doesn't matter. You never know what it's going to be."

She could see the driveway from where she was sitting. (In the morning, when Cal woke up, she had louvered the blinds to let in the light.) Cold white skies, cold white light, and Paul was parking his car against the curb. He got out and walked through the grass to the steps, an image broken into slats or lines, and then under the portico and out of sight. She could hear the front door while Stephen was talking.

"So yesterday we finally had a fight. The whole Christmas thing in Connecticut was basically just a lot of bullshit politeness. I said, what do you want from me. I'm hanging around the whole time, you don't want to talk to me, you don't want to *do* anything, I'm starting to go crazy. I don't even think you want to be in the same room, and she said, Help, I want help, and I said, Tell me what to do. I'm not your mother, you have to tell me. So today this morning at five a.m. when the baby woke up she brought her into my room. She said, your turn, and I took her into the den, and for the next . . . I don't even know how long it was. Eventually she got hungry and there was nothing I could do. But for a couple of hours . . . we danced, we sat on the couch, we watched TV, this little warm thing, and I thought, it suddenly occurred to me, I can do this. If that's the problem, I can do this again. I just wanted to call you . . . I wanted to talk."

"I want to see you, too," she said. Paul had walked in the door, she could hear it slam. The entrance hall was directly below her.

"Let's make a date. What are you doing New Year's Eve? I've been invited to this thing at Ted Greenberg's apartment—not by Ted, I should say. But we don't have to go, we could do anything."

"I want to see you before that," Dana said. "I'm flying tomorrow."

"My daughter is going the day after." Then he said, "Maybe we can all hang out."

"You don't have to . . . that's fine. I can wait, it's just that . . . Cal is staying here. Paul's going to bring him back next week. Twenty-four hours before I have to say goodbye, I start to get a little emotional. I'm sorry."

"Hey, that's all right. That's all right."

"He's very happy here, he's fine."

"You don't have to explain."

"Listen, I should probably go. Everybody's . . . they all sit around all day making plans. I don't know what we're doing."

"We'll do something fun, just the two of us. Okay? New Year's Eve—I'll book something, let me surprise you."

"Okay," she said, and hung up.

The green-tiled bathroom at the end of the hall was unoccupied. She washed her face and stared at it for a minute then went downstairs to find Paul or Cal. Susie said they were in the backyard, so Dana walked out, into the cold, letting the screen door bang behind her. It had rained overnight, the sharp grass showed every drop, and her Foxley loafers lifted at the back with each step. She had bought them on sale a few months ago. They were a little too big, and she could feel her tights growing damp at the heel; but that didn't matter, it's what she deserved.

She found them playing tennis, taking turns knocking a ball against the concrete wall. Cal was still in his shorts, his coat lay on the ground. Paul saw her. He said, "I tried to make him keep it on."

"It's nice to see him running around."

"Come on," Cal said, so Paul hit him the ball.

"Is he any good?" Dana asked.

"I think he likes it. He saw Willy doing it so he wants to do it, too. Half the talent is having fun."

"Is that what you're good at?" But she was only kidding.

A few minutes later, they walked back in together. Paul was getting cold and there were puddles all over the court. Whenever the ball landed in one, it became heavy and dirty and started spraying on contact. A very thin film of mold or moss grew in the cracks of the painted concrete and turned slimy in the rain. Anyway, he was worried that Cal might slip; he wanted to talk to Dana. Cal ran inside. There were stepping-stones between the fountain and the backdoor patio, and Cal tried to touch each one. Paul carried his coat.

Dana said, "I want to talk to you before I go. I want to have an actual conversation."

"I want to have a conversation, too. Why don't you stay over in Wimberley tonight? I can drive you to the airport in the morning.

Cal's going to have to move anyway. It might make it easier for him."

When she didn't answer, he said, "It doesn't matter. I'd like it, too."

"Okay," she said.

———

Clémence hated driving and relied on taxis or the kindness of colleagues or friends to get anywhere. She was used to accepting rides; it didn't really bother her that Kurt maybe had a slight crush. At her age, she knew how to turn this kind of relationship into something maternal—that was probably a high percentage of what was going on anyway. Kurt was a young ambitious guy. You forget when you're married with kids how much time a guy like that spends alone, you can't even really imagine it. They feel awkward around women, and that awkwardness comes across as something else, sexual hesitancy or interest. Anyway, it probably didn't have much to do with her.

Kurt drove a Saab 9-3; it looked new. He must have parents with money. The small backseat was taken up with equipment: black cases and leather bags, things with metal legs. He had stopped off at KUT on the way over. When they got in the car, he said, "That's a nice house your husband grew up in."

"It's a nice neighborhood." This is how she deflected him.

But it's true, every second morning she went for a run before breakfast and took pleasure from the quiet streets. All the houses looked different, people cared about their gardens. You got a mix of income brackets, too. There were red-brick neo-Georgians with thirty-foot pillars guarding the front door, houses that basically looked like small-town banks. But you also saw white-walled bungalows, witches' cottages, whose chimney stacks were hidden by ivy; bamboo covered the windows. Red brick, yellow brick, painted clapboard . . . Craftsman-style homes from the Thirties, Colonials (like the Essingers') from the Twenties, modernist rebuilds in the new

Austin vernacular—brightly painted boxes with pre-rusted metal towers rising out of them.

The park with the creek running through it was really just a grassy field; the footpath on one side was lined with old pecans. Most of the streets had sidewalks and were wide enough anyway for kids to play football in them or ride their bikes.

Variety and modesty and comfort, neighborliness and individualism—this is what it suggested, old American virtues, though in fact the Austin that Nathan felt nostalgic about existed only in pockets like Hemphill Park. Even here the people who could afford to buy or rent now were lawyers and tech types, businessmen. The high-school history teachers and part-time musicians had been priced out. When Dodie died, they'd tear down her house and build a new one.

Kurt was happy to talk about Austin, too. It seemed like moving here involved a certain amount of self-consciousness. Pretty much everyone he knew came from out of town, places like Richmond or Denver or Brooklyn or Palo Alto. It didn't even matter anymore. The city was changing so fast that the restaurants and bars and music joints you wanted to go to, even some of the parks and neighborhoods, probably weren't around five years ago. There was no real advantage to being native. He had done some prep work yesterday, talking to Joel Beigott on the phone, just to see what he wanted to say. Joel said, it used to be that the way you could recognize a real Austinite is they knew the shortcuts and places to eat and now you can recognize them because they don't.

They crossed over North Lamar into Pemberton Heights, then swung onto Mopac and headed downtown. The shiny new skyline spread out along the river to the south; even on a cold day, with low cloud cover, the Frost Tower gleamed like brass. One of the advantages of not driving is that you can stare out the window.

But she was also thinking, Nathan has ambivalent feelings about going home, which often, in one way or another, I have to deal with. They'd had a fight or muted argument before breakfast. Julie was moping around, lying in bed and then wasting time in the bathroom, refusing to get dressed. Nathan eventually lost patience.

"Snap out of it," he said. "Nothing happened."

All of this took place in the dark of the back apartment, around the pool table, on the brown linoleum floors, with the bathroom fan humming in the background, and Margot lying feverish in bed.

"I thought you were on my side." Julie looked genuinely surprised.

"What Ben did was not forgivable, but it was also not a big deal."

"Not forgivable is too strong," Clémence said.

"You don't forgive someone who picks wings off ants. You don't punish them, but you stay out of their way."

"I don't think that's what happened, Julie is . . ."

"I'm not some helpless . . ." Julie broke in.

"It was an analogy. I'm talking about the intention, I'm talking about the pleasure."

"I can look after myself."

"Then do it," Nathan told her.

Afterward Clémence tried to reason with him, or soften him up. "You're too absolute in these things." And then, uncomfortably echoing what David had said to her: "He just wanted attention. They're moving to England and he feels out of control."

"Excuse me, this is not a cry for help. It's something deliberate, it's weird."

The argument didn't matter much, except that it touched on a deeper disagreement between them, that he was intractable. So he gave in to her sometimes, to show he could give in. He had promised already to say nothing to Ben, but it made him resentful—of her. And Julie was still mad at her father. She felt like, you didn't stand up for me. For some reason she thought of it as his responsibility. So the wheel went round.

Meanwhile Clémence couldn't help noticing at breakfast that Susie and Ben . . . he sat next to his mother, there was a tone in his voice. When he asked to be excused he glanced at her; she let him watch TV.

He looked chastened, which was a good thing, but it also meant that by crawling out of bed at two in the morning to throw stones at the window where her daughter was sleeping (and scaring the shit out of her), he got out of his system whatever spirit of protest or rebellion had made him do it. And afterward there was tenderness and reconciliation, there was forgiveness, while for Julie . . . But you can't get involved in this kind of thing. You have to be the one who doesn't get involved.

Which is partly why she didn't want to come. She liked her in-laws but when the storm blew down from Canada, she thought, let's stay in Cambridge and light fires. We can go sledding. Let's have Christmas as a family. *We're* the family. But Jean called so they went.

From Mopac they merged onto 290 and then turned onto I-35. Kurt explained himself: There's construction around the university, the road is down to two lanes. I thought it might be quicker to get on farther south. Clémence was always amazed by the brain space driving takes up. People develop this intimate knowledge of uninteresting facts, it's part of what makes them feel alive, like they're living somewhere. Traffic started picking up. Christmas was over, there were trucks on the road. It seemed likely that Liesel and Susie and probably even Jean and Paul found it annoying that she was making this program about Austin. They thought she would get it wrong, even though Jean and Susie hadn't lived here for more than a decade, and Paul only moved back last year. For them Austin was really a house, it was really a childhood. Maybe even Nathan found it annoying.

For them it was like a source of reality, it was like a reservoir they could draw on. As if everywhere else, and even the rest of their lives, was slightly unreal—their jobs and marriages and kids. The fact is, Kurt probably knew Austin better than any of them.

When she first met Nathan, he was twenty-eight; she was thirty-six. Somehow the age difference mattered, it was part of the attraction. At that stage, he was still clerking for Judge Schuyler and applying for tenure-track jobs. Unsure of himself, waiting for recognition.

Clémence seemed to him like a public figure. She covered the White House for *The Sunday Times*, after spending three years in Tehran. But she was tired of living like a foreign correspondent. She wanted to write a book, she wanted to buy a house. Of course, part of what she liked about Nathan was his attitude to family — this is always how it starts.

Had she put his career and worldview ahead of her own? At some point they decided she should quit *The Sunday Times*, to go free-lance, which made life easier with the kids. But that was also because she had a chance of moving into broadcasting. They were more likely to meet, at a dinner party, somebody who had heard of *her*. Yet Nathan had ambitions she didn't share, they recognized that. He wanted to be a Supreme Court judge, he wanted to shape the history of the nation, and the question was, how much of your ordinary life are you willing to sacrifice? You, and your children, are the ordinary life. But ambition made him unhappier than it made her, and slowly that kind of unhappiness . . . it's very persuasive. You give in to the logic behind it, you make allowances. From the beginning she understood what the deal was: to be on his side. And when she met his family, she understood why. Liesel was a loving mother but sometimes short of sympathy for her eldest child. You fight these fights with your eldest child that make sympathy difficult. Poor Julie.

It was good to get out of the house. There was a danger of getting caught up in it all, which helped nobody.

Manzano Lane was visible from the highway. A big billboard, fea-turing an apple tree and a cart filled with apples, appeared by the side of the road, above one of those high flimsy-looking pine fences designed to keep out sound. There was an access lane, and Kurt drove up to the barrier, which was raised, and passed slowly by the security booth. The guard inside didn't seem particularly interested. "My im-pression is, this is a mid-market community," Kurt said. There were signposts at the street corners advertising various trails, and a bike lane running by the side of the road. But some of the land looked undeveloped, they saw tractors sitting in dirt, orange plastic netting flapping around, and it's possible some of the funding stream had dried up.

Clémence had a camera out and took pictures through the window. Plots were arranged in cul-de-sacs and crescents. The developers had tried to create a sense of variety by mixing one- and two-story buildings; some of them had brick siding or limestone pillars or both. But the general impression was of sameness. The houses looked boxy and odd, they had slanted roofs that ran into each other, they were painted in primary colors. There was a park or open grassy area in the middle, but on a cold day nobody seemed to be using it, not even the dog walkers. Kurt's Sat Nav had run out of information, they were drifting along.

Joel lived on something called Autumn Corner, and they found it eventually—a row of saplings, no more than three feet high, had been staked along the sidewalk. Every house had a driveway, and Joel's had two cars backing into the road, a pickup and a bright red Toyota Corolla, so Kurt parked along the curb. There weren't any signs telling him not to. As soon as Clémence got out of the car, she could hear the highway. It was like a white-noise machine, with little variations inside the general hum. "Where the hell are we?" Kurt said, as they walked up the poured concrete footpath to the front door.

———

Judith had sent an email around, she had also posted a message on the Facebook page of the Northeast Jewish Center in Yonkers, where maybe four or five times a year Rose went to synagogue. But the service was scheduled for twelve o'clock at Laurel Grove cemetery in Port Jervis. Bill's parents were buried there, too. It was about an hour and a half in the car from Yonkers, maybe a little more, depending on traffic. You skirted various state parks and drove through the empty countryside of upstate New York.

Bill and Rose grew up in Port Jervis; he hadn't been back there since his mother died, twenty years before. Mourners were supposed to meet at the cemetery office, not the grave. He didn't expect many to come but had called the secretary at Temple Beth-El, where they used to go to synagogue as children; she put an announcement on the website. Afterward, back in Yonkers, they were having a reception at Rose's house—sitting what Judith called "mini Shiva." Bill had spent the morning buying food while Judith covered the mirrors and set out candles. Everything was ready.

They arrived at Laurel Grove half an hour early. Judith wanted to sit in the car and wait, with the heating on, but Bill walked around. It was a cold bright day. The cemetery occupied an island in the Delaware River—Pennsylvania lay across the water. It was caught between two highways, Route 6 and Interstate 84. The grounds were dotted with pine and oak and sycamore, picked out in white by the snow, but you could also hear through the clear air a constant stream of cars, making little zip sounds, zip, zip, zip, as they passed by. It was the sound of life, busyness, urgency, but it also suggested to Bill the passage of souls. With the headstones all around it was hard not to make the connection. A machine had cleared the roads, pushing the snow to the side, but it meant that some of the plots were sitting under four-foot drifts. He was sweating lightly by the time he got back to the car.

Only eight people showed up—Bill counted them as they stood around in the cold. Including the new rabbi at Temple Beth-El, a fat young man with a scratchy beard; he was red-faced and cheerful, too. He wanted to impart his own good mood. They were one person short of a minyan, even if you counted the women, so he called up his cousin, a screenwriter from LA, who was staying at his house.

Ten minutes later the guy arrived, wearing a borrowed jacket over jeans and Nike running shoes. But he made a likable impression, he didn't seem at all put out. This is my kind of crazy afternoon, that was the impression he made. The cousins had a good relationship, you could see their breath when they talked. You owe me lunch, the guy said, but he was smiling, and the rabbi said, For what?

The secretary at Temple Beth-El was old enough to remember Bill's mother. She carried her handbag in both hands, hugging it to keep warm. Laurel Grove is large and they ended up taking three cars to the burial site, driving along slowly behind the hearse. Bill's cousin Doris was there, too, with her husband. They were perfectly friendly but rode with the secretary, and Bill wondered if they still held a grudge because of Liesel. But you can't really tell after so much time—the distance has been created.

When he got out of the car, Bill saw the hole in the ground, beside his parents' graves. He went up to Doris and said, "Did you ever see Rose? Did you keep in touch?"

"Every New Year we included her in the family round-robin."

She didn't look well. Her skin was colorless, like she was missing a layer of paint. To make up for that she had put on bright red lipstick. Her husband wore a suit and tie and gloves but no overcoat. He said, "I went to Dallas last month. On business. They took me out to eat at some restaurant, it's the place everybody goes. The food arrived—I had a plate of meat this big." He held his hands apart. They lived in Westchester, in a very small house; their son was forty years old and single. Doris was one of these people who concerns herself with the family tree, maybe to make up for the fact that she didn't have grandkids. For most of her life she had been underemployed, and you felt that, too, in her restless hemmed-in manner. But she showed up, whatever the reason; you get points for that.

Two young men from Kaplinski-Sternau, the funeral home, slid the coffin into the ground—the hearse had backed up to the spot. For some reason, his sister was inside; she was lying there.

The rabbi gave a short sermon, he had asked Bill beforehand to corroborate certain facts. Because that's all he knew about Rose, he had never met her. She was born in 1941 and graduated cum laude in 1963 from Syracuse University, where she joined Sigma Delta Tau.

She received her master's in education from Teachers College, New York, and worked for three years . . . There were details about her marriage, too, her husband and their daughter and Michael, her beloved grandchild. Events clustered in the Sixties and Seventies, and after that the facts thinned out. Is this what it felt like to live her life, too, Bill wondered. There was something impersonal about the list but also moving. So that's who she was.

"Do you want to say a few words?" the rabbi asked.

Bill shook his head. What he felt was not for public consumption, there was no need. But Judith stepped forward. Something had happened to her, sitting in the car; it's like she'd taken a nap and had just woken up. She seemed sleepy but also somehow freshly rinsed.

"I didn't bring anything suitable to wear."

Her voice was clear and loud.

"When the hospital called, I just kind of threw everything in a suitcase, I had to find somebody to look after Mikey. Which meant a long conversation with my ex-mother-in-law. (No picnic, believe me.) I had to pack for him, too. So I didn't bring anything black, and this morning, when I was getting dressed . . . but then I remembered. Of course, I'm staying at Mom's house. Everything she owned — half of it's black. When she started putting on weight ten years ago, that's what she felt comfortable in. So I'm wearing one of her dresses. Which is why it's so big."

She laughed sweetly and, Bill thought, like somebody who is confident of charming, of receiving love. This was Rose's doing, for better or worse.

A pile of dirt by the side of the grave had a shovel sticking out of it. These bullshit rituals annoyed Bill, there was something ye oldey about them, part of the world he grew up in and from which he'd been cut off after marrying Liesel. But maybe the problem was that he basically believed in them. He didn't want to wait in line and shovel dirt on his sister's grave, he didn't want to be complicit, but he did it anyway. Judith handed him the shovel, the dirt made an audible thud and he turned around and gave the shovel to the next guy, feeling—that's the last you'll see. Everybody was cold, nobody wanted to be there; they wanted to get in the cars.

Afterward Bill said to Judith, "Maybe we can drive by the house for a minute. I haven't been back here in twenty years."

The streets were quiet at lunchtime, and they stopped off at the Erie Hotel for a bite to eat. Bill had a Reuben sandwich. "My father used to meet clients here," he said. "But it was called something else." From their table in the window (the restaurant was mostly empty), they could watch the occasional traffic on Jersey Avenue. The awning dripped, the sky was bright blue, there was a parking lot over the road and a church behind it. Small-town America. A couple times a year his father drove them to Manhattan, for a ball game or to visit his sister, and Bill was always grateful afterward to get back home. He waited for Judith to order coffee, then paid for both of them and they walked back to the car.

It didn't take him long to find the house. Liesel always said, you could have been a black-cab driver. He had a head for directions, they were part of the information a responsible person should store in case of emergency. "Do you want to go in?" Judith asked. They were parked by the curb with the motor running. He switched off the engine but didn't move. It was a funny old house, on a corner plot—his mother liked to say they lived on Roosevelt Avenue, but really the front door opened onto Watkins. The present owners had built an extension at the back. The yard was covered in snow. Judith said, "There's no point just sitting here," so he got out, but he didn't have the nerve to ring the doorbell. He let her do that.

"I don't know who lives here now," he said. "They're probably away."

But their car, a Mazda 6, sat in the driveway. The door opened and a man put his head out. He hadn't shaved, he looked about thirty years old. He wore jeans and a T-shirt, under a bathrobe.

Judith explained, and Bill said, "I sat in that kitchen, doing homework." He could see it at the end of the hall, where he used to come in from the cold, tracking snow. His mother shouted at him, take off your shoes, then got down on her hands and knees with a dirty towel, to wipe up after him. It was cold now, and he stood on the porch, peering in. The sink was still under the window, overlooking the yard; everything else was unrecognizable.

"I'd invite you in but this is not a good time." His wife had just had a baby, she had just gone to sleep.

"The baby or the wife?" Bill joked. Company of any kind cheered him up.

"Come back in like six months," the guy said. He was trying to sound like the crazy parent, the one everybody leaves alone.

Judith was unimpressed. "We'll be very quiet, we just want to look around."

"I'm sorry, no." He had stepped outside, onto the porch, and shut the door quietly behind him.

"We buried my mother today," she said. "She grew up in this house. Uncle Bill just wants to see it again." The sweet or sleepy tone had gone; she was angry, and the man held out his hands in a gesture of, what can I do.

"Look, I'm not kidding," he said. "We've had a tough couple weeks."

Bill turned to his niece. "I'm okay."

"It's not okay," she said. "He should let you in. People think they're the first person ever to have a baby."

"I'm trying to be a nice guy here," the guy said. "I'm trying not to be a dick, because what I really feel like saying is, get the fuck off my property."

"Come on, let's go," Bill said, but Judith wasn't finished.

"I'm sorry your wife is taking it like this."

The fact is, black suited her. Her pale and red coloring, her mother's complexion, stood out against the black neckline—her cheeks were bright with cold. She wasn't particularly attractive but she had brass.

"Like *what*?"

"That's part of your job, too. You know that. Not to give in to unreasonable demands."

"I have no idea what you're talking about."

"These things can be signs of postnatal depression. Obsessive concern with sleep or weight gain. Negative thoughts, general irritability. A feeling like you can't really cope. These things are all signs."

"I'm going inside," he said. "If I have to come back out, I'm calling the police."

Bill noticed he had been standing around in his socks. "Let's go," he said, and this time they went.

"What a prick," Judith said.

Her anger had turned into something else. They were sitting in a rented car on a cold day in December. Her mother was dead. She had lost her temper, it was like stirring up dregs. You have to wait for them to settle again. The drive back to Yonkers would take an hour and a half—more if they hit rush hour on the Tappan Zee Bridge. Then, when they got there, she had to put on a social face again, people were coming at five. Maybe no one would show up. Anyway, she was going home tomorrow, she would see Mikey.

Bill turned the heating on, but before heading back, he drove around the neighborhood. Some of the houses were hidden by trees, they had wide front yards. He crossed over Kingston Avenue toward the river. There was a car dealership on the corner, with a Christmas tree in the lot and bunting strung up on poles along the sidewalk. The houses on the other side were more modest, the plots were smaller, and he stopped outside a white clapboard bungalow built on a sloping yard, so that the basement walls were visible to the rear. There was a narrow driveway with a garage, a small front porch, two or three steps leading up to it. No fence, no bushes, no trees in the yard, which was covered in white.

"This is the house we were born into," Bill said. "Rose, too."

Bill stayed in the car and Judith didn't suggest getting out. The road dead-ended in the park where he used to play baseball. He stopped there for a minute as well. You could see the river—sunlight reflected endlessly off the water and dripping trees, you had to squint. On the far side was the golf course where he caddied in the summer. Driving back to the interstate, he passed his high school.

"Every day we walked to school right by our old house," he said.

"Who lived there after you?" Judith asked.

"The Manolo sisters," he said, in his football announcer's voice. She was trying to make it up to him, to let him reminisce. So he reminisced. "Their father owned a restaurant on Main Street."

Later she said, "I'm sorry I lost my cool back there," and he turned to her in the car.

"Don't worry about it. He had it coming." It didn't matter if he did or not.

When they crossed the Hudson an hour later, the sun was going down behind them—down the length of 287, flashing off cars. Everything shone. It put a blind spot in his rearview mirror, he adjusted the angle. Already it felt like time had passed, distance had come between them and the funeral, who knows when he'd go back to Port Jervis, maybe never.

—

Susie was going stir-crazy, she needed to get out of the house. Willy had spent most of the day in front of a screen. At lunch, he ate a little vegetable soup, whizzed up. He ate Ritz crackers. She gave him Tylenol and that got the fever down. If he was well enough to play Minecraft, he could sit in a car. He could sit in a car playing Minecraft. Margot was reading a book, *James and the Giant Peach*, lying on the sofa in the living room like a good girl, with a cup of warm milk on the coffee table. This annoyed Susie a little, but mostly it stressed her out. Dana kept apologizing. Cal was outside, in the cold, running around.

"This is what happens," Susie said. "If everyone gets on planes in December, kids with different colds, this is what happens. It's not your fault. The only thing you can do is wash your hands, but what does that do. They're kids."

Dana couldn't tell if she was being reproached.

At three o'clock they finally reached critical mass. Clémence was back, Nathan was willing to go out. They started marshaling troops. But Margot didn't want to go, and Willy didn't want to go. Clémence offered to stay behind with the kids, but Nathan nixed that. He hadn't seen her all day. So David offered, and Susie felt again the force of comparisons.

"I want to do something as a family," Susie said. "I want to do something where you actually participate."

Julie said, "What should I wear? Do I need a coat?"

"Yes, you need a coat. It's freezing outside."

"So why are we going?" she asked.

"Because everybody's crazy," Jean told her.

They needed three cars. Jean and Henrik drove with Paul and Dana and Cal. Susie and David had their boxy Kia Soul, one of those stupid-looking cars they give you at the rental agency, and Nathan drove Liesel's Volvo, with Clémence and Julie and Margot in the back. In the end they decided to go to Mount Bonnell. It seemed to involve the least amount of time or disagreement. "We can get out, we can walk up the steps, we can look at the view. We can go back home." Nathan was in one of his perfectly reasonable moods. Tension in the family sometimes had this effect on him. He didn't try to impose his will, and to the extent that it didn't cost him anything, he went along.

"I want to show the kids the peacocks afterward, at Mayfield Park," Susie said.

"Then you can show them. Nobody's going to stop you."

Dana took her camera.

It's a ten-minute drive, over Mopac and into the hills. The houses thin out toward the top, and by the end, the Volvo struggled up the gradient. There are terraced gardens, heavily irrigated, gated drive-ways, and somewhere, in the slopes above, a metal and glass Mod-ernist box, set between trees, that Nathan coveted. The road passes by the steps leading up to the summit—you park at an angle against the limestone rock face. Even on a cold day in December, people came. It's the holidays, they're stuck at home with family, the house is crowded, everybody gets antsy and bored. So they go to Mount Bonnell. It's a festive thing to do, let's get out of it all and stand above it and look down.

David parked and turned to Willy in the backseat. "I can carry you, if you want me to carry you." But Willy said he could walk. When they got out, into the cold, Susie took his hand. It was clammy and hot, and she had a moment of hesitation, of anxiety, but Willy was feeling calm and trusting, he clung to her, and they started climbing. There are ninety-nine steps cut into the mountain, between slopes covered in laurel and cedar, which hang onto the slippery loose sur-face of the rock.

Willy said, "Where will we live, when we go to England?"

"I don't know yet. We'll find somewhere nice."

"I mean will we live in a house?"

It took her a minute to find out what was worrying him. He thought they might live with other people. Maybe he had overheard something and misunderstood it. Ben was listening, too, walking next to her on the other side. David carried May in the BabyBjörn; the steps were putting her to sleep, he was a few paces behind. Some power had shifted, this is what he felt, or some problem had resolved itself, and Susie, talking, felt it, too. She said, "In England they have different kinds of houses . . . a lot of people live in what they call ter-races. We have them, too, we call them row houses, but they're not as common. That's where there's a house next door to your house, they share a wall, but you have your own front door. In England they call apartments flats . . ." And so on. She was conscious that David was paying attention.

By the time they reached the top, she was out of breath. The summit was semi-crowded. Under a kind of gazebo, people sat on the limestone walls, drinking from water bottles or taking pictures.

Paul and Dana were there already. Even on a cloudy day, you could see for miles. A wide stretch of Lake Austin lay below them, crusted with mansions, boat docks, and waterfront lawns. Their driveways were paved for multiple cars. But beyond the shoreline, trees partly obscured the houses, and you had a sense of the continent expanding around you. Forest and overcast sky mirrored each other, rolling into the distance in irregular cloudy patterns. Dana said to Cal, who had jumped off the wall and was climbing through the undergrowth beneath it, "Come on, Cal, not there. There's a sign, it says . . ." and Jean called out, "I've got something in my pocket you might like," but he wasn't listening. Paul eventually went after him, and Liesel arrived at the top, looking red in the face, under her white hair. Nathan walked with her, she had taken his arm.

"*Sag mal*," she said, "*ich muss mich eine Minute hinsetzen*." I have to sit down. Clémence had carried Margot for the last few steps—she hung on her mother's neck. Julie wasn't talking to anyone.

There's nothing to do at the top but look around and go back down. Nathan made an effort with Henrik, but he felt some resistance. Maybe that was just his manner. Henrik spoke slowly and deliberately. He said to Nathan, "Jean says you organized a conference on the use of drones. In Israel." But this wasn't what Nathan wanted to talk about. In his experience, people (especially Europeans) brought it up when they wanted to pick a fight, when they were looking for a source of disagreement. Sometimes he liked to disappoint them.

"Really what interests me," he said, "is cultures of training. Often what you're arguing about in government is how to make decisions. Not just how, but *who* . . . that's what the drones discussion was about, and people make decisions according to their training. Politicians go through a certain kind, they're used to looking at problems in certain ways. Lawyers go through another. As it happens, I like

legal training, it's got a long history, it's rigorous, but more importantly it's also predictable, it's also regulated—there are professional
bodies that assess acceptable and unacceptable practice. If you had to
pick who should make decisions, I'd pick the lawyers. With certain
caveats."

Henrik could tell that he was being lectured to. He wasn't interested in that. His response to this kind of performance was to play up to
it. He kept asking questions. Let him talk.

Jean asked Clémence, "Did you get what you needed?"

"I don't know what we got," she said. "You never get what you
need, right? And if you do, you're doing it wrong . . ."

But they stayed two hours with this Beigott guy, they probably
got an hour on tape. Whenever you talk to people it turns out that
the story is more complicated than you thought it was, and usually in
quite boring ways. It's true he sold the house on 37th Street, partly to
pay for his mother's care. But he was ready to move out anyway. He
got sick of the frat-house atmosphere at Christmas, people left beer
bottles in your front yard, they honked their horns. His daughter was
there when we interviewed him, we talked to her, too. What it was
like growing up, etc.

Anyway, she's twenty-seven years old and living at home again.
She got a DUI and lost her license, which basically meant that she
lost her job—she was working as a courier. Part of the gig economy.
Which meant she lost her apartment. Anyway, you can see where this
is going. So now she's stuck in the middle of . . . the nearest town is
Kyle. I mean, there's nothing there, no bus service, nothing, taxis are
too expensive, so anytime she wants to go anywhere, her dad has to
drive her. Which he says he's basically fine with, because it means he
can keep an eye on her, he doesn't trust her. And the truth is, they
have a bickering kind of relationship, she rolls her eyes at him, but
they also seem very close, they get along. So it's not really clear what
any of this adds up to. Joel says he's perfectly happy, he likes the
fishing at Quarry Lake. When you walk in the house, there's a canoe

paddle next to the front door. But if he shot himself tomorrow, I wouldn't necessarily be surprised.

Clémence when she talked showed a lively use of hands. Her accent was always hard to place, you could hear the French in it, you could hear London. Liesel listened, too. She said, "Nobody wants to live out there, nobody wants that."

And Jean said, "She's not saying they do."

"People want to live where you can walk to a store."

"Mom, you didn't listen, that's not what she's saying."

But Clémence broke in, "It was a relief to get back to Wheeler Street afterward. It makes you think, everyone we know, people like us, what we do is move from island to island."

They had started to walk back along the trail. It descended gently to the road level a hundred yards on from the steps. On your left, the ground gave way to loose rock and undergrowth; it sloped steeply toward the water, and a certain amount of parental attention was absorbed by making sure the kids didn't fall off the cliff—Susie and Dana trailed after Cal and Ben.

Paul said to his brother, "Nobody asks if you're okay."

"What do you mean?" But Nathan knew what he meant. "Once a week I inject myself with Avonex. Or Clémence does it. I get my liver tested. When I see my doctor he checks for signs of depression. That's one of the side effects. So far as I know, and these things can be incremental, I haven't had another episode. The longer this goes on like this the better."

"Do the kids know?"

"The kids do not."

"Does anybody know?"

"Anybody I have some kind of professional contact with, where it might be relevant. This is the first thing I tell them."

Paul walked with his head down; there were bits of white limestone underfoot, like loose chalk. He said, "It feels weird to me that we don't talk about it, but we don't want to talk about it all the time.

We like to think of you as indestructible."

"I'm fine. I try to look after myself, I try not to drink too much. I try to get some sleep. All these things are good for me."

"Even when it pisses us off, it's important for us to think of you as indestructible. It's important to know that you're always right."

"I'm mostly right," Nathan said.

At certain points, the underbrush gives way, and the view opens out over the water and the forest beyond. Susie said, "Let's get a picture." Dana when she wasn't chasing after Cal had been using her Leica. It gave her an excuse not to talk to people. But views are the hardest thing to photograph—they look like views.

Nathan, softened by Paul, still had to make his usual objections, but he got overruled. They all lined up, even the kids. Even Julie. Nathan had to say to her in the end, "Come on, I don't want to do this any more than you do." She stood next to Henrik and Jean on the far side, away from her family. Dana backed up on the gravel; everybody looked cold. "Smile," she said. "Say *queso*."

Some of them said it and some of them didn't and she took the picture. A white path in the foreground, a few rocks, a layer of trees. The sun was going down behind them, red and cool and wrapped in cotton, and she had to adjust the exposure on her camera. She took several more shots. You could just see the edge of the water around Henrik's shoulder, gleaming flatly. Their shadows stretched toward her like ghostly arms. People behind them had stopped for a moment, waiting to pass, and Paul said, "Now you."

"What do you mean?"

"Let's get one with you in it."

"That's fine. It doesn't matter. I don't . . ."

But he asked a guy in a Michigan sweatshirt, who was walking with his arm around his girlfriend. She looked Asian or Latina, it was hard to tell. "Excuse me," Paul said. "Do you mind . . ." and Dana had to give in. The guy unwrapped his arm and she handed him the camera, lifting the cord from around her neck. She stood next to Paul, who stood next to Nathan, with Cal and Margot and Willy in front of them. Liesel was in the middle, with Henrik and Jean and Julie on her other side. Susie, Clémence, and David made another little row. May still slept against his chest; Susie had a hand on Ben's hair.

"Now we're all here."

"Except Bill," Jean said.

Afterward, Dana retrieved her camera, and Paul asked her, tenderly and curiously, "Why didn't you want your picture taken?"

"I don't like to . . ."

"You used to be a model."

"Yeah, well," she said.

Before they reached the street again, David took Susie aside. "I don't want to be shut out from these conversations." He spoke in an undertone; there were people around. He was almost pleading with her. "I want you to talk to me about Ben, and not anyone else."

"Fine," she said.

"I don't want you to be angry that we're going to England."

"I'll get over it."

Cars went past with their lights on. You could see pockets of mist rising in the glare of the headlamps. The Kia was still warm from the ride over, and they shut the doors quickly and drove back to Wheeler Street. Susie had given up on Mayfield Park—they could see the peacocks another day.

The first thing they had to do, on getting home, was make supper for the kids. In Austin, even the big kids ate early. The dinner service functioned on a couple of sittings, otherwise there wasn't room around the table. Anyway, it got too crazy. Nathan wanted to fry some fish, by way of appeasement—for Julie's sake. There was cod in the freezer and he'd taken it out before they drove to Mount Bonnell; it was dripping on a plate. He took flour from the cupboard and sprinkled it over the tiled kitchen counter. Susie, whose kids didn't like fish, cut up vegetables next to the sink. She put a pot of water on—they could eat pasta.

Nathan said, "There's plenty of fish."

He mixed salt and pepper in with the flour, and poured oil in a pan, letting it silently gather heat on one of the burners. Nobody talked much. The kids were next door, watching TV.

Twenty minutes later, Paul came down. He said, "We're taking off now. You should say goodbye to Dana, in case we don't make it to breakfast tomorrow morning."

"What?" Susie said. "What about supper? Cal needs to eat."

"There's some Bolognese in the fridge at home. We can all eat together."

He had Cal's suitcase in hand, loosely packed. It didn't matter if they left some of his things upstairs, he could pick them up another day.

Dana said, "I'm flying out tomorrow. Paul thought it might be a good idea to move Cal over tonight. I can sleep in the spare room."

"Ben, Willy," Susie called out. "Say goodbye to your aunt. They're leaving."

But she had to go into the TV room and turn off the TV. Dana kept saying, "Don't bother, I'm sure we'll see you in the morning. Otherwise, I'll feel stupid coming back."

"What time's your flight?" Nathan asked her.

"Twelve o'clock."

"We're pretty much on your way anyway," Susie said.

She had walked in again and stood with her hands folded, feeling foolish and formal, as if the occasion should be marked. She had the sense that maybe she hadn't talked to Dana much. You always assume there's more time. With the kids around, most of the time you're just fighting fires . . . that's not really true. You put it off, because you don't want to have the big conversation, but now she felt remiss.

"It is not on the way," Paul said, and Susie shouted again, for the kids to come.

Somebody had to tell Liesel, who was in her study. Jean came down, too—Henrik had been taking a nap upstairs. Everybody gathered in the entrance hall to say goodbye; Cal was clearly a little freaked out. He clung to his mother, who carried him, which made it hard for her to hug anyone else. Paul got slightly annoyed.

"Let's not make this a big deal."

"I'm sure we'll see you tomorrow anyway," Nathan said. The fish was in the pan—he had to get back.

"I won't say goodbye," Liesel told Dana. "But I'm very glad you came."

Her eyes shone a little, her emotions were near the surface. Dana leaned over in spite of her son and put an arm around her. She was moved, too, and closer to tears than she had any reason to be. "I don't want to go," she said, and Paul couldn't tell what she meant. He got bored standing around and carried the suitcases to the car, then waited on the front porch by the open door.

"If we don't see you for breakfast, we'll stop by after the airport," he said. "Cal, come on, Buddy. You're not really going anywhere."

"Shut the door," Susie said. "You're letting the cold in."

Afterward, they gathered in the kitchen, which smelled of the fish. Susie slid spaghetti into the pot, the water was boiling now, and heat and steam fogged up the window over the sink.

Liesel said, "Maybe later we can light the tree again and sing songs."

"I don't know what you're looking so pleased about," Jean told her.

"What do you mean?"

"I don't know what you expect to happen tonight, but it's not going to happen."

"Do we have to have this conversation here?" Susie said.

The kids had sat down at the table. Julie and Ben were arguing about something—*American Pickers*, which is what they'd been watching. Willy looked pale. Sounds echoed in his head, and he had the feeling you get in an indoor swimming pool, of faint distortion. The smell of boiling water . . . he felt hot and cold. Margot was still reading, turning the pages of her book in a mechanical way.

"I don't expect anything," Liesel said.

"Yes, you do. But it doesn't mean anything, she's just staying over to help Cal settle in."

"He sleeps at Paul's house all the time, whenever he comes to stay."

"But not usually with Dana here. It's confusing for him."

"That's what I mean."

"You're not making sense," Jean said, but her mother snapped.

"Stop telling me this all the time, that I don't understand, that I'm not making sense. I understand more than you think."

"In this case, I don't think you do."

"What do you mean?"

But Jean was unhappy now, too. She didn't want to say it. "She's seeing somebody else, in New York."

"How do you know this?" Liesel asked.

"She told me." And then, when nobody said anything, Jean added: "Don't shoot the Essinger," to make a joke of it, but her eyes were wide with apology or shame, and she was looking at her mother.

"When did she tell you?" And Nathan asked, "Does Paul know?"

"I don't know. I don't know what Paul knows. She told me in the Spider House a couple of nights ago." After a moment, she said, "I didn't think it was my secret to tell."

"So why are you telling us now?"

"I don't know," Jean said. "I didn't want you to get your hopes up."

But Liesel was angry now. "I don't see how she can come here like this, and not say anything, for a whole week, and pretend that nothing is going on. I don't understand her."

"She said something to me," Jean said. "You invited her."

"Listen, I'm trying to get the kids something to eat, can we do this elsewhere?" Susie carried the pot to the sink and poured the pasta into the colander. Steam rose.

"What does it matter, the kids don't care," Nathan said. Julie and Margot had started eating—the fish was hot, and Clémence sat with them, to regulate the ketchup. There were bowls of cut cucumber and carrots. She ate one and looked at her husband, a warning look, but he ignored her. "They're not even listening."

"Of course they're listening," Susie said. "Of course they care."

"What don't we care about?"

Julie had cheered up. For some reason the presence of adult disaster put her on good behavior.

"None of your beeswax," her mother told her.

Liesel had gone red in the face. "I'm upset now. I don't understand her at all. She's a very cool customer."

"I don't think any of this is her first choice," Nathan said.

———

"That felt a bit rushed." Dana was putting Cal in the backseat, leaning over to reach the buckle.

"What do you mean?"

"I don't know, like we were making an escape." She got in herself and closed the door. "We could have waited for Cal to eat with his cousins."

"I had food at home. I made it so we could eat together."

She waited for him to turn the car around. "It just felt like . . . I've been there all week. I don't know."

"If you want to go back, I can take you back."

He was driving across the bridge, over the creek. The grass was covered in fat leaves, which glowed in the dusk, pumpkin-colored. Lights had come on in the houses overlooking the park.

"I don't want to go back."

"You said you wanted to do this."

"Okay."

"If it matters to you, we can go back in the morning. We can have breakfast with everyone else."

"Yes."

"I thought, after a week, you'd be glad to get away."

"I am glad, I mean it's fine. I like your family," she said.

By the time they crossed the river, night had fallen. Paul let Cal play with his phone, he didn't want the kid to go to sleep. They took I-35 and the headlights streaming against them were like the bombs in *Space Invaders*, repeated blips. The quality of the graphics was very basic. Neighborhoods with parks and swimming pools passed by below them, front yards, driveways, places where people lived, but it all seemed a little abstract, and Dana had the computer-game feeling you get, where life is made up of simple data and measurable tasks. In the dark she could sit in the passenger seat and look out the window and not feel observed. Paul wanted to talk.

"What do you think of Henrik? I had a good time with him last night."

He wanted her opinion because he wanted to have a certain kind of conversation, which she didn't want to have. She said, "I think he's sexy," partly joking, and to put him off. But maybe this was the wrong thing to say, it sounded like flirting.

"He seems to me somebody who's still open to experiences. A lot of people his age aren't anymore. That's attractive."

More and more, he sounded like his father. She was the teenage babysitter, being driven home.

What surprised her is that she felt guilty about Stephen. Would she mention it to him, that she spent the night at Paul's place? Would he care? This morning he asked her . . . it wasn't really clear what he was asking. To have a baby with him. They hadn't even had sex. All day this phone call had been running through her head.

A therapist once told her, people create the situations they want to respond to. And it's true, something had to change. She wanted to leave their apartment and get a place of her own. Maybe she could move in with Stephen but that seems like, just substituting . . . and it isn't fair on Cal. With everything up in the air, at least, his home, where he was born . . . but how much of your life can you live like that, according to the needs of a four-year-old boy? I'm thirty-one now. In two years he's going to be in school full-time, and after I drop him off, what am I going to do. I need something to do. She was sick of living in the . . . what Jean called the self-expression economy. Freelancing, taking photographs. She wanted to do something where it was important you showed up on time and did your job. At least I think that's what I want. Until she came to Austin she had no idea how unhappy she was.

It's a fifty-minute drive to Red Hawk Road, the last half through empty landscape. Once you turn off I-35 you hit the real dark, there are depths of it, which you start to feel like pressure in your head. Like swimming to the bottom of the pool. Paul said, "I've been reading a lot of different things." She said, "What are you reading?" but didn't listen to the answer. Behind her, in the car, Cal was still playing on the phone—she could see his face in the glow. The game made a noise but much of it was drowned out by car noise.

Paul kept his eyes on the road. "It's a shame we're not arriving in the light."

"I've seen the house before."

"I know, but I've been . . . working on the backyard."

"I'll see it in the morning," she said, which changed the tone and frightened her a little.

He wanted to know what was going on at Wheeler Street. "I've been feeling bad all week for leaving you to . . . leaving you there alone."

"Without your protection?"

"You know what I mean. It just feels weird."

"I'm sorry if you didn't want me to come," she said.

"That's not it. That's not what I mean at all. You know that."

If she responded, it would be like saying she wanted him to reassure her. But that's not what she wanted. They were going past a stretch of cookie-cutter houses, beige siding, a recent development, which meant that the streets were decently lit. But then at the traffic lights they turned off again onto one of those Texas highways named after a number, which quickly led them back into nothing much—trees and telephone poles by the side of the road.

He said, "I feel like I'm in the middle of an argument with Nathan."

This is something they used to fight about—that he wouldn't talk about his family with her. She felt left out, so maybe now he was trying to make an effort. But it sounded over-rehearsed.

"What's the argument?"

"We were talking about it yesterday at this brunch thing. He wanted to schmooze the judge, I don't know. He kind of left me waiting around for him. Sandra Bullock was there, I could have . . . it was stupid, it didn't matter. Nathan said that we have this chance to live unusually good lives, but you have to make certain sacrifices."

"What's he talking about?"

"He means . . . I said to him, not everybody wants to be Judge Kirkendoll. He's very ambitious, I used to be, too. But you don't interact with the world and come out of it a better person. That's something I've learned this year; you come out worse. Which is why people like children, because they haven't interacted yet."

Maybe he was trying to niggle her, in which case it worked. He wasn't arguing with Nathan, he was arguing with her—about living in New York, about moving to Texas, to the middle of nowhere.

"You heard about Ben, right?" Her voice was rising; she tried to keep it down. "He got up in the middle of the night to throw stones at Julie's window. That's not . . . I wouldn't call it innocence."

They had reached the outskirts of Wimberley, such as they were. Dana could see lights, but then the road doubled back and they headed away from them again. "Come on, Cal," Paul said, turning around in his seat. The boy was nodding off; the iPhone lay in his lap. "We're almost there, just hang on. We can all have supper together."

He switched on his brights, and there was a flash of water ahead of them. It had rained heavily overnight, and the road ran down through the channel of a river. She had forgotten that part, the only time she ever came to his house was last summer. A kind of concrete platform served as the intersection; maybe half a foot of water lay across it, a moving surface.

"Jesus," she said, but he plowed right through.

You could feel the weight of water against the tires, and then they pulled up the ramp on the other side. Her heart was racing, and suddenly the vague uneasiness she had felt, and which had been building in her, turned to fear. The houses were set far back and apart from each other at the end of steep drives. She could see the river below them, a different-colored darkness; they were going along the side of it. Paul kept his brights on—nobody else was on the road.

"You don't think he learned that at home, do you?" he asked. "You learn that kind of thing at school."

After a pause, she said: "You don't think kids should go to school?"

Paul could feel the atmosphere changing. "I have two years of Stanford. You went to Amherst. My brother is the smartest person I know. And yet when it comes to educating our kids we farm it out to other people. The most important thing . . . what they think and know, teaching them to think, we let other people do the work—we don't even pick the people. We let the state do it, or whatever. It doesn't make sense."

Then his house appeared, a low-roofed box, illuminated by little lights in the grass. She said, "Maybe I'll be a teacher. That's something I've been thinking about."

She wanted to change the tone.

"What age?" He was parking the car.

"Kids. Elementary school."

"You'd be a very good teacher," he said.

"I don't know. I don't know that I'm somebody kids warm to."

"That's not the job." But he hadn't contradicted her, which he realized. "Kids love you," he said. "Cal loves you."

"Of course, I'm his mother . . ."

But he wouldn't be put off. "You're very good with Cal, he's a good kid. I see him with his cousins, he's very confident. That's you, that's not me."

The house was cold when they got in—because of the concrete floor and the wall of glass at the back. There was a stove, and he wanted to light the fire; this was part of his idea. He didn't like to run the heating when he wasn't around, he liked to get by on natural heat. Being cold, lighting a fire, warming up, these things gave him something to do. But he turned on the heating now and put a pot of water on to boil. He drew the curtains. Dana felt like she should take off her shoes. Cal was running around—there was a ball his father let him kick inside the house, one of those plastic inflatable balls you get for a dollar. She wanted to tell him not to, but it wasn't her business.

"Give me something to do," she said.

But there was nothing to do; he gave her a glass of wine. She was starting to freak out and trying hard not to show it, so she seemed a little cool. Even after a year the place looked under-furnished—sounds echoed, and you could feel outside the house, beyond the curtains, empty landscape. There were prairie dogs, possums, skunks, coyotes out there; even bears. Rattlesnakes and bats. Animals outnumbered the humans. Cal seemed happy at the table. It didn't matter if he made a mess—the floor was easy to clean.

She said, "This is very good," meaning the sauce, which sat in a cast-iron pot on the stovetop of his industrial oven. Paul bought the beef from a guy he knew who kept his own cattle, a writer who was on the staff of *Texas Monthly*. Every year he killed a few and sold them to friends. Paul put the meat in the freezer and worked his way through it. Dana thought, it must be weird for Cal, seeing us like this, eating together. He didn't seem to mind, but also, with him around, this wasn't something she could talk about. It cut off other conversation. Paul told her about the meat.

Afterward, she gave her son a bath.

Paul watched her from the bathroom doorway. "I'll clean up," he said.

The sense of orchestration, which she felt strongly, didn't actually require from her any reaction—she could just go along with it. At home in New York in their apartment he often used to cook while she put Cal to bed. He cared about food more than she did, it was part of his job to pay attention to what he ate. Sometimes when she turned off the light and emerged, he gave her a glass of wine and went in to kiss their son goodnight. Then they ate supper. It never occurred to her at the time that this narrow and limited life would end. Because it was fine with her.

Cal's bedroom had one of those plastic Ferraris with a mattress inside. This is where he slept without her. The floor had a thick carpet covered in toys; she got down on her knees to put on his pajamas. It was late, past his bedtime, he had wet hair, but Paul said he would read to him in front of the fire. He seemed to be in control. The fire was going brightly now, he turned off most of the lights, and Dana was aware of an intensification of her feelings, which had to be kept in check. She poured herself another glass of wine and listened to him read.

He said, "Do you want to put him to bed?"

"It's your house."

"He won't see you for a week."

"Sure, I can put him to bed."

But there was something missing in her, something absent, which Cal noticed. She said, "Come on, big guy," and carried him from the sofa. He had brushed his teeth, he had done a pee, he was very tired. But when she turned off the light, he wouldn't let her go—he held onto her hand. His bed wasn't really big enough to lie down in, but she tried. "I'll just lie with you here a minute, until you fall asleep." Her head was propped against the wheel of the Ferrari, her legs fell over the side. She was quite uncomfortable but waited anyway, partly because she didn't want to face Paul, and this was also a gesture—of self-assertion. I'll come when I want to come. But Cal wouldn't go to sleep. When she tried to get up (her neck ached), he grabbed her shirt. Her eyes were used to the dark by this point, and she could see his expression.

"Lie on top of me," he said.

So she lay on top but it wasn't enough. And he was starting to get on her nerves—she didn't like to be pulled at. "Go to sleep," she said. "I want to talk to Daddy."

In the end, Paul had to come and put him to bed. She left them to it. She was very close to the edge, but it took him a few minutes and she had time to calm down. When he came out again, he said, "I told him I would give him your cardigan," so she took it off. It was warm in the house by this point, but not that warm. And then Paul closed the door behind him, making the face you make when you can't tell if something's going to work. But Cal stayed quiet—he didn't call out.

"What do you want to do?" He opened another bottle of wine. "Do you want to watch a movie?"

In a corner of the L-shaped living room, Paul had set up a projector. There was a blank wall in front of it; a soft gray sofa faced the wall.

"Sure, I'm easy." He leaned in to kiss her, and she let him. "Let me just go to the bathroom for a second," she said and took her purse.

The bathroom was large, with a window overlooking the backyard, which sloped down to the river. There were no blinds or curtains, but you couldn't see much, because the overhead light reflected off the glass. The bathtub was still full of Cal's toys. They were wet and slimy with bubbles—Dana hadn't bothered to put them away. She sat on the toilet seat with the lid down and took out her phone. She didn't know who to call but she had to call somebody. Maybe Jean . . . she tried her number, but it was an English cell, and the dial-tone sounded funny. No one picked up, so she called the number at Wheeler Street and Nathan answered.

"Hello." She could hear singing in the background . . . they were probably sitting in front of the tree. Liesel had said she wanted to light the candles. It was nine o'clock.

"Can you pick me up?" she said. "I don't know any taxis around here."

"Is something going on, are you all right?"

"I'm fine. I just don't think this is a good idea."

"Okay," he said. "Give me a minute. Let me think." Then he said, "I can come get you, but it will take me almost an hour to get there."

"That's fine."

"Is everything okay?"

"Everything's fine. I'd ask Paul to drive me but Cal is already asleep."

After washing her hands and face (and drying them on Cal's towel), she emerged from the bathroom. Paul was waiting; the projector hummed faintly overhead. She didn't say anything. They sat on the sofa and watched *The Breakfast Club*, which was one of the movies he had on DVD. When he tried to kiss her, she kissed him back, but then she wriggled out of it and said she wanted to watch. He was clearly just sitting there waiting for it to end, he was biding his time, and she found this so unpleasant that it kept her going until Nathan arrived.

Nathan put down the phone and sat at his mother's desk without getting up. His grandfather's letter lay next to the computer, along with Liesel's translation; she used a little metal donkey as a paperweight. Next door, they were all singing Hanukkah songs, one of the ones with a marching cadence: *Mi Yimalel*. When he came back into the living room, he saw that Henrik had fallen asleep on the couch. The fire was lit, Jean was sitting at his feet.

She said, "What's wrong?"

"Nothing. Walk with me to the car."

"What's going on?" Clémence asked.

"I'll tell you later," he said, and Jean followed him out.

Nathan still had the keys to the Volvo, which was sitting in the drive. Jean wore only a T-shirt, it was really very cold. She said, "Who was on the phone?"

"Dana. She wants me to pick her up."

"Why?"

"She didn't say, but I think I should go."

"Let me go, you don't like driving at night."

"No, I talked to her, I should go. I think this could have real repercussions, you shouldn't have to deal with it."

"Why should you?"

Julie had followed them out, she was standing in the doorway with the door open—letting in the cold. Nathan called to her, "Go inside. Nothing is going on. It's fine," but she came out in bare feet anyway.

"If nothing's going on, why are you standing out here?"

She had followed them down the steps, and her father put an arm around her.

"I have to pick up Dana."

"What's wrong?"

"Nothing's wrong. She asked me to pick her up."

"What about Paul?"

"Look, I don't really know what's going on. But I guess I'll find out."

"You don't like driving at night," Julie said.

"Let me go," Jean broke in. "He won't get so mad at me."

"There may be some truth in what you say, but I feel like, I said to Dana that I would come."

"Call her back. Call Paul."

"The sense I got from her is that's not what she wanted me to do. She wanted me to come."

"What about Paul?"

"I don't know," Nathan said and got in the car. Clémence had come out, too, she was standing on the front porch. Somebody called out, "Shut the door."

Julie asked, "Can I tell her what's going on?"

"You can tell her."

He had driven out to Wimberley four or five times in his life. The first part was easy enough, you pulled onto I-35 and at this time of night, the access road, which could be tricky, was usually clear. Later, if he needed to look on his phone, he could stop at a gas station or whatever, but he thought he'd remember where to go when he saw the exit signs. He told himself, I have to be careful how this plays out, but he had at least fifty minutes in the car to think. Part of what bugged him was his own sense of responsibility. Because if it had to do with sibling rivalry, or some kind of controlling instinct, which you get used to acting on as a big brother, Paul could reasonably reproach him for it afterward. But the truth is, he didn't want to go, and if somebody else could have picked up the phone and spoken to Dana, he would have let them go. He was almost sure of that. He felt sick about it, but he also needed to concentrate. One of the reasons he didn't like driving at night is he worried about falling asleep.

It was ten o'clock by the time he pulled up at the house. The outside air had a kind of crystal quality. For the last ten miles, he had driven with the windows open. Paul answered the door. The lights were off behind him, Nathan could see the fire dying in the stove and the flickering of the movie against the wall. The sound was low, and Dana had stood up, too.

"Hey," Paul said, surprised. "What's up?"

"Dana called. She asked me to pick her up."

"What are you talking about?" And Dana said, "I called him."

"What's going on?" Paul said, and Nathan knew that whatever came out of tonight was going to be worse than he feared.

"I can't stay here. It's too weird. We're not even talking about anything."

"So let's talk."

"That's what I wanted to do."

"No, it's not," Paul said, and she knew he was right.

"I don't want to live with you out here, that's not what I want."

"Do we have to do this now?"

"I don't want to . . . homeschool Cal, I don't want . . ."

"No one's talking about that."

"You were talking about that."

"So send him to school, I don't care." His face, under strain, looked hollow; he had lost weight, it was the face of a homeless man.

Dana said, "Let's talk tomorrow."

"Okay, so let's talk tomorrow."

"I can't sleep here tonight."

"What are you talking about?" He was speaking too loudly and knew it, he sounded like somebody it's reasonable to be afraid of, but he couldn't help himself.

Nathan said, "Paul. Nothing good can happen tonight. Let me take her home and we can talk in the morning."

"What's Cal going to think when he wakes up and she's not here?"

"You can bring him in the morning," and Dana said, "We can wake him up now and take him home." She wanted to see him, to hold him, but Paul was closer to the bedroom door.

"You're not waking him up, that's not going to happen."

Suddenly she started shouting. "Cal!' she shouted, "Cal!' but not really loud enough to wake him, and she knew it. It was a protest and she felt stupid.

Paul told his brother, "This is what you're getting involved in, this kind of craziness?"

Nathan looked at him, utterly helpless, almost childish. "I don't know what to do. I don't know what I should do."

Paul had never seen him like this, or not in thirty years.

"Go home," he said. "Turn around and go home."

"I can't do that. You have to make this easier for me. You have to help me out."

But in the end, he didn't have to do much. Dana hadn't unpacked yet, her suitcase was by the door. She said, "I want to give him a kiss, I want to see him," but Paul wouldn't let her. He stood in front of Cal's bedroom and she didn't want to go near him. Nathan said, "Come on, Paul," but he wouldn't budge. "Don't act like I'm the dangerous one here. This is crazy." Dana was frantic now. "Bring him in the morning. Let me see him in the morning," but Nathan persuaded her to come away. Afterward he told himself, it could have been worse. If she had tried to get in his room, it could have been worse. As they walked outside into the cold again, and got in Nathan's car, Paul followed them. You could see their breaths in the garden lights; a few flakes were falling. Footsteps echoed under the low sky. Nathan backed out of the drive and watched his brother standing there, by the open door.

There wasn't any traffic on the drive back. Nathan hadn't been at the house more than ten minutes; he got back to Wheeler Street around eleven o'clock. Dana in the car was almost flat with grief; she was cold, too. She had left her cardigan behind. Nathan turned up the heat. "I'm sorry," she said. "None of this is your problem."

"I don't want to ask you what happened, or what's going on. I don't want to know anything Paul doesn't know, or be part of any conversation without him."

"Okay."

"I'm trying to get through this without doing permanent damage to any of these relationships."

"Okay," Dana said. In fact, she fell asleep on the road, and Nathan had to wake her up. Liesel was waiting in her study — he could see the light on. Jean was up, too; Henrik had gone to bed. She met him in the hall and said, "Clémence asked me to say, you should wake her up when you get in. I told her what happened, as far as I knew."

"That's fine."

Jean said to Dana, "Can I get you anything, do you want a cup of tea?"

"I just want to go to bed. I don't want to see anybody."

They were speaking quietly — sound carried in the stairwell, and Susie's family was already asleep upstairs.

"Your bedroom is still . . . I mean, just go to bed," and when Dana went to her room she noticed that she had clean sheets. There was a fresh towel on the blanket. Cal's mattress was put away, too.

Jean said to Nathan, "What happened?"

"I don't want to talk about it. Paul was completely blindsided. This isn't going to go away."

"What were they doing?"

"So far as I can tell, they were watching a movie."

"So you took her home?"

"That's what she asked me to do. I don't know if I did right, I didn't want to gang up against her."

"I'm sure you did what you could."

"Well, I don't know. Listen, I'm tired, I'm going to go to bed. There'll be a lot of conversation in the morning, which right now I don't think anybody can face."

"Don't forget to wake Clémence," Jean said, and put her arm on his shoulder.

The phone rang, and Liesel picked up. Bill had said he would call her tonight after everybody left. She wanted to talk to Nathan but she couldn't face Dana and had waited for her to go upstairs. Then the phone rang and she missed them both.

Bill said, "Well, it's over," and Liesel said, "How did it go?"

"The funeral was what I expected it to be," and he started talking. He mentioned that he went to visit the house in Port Jervis, he told the story. Honestly, he said, after living with Judith for a week, you can't help but . . . admire her. She fights every fight. But the reception at Rose's house was something else. Twenty, thirty people came, and not just seat-fillers from the synagogue. Rosario came, with her two kids. This was Rose's cleaner, who worked for her for thirty years. Her daughter is a junior at Manhattan College, studying communications. She wants to be a sports reporter; her son is going to be a freshman next year. He's on the baseball team. Both of these kids had vivid memories of Rose, they were extremely articulate . . . Good company. It took them two hours to get here from Oceanside, which is where Rosario lives now. Let me tell you, the number of people she formed meaningful relations with, given the limited means at her disposal. I mean, for the last five years of her life, Rose hardly left the house. And this evening they just kept coming. Thirty, forty people, they ate up the food, the living room was full. We had to bring in dining chairs from the kitchen. The last person left at ten o'clock. Judith went right to bed, it's been a long day. Our flight isn't till one o'clock. I told her, we can clean up in the morning. And then he said, "What's going on with you." It was as much a statement as a question, he'd been talking too much.

"Something happened with Paul and Dana," Liesel told him. "I don't know what. She was supposed to stay the night in Wimberley, but Nathan had to pick her up. Jean says she's seeing somebody in New York, but she never said anything to the rest of us. I don't think Paul knew."

It was the first tug on the cord, pulling him back.

FRIDAY

It snowed overnight, enough to leave a crust on the lawn. Liesel looked out on a blank garden, two of the kids were already out there, making tracks. Even with her glasses on, she couldn't see who they were. Her eyes were bad, especially in the morning, and the children flickered in a white half-light. Different-shaped smudges. Every five or ten years it snowed in Austin, enough to stick, and when it did, the garden looked like it might be anywhere. It might be Germany or sixty years ago. One of the kids was pulling the other one along on ... maybe it was a trash-can lid. There was a lid with a rope attached to it. What was happening to them was happening in the depths of their own childhood and they would look back later as if it lay at the bottom of a deep well.

Usually Liesel went down to breakfast in her nightgown, but today she got dressed; she wanted to walk outside. Nathan came out to join her on the patio. He wore pajamas and a sweater and his running shoes, without socks. The kids were Ben and Julie. Ben pulled Julie but the lid wasn't really big enough, she kept having to balance herself on her hands, which were red with cold.

She said, "Pull harder."

"You're too heavy."

"That's your problem."

"When's it my turn?"

"When I say so," but she had to kick herself along, it wasn't that much fun. Her hands had gone numb and snow trickled into the gap between her shirt and her pants.

Clémence pushed open the sliding door and stood in the doorway.

"Excuse my *dishabille*," she said to Liesel. And then to Nathan: "Is Julie warm enough?"

"She's fine."

"I don't want her to get sick, too."

"We're all going to get sick."

"How's Margot?" Liesel asked, and Clémence told her, "She slept a little better."

"I'm so happy it snowed." Liesel could see her own breath and feel the skin on her face. She could feel that her cheeks were red. "I just hope it doesn't mean . . . Bill's landing at four-thirty."

Nathan was staring at the kids. She couldn't tell what he was thinking.

"I'm sure that by then everything will be melted, it will be sixty degrees out."

Then he walked out into the backyard; his sneakers crunched on the frozen grass. "Come on, people," he said. "Let's see if we can make something." He bent down and swept his arm against the lawn to cause a pile-up, but the surface layer was hardly an inch thick. The snow was dusty, too; it puffed in his face and stuck to his eyelashes while Liesel watched him.

The white light woke Dana—she had left the blinds half-open when she went to bed. It took her several hours to fall asleep, because she had slept in the car, and because Cal wasn't lying on the floor beside her, and because . . . The panic she had felt rising up inside her in Paul's house had turned into shame. She was ashamed of the way she sat on the toilet and called Nathan and then walked out again like nothing was going on. She was ashamed of causing trouble for Nathan, too, for the Essingers generally, of disappointing Liesel and accepting her invitation in the first place. In the mood she was in she couldn't give a reason for any of these decisions. She was making decisions like this because there was nothing in her life that she knew she wanted or was striving toward and so she had no reasons for doing anything. She might as well move in with Stephen in New York and have another baby or move to Wimberley or move home again when her parents got back from their cruise. Her mother could help with Cal; she could save money, and not rely on Paul so much. She could rely on her parents instead. She didn't want to do any of these things.

She got up anyway, and dressed, and repacked her suitcase. Her bedroom window overlooked the driveway and the road and she checked to see if maybe Paul had come but she couldn't see his car. The only thing she really wanted was to see Cal before she left, but it was only seven-thirty—of course they hadn't come. To get here by now Paul would have had to wake Cal around six o'clock and get him dressed and give him something to eat, and then set out maybe by a quarter to seven. But she was leaving in two hours, she didn't have much time. It also wasn't clear how she was getting to the airport, and maybe right now she should just order a cab, but that might look like a statement. Probably someone would drive her. She didn't want Paul to drive her. The conversation they needed to have wasn't something they could finish in a half hour on the way to the airport . . . and she didn't want Cal to be deserted by both of them at the same time, or have to say goodbye to her again at the airport or have to listen to them argue in the car. She didn't want to go down to breakfast. She couldn't face anybody, but she had a kind of courage of appearances. It's what she'd been brought up to do: show your face and make polite conversation. As a woman generally, her mother had taught her, you should learn to accept a certain amount of unwanted attention gracefully. This didn't always serve her well, but she stripped the bed and left a pile of sheets on top, then carried her suitcase downstairs.

Henrik was pouring coffee by the sink when Dana walked in. He had his back to her and didn't turn around. Jean stood by the kitchen counter, waiting for the toaster to pop. She said, "Morning," and Susie looked up. Willy was sitting on her lap, and May was in the high chair, playing with Cheerios and throwing them on the carpet. Clémence sat with her elbow on the table and her hand in the air; there was an ice pack around her wrist. Then Liesel stomped in the backdoor and cleaned her feet on the mat. A scattering of snow fell and melted on the wooden floor.

"Everybody's up," she said cheerfully.

Except David, Susie said. May had caught Cal's cold. "I don't think she feels terrible, but she's all stuffed up and can't breathe. You can't explain to her why, and so basically she spent all night saying, why, why, why, unless we walked her up and down. I didn't want to wake the house."

"I didn't hear anything." Dana had blushed a little; she poured milk into a bowl of raisin bran.

"It doesn't matter if you wake us up," Jean said, and Henrik added, "If I wake up, I think, this is not my problem, and go back to sleep."

"You do not go back to sleep."

"I'm sorry, all this is my fault. I brought disease into this house."

"Dana, this is not your fault. Henrik woke up at half past three anyway. Just as I get over jet lag he drags me back in."

"It's nobody's fault, it just is what it is. David did the three a.m. shift, which is why I told him to go back to bed."

"What happened to your wrist?" Dana asked.

"She had a fall," Jean said, teasing her.

"I did not have a fall. I fell, there's a difference." Clémence had slipped on the dusty snow, walking across the patio. She said, "It's fine, it's just a sprain, I think I can move it."

"You *think* you can move it?"

"Is this moving it?" and she wiggled her fingers. Dana thought, I'm back in the middle of it all again. But she was going away.

Susie had made the ice pack, grabbing a handful of cubes from the freezer and squeezing them into an old blue plastic *New York Times* delivery bag. She kept saying, "Leave it on," but Clémence got tired of holding her hand in the air. It made her feel frail. She was turning fifty next year and didn't want Nathan to think of her as somebody he had to look out for—she was conscious of the age gap. But there was nothing she could do, she really couldn't use her hand. So she

sat there "in state," as she said, and let Jean bring her breakfast. Dana
kept looking at the hallway. She ate her cereal and watched the clock.

Nathan gave up trying to make something out of the snow, there
wasn't enough. He liked doing stupid practical physical stuff with
the kids, because it kept his mind off other things, but he was feeling
cold now in his pajamas. The knees of his pants and the sleeves of his
sweater were wet. He could smell the wool and feel the cotton against
his skin as the thin material shifted and made contact and then hung
loose again. But he didn't want to go inside, and see Dana or Paul—if
Paul decided to show up. He hoped Paul would come, for his sake,
Nathan thought. Because it would mean he was a reasonable human
being. Last night he didn't have any trouble falling asleep but he
woke up at three in the morning and went over the arguments in his
head. There were the justifications he could use if he talked to Paul
and the other arguments he had with himself. They bled together.
At four or five he fell asleep again and then woke up again with the
unusual light. When he saw it had snowed, and Liesel standing there,
he went outside.

And then Margot came out in her nightgown and a thick blue
terry-cloth robe and her mother's leather boots, which she could
hardly walk in. "What are you doing?" she asked. She had followed
them into the yard along the stepping-stones, from which the snow
had melted. It was still cloudy, and the low white sky seemed to
contain the light—they were caught in the middle.

"What are you wearing?"

"They're Mom's."

"I know they're Mom's. Did she say okay?"

"She lets me. What are you doing?" she asked again.

"Nothing. Going in."

"Why do you always stop when I come?"

Her voice sounded normal, maybe the fever had passed; but her
question genuinely surprised him. Julie was more predictable. Nathan

had interesting conversations with her and liked their arguments, but she rarely said or noticed something that he hadn't thought or noticed himself. But Margot was like her mother, he couldn't always guess what she was feeling.

"I'm just cold. You must be pretty cold, too." But that didn't really answer her question. "Okay," he said. "There's something I wanted to try anyway."

He had an idea of turning the court into an ice rink. There was a hose at the back, connected to a water fountain that Bill had put in next to the sycamore. (Paul used to practice out there hour after hour in the summer, hitting balls against the concrete wall.) It dripped but it worked, and Nathan hooked up the hose to the faucet and pulled the other end through the snow. The kids were watching him with a certain amount of expectation. He told Ben to turn on the faucet and slowly the hose shifted in its coils and he felt the pressure of the water under his thumb. As far as he could reach, he sprayed the court, standing on the stones by the edge. But it wasn't quite cold enough, which he knew.

"Just wait," he said; he could sense their disappointment. The snow was turning to slush and he felt unhappy and self-disgusted. "Let's go. We can check again in an hour if the temperature drops." Margot let him carry her back to the house.

Liesel was telling a story when they walked in. Susie said, "Shut the door," good-humoredly; it became a kind of refrain. Ben and Julie were messing around outside. Dana thought, just close it, just close it. As an only child, she wasn't used to the amount of interaction. Eventually Liesel started again.

Once in winter the fjord froze over—Nathan has heard this already, she said. Klaus, her brother, woke up first and went down to the beach, then came back to tell her what had happened. It's amazing how flat the ice looked, like a parking lot. They could have walked to Denmark but didn't dare. But they walked a hundred yards out, and she remembers that what surprised her most was how low their house seemed above the shoreline. She thought of it as high in the hills because of the steps from the garden to the beach, and the woods in between; but from the water it looked like you could throw a stone and break a window. In fact, they threw stones on the ice, which skittered and made a sound like the end of the world. None of the ships could get out of the harbor; it lasted for two weeks. She noticed that Dana kept looking toward the hallway.

Nathan said to his wife, "What happened to your hand?"

"I fell on the patio."

"She had a fall," Jean said.

"Does it hurt?" he asked tenderly, and his tenderness comforted him.

"It's fine. Susie made me put on this ice pack. It hurts because it's cold." The bag had started to drip.

Then the phone rang and Liesel made a show of hurry, pushing her chair back and maneuvering her legs around. Her chair was at the end of the table, near the wall. She stood up painfully and answered. Cal ran in, wearing brand-new corduroy pants that were still a little stiff, a Christmas present, and Liesel said, "Get me a pen, get me something to write on." It was Bill, she wanted to write down his flight information—he never used email. Jean gave her an envelope and Paul followed, carrying a bag of pastries from Texas French.

Nathan said, "Tell him I can pick him up."

"Okay, okay," Liesel said. "*Ich freue mich sehr.*" I'm very pleased. "Everybody's missed you. Nathan says he can pick you up."

Paul put the pastries on the counter, next to his car keys.

People had mostly finished breakfast but Jean unwrapped them anyway and laid them out. Dana was trapped between the table and the wall, but it didn't matter, because Cal wanted to sit next to Ben. It's annoying, Ben thought, the way kids follow you around. For some reason, he felt uncomfortable around his cousin. I don't know why I didn't tell anybody that he was there, too. Already the terms he used for describing that night were becoming vaguer. He had started to believe, it's because I wanted to protect him; but instead of feeling generous he felt annoyed.

Dana said, "All I do here is eat, I must have put on ten pounds."

"I don't know where you put them," Clémence said. She was conscious of Julie's presence and thought, women shouldn't boast or complain like this. She worked hard to keep her own weight down but also thought you should never talk about it.

Already Susie had started on the first round of dishes, but nobody else had gotten up. They picked at the scones. Liesel turned in her chair (she had hung up and sat down again) and brought out a pot of good honey. Dana thought, this is how the day goes every day, it's all going to go on without me. Partly she was relieved to be getting away. She could feel whatever she wanted now that Cal was there, whereas before all she could do was wait to see if he came. She tried to say something to Paul, to have some kind of exchange, but he wouldn't look at her.

Henrik asked if he still went running with Lance Armstrong every Sunday.

"Running or biking," Paul said, with a full mouth.

"Do you think I can come, too? I won't be able to keep up for very long. I am still a little weak."

"I don't know if it's happening this Sunday."

"Are you training for something?"

"Not really. I signed up for the Boston Marathon, which is in April. A friend of mine is having a kind of Stanford reunion that weekend. It's his birthday or something, he's got a house near Lincoln. I told him, maybe I'll go. I haven't made up my mind."

"Of course you're welcome to stay with us," Nathan said.

Paul didn't respond, and to break the silence Dana asked, "What time do I need to leave for the airport? My flight leaves at twelve. Should I book a cab?"

"You should absolutely not book a cab," Susie told her.

Jean said, "I can take you."

It was nine o'clock now, they had at least an hour. Dana reminded herself, there's nothing you really have to do, just sit here. So she sat there.

They all lined up in the front yard to see her off—it was pretty cold. Take two, Jean almost said. Liesel told Dana, "I'm very glad you came," somewhat formally. When Dana gave her a hug she closed her eyes. She thought, I might not see you again. Paul stood around impatiently.

"Let's not make this a big production. She has to say goodbye to Cal."

But Cal kept running away. Ben was in the living room, looking at YouTube videos on the iPad; it was the only place that got reliable reception. In the end Susie had to take it away, because Cal wanted to watch. Dana said goodbye to him in the hallway with nobody else around.

"You're my guy," she said. "Just you. You're my guy."

He hugged her but also quickly wriggled out and Paul chased him down and carried him by force to the driveway in his arms—a big kid, with his head turned away. Offering him to Dana, like a bouquet.

"I'll see you next week." She kissed her son's hair, before getting in the car.

"Wednesday," Paul said, and suddenly her heart went out to him.

"So what the hell happened last night," Jean asked her, as they drove away.

"I don't know. I panicked, I fucked everything up."

"Is everything fucked up?"

Dana didn't answer at first but then she said, "I'm worried about Paul. I just didn't want to be stuck out there with him."

"I'm worried about Paul, too." She had to concentrate a little, merging onto I-35. "So is it serious, this thing with this guy in New York?"

"I can't really think straight about anything right now." But Dana didn't want to put her off; she was grateful for Jean's directness. All morning long the sense of ordinary life proceeding had weirded her out.

"Have I fucked it up with you guys, too? I mean, will I see you again?"

"You'll see us again," Jean said.

There wasn't much traffic, and they reached the airport (the control tower, the hotel, the wide flat parking lot surrounding it, glittering with cars)—sooner than Dana wanted. It was warm in the car with the heating on, and she felt reluctant to get up or leave or do anything that required competence or effort. The snowfall was thin enough that only a little slush survived on the roads or built up by the side of the highway and melted there. But some of the parked cars had a clean white thatch, and she knew that in New York the snow was piled up, dirty, she'd arrive in the dark and have to go back to a cold apartment on her own. Maybe she'd call Stephen from the airport; he wanted to take her out, but at this stage in her present frame of mind that might not be a good idea, and she was still in the zone where calling him felt like a betrayal and compounding of errors. But the thought of her childless apartment . . . the next few days, the quiet after the crowds, which only an hour ago she'd been happy enough to get away from.

Two or three times in her life, in the first few months after dropping out of Amherst, when she moved in with the guy who would become her first husband, and then several years later after he divorced her, Dana had suffered from depressions severe enough that her mother had almost insisted she take Prozac or some equivalent. She agreed to see a therapist, partly just to get her mother off her back. Her mother, who was even-keeled and almost terrifyingly cheerful and social, had been on antidepressants more or less since Dana was a kid. She considered it almost a natural part of adulthood, and Paul had always resisted the view of the world that made this seem reasonable. It's one of the things she liked about him, that he didn't buy it. But given what he was doing to himself now . . . and she felt like, after this week, she couldn't rely on the part of her thinking that had been shaped by her relationship with Paul, which was substantial, but still somehow depended on Paul for system updates, which she didn't have access to anymore or didn't want. But without him, she had to start again, she had to think through a lot of things again, like attitudes to Prozac and a hundred other things. But you don't have to do it now. You just have to get through the week, until Cal comes back.

When Jean pulled in to the terminal, Dana said again, "When will I see you?"

"If we get married, I'll invite you to the wedding." But this wasn't a joke or a flippant remark, she had obviously been thinking it through. And Jean had tears in her eyes when she got out to help with the suitcase, then waited in the car until Dana had walked through the revolving door and turned to wave and somehow (at least this is what it felt like) release her.

When they were gone Susie said to Paul, "Let's go for a walk. Just wait a minute while I put May in the stroller. She had a bad night last night. Maybe she'll go to sleep."

"What about Cal?"

"He's happy, he's fine," but Paul went to look for him anyway.

He found him in the playroom next to the kitchen. The TV was off. Clémence was reading to Cal and Margot on the sofa, holding the book with one hand and bending the spine with her thumb. Her reading manner was very performative. You could tell she was used to the microphone. Paul felt uneasy, listening; it was like watching someone look at herself in a mirror.

"How is she feeling?" he asked. Margot still seemed pale.

"She says her ear hurts."

"That's what happened with Cal."

"It's her father's fault. He dragged them out in the snow."

"I guess it doesn't snow here often." But he didn't know why he was defending Nathan; it's not what he felt like doing.

"They get snow in Cambridge all the time."

"Cal," he said. "Do you want to come for a walk with me and Aunt Susie?"

But Cal didn't answer, and Clémence said, "Go, he's fine."

"We can play in the park," but the boy shook his head.

"I'll keep an eye on him," so Paul left.

They walked in the road because the sidewalk was still icy. Already the snow had started to disappear. It dripped from the trees and looked almost bluish in the grass. Kids were out, playing in their front yards, but the park itself was pretty empty. The creek in the middle had swollen with the runoff, everything tinkled and gleamed. You could feel the heat of the sun building slowly under the layer of cloud.

"What happened last night?" Susie said.

When they were kids Paul went back and forth between his brother and sisters. They fought and formed alliances and switched sides. You spent your whole childhood in the middle of these relationships, then you grew out of them. But maybe he hadn't gone anywhere because he was still in the middle. Susie's pretty-enough face was still his sister's face, though she was almost forty. Her breasts were heavier and she carried the weight of her children on her hips and dressed in comfortable hippie-mom clothes. None of that mattered. There are four or five people in the world you can have these conversations with, and she was one of them.

"I can't tell you how angry I am at Nathan."

"He didn't want to do it," she said.

"I don't know what he told you."

"He didn't tell me anything. I talked to Jean."

"What did Jean say?" But he didn't wait for the answer. "Nathan throws his weight around, he thinks it's his job to play arbiter. Not everything is his problem."

"Paul, he loves you. Honestly, he's incredibly upset. He didn't know what to do."

"How do you know he's upset if you didn't talk to him?"

"I can see it. It's not very hard to see."

"He should have called me. When Dana called, he should have called me and said, what's going on. Basically, he acted like I couldn't be trusted—like I'm one of those guys. This is bullshit."

"I'm not going to argue with you. Sometimes he overthinks things, he believes in due process, but this has nothing to do with what he thinks of you."

"We had supper together like a family. We were watching a movie."

"She called and asked him to come."

"So he says, let me talk to Paul. That's what he says. Or he calls me himself."

"Maybe he should have. But that's not what she asked him to do."

The park has a road running through it, a bridge over the creek, and houses on either side overlook the green. They walked on the empty road under the shade of the trees. No cars came, or if they did, the road was wide enough to let them pass. May slept. Susie had pulled the rain cover down to keep off the drips.

"Have you talked to Dana?" she asked.

"Last night she drove off in the middle of the night without saying anything and this morning—you've seen our interaction."

"I mean have you had any kind of conversation about any of this in the course of the week?"

"We were talking all the time, we were getting along. I thought we were getting along."

"Has Jean said anything to you?"

"About what?"

"She said she's seeing someone in New York."

"Who said?"

"Dana, this is what she told Jean. We assumed you knew."

"No," Paul said. "I didn't know."

"I mean, what do you want out of all this? Do you want her back?"

"I never . . . I wanted to get out of New York. I wanted to live a different life. I'd be happy for her to be a part of it."

"I don't think that . . . I'm not sure that's going to sell it to her."

"I shouldn't have to sell it." Then he said, "I didn't sleep much last night. I can't think straight."

They had reached the end of the park and Susie asked, "Do you want to keep going or do you want to turn around?"

"Maybe we should go back. I don't like leaving Cal."

Some of the houses they still had associations with, but many of them had been rebuilt or spruced up, repainted. The front yards looked different. When they were kids, nobody cared much about their yards—or at least, they didn't notice. Now it all looked like real estate. Susie wanted to say something comforting but she didn't know what. Paul when he was unhappy went inward; you had to throw down a line. Or just leave him alone, but when you see someone for one week a year, that doesn't work anymore. She felt, both of them have reasons to feel what they're feeling or to act the way they're acting, they should be able to see that.

Paul said, "Marcello advised me once, if you make some money, buy a house in the country, pay off the mortgage, put it in your name. Even if you get married. So afterward if anything happens, if you get divorced, you have something permanent in your life, that's always there, which you can go to. Even if your kids start to hate you, it's there. When he said this to me, I thought, these are the sorts of people he usually deals with, people for whom this is good advice."

"You are not those people."

"Well, at least I have a house."

"Nobody hates you."

"I don't understand how Nathan can get in a car and drive for an hour instead of calling me. I don't understand how he can know me and do that."

"He wasn't thinking of you, he was responding to Dana. He was trying to behave honorably."

"We don't have to go over all that again," Paul said.

When they got home, he helped Susie carry the stroller up the steps. May was still asleep, and they left her in the front hall. Then Paul went to look for his mother—she was in her study. He knocked because the glass door was closed, then he slid it open and went in.

"So did that turn out how you planned?" he said, joking, or pretending to joke.

"I didn't plan anything!" Her emotional response was instantaneous.

"How long did you know she was seeing somebody in New York? Did everybody know? Was anybody going to tell me?"

"*Mensch du*, we didn't know—nobody knew." Sometimes when Liesel was upset she sounded outraged.

"Jean knew, Nathan knew, Susie knew."

"She told us last night, we only just found out." Then she said, "Don't be angry with Jean. She thought you knew anyway, she didn't want to interfere."

"I'm not angry with Jean, I'm angry with you."

"I messed up."

"What did you think would happen when you invited her?" But he heard himself shouting and tried to keep his voice down. "What am I supposed to do now? What am I supposed to go back to?"

"You don't have to go back anywhere."

"I can't stay here," he said.

"Why not? You can sleep in Dana's room. I just have to change the sheets."

"Don't treat me like a kid," he said.

As he walked out again, Liesel thought of Klaus, her brother, who had the same narrow boyish face and dark complexion. Sitting in his apartment, half-deaf, getting angry on the phone. She used to say that Paul was her happiest child, he didn't have to work at it. Just give him a ball. Bill said the same thing. He's happy hitting that ball against the wall—by the hour, Bill said. He's got this endless patience for playing by himself, but now he was thirty-five years old and this kind of patience didn't help him, it was part of the problem.

Nathan ran into him in the hallway by the stairs. He said, "I've been trying to find you, I want to say something," but Paul wouldn't stop or look at him.

—

When Dana took off from Austin, Bill was on the runway at JFK. They passed each other midair somewhere over Tennessee. Since seven in the morning, he had been cleaning up the house—Judith helped. They filled garbage bags with food and napkins and paper cups, they vacuumed the living-room carpet and mopped the kitchen floor, they emptied the fridge, because who knows when they were coming back. At some point they had to instruct a realtor but maybe they could send the keys. There were still a lot of decisions to get through first. He unplugged the fridge and opened the doors and rolled a towel against the bottom on the linoleum tiles. He didn't like throwing out good food and ate some of it as he went along—babka from Polanka's and dry challah and bagel halves with a little cream cheese. He said to Judith, "Should I make you something for the plane?" but she was sick of all this food, she wanted to wash her hands of it.

"I'll eat at the airport, I don't like eating in the air."

If Bill ate a big breakfast, he skipped lunch. He could eat again when he got to Austin.

For some reason, they had run out of conversation. Judith was preparing herself already, she had to go home. She had to be a mother again and deal with her soon-to-be ex-husband and in-laws, she had to get used to being a grown-up and making a hundred daily decisions for herself. So she was perfectly friendly but held back. Their strange five-day intimacy, which was partly inherited from Rose, by shared grief and the roles that were sanctioned by it, by living in her house, attending her at the hospital, dealing with her funeral, was over. Their lives wouldn't really have much to do with each other anymore; they didn't really know each other that well. What Judith had to go back to, as a single mother, living in Chicago, accepting the support of her girl-friends, complaining about the things you complain about, this was not within the range of his experience. And his life to her must seem equally incomprehensible. The way he conducted his relationship with his kids, with Liesel, his frustrations with the university, the pleasure he took in his house, the Texas weather, all of this was foreign to her, too.

Even in the car, on the way to the airport, they didn't talk much. The roads were clearer but there was still a lot of Christmas traffic, even at lunchtime. She was flying Delta, terminal four; his flight left out of terminal eight. He dropped her off first, because she always worried about missing flights. They had plenty of time but Judith had reached the point where any task or diversion that stood even symbolically between her and the moment she would see her son stressed her out. And by that point Bill was perfectly happy to be on his own. So he pulled over at the curb, got out, carried her bags to the sidewalk, gave her a hug and said, "If you ever need anything, give me a call. I'm talking about money, too. We'll be in touch about other things as well. Okay," he said, and she said, "Goodbye, Uncle Bill." Then he drove around looking for the rental car drop-off. It was a relief to get rid of the key.

Only after collecting his ticket and passing through security—everywhere you go, you wait in lines, you have your hands full, you unzip, unbelt, take out your documents and put them back again, take off your jacket and put it on again, zip up, belt up, move along—when he was sitting in his aisle seat on the plane could he relax enough to think or feel. What a week; at least it was over; you don't have to live through a week like that again. You don't have to live through it again because Rose is dead. The life that had been made for him was gone, his childhood, the house he grew up in, they were buried with his sister. All that was left was the life he had made for himself. For the journey, he had brought along one of her novels, a Lee Child thriller. He read it and sometimes stopped reading and looked out at the blue winter afternoon sky, and the clouds below it, then turned back to the book. It mostly held his attention. The flight was a long flight, over four hours, but there was nothing else to do—nothing he had to do, nobody needed him, nobody could reach him. Nathan was picking him up.

Also by Benjamin Markovits

A Weekend in New York

Paul is a mid-ranking tennis professional on the ATP tour. His girlfriend Dana is an ex-model and photographer, and together with their two-year-old son they form a tableau of the contented upper-middle-class New York family. But Paul's parents and siblings have come to stay in the build-up to the US Open, and with summer storms brewing, several generations of domestic tension are brought to boiling point . . .

'Elegant, absorbing . . . What a fine ear Markovits has for the way people talk.' *Guardian*

'In tender, compassionate prose and a deftly compressed time-scheme, Markovits glints through desire, ennui, misunderstanding, and love, illuminating his family so they collectively glow like a human panorama.' Jonathan Lethem

'Sophisticated and engrossing . . . This subtle, ruminative novel of family life, generational conflict and compromise marks a novelist coming into his own.' *Literary Review*

Newport Community
Learning & Libraries

faber

Ringland
16/4/60
Library